Matchmaker

IVY SMOAK

This book is a work of fiction. Names, characters, places, and incidents are fictitious. Any resemblance to actual persons, living or dead, events, or locales is purely coincidental.

ISBN: 9798734128121

Cover photo by Michelle Lancaster
www.michellelancaster.com

2023 Edition

To my amazing readers who always have kind words to say.

I write for you.

CHAPTER 1

Thursday

I blew my whistle as Jefferson kicked the ball…nowhere near the uprights. The football flew way left and into the parking lot, hitting the top of the principal's car, setting off a blaring alarm. I cringed. Back when I used to be on the Empire High football team, our kicker was terrible and we still won all the time. But Jefferson's ineptitude was on a whole different level. He hadn't made a single field goal yet. Not even during practice. I knew we were only a few weeks into the season, but I'd already heard the whispers that Jefferson was going to be the worst kicker in the history of Empire High. I wanted to prove those whispers wrong, though. Jefferson deserved a fair shot, just like everyone else on the team.

I blew my whistle again. "Everybody in!" I waved the team over.

They were all out of breath, and to me that meant we'd had a good practice. We weren't supposed to be done for another half hour. But we were ready for tomorrow's game, despite Jefferson being better at hitting cars than doing anything useful on the field. If I cut the team a break today, they'd work that much harder when I needed them to.

Besides, I needed to have time to shower before heading over to Penny's. I knew it was inappropriate to hang out with her. Especially one on one. But I didn't really care about the consequences. All I knew was that being alone with her sure as hell beat going back to my empty place.

I realized the whole team was staring at me while I daydreamed about being alone with the one woman in this city that I couldn't be with. I cleared my throat. "Okay, let's do sprints," I said.

There were a few groans.

"Come on," the captain, Smith, said as he pulled off his helmet. He was still catching his breath from the last drill. "We're going to be too tired to play in the game."

I laughed. "I'm just kidding. Let's call it an early day. That is…if you think we're going to win tomorrow?"

"Of course we're going to win," Smith said. "With me as the quarterback it won't even matter that we can't make a single field goal."

A few players snickered.

I glanced over at Jefferson. Everyone was literally standing a few feet away from him right now. Like he had some kind of contagious disease. Jefferson was the only freshman on the varsity team. He was also a scholarship student. The combination of the two would have been bad enough. But his terrible kicking made it even worse.

"We can't win unless we all show up. And nice try, Jefferson," I added. "A few more practices and I'm sure you'll be knocking them through from 50 yards out." *Hopefully*. I had a soft spot in my heart for scholarship students. And I wanted the team to accept him. I knew he'd been having a hard time at school because a few kids on the team had laughed at him just for walking onto the field for tryouts. And Smith swore it was an accident, but a ball had been thrown right at the back of Jefferson's head when he went to try his first kick. I gave him a spot on the team because I wanted to help. I was hoping that despite the fact that he was scrawny, he'd magically have a golden foot. I was wrong. And I was pretty sure being on the team was just making his social life worse.

Jefferson pushed his glasses up. The kid was beaming.

"Go Eagles on three." I put my hand out and they all threw theirs in too.

"One, two, three…Go Eagles!" we all yelled at the top of our lungs.

The team dispersed. But Jefferson hung back. "Coach Caldwell?"

Hearing the students call me that still seemed weird. I had started volunteering as the assistant coach several years back. And when Coach Carter retired last year, the head coach position had landed in my lap. I'd almost turned it down. But now I was glad I hadn't. Coaching these kids was always the highlight of my day. It wasn't like I had much else going on. "What's up, Jefferson?"

"My mom wanted to know if she could bring some snacks for tomorrow's game? She noticed that there haven't been any at the last couple games. And that maybe everyone would like them?"

I smiled. I remembered when I played youth football and all the parents used to bring snacks and juice boxes. It wasn't standard practice for our games at Empire High. But I didn't blame Jefferson or his mom for not knowing that. I was pretty sure they were more used to attending chess club than sporting events. And honestly, what could some snacks hurt? Surely the other players would like that. Maybe it would help. Although the combination of being a scholarship student at this prestigious school and being the only freshman on the team was an uphill battle. In a few weeks the students would have to accept him though. All it was going to take was him kicking a last second field goal to make everyone rally around him. I just needed to figure out a way to make him stop hitting cars. "Sure, that sounds great."

"What's your favorite snack?" he asked.

"Oh…um…"

"I think my mom kind of wanted to thank you for letting me join the team. It was her idea for me to try out, but I never thought I'd make it." His glasses slid down his nose when he spoke and he quickly shoved them back up.

"I see a lot of potential in you. That's why you're on the team." I slapped him on the back.

He smiled even though he lost his footing a bit.

"I'm sure the whole team will love whatever you bring. And I'll eat anything." With how much I worked out, any extra calories wouldn't be an issue. Another result of having too much time on my hands. Work. Coach. Exercise. Rinse and repeat.

"Okay. Thanks, Coach Caldwell. See you tomorrow!" He hurried off, nearly tripping over his own feet as he went.

I shook my head and grabbed the footballs that were left on the field. I shoved them into the equipment bag as I wondered about what else I could do to help Jefferson fit in. More encouragement might just make the other players resent him. Some kind of party, maybe? I shook my head. That was probably overstepping a bit. Hopefully Jefferson's mom would bring something to the game that would make everyone suddenly love him. My mom won people over with her cooking all the time. My stomach growled just thinking about a home cooked meal. Takeout every night was getting a little old.

My phone buzzed in my pocket as I finished zipping the equipment bag. It was a text from Penny:

"Are you still coming over?"

I smiled to myself and texted her back. "Is this you begging?"

My phone buzzed almost immediately. "Ha. Ha. Very funny, Matt. I'm checking in because you keep canceling on me at the last minute. I don't want to sit here like an idiot all alone on the couch again. I don't like being stood up."

I pictured Penny sitting on the couch, looking not at all like an idiot. She couldn't look bad if she tried. She was beautiful. Intoxicating. She was a breath of fresh air in this city. And just texting her stirred something inside of me. Her unruly red hair was just begging to be wrapped around my fist. Her plump lips begging to be kissed. The last few times we'd hung out, she'd worn these little shorts that showed off just a glimpse of the bottom of her perfect ass. I didn't want her to be alone on a couch. I wanted to be on top of her on that couch.

And I was pretty sure I was going to hell. Because Penny wasn't mine to be thinking of. She was James' wife. I shouldn't have been thinking about fucking anyone's wife, let alone one of my best friends'. Something was seriously wrong with me.

I ran my fingers through my hair and sighed. "Maybe we should do it a different night," I texted back.

"Please, Matt. James is working late tonight so he won't be home for a few hours. It gives us plenty of time."

I was pretty sure she didn't even realize how suggestive that sounded. Or...had she made it sound suggestive on purpose? For just a second I let myself think that she desperately wanted me too. *Stop.*

Penny was fun. And kind. And sweet. And yes, beautiful. But I knew I wasn't actually in love with her or anything crazy like that. My friends teased me about it. But they were all joking. Because they knew the truth. My heart was too cold for love.

I looked up at the stands. Sometimes during the games, I'd look up there. And if I squinted and let the cheering faces blur together, it was like I could make out

Brooklyn in the crowd. My high school girlfriend. My fiancée. My everything. Something about being in this stadium brought her back. Like I could just reach out and touch her. The familiar sounds of helmets clashing and the smell of freshly cut grass made it seem like Brooklyn was here with me. Smiling and cheering. Alive. Happy. Mine. Frozen in time. Always frozen in time at 16.

I closed my eyes. I lost the love of my life when I was a student at Empire High.

And I was just pissed that James had gotten the life I always wanted. It almost felt like he had taken it from me. I thought that feeling would fade over the years. But it hadn't. James had everything.

I opened my eyes and stared at the empty stands.

And I had nothing.

My phone buzzed again and I looked at Penny's new text.

"Is it because you're worried I'll tell someone? I promised you I wouldn't. It can be our little secret. I promise, Matt."

Yeah, she had no idea how suggestive she sounded. Our little secret? It felt like there was a knife twisting in my chest. It reminded me of the times that I had treated Brooklyn like a dirty little secret right here at this school. She'd been a scholarship student, just like Jefferson. She hadn't belonged in my world. I'd forced her into it. And now? Now she was gone.

The cool autumn breeze blew and I felt a chill run down my spine. I loved the fall just as much as I hated it. Brooklyn and I had shared one season together. I'd met her in the fall and she'd passed away before the seasons changed. All I knew was her in the autumn. So I loved the fall because it reminded me of her. But I also hated it because it reminded me of losing her.

So I kept myself preoccupied with coaching. Or maybe a part of me was just stuck here at Empire High. Frozen in time. Everyone else had moved on with their lives, but I couldn't.

I looked back down at my phone. I'd always be stuck here. But Penny knew how to make me feel better, at least for one night. She reminded me of Brooklyn more than anyone else ever had. And tonight, I just needed someone to raise my spirits before I went home alone.

I texted her back as I made my way to the parking lot. The principal's car alarm was still blaring. And there was a little dent on the hood. I hurried past it, hoping no one would make the connection that it was Jefferson who had caused the damage. I didn't need anyone else telling me to cut him from the team. "Okay, I'm coming over now."

"Yes! I can't wait! This is going to be so much fun. You have no idea how long I've been looking forward to this. Get your butt over here."

Suggestive as hell. Now I was thinking about her ass. *Stop it.* I shoved the equipment bag into the back of my car and slammed the door.

I looked back at the stadium once more and took a deep breath. It had been 16 years since Brooklyn died. But I couldn't seem to move on. How could I? I'd promised her forever. And I wasn't a liar.

I swallowed down the lump in my throat. That's what she'd called me right before she died. A liar. If I could go back, I'd do everything differently. But there was no going back. There were no do-overs. I'd fucked up. I'd fucked everything up.

Another text came through. "This is going to be the best night ever!"

No. It wasn't. But being with Penny would help. She'd distract me for the night. She'd make me forget. Because she was one of the only people in my life that didn't know about Brooklyn. She was the only person who didn't look at me like I was broken. And I didn't care that she was James' wife. I needed her.

CHAPTER 2

Thursday

I made a right toward my apartment building and slammed on the brakes. I was pretty sure my heart stopped beating. Horns blared behind me as I stared at the woman whose blonde hair was swirling in the autumn breeze, covering her face. *Brooklyn?* My knuckles turned white on the steering wheel as the blonde woman slowly turned toward me. I held my breath. And for just a second, I let myself hope. Because I was a fucking idiot.

There was a scowl on the woman's face. A face that looked nothing like Brooklyn's. She was staring at me like I was a lunatic with a death wish. Maybe I was crazy. I didn't want to die though. I knew all too well what damage a life cut short could cause.

Another horn honked behind me. And then it was like a symphony of horns. *Fuck.* A taxi swerved around me and the driver lifted his middle finger in the air as he blew past me.

Asshole. The horns started up again and I pressed down on the gas. My heart felt weird in my chest. Like it was beating out of sync.

I made a quick U-turn. I didn't care about changing out of my sweaty clothes anymore. I just needed a drink. It wasn't like I needed to make a good impression on Penny anyway. Her husband was practically a brother to me. Which made her practically a sister. My stomach rolled over. I sped into her apartment building's underground parking garage and pulled into one of the empty spots next to James' extensive car collection.

I sat there for a few minutes trying to catch my breath. It had been a while since I thought I'd seen Brooklyn walking around the city like a ghost. But every now and then some random woman with blonde hair made me freeze. It was never her. And every time it happened, it messed up my breathing and made it feel like someone had turned me inside out.

Breathe in. Breathe out. Brooklyn used to get panic attacks all the time. She'd left them with me. Just like she'd left me with a hole in my heart and an overactive imagination. I ran my hand down my face and then climbed out of my car. A drink would help.

I let myself into the apartment building and nodded at the man standing at the front desk.

"Good evening, Mr. Caldwell," he said. "Mrs. Hunter's expecting you."

Mrs. Hunter. I wasn't sure why it bothered me so much when people called Penny that. I tried to give the attendant a smile even though I was still having trouble catching my breath. I hit the elevator button and stepped inside. *Breathe in. Breathe out.* As soon as the doors closed, I let the back of my head rest against the elevator wall. The doors dinged open far too soon. I walked out onto Penny's floor and looked up at the cameras that were pointed toward the elevator. James' security team would be watching me. It was possible that even James was watching. It didn't matter if Penny promised our meeting would be a secret. It would never be secret here.

I should have turned around right then. But I knew on the other side of that door was a scotch and someone who wouldn't make me feel like I was crazy. I knocked.

Penny opened the door with a huge smile on her face. "You came!" It was like her cheery words caught in her throat and died at the sight of me. "Matt, are you alright?"

"Fine." I stepped past her. "I just need a drink."

"Okay..." she said, following me into her huge kitchen.

I could feel her eyes on me as I took out a glass and poured myself some scotch. I knew I was being rude. But I took a huge sip anyway before turning back to her. "Sorry. Do you want some?" I set the glass down on the counter with a clink when I realized my hand was shaking.

She laughed. "As good as a drink sounds right now, I can't. I'm breastfeeding."

My eyes wandered to her breasts and I didn't even try to hide it. *What the hell am I doing?* She was breastfeeding her baby boy that would one day call me Uncle Matt just like her daughter did. I grabbed my glass, downed the rest of the burning liquid, and tried not to cough. "I'm sorry. I just stopped by to tell you that I need to cancel our plans for tonight. I'll catch you later." I tried to walk past her, but she grabbed my arm.

"Matt." Her voice was laced with concern. But I barely heard it. Because it was like the fire in my throat had somehow transferred to where she was touching my skin.

I pulled back. "Penny, I've had a really shitty day and I don't want to pretend that everything is fine. You know I don't want to do this."

"I'm not asking you to pretend anything. And I thought you did want this?" She pulled her arms across her chest like she was hugging herself. Like she was trying to protect herself from my wrath. "I'm sorry, Matt. I didn't mean to pressure you." She shook her head. "I didn't realize I was doing that. I thought...I just..." her voice trailed off. "I'm sorry."

Fuck. I hadn't meant to upset her.

She was blinking fast like she was about to cry. I'd noticed her doing that more and more recently. Like there was something in her life that was making her unhappy. She was hiding something. And her secrets drew me closer. It was one of the reasons why I'd agreed to meet with her like this. I wanted her to let me in. Even though I wasn't the person she should be opening up to.

She blinked faster and all I wanted to do was pull her into my arms. And kiss away the tears before they had a chance to fall. I took another step back from her.

She hugged herself even tighter and forced a smile onto her face. "I'm sorry you had a bad day. It's okay if you want to go. I have a little work I need to finish up anyway."

I just stared at her. Because I didn't really want to leave.

"But I'm here if you wanna talk about it," she added.

I pressed my lips together. It was a bad idea. My breathing had finally evened out, but I still felt shaky. The last thing I needed was for Penny to see me like this. But I found myself nodding. "Okay."

"Okay you'll stay?"

"Yeah. I'm going to need another drink though."

"Do you want something to eat too? Ellen made a delicious chicken casserole for dinner last night and we have some leftovers."

Her housekeeper, Ellen, was a great cook. And the thought of a home-cooked meal made my stomach growl. I nodded.

"Great. Go sit down and I'll warm some up for you and grab you another drink." She turned her back to me.

I retreated to the living room. Not just because I needed a minute to calm down. But it seemed like she needed a minute to compose herself too. I sat down on the couch. I was still in my sweatpants and t-shirt from practice. I'm pretty sure I smelled from running sprints with the team. And I probably looked like death after thinking I saw the dead walking along the busy streets of Manhattan.

I leaned forward, placing my elbows on top of my knees, as I stared at pictures of Penny's happy family on the wall. There were several framed pictures from James and Penny's wedding day. I was standing right next to James with a huge smile on my face. A fake one. But I wasn't sure anyone could tell.

It should have been me.

I looked down at my hands. I wasn't a homewrecker. I wasn't actually here to sleep with Penny, despite my wandering thoughts. The only reason she'd invited me over was because she'd offered to help me with online dating. I didn't want to date. I didn't date. Ever. But I couldn't pass up spending more time with Penny. We rarely ever hung out one on one. And here she was, offering. She'd even said she wouldn't tell anyone about it. Our little secret project. One I figured I could drag out for as long as I wanted. Because we didn't have the same end goal.

Penny pictured me having a life like her and James. Happily married with two kids.

But I didn't want that. I would never get married. And I'd never have kids. I'd given up on that dream when I buried the love of my life.

"Here you go," Penny said, setting down my glass and a plate piled high with steaming deliciousness.

"Thanks, Penny." I grabbed the plate of food instead of downing another glass of scotch. I practically sighed around my first bite. *Definitely better than takeout.*

"I thought you were coming from work?" Penny asked.

"I did."

She stared at my sweatpants but didn't say anything else about it. "So, bad day at the office?"

I shrugged. "Something like that."

She sat down next to me and pulled her legs up beneath her on the couch. "I was really excited about tonight. Honestly, I've been looking forward to it for months. And when you finally didn't ditch me, I figured it meant you were excited too. But we don't have to set up a dating profile for you tonight. We can just talk."

I really would prefer just talking to her. "How are you doing?" I asked. She'd been through a lot. We'd almost lost her. We'd almost lost her baby boy, Liam. And I could see it in her eyes. She was still holding on to something there. And I think maybe when we almost lost her, it reminded me of losing Brooklyn. Maybe that's why I kept feeling like I saw Brooklyn on the streets. Like my past was somehow swirling with my present.

"I'm good." She laughed and pretended like she meant it. "I kind of thought we'd talk about why *you're* upset today." She leaned back on the couch, resting her head in her hand. "Or why you keep postponing trying to find your soulmate."

Soulmate. The word sounded bitter instead of hopeful. I took another bite of casserole to stall. Because talking led to the truth. I wasn't going to talk to her about Brooklyn. One of the reasons I liked hanging out with Penny was because she didn't know about my past. "No, let's go ahead and set up this dating profile you're so obsessed with." Besides, actually going through with this was the best pretense I had to keep coming back here and hanging out with her.

"Really?" A huge, crazy smile spread across her face. Fine, she didn't really look crazy. She was always beautiful. And I could easily imagine pushing her back on the couch. My fingers tangled in her hair. That blush on her cheeks just for me. I'd kiss that smirk right off her perfect face.

And I wouldn't need to go on some stupid dating app and play pretend. I knew for a fact that I'd never find someone. But it wouldn't be half bad having Penny to keep my bed warm.

I hated that I wanted that. But I couldn't deny it was true. She reminded me so much of Brooklyn. She was sweet and kind and hopeful, despite everything she'd been through. Her laugh filled a room in the same way Brooklyn's had. Her voice even sounded similar. I wasn't sure if it was a slight Delawarean accent or what. But when she spoke, I always found myself drawing closer to her. Like she could help me remember everything I'd lost. Even if just for one night.

Yeah, I knew I shouldn't have been thinking about James' wife in that way. But I didn't feel like chastising myself right now. And I couldn't sit there and deny that she was hot. Gorgeous with a whole lot of crazy currently directed at me.

"Stop it," I said.

"Stop what?" she asked. But her smile didn't disappear. If anything, it grew.

"Stop staring at me like you're about to do something weird."

Penny laughed. "I'm not doing anything weird. *You* came to *me* for help." She rubbed her hands together in evil joy. "So what dating app were you thinking? I'm a little out of my depth here. James and I met before this whole online dating thing had gotten popular. I never got to experience any of that."

"I thought you said you knew what you were doing."

"I do." She laughed. "Forget everything I just said. I'm a very skilled matchmaker. You came to exactly the right place. And I know which app I want to use. I saw a commercial the other day about compatibility and percentages. Apparently true love…"

True love? Give me a break. "Yeah, I'm out," I joked and pretended to start to stand up. But I wasn't going anywhere. Joking around with her was one of my favorite things.

"Matt." She caught my arm and I tried to ignore the spark that her touch ignited on my skin. *Again.* It kept happening. And I wanted to pretend it was nothing. But it didn't feel like nothing to me. It had been a long time since I'd felt something like that. A really long time. It was one of the reasons I'd come over here like an idiot, pretending to ask for her help.

But she felt it too, right? My eyes locked with hers. We both stood frozen for just a few seconds.

I wanted to kiss her. I ran through the consequences in my head. James would hate me. Despite years of trying to forget how much he'd fucked up my relationship with Brooklyn, a part of me still hated him. So I didn't really care about that. Our friendship was built on a foundation of rotten wood. It was doomed to collapse eventually. But if I kissed James' wife, Rob would never forgive me either. He'd choose his brother over his best friend. Worst of all, my brother, Mason, wouldn't even have my back on this one. There'd be nothing he could say to defend me. I was crossing too many lines. I'd lose everything. But what did I really have anyway? Some half ass friends that pretended the past meant nothing when I was fucking drowning every day? They didn't understand. They didn't even care.

I swallowed hard. There were two things that could happen immediately if I went for it. Penny might slap me and kick me out. Or… My eyes landed on her lips. Or she might kiss me back.

CHAPTER 3

Thursday

I leaned forward, my eyes glued to her lips. Every thought swirling through my mind was telling me to stop.

Penny's eyes grew round.

But I didn't stop. Because my heart didn't agree with my head. It was broken, and I just needed one night to help heal it. I was so tired of feeling fucking broken.

But I didn't get a chance to find out if kissing Penny would numb my pain. Because she removed her hand from my arm like she knew exactly what I was thinking. She quickly wiped the side of her mouth, as if I'd been staring at her because there was something there. And not because I wanted to kiss her senseless.

"Is there something on my face?" she asked, ignoring the fact that I was leaning even closer.

I swallowed hard, my thoughts still swirling with desire.

"Matt?"

I wasn't even sure what her question had been. "Sorry, what did you say?"

She laughed. "Why do you keep looking at me like that? I have something on my face, don't I?" She wiped the side of her mouth again. "I was eating ice cream earlier and I…" her voice trailed off as I reached out and ran my thumb right beneath her lower lip.

She didn't have anything on her face. But I'd use any excuse to touch her. "There," I said, letting my fingers rest along her cheek for just a moment. "I got it."

"Thank you." She cleared her throat.

I reluctantly let my hand fall from her velvety skin. She wasn't mine to touch. But touching her made my heart feel like it was beating better.

"So back to the app." She looked down at her phone. "It's time to find you someone to settle down with."

Why the hell did I agree to this again? I didn't want her to download some stupid app. I just wanted to spend more time with her. I didn't want to fucking find the love of my life on some random dating app. I'd already found that back in high school. And it had all been taken away from me. So I no longer believed in love. All I knew was that hanging out with Penny made me feel better for some reason. I was doing this to spend time with her. Not to fall in love. Not to find someone to settle down with. That wasn't in the cards for me. Ever.

I leaned away from her. If Penny knew how beautiful she was, she would have known I was about to kiss her rather than worrying about something invisible on her face. If she was mine, I'd let her know how beautiful she was every day. Which her shitty husband was apparently neglecting to do.

"Give me a second to download the app," she said. "And while we wait, you can tell me all about your ideal girl."

I stared at her. I didn't want to talk about this. "I don't have a type."

Penny rolled her eyes.

I loved when she did that. Like she was begging to be spanked. *Stop.* "Well, if you insist, I really like girls who roll their eyes at me."

"I don't think that's an option," she said as she looked up from the app.

I smiled at her.

And then she blushed and laughed awkwardly. "Stop making fun of me."

"I wasn't making fun of you, Penny." I couldn't help it. My eyes fell to her lips again.

She shook her head. "True love is serious. So you need to take this seriously," she said, using her commanding mom voice that worked so well with her daughter, Scarlett. *Sometimes.* Scarlett tended to do whatever she wanted. She was freaking adorable and I was one of the people who spoiled her the most. The little girl could do no wrong in my eyes. I'd never said no to her before, and I was pretty sure I never would. Maybe it was the same with her mother.

And there was something sexy about her using that demanding voice on me. I usually liked to be in control in the bedroom, but I wouldn't mind giving her a turn. *Seriously, what the hell is wrong with me?*

"Ideal girl," she said. "And go."

"Hm." I put my arm on the back of the couch, dangerously close to touching her. "Petite. Red hair…" I stopped talking when her eyes snapped to mine.

"This is all very funny, Matt. For real though. How am I supposed to find the girl of your dreams if all you want to do is mess with me?" She pushed her red hair behind her ear and looked back down at the app downloading on her phone.

I wasn't joking. She was my ideal girl. But she'd never be mine. I knew that. And yet…I was sitting here like an idiot anyway. "You promise this stays between us?" I asked. For some reason, I wanted this whole dating app thing to be a secret. I knew she'd already agreed. But I needed to know for real.

"I promise. It can be our little secret. Now describe your ideal girl."

"I don't know. Hot. Nice."

She laughed. "Hot and nice? Did you think I was going to set you up with a mean uggo?"

Honestly I had no idea who she was planning on setting me up with. Because it didn't seem like she had any idea what she was doing.

"You know what, let's circle back to that vague answer later. I need some of your hobbies and interests right now." She started typing in the app. "And by hobbies, I mean things besides sleeping with random girls with huge boobs. Actually, now that I mention it, I do know your type."

I laughed. "That's not my type."

"Then what is?"

"I already told you. Petite redheads." I winked at her.

She grabbed a pillow and threw it at me. "You're incorrigible."

I easily caught the pillow before it smacked me in the face. I liked when she was feisty. "Hobbies, huh? Well..." my voice trailed off as I thought about it. "I like to work."

She shook her head and typed something into her phone. "I need more than just what you do for work. Tell me something you do for fun. Other than being the best babysitter in town."

I smiled. I was a pretty badass babysitter for her kids. Rob's too. But I didn't really know what else she wanted me to say. "I like to work out."

"Work and work out? Do you have any hobbies that don't involve the word 'work'?"

"I'm the head coach for the Empire High football team. It's a volunteer thing, so you can't say that's work."

She lifted her head and stared at me. "How did I not know that?"

"You never asked."

"You sit in our living room every Sunday watching the Giants. You never thought to mention you were a volunteer football coach at your old high school?"

I shrugged.

"Interesting." She typed something into her phone. "That's actually really good. I can work with that. Smile for me."

"What?"

She snapped a picture of me with her phone with my mouth open in mid-question. She looked at the picture and smiled. "Perfect," she said.

"Are you using that as my profile picture?"

"Yup, it'll do."

"Let me see it." I reached out for the phone.

She laughed and pulled it away. "No, it's fine, I swear."

I tried to reach around her, sandwiching her between me and the couch. "You're sabotaging me."

"I'm not sabotaging you!" she said with a laugh, trying to squirm away from me. She pushed on my chest to try to shove me away.

And for just a second, I let myself relish the fact that I was on top of her. On the couch. Just like I'd pictured countless times in my head. I could smell the scent of her floral shampoo. It swirled around me, drawing me closer. Her lips were only a few inches away from mine.

The front door clicked opened and I jumped off the couch. It was one thing to dream about kissing Penny. It was another to actually do it. Especially right in front of James. I could bench press more than him, but James had always been a good fighter. I wasn't sure I'd win that fight.

But it wasn't James coming through the front door.

"Uncle Matt! Uncle Matt!" Scarlett darted right past her mother and jumped into my arms.

"Hey, Scar." I kissed the top of her head. "What have you been up to today?"

"Ellie took me and Liam to the zoo. And I got to watch the red pandas."

She'd become obsessed with red pandas recently. I was pretty sure she liked that their fur was the same color as her hair.

"That sounds like fun. Did you get to feed any?"

Her jaw actually dropped. "I can feed them? I didn't know that was allowed! Ellie, can I feed them next time?"

I glanced into the foyer to see Ellen lifting baby Liam out of the stroller. She was the most patient person I'd ever met. She didn't even care that Scarlett called her Ellie instead of Ellen. She walked into the living room with Liam in her arms. And she shook her head at me, giving me a pointed glare. "Only Uncle Matt is allowed to feed them. Next time you go with him, he'll let you."

Oh shit. Ellen could dish it out too.

"Really?" Scarlett looked up at me with her big doe eyes.

"Sure." I'd figure it out. Anything for her. I looked over at Penny. Anything for her too.

"You're ridiculous," Penny mouthed silently as she took Liam from Ellen.

Scarlett gave me a big hug and then turned to her mother. She stood up on the couch and looked down at her baby brother. "He was a good boy today. He didn't cry and scare the animals like last time."

"Is that so?" Penny tickled Scarlett's side.

"Scarlett," said Ellen. "Let's go get you a bath before your daddy comes home."

"Okay. Uncle Matt, tell my Mommy when we can go to the zoo. I'm always free." Scarlett jumped off the couch and started running toward the stairs.

She was so freaking cute.

Ellen took off after her.

I watched in silence as Penny stared down at her son. The son she almost lost. The miracle baby sitting in her lap. Liam started to whine. And it looked like Penny was about to cry again.

"Penny?"

She blinked fast and didn't look up at me. "Yes?" Liam started to really cry now. "Shh, baby boy."

"Are you okay?"

She laughed, but it sounded forced. "I'm fine."

Fine. Women's universal word for not okay, as far as I could tell. "You know you can talk to me."

"Hm?" She finally looked back up at me. She shook her head like she'd been lost in a trance.

I pulled Liam out of her arms and cradled him in mine. Liam immediately quieted down in my arms. "I can tell when something is bothering you, Penny."

She pulled her eyebrows together in an adorable frown. "I can tell when something is bothering you too."

"A standoff, huh?" I looked down at Liam. He looked just like James. A head of dark hair and a rather serious face. But he had blue eyes like his mother. I used to want kids. And this was the closest I would ever get. *This should have been my life.*

"I always wanted kids," I said, breaking the awkward silence. "Four of them. I don't really know why." But I did. Because my brother and I were practically raised with the Hunter brothers. The four of us against the world. The Untouchables. Before everything broke.

"You're going to be a great dad," Penny said. She didn't look comforted by my words at all. Instead, she looked even more upset.

But I didn't get a chance to ask her why. Because James walked in the front door. Penny plastered a fake smile on her face. I could tell. I'd been wearing one for half my life.

"Hi, James!" she said and stood up.

"Hey, baby." He leaned down and gave her a kiss on the lips, pulling her against him.

Message received loud and clear. I turned away.

"Hey, Matt," James said. "I thought our dinner was Saturday night..."

"It is." I stood up. "I just stopped by to say hi."

James gave me a weird look and pulled Penny closer.

I clenched my jaw. As much as I was tempted to, I wasn't going to ruin his life. Not like he'd ruined mine.

"Since you're already here, you're more than welcome to stay for dinner," James said. "I'm sure Ellen made enough."

"I already ate," I gestured toward the plate of leftovers. "And I actually have plans tonight." I didn't. But I didn't want to sit here as the odd third wheel. Or like I was one of their kids.

Penny looked up at James. "Did you know that Matt volunteers as the head coach for the football team at your old school?"

"Yeah."

"What? How did everyone know this but me?" She turned back to me. "When's your next game? Maybe we can come? I've never even seen your high school. It'll be so much fun."

"Tomorrow night," I said.

James ran his fingers through his hair. A nervous tic. "I have a lot of papers to grade tomorrow."

"That's okay," Penny said. "I've been meaning to get together with the girls anyway. I'll ask them to go with me. I bet Bee and Daphne would love to see Empire High."

She was right - I was sure Mason and Rob's wives would love to see where we used to go to high school. And honestly, that sounded better than having the guys there. None of my friends had stepped foot back in that school after graduation besides me. I think they were terrified of the ghosts of their past. And they'd all moved on. I was the only one who kept going back. I was the one who was stuck there.

"This is going to be so much fun," Penny said. She was smiling for real again. And I was happy it was because of me.

"Great. I'll see you tomorrow, Penny." I winked at her.

James frowned at me.

But Penny's smile grew. And that was all I cared about.

She waved goodbye and I left before James could pull me to the side and tell me to fuck off. It wasn't like Penny and I were going on a date. I'd be on the field the whole time and she'd be with our friends. There'd be zero funny business going on.

No, I didn't kiss Penny. But I still felt a million times better than I had after practice. Penny was the breath of fresh air I needed.

When I was in the hall my phone buzzed in my pocket. I pulled it out and saw the name flash across my screen. *Mr. Pruitt.* My blood ran cold. Why the hell wouldn't he leave me alone? I clicked out of the text without reading it. I knew exactly what it would say. He sent me the same text every few months for years. Telling me we needed to talk. That it was important.

But nothing that came out of that man's mouth was important to me.

My heart started beating the same way it had when I thought I'd seen Brooklyn walking around the streets of the city. None of my ghosts were leaving me alone tonight.

I needed another drink. And to talk to someone who actually understood. Someone who hadn't frozen me out. I fired off a text and headed to the closest bar.

CHAPTER 4

Thursday

"Hey man," Tanner said and slid into the stool next to mine. "What's up?"

I could always count on Tanner. No matter what he had going on, if I said I needed to talk he'd show up within 10 minutes. Honestly, I didn't know how he managed it with the ridiculous traffic in this city. It was like he could teleport or something.

I didn't respond. I just downed my glass and slammed it on the bar top.

Tanner grimaced. "That bad, huh?"

I nodded. My parents had forced me to go to therapy after Brooklyn died. And I did that whole thing for years. But it didn't help. I just needed someone I trusted to talk to. Back and forth. Not someone staring at me taking notes. My best friends growing up didn't want to talk about Brooklyn. Or anything high school. I got it. I was pretty sure they felt as guilty as me. But they'd all moved on. And I…couldn't. Tanner was my only friend who seemed to care to listen. And he'd become my therapist of sorts. He never seemed to mind me talking about the past. He liked talking about his too.

I slid my phone over to Tanner.

He looked down at the text from Mr. Pruitt. "Again? What a dick. It's like every time you start to move on, he pulls you back into this shit."

It was kind of Tanner to say, because we both knew I was never even close to moving on.

"Maybe you should just answer him and get it over with," Tanner said as he ordered us another round.

"I have nothing to say to him."

"I know. But he clearly has something to say to you." He handed me my phone back.

I looked down at the text. I could practically hear Mr. Pruitt's voice: "Matthew Caldwell, it's Richard Pruitt. We need to talk. It's urgent. Please stop by tomorrow at 7 pm. The staff is expecting you." He even put his address.

Pretentious prick. Why would he just assume I was free tomorrow at 7? I wasn't. And I knew his freaking address. His apartment was ingrained in my head, no matter how hard I tried to forget. The last place I ever saw Brooklyn. Her crying in the foyer. I'd left her alone with that monster. My stomach turned.

Tanner leaned over to see some of the previous messages. "Today's message is different than the others. Apparently now it's urgent."

"Everything with Mr. Pruitt is urgent."

Tanner laughed. "Why do you still call him Mr. Pruitt?"

Tanner was weird about titles. It was respectful to call someone Mr. or Mrs. that was older than you. Especially someone that I grew up around. I'd never heard Tanner call anyone Mr. or Mrs. even if they were 50 years older than him. "I just always have," I said. I hadn't spoken to Mr. Pruitt since the funeral. He'd let me take a few of Brooklyn's things. And that was it. He was going to be my father-in-law. And now I wanted nothing to do with him. Because as much as I blamed myself for what happened to Brooklyn? He was the real reason she was dead. And even though Brooklyn was his daughter, I was the only one that seemed to care that she was gone. Mr. Pruitt could go to hell.

"Want me to set his car on fire or something?" Tanner asked without a hint of humor in his voice.

I laughed even though he definitely seemed serious. Car fires sounded a lot more like something Mr. Pruitt would do. And I didn't want to stoop to his level. "Maybe some other time."

Tanner shrugged. "Just let me know. In the meantime, maybe you should change your number again."

I'd changed my number five times. The messages still came. Mr. Pruitt was officially stalking me. "I'll just ignore it."

"You can't ignore it if you get this shaken every time he texts you," said Tanner. "Living life in fear is no way to live."

"I'm not living my life in fear. And I'm not shaken."

"Whatever you want to call it. These messages clearly get under your skin. And if I've learned anything in my time on this earth, harboring resentment is no way to live."

His grand proclamation was a little shaky since he was a few years younger than me. "It's not just his text that's bothering me." I stared down at the glass the bartender had just placed in front of me. "I thought I saw her again." I didn't tell him that I almost got in an accident because of it.

Tanner winced. "I'm sorry, man. Did that thing happen again? Where it was hard to breathe?"

I nodded and lifted the glass. "I hate the autumn." All the memories came flooding back every fall. It was like she was still here.

"It'll get better. The memories. They won't feel so painful soon. One day you'll be able to appreciate the way the fall reminds you of her."

That was another reason why it was so easy to talk about Brooklyn with Tanner. A girl that he was dating died when he was pretty young too. He didn't grow up around here. All I knew was that it had something to do with an arranged marriage. His parents were old fashioned or from a different country or something. He never gave me all the details. But I saw the ghosts in his eyes too. It was fine that he didn't want to talk about it. Sometimes I didn't want to talk about Brooklyn either.

"You're sure you shouldn't see a doctor about that?" he asked. "The trouble breathing thing?"

It was nice to have one person in my life other than my mother that was concerned about me. But I had a handle on this. "I'm not going to see a doctor about having panic attacks caused by visions of my dead girlfriend. They'd lock me up." Besides, I knew how to make them pass. Brooklyn had taught me how to help her breathe when she used to get panic attacks. Now I could help myself. I didn't need anyone's help.

"They won't lock you up." Tanner took a sip of his drink and stared straight ahead, lost in thought. "So…did you hang out with Penny tonight before texting me?"

"How did you know that?"

"You always run to Penny when you're sad. And to me after because you feel guilty about hanging out with her."

Fair enough. I sighed. "Yeah. I did."

Tanner's eyes lit up. "Don't tell me…you finally got the balls to kiss her."

Unlike the rest of my friends, Tanner had no loyalty to James. And he had this weird thing about true love. Like what was meant to be was meant to be. Destiny. Fate. All that.

I laughed. "No." I pressed my lips together. "Almost. I don't know. She seemed so sad tonight. What the fuck is wrong with me?"

Tanner clapped his hand on my back. "Nothing is wrong with you. It's normal to not want to be alone when you're having a shitty day. And Penny's probably sad because she's in love with you and trapped in a terrible marriage. If you sleep together, you'll know for sure."

I wasn't sure if that was true. I knew I loved Brooklyn long before we'd slept together. But Tanner had this philosophy that you had to sleep with someone in order to know if it was true love. I believed the opposite. To me sex had nothing to do with love. No strings attached. Just the way I wanted it. Speaking of which. I scanned the bar and locked eyes with a tan brunette laughing with her friends. I could use a distraction tonight. She caught me looking and flashed me a mischievous smile.

"So if you didn't kiss Penny, what did the two of you do?" Tanner asked.

"She's setting up a dating profile for me on some stupid app."

"What?" Tanner leaned forward so that I'd stare at him instead of the brunette with sex eyes. "You're going to start dating? Why didn't you tell me? You don't need a ridiculous dating app. Those things are useless. Their algorithms know nothing about true love. Delete it. I know plenty of single women to set you up with." Tanner pulled out a binder from…somewhere.

I blinked. I was pretty sure that binder hadn't been there a second ago. "Where the hell did that come from?" I asked. "Did you walk in here with that thing?"

"Of course I did." Tanner flipped open to a random page.

"But you…" I shook my head.

He continued scanning the pages, ignoring me.

I'd had too much to drink. But I was sober enough to know that I didn't want to go through this binder. Because each page he flipped past contained a headshot of a woman accompanied by a detailed profile.

"Ah. Right here." Tanner pointed to some rando on the page.

"I'm really not interested in your weird binder full of women." I pulled it away from him and closed it. I didn't want Tanner's rejects. Hell, I didn't even want to date anyone, so this conversation was pointless. "I'm not actually looking for anything. You know that. It's just a ruse to hang out with her."

"Oh. Well, that's brilliant. You get one on one time with Penny to get her to fall in love with you. Nice plan."

I shrugged. I was pretty sure it was more idiotic than brilliant. And it wasn't really about her falling in love with me. I just liked spending time with her. *And constantly dreaming about fucking her.* Yeah, it was a problem. But for some reason I had no desire to squash it.

"Well, if you do go on any dates, make sure you introduce me to the girl before you sleep with her."

I looked over at him. "Why?"

He shook his head. "Because if you sleep with her it could be true love, and I want to make sure she seems like a good fit. After all, I'll be hanging out with her a lot too if you get hitched."

So he willingly wanted to be a third wheel on my dates? I'd been actively avoiding that same scenario with James and Penny tonight. Who actually wanted to be the third wheel? Yeah, Tanner was a weird guy. But he was also my best friend. Which probably made me just as weird. "What about her?" I asked, nodding over to the brunette. "Think she could be a good fit for me?"

"Wingman on duty." Tanner saluted me before sliding out of his seat. "I'll go see." He had the brunette laughing in two seconds flat.

I'd never tell Rob, but Tanner was an even better wingman than him. Women just melted into a puddle at his feet. I would have been jealous of his game if I didn't think I was just as good.

Tanner whispered something in her ear and she laughed again. And then he walked back over to me, without the girl on his arm. "Nope," he said and sat back down. "Definitely not a great fit for you."

Honestly, that sounded perfect to me. I went to stand up to go talk to her.

Tanner grabbed my arm. "Seriously? I just said she isn't a good fit for you. I told her you owned a finance firm and she asked what a finance firm person does." He blinked at me. "Finance firm person. Who the hell says that?"

"It doesn't matter if she understands what I do. I'm not going to marry her, I'm just going to fuck her."

Tanner shook his head. "I don't get it. You had young love. You know how wonderful it felt to have that. And now you just never want it again? Don't you miss it?"

"Do you?"

He exhaled slowly and then took another sip of his drink. "Yeah. Every fucking day." He didn't offer any more.

I sat back down. "Then why aren't you trying to find your *true love*?" I sounded ridiculous saying it out loud. But actually, unlike most people, I did believe in it. Because I'd had it and lost it. And I'd never have it again.

He took another sip of his drink. "I am. I just...haven't found her yet."

Tanner dated a lot of women. Every time we went to any high society function, he had a beautiful woman on his arm. Always a *different* beautiful woman. Same as me. So I wasn't sure why he was judging me here.

"Well, same with me," I said.

He narrowed his eyes at me.

Sometimes I hated that he was part friend part therapist. "Fine," I said. "Every woman I go on a date with is someone I 100% don't see myself with. Happy?"

"No, that doesn't make me happy. What would make me happy is if you let me find you someone instead of Penny. Well, not instead of. If you want Penny, I'm all for that. I just mean, if you are actually looking for someone, you should let me handle it instead of her. She has zero experience. She's an amateur."

"I thought you liked Penny?"

"I do. But she's not a matchmaker."

"She kind of helped push Mason to Bee. And Rob to Daphne. In a weird roundabout way. She didn't actually introduce any of them."

"Great. Two sort-of success stories. And even that's stretching it. I've introduced hundreds of happily married couples."

I lowered my voice so no one nearby could hear us. "Tanner, you own a sex club. Not a matchmaking service."

"It's not a sex club. How many times do I have to tell you this? It's a club to find true love. If you would just come see..."

I laughed. I was just messing with him. It was hilarious that he truly thought he didn't own a sex club. I was in charge of all his finances. And there was no other way to describe those expenses. "I have to politely decline the offer. Again." Yes, I was pretty sure it was a sex club. But the way Tanner talked about true love did freak me out a little. I didn't want that. And if there was any possibility of stumbling upon it in his club, I wanted nothing to do with it. I liked being alone. I ran my fingers down the condensation on my glass. No, I liked being with Penny.

He shook his head. "Excited for your game tomorrow?"

I didn't mind the change of subject. I'd heard enough about true love for one night. And it was actually really nice that he always came to my games. Mason, Rob, and James never stepped foot in our old stadium. "Yeah, it's going to be fun. Penny's coming. And Bee and Daphne I think."

"Great. I'll sit with them."

"You can't harass Penny about the dating app thing. It's our little secret. I wasn't even supposed to tell you about it. And I don't want anyone else knowing about it either."

"I wasn't going to harass her. I might ask her some questions about how she feels about you though." He downed his drink and stood up.

"Please don't do that."

He laughed and picked up his binder full of women. "Just you wait and see. I'm going to matchmake her to you before she can matchmake you to some rando."

"Tanner..."

"I have to get going. I'm going to be late for a date at my *sex club*." He put the last two words in air quotes. "Let me know if you change your mind about the car fire," he said a little too loudly as he started walking away from me. "I'll see you and the lovely Penny tomorrow." He waved his hand through the air and disappeared out the door as quickly as he'd come.

I would have gone after him, but he'd left me with the check. I knew how much money he had because my firm was responsible for investing it. Yes, I was rich. But he was a hell of a lot wealthier than me. *Cheap asshole.*

CHAPTER 5

Friday

I should have been watching the team warm up, but my eyes kept wandering toward the stands. The last time I'd been this nervous for a game was way back when I was playing. Specifically homecoming game sophomore year. I remembered that day perfectly. When I was more focused on winning Brooklyn back than winning the game. I'd won both. Although, Coach Carter had almost made me sit out the second half after my stunt in the homecoming parade. It was all worth it though. To see Brooklyn smile.

Just thinking about her made my chest hurt. But for the first time in ages, my eyes weren't scanning the crowd for a ghost. I was searching for Penny. So far though, Tanner was the only person I recognized in the crowd. He waved at me and walked over, stopping on the track that circled the field.

"Ready to impress Penny?" he asked, but then frowned. "Whatever are you wearing, dear boy?"

I looked down at my gray sweatpants and Empire High t-shirt. My whistle dangled around my neck and I had a clipboard tucked under my arm. "I wear this to every game." It was pretty much my coach uniform.

"Exactly. Every game. But this one is important." He shook his head like I was ridiculous. "The coach over there is wearing a fitted suit." He pointed at the douchey coach for Calver Academy.

"It doesn't matter what I'm wearing."

"I thought you were trying to woo Penny? Speaking of which, is she here yet? I want to sit with her and her friends."

"You are definitely *not* sitting with them."

"Why?"

"Because you'll talk too much." I'd sworn Penny to secrecy about the whole dating app thing. And I'd gone and blabbed to Tanner about it. I was seriously regretting both things right now. Because if she found out that I'd broken our code of secrecy, who knew who she would tell? Actually, I knew exactly who she would tell. She'd tell James. And his brother, Rob.

Tanner laughed. "Exactly. I'll find out everything you need to know about her."

"I know everything about her." Except what her lips tasted like. And how her body felt beneath mine.

"There's plenty you don't know about her," Tanner said. "Like all of the important things."

"What important things don't you know about who?" Penny asked.

Tanner and I both froze. We hadn't seen her walk up. Bee and Daphne weren't with her. But she was balancing Scarlett on her hip.

"The blonde over there," Tanner said, hitching his thumb over his shoulder. "Matt has the hots for her."

What the fuck? I was pretty sure he was pointing at a high school student.

Penny just laughed. "Hi, Tanner, it's good to see you again."

Tanner smiled at her in a way that had me frowning.

"Hi, Mr. Tanner," Scarlett said very politely. But then she turned to me with a huge smile on her face. "Uncle Matt!"

"Hey, kiddo." I ruffled her hair. "Have you ever been to a football game before?"

"No." She shook her head. "But Mommy said I could have a hotdog if I came with her."

I laughed. "She's correct." I pointed over to the concession stand. "There's hotdogs and even soft pretzels." I knew how much she loved soft pretzels.

"Pretzels! Mommy, I need one of those too." Scarlett turned back to me. "Mommy said I could have whatever I wanted so she wouldn't have to sit alone."

Penny shook her head, but she looked a little embarrassed. "Bee and Daphne were both busy."

I tried not to stare at the blush crossing her cheeks. God she was beautiful.

"No problem," Tanner said. "I'll sit with you ladies. This is going to be so much fun."

Fuck me.

"Oh, that'll be great!" Penny said. "Let me go get Scarlett the hotdog *and* soft pretzel I promised her and then we'll meet you in the stands?"

"Perfect."

"Good luck," Penny said to me. "I hope you guys win."

"We'll definitely win," I said.

Penny whispered something in Scarlett's ear.

"Oh yeah. Go Eagles!" Scarlett yelled. "Did I do it right?" She looked up at Penny.

"Exactly right." Penny kissed the top of her head, gave me a thumbs up, and headed over toward the concession stand.

"What the hell was that?" I asked Tanner when Penny was out of earshot.

"What the hell was what? I thought that went really well."

"You told her I have the hots for some random high school student."

"Oh. That." Tanner shrugged. "I wanted to see if she got jealous. It didn't seem like it to me, but I promise I'll get to the bottom of it over the next couple hours."

"I don't want you to talk to her at all. Especially about any of that."

"But I'm your wingman. We can't forgo this opportunity. When else will I have a chance to decipher all her secrets? Scarlett looks like she's around the age of a kid that will probably need a nap after all that food. Which gives me a couple hours to talk to Penny one on one. I've got this. Trust me."

I usually trusted him. But I didn't want him to do any of that. "Tanner..."

"Go Eagles!" he said and started walking away from me.

"Tanner!" I hissed.

He ignored me, walked up into the stands, and sat down where there was enough seating for three.

The scoreboard made a beeping noise, signaling it was time for the game to start. My team ran out for the coin toss. But my mind was in the stands. So much so that I hadn't even realized that we were down a kicker.

"Where is Jefferson?" I asked.

"Here!" Jefferson said as he rushed onto the field balancing a few trays of cookies. So many cookies. And in a super wide variety. It seemed like maybe Jefferson was more of a baker than a kicker.

"Sorry I'm late," he said. "My mom and I had to finish the last batch of cookies. It took longer than we thought."

Several guys on the team snickered.

"Perfect timing," I said and grabbed the trays from him. "We'll eat these after the game. Sound good?"

Jefferson nodded with a huge smile.

Hopefully they were the best damn cookies ever. Because if the game was anything like the one last week, Jefferson was going to miss a minimum of 3 PATs and a field goal.

I pulled out my clipboard and went over the plan for our first few plays. "Now let's get out there and bury Calver Academy before halftime!"

Smith nodded. "We got this, Coach Caldwell."

I knew that they did. I just really hoped that this time Jefferson would be a part of that victory. And that for once we didn't win in spite of him. "Go Eagles on three." I put my hand out and they all threw theirs in too.

"One, two, three…Go Eagles!" we all yelled at the top of our lungs.

***

It was really distracting having someone I cared about in the stands. Not that I didn't care about Tanner. He came to all my games, which was really nice of him. But I didn't care about him the same way I cared about Penny.

Mason and Rob teased me about having a crush on her. So much so that I knew Penny had worried about it before. She'd even confronted me about it. But I'd told her they were idiots. And that the two of us were just friends. It was mostly true. I fantasized about her. But I knew it was just a patch on a wound. I didn't love her. I didn't love anyone. My friends refused to drop it though. They just kept on teasing me. And James' teasing felt a lot more like threats. He'd made it clear several times that Penny was off-limits. It was probably why I kept thinking about her. I always wanted what I couldn't have.

Although in this case, maybe I could have Penny. Because I could feel her staring at me. And it made the hairs on the back of my neck rise.

I turned around to look at her. But instead of Penny staring at me, there was another woman's gaze pointed at me. She looked vaguely familiar. But I couldn't place her.

A smile crossed her face and she lifted her hand and waved to me.

Fuck. I swallowed hard. I remembered. Specifically, I remembered that hand around my cock a few months ago. We'd met at some bar. We'd fucked at a nearby hotel. And I'd left in the middle of the night like I always did. No exchanged numbers. No promise of ever speaking again. I always bounced while they were sleeping. To avoid an awkward next morning. To avoid ever seeing them again. Yet...here she was.

I immediately turned back to the field. Jesus, was she stalking me? I tried to discreetly look back over my shoulder. She was still staring and smiling. She waved again. And a little farther up in the stands, Penny was deep in conversation with Tanner.

Now I had some one-night stand here *and* Tanner talking to Penny. Could this night get any worse?

I watched as Jefferson's extra point sailed way to the right, nearly crashing through a window of a nearby skyrise. It bounced off the brick wall and then knocked into one of the floodlights.

Damn it.

He came running off the field.

"Good try, Jefferson." I put my fist out for him to bump and he awkwardly shook it. *This poor kid.* "Did it hit your laces again?"

He looked down at his cleats and shrugged. "I'm not sure. I tried to make contact with my instep like you said. Did it look like I hit my laces instead?"

I honestly wasn't sure. Because I was too busy thinking about what Tanner was saying to Penny. And whether or not I had a stalker situation I needed to deal with.

"We'll keep working on it next week." I tried to give him an encouraging smile.

"Have you tried a cookie yet?" he asked.

"Oh. No. Let me try one."

I took a bite. "This is great." I finally got to tell him something positive and truly mean it. His cookies were delicious. Which was good, because if they were as bad as his kicking, I'd for sure get food poisoning.

The rest of the game was painfully slow. Tanner and Penny had not stopped talking for a second. And to make matters worse, Scarlett was sound asleep on her lap. Which meant Tanner was probably grilling Penny about her sex life or inviting her to his sex club or something else wildly inappropriate.

Empire High won by two touchdowns, but only by twelve points, thanks to missed PATs by Jefferson.

As the team came off the field celebrating, I gestured toward the cookies. "Great game, guys. To celebrate the win, Jefferson brought us all a treat. Go Eagles!"

"If only he could kick a field goal," someone said under their breath.

I didn't see who said it or I would have called them out. "It's a team win. We celebrate as a team."

"Jefferson sucks," added someone else through a fake cough.

The whole team laughed.

"We're celebrating our team win together right now," I said more firmly.

Smith rolled his eyes at me. And not in a cute way like Penny did. But in a disrespectful way.

"Everyone eat a damn cookie or I'll have you running sprints until Monday morning!" I wasn't sure what made me snap. Maybe it was the frustration of not being able to help Jefferson fit in. That I just kept making it worse somehow. Or maybe it was the stress of who was in the stands. I didn't know. But I did know what it was like to be on the team. They'd all be going to a house party tonight. Drinks. Drugs. They didn't want cookies. I'd basically set Jefferson up for failure.

I grabbed a cookie and bit into it a little more violently than necessary. "Now," I added and pointed at one of the trays.

The team slowly obliged. But I knew I hadn't helped Jefferson at all. I'd just made myself look like a dick and showed favoritism toward everyone else's least favorite player.

Jefferson pushed his glasses up the bridge of his nose as he watched everyone grab a cookie.

"These really are great," I said with my mouth full.

He smiled, but it didn't look like he believed me.

I felt defeated. I was trying my best, but I was just making his life at Empire High worse. There had to be a way to improve his game. I just…didn't know what it was. I patted Jefferson on the back. "We'll keep practicing next week, okay? I know you've got this."

He nodded and then went to pick up his trays of cookies, one of which had gone entirely untouched.

"Great game," Penny said as the stands emptied. Scarlett was asleep in her arms, and Tanner looked very pleased with himself.

"Thanks. Here, let me." I lifted Scarlett up. She really was getting heavy.

I felt someone staring at me. I looked over to see the one-night stand no longer smiling. Actually, she seemed rather horrified. She looked back and forth between me and Penny and then retreated into the crowd.

Weird. I looked down at Scarlett. *Oh. She thought…* I lifted my gaze to meet Penny's. That woman must have thought that this was my family. Scarlett my daughter. Penny my wife.

And for the first time in ages, I wanted it. I wanted a family. A wife. A fucking life. I immediately pushed the thought away. I'd made a promise to Brooklyn. To love her and only her. And despite what she thought before she died, I wasn't a liar. It was like I could feel the guilt twist around my chest. *I don't want a family. I don't want a wife. I'm fine.*

"Do you guys want to grab milkshakes or something to celebrate?" Penny asked. "I know there's a diner down the street. I could really go for a chocolate milkshake right now. It feels very high school."

Tanner laughed. "Sounds good to me. Although back in my day milkshakes didn't…" he cleared his throat. "Sorry, something in my throat. They weren't popular, I mean." And then he nudged me in the ribs. Which in Tanner speak meant he had something to tell me. Which meant he'd grilled Penny. And he had answers.

"Yeah, let's get out of here." I needed those answers. And I needed to be as far away from this stadium as possible tonight. Because I couldn't stand here thinking about a possible future without feeling like a monster.

CHAPTER 6

Friday

"So Tanner has a few ideas about your potential dating prospects," Penny said.

I choked on my milkshake.

She started talking again, oblivious to the fact that I was going to die a slow painful milkshake death. "And it will be kind of nice to have his help because James doesn't exactly like us hanging out alone. He's got it stuck in his head that you want to sleep with me." She laughed like the thought was ridiculous.

It wasn't. It really, really wasn't.

"Don't worry, I promised him that you don't have feelings for me like that," she said. "But he's being really stubborn about this. You know how he gets a little over-protective sometimes."

"Oh yeah," Tanner said, slapping me on the back to help with my choking. "Sorry, I forgot to give you a heads-up. During the game I found out that James knows about Penny helping you find true love."

Clearly. How the fuck did James find out? What the hell was going on?

"It's cool," Tanner said. "We have a solution to work around that. A loophole, if you will."

I ignored him. "Penny, you promised you wouldn't tell anyone," I said.

"Right. Any *random* person. Or like one of our friends. But I tell James everything. You know that. I don't know how to keep a secret from him. Besides, we have cameras all over our apartment. He wanted to know why you were there. And don't look at me like that. Tanner was the one that brought it up at the game. So we're even. I told my husband and you told your…your Tanner."

My Tanner? I didn't have time to digest how gay that sounded. Because James was going to kill me for sneaking around behind his back with his wife. I was having dinner with him and Mason and Rob tomorrow night. Which meant I probably wouldn't live to see Sunday.

"I'm sorry," she added. "I really am. James asked and I couldn't lie. You know I'm a terrible liar."

She was. But still. *Fuck.*

Tanner cleared his throat. "Anyway, back to what I was saying. Penny's going to let James know that I'm helping you find true love too. So it's no longer an issue of the two of you hanging out."

If he said "true love" one more time I was going to snap. I'd told him that this stupid dating app thing wasn't about finding true love. It was about getting to hang out with Penny one on one. Not hanging out with her and Tanner. What was he doing?

Penny took a sip of her milkshake.

And for a second, as her lips wrapped around the straw, I forgot that I was pissed at her. God, I just wanted to feel those lips around my cock. *Stop.*

"It's a good thing you did tell Tanner," Penny said. "He told me he has a whole binder full of potential suitors." She frowned. "No, that's not the right word. Suitresses? Maybe?"

Tanner nodded. "Yes, it's a bit of a dated term, but suitress is the female equivalent to suitor. I'm impressed that you knew that. I haven't heard the term in years. And I do indeed have a binder full of suitresses."

I didn't need his binder full of women. We'd literally just talked about this last night. Did he have severe memory loss or something?

"Mommy?" Scarlett said, yawning awake from her nap. "I need to use the potty. Please," she added.

"Okay," Penny said and scooped her up into her arms. "Be right back." She practically sprinted to the restroom.

Scarlett liked to give very little warning before she needed to use the bathroom. In that one way she was just like her father. Very uncaring of the consequences of her actions. Fine, she also had brown eyes like James. Otherwise she was as sweet and beautiful as her mother.

"So this is going very well," Tanner said.

I turned to him. "Really? What part of this conversation do you think is going well?"

"You weren't going to be allowed to hang out with her anymore. So I inserted myself into the situation to appease her husband. You're most welcome."

"Tanner, I don't actually want to find love. I told you that."

"Yeah, but I had to continue with the charade. Did you expect me to tell her that this was all a ploy just so you could sleep with her?"

Fair point. "No, of course not." I didn't need James and Penny both mad at me.

He looked over to see that Penny and Scarlett were still in the restroom. "Hmm…too bad."

"What's too bad?" I learned a long time ago that you had to ask Tanner questions when he left stuff open ended. Waiting in silence for him to fill in the blanks never worked. He always acted like he had all the time in the world and would literally make you wait and wait and wait some more.

"Because she also agreed to sleep with you tonight. Room 904 at your usual place."

Wait, what? I would've choked on my milkshake again if I'd just sipped any. "What are you talking about?"

He lowered his voice. "I told her that it's better to get you out of her system than to let this unresolved sexual tension between you go on any longer in its destructive path."

My heart started beating faster.

"But I'm assuming you can convince her that just this once isn't quite enough. I'll leave that to your performance in the bedroom tonight."

"You're kidding me right now."

He laughed. "Do I ever joke about true love? And you're going to have to pull out all the stops, because it sounds like James knows his way around the bedroom quite well."

Why would I want to know that? I couldn't question him any further because Penny and Scarlett sat back down.

I swore Penny blushed when she met my gaze.

This was really going to happen. I was going to sleep with Penny? For just a second I thought about James. But I squashed it back down. James never gave a shit about my feelings. Why should I care about his?

"So what's the plan?" Penny asked. "I know you're going out with the guys tomorrow, but maybe we can all get together on Sunday?"

Sunday? But Tanner said...

"Out with the guys?" Tanner asked and looked over at me.

I wasn't actually going to go get drinks with them after I fucked Penny tonight. She must realize that. "James, Rob, and Mason. You're welcome to come, Tanner. I just didn't mention it because I know you don't get along super well with them..."

"Of course I get along with them. I get along swimmingly with everyone. Just because Robert Hunter is jealous of our friendship doesn't mean I don't like him."

Penny was looking back and forth between us, clearly finding our conversation entertaining.

"What are you giggling about?" I asked. I couldn't wait to silence her with a kiss. How many nights had I dreamt of that?

"Nothing. You two bicker like an old married couple." She handed the rest of her milkshake down to Scarlett, whose eyes lit up.

"We do not," Tanner and I both said at the same time.

"Point made," Penny said with a laugh.

I shook my head. "We're meeting at My Favorite Bar at 8:30," I said to Tanner. And you're more than welcome to come.

"Oh, The Dead Rabbit?" Tanner asked. "Sounds great."

"No, My Favorite Bar."

"Huh. The Back Room?"

"No, My Favorite Bar, Tanner."

"The one in East Village?"

"Tanner..."

He snapped his fingers. "Oh that swanky rooftop one?"

"The name of the bar is My Favorite Bar. None of us have ever been there, but it has good reviews."

Tanner laughed. "What a stupid name for a bar. I knew your favorite was The Dead Rabbit."

Penny shook her head. "Yup, definitely an old married couple. I gotta get Scarlett home before she falls asleep again."

"But Mommy, I haven't finished my milkyshake yet." She gave it one last very loud slurp. "Never mind." She pushed it onto the table.

Penny smiled at me. "See you both on Sunday, I guess."

She'd said Sunday. Again. What about tonight?

"Just text me the time and place," she added.

"For…Sunday?" I asked. *What about room 904?*

"Unless you're busy?"

"No, Sunday's great." She probably just didn't want to say anything in front of Scarlett.

"Bye, Uncle Matt!" Scarlett said. "Bye, Mr. Tanner."

"See you later," I said to Penny. I couldn't even hide the stupid grin on my face. I'd be doing a lot more than seeing her later.

She gave me a weird look and then laughed. "On Sunday, yes."

"*Right.* Sunday." I nodded.

Penny pulled her eyebrows together. "Are you feeling okay, Matt?"

"I'll be feeling a lot better after tonight."

She nodded. "I'm glad you liked the milkshake. We're gonna leave now." She gave me one last weird look, waved, and walked away.

Tanner burst out laughing.

I just stared at him.

"You thought I…" he laughed harder. "That she was going to…" He could barely catch his breath. "Tonight in a hotel…" He doubled over laughing.

Oh fuck. This was just one of his stupid pranks. Why did he always find it so funny to mess with me? Of course Penny wasn't going to sleep with me tonight. For Christ's sake, she had Scarlett with her.

"I got you so good," Tanner finally said when he stopped laughing. "Pretty sure the only person getting laid tonight is James." He slapped me on the back as he stood up to go. "You're so gullible."

"And you're a terrible friend."

"Terrible *best* friend, thank you very much. I'll see you tomorrow night at My Favorite Bar." He touched the side of his head like he was about to tip a hat. But he wasn't wearing a hat. He shook his head, looking momentarily confused, and then hurried out of the restaurant.

The waitress came over and handed me the bill. What the hell? He'd jilted me with the check again.

***

I walked up the steps of my brownstone on one of the quieter streets in the city. All my friends lived in swanky apartment buildings. The first apartment I'd bought was just like theirs. I'd hated that place. All the white walls and modern furniture and appliances. It was like there was no life in it. It made me feel claustrophobic. I'd sold it for a loss because I couldn't bear to live another second in that empty hell hole.

When I was growing up, my favorite place to be at my house was the kitchen. It was warm and light and happy. I think I'd been chasing happiness my whole adult life. Even though I knew it wasn't possible. So I bought a place that felt like a home.

But it still felt like I was suffocating. I unlocked the door, switched on the lights, and tossed my keys onto the little table in the entranceway. The place was a steal when I bought it. A complete fixer upper. There'd been a freaking hole in the ceiling of the dining room with no explanation.

I'd been sold. And I'd been fixing it up in my spare time for the last several years. It was better when I kept busy.

But now I'd almost successfully fixed everything that needed fixing. The kitchen was brand new. The three bathrooms too. I'd sanded and refinished all the hardwood floors. I'd even managed to fix the leaky roof by myself without falling off the damned thing.

It was almost complete and I had no idea what to do next. This place wasn't meant for a bachelor. Somewhere along the way in renovations, it had turned into more of a family home instead of a home for just me. I needed to call my real estate agent. As soon as possible. When I was living in a rundown brownstone, I was fine. But seeing the place fixed up made my chest ache. I wasn't a family man. And I couldn't be here anymore. I needed a one bedroom, one bathroom…something. Maybe something between a family home and a soulless apartment building. I just had no idea what that was.

I walked up the stairs, past my home office and a second bedroom I never went in, and down the hall to the master.

I turned on the shower and stared at the double sinks I'd put in. A his-and-hers sink? What the hell had I been thinking? This place was worse than the empty, lifeless apartment building I used to own. There was life here. A life I wasn't going to have.

I pulled off my Empire High football t-shirt, kicked off the rest of my clothes and stepped under the steaming hot water.

And as soon as I closed my eyes under the stream of water, I saw Brooklyn's face. I always saw her face when I closed my eyes. She was spread out naked, tangled in my sheets. The morning sun lighting up her face.

I tried to ignore the image of her as I soaped myself up. But I could feel myself getting hard just thinking about her. *Fuck*. I pressed my forehead against the cool tile. Yes, I saw Brooklyn when I closed my eyes. And whenever I thought of her, I either got angry, mopey, or…desperate to have her. I found it best to get her out of my system as quickly as possible, despite how I felt. When I was angry, I'd go for a run. When I was mopey, I stuffed that emotion down by focusing on work. And when I wished she was beneath me?

I wrapped my soapy hand around my cock, picturing her hand instead. No, her mouth. God, her perfect little mouth. Her looking up at me innocently. Because I was the only person she'd ever sucked off. I was her first and only everything.

Seeing how hard she made me used to get her off. The first time she spread her legs for me was because she knew how badly I needed her. I pictured that first time. In her skirt that was too short. In her blouse that was cut too deep, showing off the tops of her large breasts. I'd been doomed since the first time she'd walked into Empire High. She's been mine before we ever spoke. And we both knew it.

I stroked myself faster, picturing her here with me in the shower. Her back pressed against the tile. Her tits against my chest. Her screaming my name.

I should have tried to think about anyone I'd fucked over the past few months instead. The girl from the café down the street. Or the random woman stalking me at my games.

But all I saw was Brooklyn. Her legs wrapped around my waist. Her fingers buried in my hair. Her trying to stifle her moans so we wouldn't be caught.

Fuck. Stream after stream of my cum landed on the tile floor. My breath was ragged as my hand stopped. I didn't want to open my eyes. I didn't want to leave the image of her alone in the shower. I didn't want her to disappear.

That was the other thing about thinking about her when I was hard. As soon as I wasn't, the mopey shit started. My arousal gave way to guilt. If I'd protected her, she'd still be here. I could still touch her. Hold her. Kiss her.

I was sick. I was lusting over a ghost. I pictured her when I was alone. I pictured her face when I closed my eyes with other women. I saw her everywhere.

I felt my stupid tears mix with the water falling down on me. I knew I needed to stop thinking about her. But I couldn't.

I just needed to focus my energy on something else. I'd call my real estate agent. I'd find a new place to fix up. A smaller place with less room to grow, or just another flip. And I'd get back to work. MAC International didn't grow itself. I took a deep breath as I rinsed the soap off myself. That was the best part of owning an international finance firm. You could work all night.

CHAPTER 7

Saturday

I looked out the window at the city speeding by. All my friends had personal drivers, security, the whole shebang. I had the money to live their lifestyles. But I preferred to take a taxi or drive myself. I preferred to do a lot of things differently than my friends. And the thought of someone following me around all day, watching me unravel more each day…I couldn't stand it.

"Matt?"

I shook my head. I'd spaced out while listening to my real estate agent, Bill, go over some details on the phone. "Yes?"

"Are you sure you want to sell?" Bill asked. "I was under the impression that you were fixing it up for yourself. I didn't realize you'd be looking again any time soon."

I kept my eyes glued out the window as the taxi sped up. "I outgrew it." I found myself scanning the people walking along the sidewalk. Looking for…I didn't really know what I was looking for anymore.

"It's three bedrooms, isn't it? That's a lot of room for growing."

"Yeah, but I use one for an office. And one for…storage. I want a home gym."

"It has a basement."

"Are you going to help me sell it or not, Bill?" My voice came out sharper than I meant for it to. I'd spent my whole Saturday working at the empty offices of MAC International. The last thing I wanted to be doing was driving to go meet my friends for drinks. I just wanted to go home. Or to a hotel. Maybe a hotel would be better.

"Of course I'll help you sell it. But if you hold on to it for a few more months, the market will be better. The spring market..."

"Is saturated. We'll be one of the premiere listings of the winter."

"Okay," Bill said. "I'll get the paperwork started. Do you have a number in mind?"

The taxi pulled to a stop outside the bar. "Whatever you think is good."

"You don't have a specific number? I know you put a lot of work into the place."

"It doesn't matter."

There was an awkward silence as I stepped out of the car. I knew my request was unusual. People flipped houses for a profit. Not for...whatever the hell I was doing. "I just did it for fun," I added. "I don't care about the return." I stopped outside the bar. The wind had picked up and I wished I'd worn a warmer jacket.

"So let me get this straight," Bill said. "You spent all your weekends and free time the past several years renovating a house for...fun?"

"Yeah." It was a lie and I was pretty sure we both knew it. But I wasn't about to tell him that I needed to stay busy just to keep from drowning. That I meant to stay there forever. That I stupidly renovated it into a family home without even realizing it until it was too late. That being there made me feel even more alone.

"Well, I'll need to come see it to get a proper listing price. I haven't even seen the bathroom renovations yet. Can I stop by tomorrow?"

"As long as it's before noon. I'm going to be preoccupied the rest of the day." I wasn't sure how long Penny would want to hang out. But I hoped to have her attention for as long as possible. I didn't want to spend another Sunday at the office. Or watching football at James' place as the seventh wheel. People thought being the third wheel was rough. The seventh? So much fucking worse.

"Sounds good. I'll be there by 10."

"Great. See you tomorrow." I hung up and stared at the doors of the bar. I cracked my neck, took a deep breath, and forced a fake smile on my face before walking in.

Despite the fact that it was called My Favorite Bar, I knew for a fact it wouldn't be my favorite. It was too bright. Too cheery. I liked to drink in peace.

Mason and James were already sitting at a high-top in the back corner. I made my way past a table of drunk bridesmaids. One of them backed up, almost falling into me. I grabbed her arms to help steady her before her drink could spill down the front of my shirt. For a few seconds she just stared up at me with dilated pupils.

"You okay?" I asked.

"I am now." She blinked up at me, batting her eyelashes.

Not happening. She was clearly plastered. And I had enough on my mind with the fist fight I was about to walk into with James. Sex was not a priority tonight. The woman didn't move to stand on her own, so I politely tilted her upright and stepped away from her before she could say anything else.

"Hey," I said and slid onto the barstool next to Mason.

Mason looked over at the girl I'd rejected and then back at me. "You feeling okay, man?"

"I'm fine."

He nodded. "You look tired."

"You look like shit too."

He laughed. "Touché. I'm trying to land a new client who has these ridiculous requests. He's impossible and I've been spending way too much time in the office."

"I was at the office all day today too." I could feel James staring at me, but I didn't turn to him.

"A problem with one of your clients?" Mason asked.

"No. Just...catching up on some stuff."

He nodded. It looked like he wanted to ask me another question, but instead, he took a sip of his drink.

I'd first learned to master my fake smile around my family. Mason had been really concerned about me after Brooklyn died. And I hadn't wanted to talk about it. So I pretended I was fine. And I was pretty sure that he pretended that he thought I was fine. But it worked for us.

I lifted up the scotch they'd ordered me and tried to ignore how awkward it was that James hadn't said a word since I'd arrived.

"Did you finish all those papers you had to grade?" I finally asked him, hoping to break the awkward silence.

"Yup," James said, his eyes trained on me. But he surprisingly didn't look mad at all. If anything, he looked...happy?

Why did he look so happy? I was pretty sure it was because he was about to try to break my nose.

"How was the game last night?" James asked.

"Good. We won again. Undefeated so far." I stared at him, waiting for him to punch me in the face or something, but he just smiled. *Weird.* "It might be fun if you guys came to a game one of these days."

"The Untouchables back at it again?" Rob said and slung his arm around my neck before hugging James and doing a weird handshake with Mason.

No one called us the Untouchables anymore. Not after we all realized that we weren't untouchable back in high school. That real life could break through a good last name and an exorbitant amount of money. I'd learned the lesson the hardest.

"Sorry I'm late," Rob said. "I swear RJ is actually aiming to kill me. Whenever I change his diaper it's like a freaking golden shower."

We all laughed, but I was pretty sure Mason and I looked more horrified than anything. We were the only ones without kids. Rob's hair still looked wet and I had so many questions.

"I have so many questions," Mason said, reading my mind.

"Right," I said. "The most important being…did you shower after your kid's golden shower or…"

"Of course I took a shower. RJ hit me right in the face." He shook his head but he was smiling. "Straight shot into my left nostril."

I laughed. "Why do you seem proud of that?"

"I think it means he's going to be great at whatever sport he chooses. Don't you think most kids just spray everything all over? My boy zeroes in on a target and hits it. He's a total baller."

James laughed. "Smart kid."

Rob nodded. "I bet Liam just pisses all willy nilly without true purpose."

"Well, I'll tell you one thing. My son has never pissed in my face. I consider that a win."

I had to agree with James on this one.

"Whatever," Rob said. "Just wait until RJ makes varsity and Liam gets cut. Now enough about piss and back to Matt's game. We really should all go to one. It would be fun."

"I'm pretty busy on the weekends," James said. Even though we were all sitting here together with nothing else to do on a Saturday night. But even as he said it, he still didn't look pissed at me.

What was his game here? I'd snuck around behind his back with his wife. He should have been threatening to kill me by now. I shrugged. "Most of the games are on Fridays." I didn't really care if they came to my games though. And I also didn't expect them to.

"Maybe we can come to the next one," Rob said. "Geez, I haven't stepped foot in Empire High since graduation. I bet the girls would like a tour. Do you think you can arrange for us to walk around the school?" he asked me.

"Yeah, probably." *As long as Jefferson stops putting dings in the principal's car.*

"Well, let us know. Even if James and Mason can't make it, I'm sure I can convince Daphne to come with me. It would be fun. And it would be nice to have a familiar face in the crowd, huh?"

James didn't mention the fact that Penny had already been to one of my games. And I wasn't going to mention it either. I cleared my throat. "My parents come to some of the games. And Tanner always comes."

"Tanner?" Rob shook his head. "Psh. That guy."

I laughed. "I really don't understand what you have against him."

Rob stared at me like I was insane. "He's just so…Tannery."

"What does that even mean?"

"I know you guys don't believe me, but I swear I've seen him rocking a man bun walking around the city in a neon green tux. And these weird little goblin shoes."

"Goblin shoes?"

"The ones with the curvy tops."

"Elf shoes?" James offered.

"Whatever you want to call them. Weird little goblin elf shoes. The guy is clearly bonkers," Rob said.

"I've only ever seen him in normal colored tuxedos," I said. "And normal shoes. And I don't think his hair is long enough for a man bun." The sides of Tanner's head were shaved, and even though his hair was long on the top, I'd never even seen him touch it, let alone pull it into a bun.

"It was him. I swear it was. He's up to something sketchy, I'm telling you."

"Of course he's up to something sketchy," Mason said. "He owns Club Onyx."

"But you didn't strut around in weird clothes when you owned it," Rob said. "I'm telling you, Matt, I really don't think you should be hanging out with him. The guy's hiding something."

I laughed. "Yeah, it's like Mason said. He is hiding something. Club Onyx is literally a secret club."

"I'm not talking about Club Onyx. He's hiding something else. I'm sure of it. And I think it would be best if you stopped seeing him."

"Stopped seeing him? What are you, my mom?"

"Nah, I'm not as good of a cook as Mrs. Caldwell."

No, he most definitely was not. "Could you just try to be nice? Tanner's supposed to join us tonight." I looked over my shoulder to see if he'd arrived yet. Tanner was rarely late, but he was nowhere to be seen.

"You invited him *here*?" Rob sighed. "To hang out with *us*? So much for a fun night."

"Rob, give him a chance," Mason said. "Yeah, he's a little different, but he's a nice guy."

Rob mumbled something under his breath.

James cleared his throat and turned to me. "Help me grab another round, Matt?"

I looked down at his glass that was still full. I'd been waiting for him to pull me to the side and threaten me to stay away from his wife. *Might as well get it over with.* "Sure." I followed him to the bar.

He didn't say a word as he waved down the bartender for our order.

"Everything okay?" I asked.

His fingers drummed along the top of the bar like he was nervous. "You could have come to me, you know."

"For…" I had no idea where he was going with this. To ask his permission to fuck Penny? That was a pretty weird request. Were they swingers? Or was he talking about something else?

"I used to be your wingman," he said.

"That was a long time ago." James hadn't been my wingman since we were teenagers. Rob had been more of my wingman before he'd met his wife. Now my only wingman was Tanner. And why did everyone I know keep wanting to insert themselves into my lack of a love life?

"It doesn't mean I couldn't help you with this stuff now," he said.

I didn't need help. Especially *his* help.

The bartender dropped off our drink order, but James didn't move to go back to the table.

"Is Penny really the best person to ask for help with this?" James asked. "She doesn't really know anything about what you've been through."

What I've been through? That was a very cordial way to say that my fiancée had died. But I knew he was implying more than just that. Penny was one of the only people in my life that hadn't met Brooklyn. Penny didn't know I was in love once. She didn't know I had been engaged. She didn't know about any of it.

I picked up my fresh drink and took a hearty sip. "No one knows what I've been through. And that includes you."

"Matt." He didn't say anything else. He just lowered his eyebrows at me as I took another sip of my drink. Like he was worried that I was an alcoholic or something. Hadn't he gotten the memo? That was him.

"I really don't want to talk about this." I took another sip.

"You don't want to talk about dating? Or Brooklyn?"

Hearing her name out loud felt like a punch in the gut. Great, he was here for me now. But he hadn't been there for me when I'd needed him to be. He'd flirted with Brooklyn behind my back. He'd kissed her. He'd fucking proposed to her. He didn't get to stand here and pretend he had my back when his favorite pastime in high school was stabbing it. "I'm not talking about her with you."

"It's been 16 years."

"It doesn't feel like that long ago to me." It felt like yesterday when I'd held her in my arms. I downed the rest of my drink and waved the bartender over to top me off. James was the only one of my friends that ever tried to talk to me about Brooklyn. We'd all made a promise not to bring her up until I said I was ready. James kept breaking that promise a few times every year. I wasn't ready twelve years ago, or five, or fucking now. We both knew that he didn't really care.

James still didn't touch his drink. "Penny said that you told her you wanted to settle down. Is that really what you want?"

I wanted a lot of things I could never have. But mostly I wanted out of this conversation. "I'm not going to talk about this with you."

"But you'll talk to my wife?"

I clenched my jaw.

"That's fine. If you think she can help you move on, I want that for you."

He was supposed to be mad at me right now. Not overly caring. "So you don't care if I hang out with Penny one on one for hours at a time?" I was purposely pushing his buttons and I didn't know why. Maybe I was the one that wanted to fight.

"I was under the impression that Tanner would be there now too. But when you put it like that..." he shook his head. "What do you want me to say, Matt? That I'll fucking kill you if you ever touch her again like you did the other night in my home? Because I'm pretty sure that's always implied."

"It's creepy that you watch Penny 24/7."

He didn't acknowledge my comment with a response. "You and I are friends. So stop acting like we're not. I know you lost Brooklyn. I know she loved you. But it doesn't mean you were the only one who lost something the day she died. She was my friend."

"Your friend? Do you always kiss your friends?"

"Do you?"

I shook my head. I hadn't kissed Penny. Yeah, I'd wanted to. But I didn't. He'd kissed Brooklyn 16 years ago though. I wasn't the dick here. He was.

"We were just kids," James said. "And I've apologized a dozen times."

"Maybe try apologizing a dozen more."

"I'm sorry I kissed Brooklyn 16 years ago out of revenge. I'm sorry. I'm sorry." He said it a few more times and I laughed.

"You can stop. I get it. You're sorry." Honestly, I believed him. I was sorry for a lot of things too.

"I am." He rested his elbows on the bar, not showing any intention of going back to our table. "And I do see it. The similarities between Penny and Brooklyn. I get it. But Penny isn't Brooklyn."

I knew that. I looked down at my glass.

"Are you going to tell her about Brooklyn?" he asked.

"No."

"Okay." He finally took a sip from his glass.

I looked up at him. "You really haven't already told Penny about Brooklyn?"

He shook his head. "It's hard for me to talk about Brooklyn too. And I made a promise to you that I wouldn't bring her up."

"Then why do you keep bringing her up to me?"

"Because you're the only one back in high school that seemed to realize that I had a problem. I think I'm the only one that sees that you have one now."

I wanted him to be saying I was an alcoholic. But we both knew what he was implying. Because I felt it. I was stuck. I couldn't move forward because I was haunted by the past. And even worse, I had no intention of fixing any of it. Every day felt like I was drowning.

"Looks like Tanner is here," James said.

Tanner had just walked in. Despite what Rob said, Tanner wasn't wearing a man bun or goblin elf shoes. But he did have some blonde chick on his arm. What was he doing? I'd told him this was a boys' night.

CHAPTER 8

Saturday

I hurried back to our table before Rob could say anything rude to Tanner. "Hey," I said, slapping Tanner on the back. "Glad you could come."

Rob didn't say anything snarky, but he squinted his eyes at Tanner. I ignored him.

"Me too," Tanner said. "Have you met Abigail?" He touched the blonde's lower back, gesturing her forward. Almost like he was giving her to me as an offering. Which was weird, because she was clearly his date.

"No," I said. "But it's nice to meet you." I put out my hand to be polite. Not that it was necessary. Tanner went through women even faster than I did. I'd never see this girl again.

Instead of shaking my hand she laughed and gave me a hug. "Nice to finally meet you," she purred in my ear. "Tanner told me you were handsome, but his words didn't do you justice."

I did not hug her back. Why the hell was Tanner telling his date that I was handsome?

Tanner gave me a thumbs up when Abigail didn't move from my arms.

Holy hell. He wasn't seriously trying to set me up with this chick? During boys' night. I'd told him I didn't want to actually meet anyone. Several times.

"What do you say we get out of here?" She booped me on the nose like I was five years old.

Nope. I pulled myself out of her embrace. "Sorry, I've had a long day," I said. "I was just hoping to hang out with my friends."

She literally pouted.

Maybe she really was just a kid. How old was this girl? And if this was the kind of girl Tanner thought I'd find *true love* with or whatever bullshit he was calling it, he'd lost it. He was as crazy as Rob said.

I sat down on my stool and pretended that awkwardness hadn't just happened.

Tanner said something to Abigail, she pouted again, kissed him on the cheek, then walked away like he'd dismissed her. "Sorry about that," he said. "I thought she might be a good fit." He sat down next to me and stole my drink.

"A good fit for Matt?" Rob asked. "Was she even legal? She looked like she was 17."

"She's 25."

Rob shook his head. "She booped his nose. I boop my daughter's nose."

"Well, she has a kid," Tanner said. "She's probably just used to hanging out with little Timmy all day. Anyway, how is everyone? It's been forever."

"It really has," Mason said. "Bee and I have been so busy. How is Club Onyx going under new management?"

"Don't worry," Tanner said. "It's still running as efficiently as ever. You'll have to stop by sometime. It's been far too long. And I've made some very interesting changes. But no business talk tonight. What about you, James? How are you?"

"Good," James said. "Penny and I have been busy too, but not with work. Liam isn't sleeping through the night. But at least he doesn't pee in my face."

"Like a boss," Rob said. "My son is going to go pro. In something. But we're more interested in what you're up to, Tanner. Especially on Tuesday nights."

"Hm?" Tanner laughed. "What about Tuesday nights?"

Rob leaned forward. "Don't play dumb with me. I saw you rocking a man bun and a leopard printed tux last Tuesday outside of One57. And a few Tuesdays before that…a maroon tux with black paint splatters all over it."

"A man bun?" Tanner laughed again and ran his fingers through his hair. "I don't think I could pull that off."

"It was you."

Tanner shook his head. "I promise you, young sir, it wasn't."

Young sir? Rob was older than him.

"But it looked just like you," Rob said. "Except without the glasses. And obviously, your clothes and hair were more…extra."

"Maybe I have a very extra twin running around town then?"

"But…"

"Rob, come on," I said. "Stop interrogating him. Besides, Tanner was with me on Tuesday night." Wait, was he? Or was that Monday? Actually, Tanner usually was busy on Tuesday nights. And Thursdays too, now that I thought about it. But I doubted he was gallivanting around the city in weird suits. He owned like a million businesses. He was just a busy guy.

"Enough about me," Tanner said. "And more about…Georgia." He said "Georgia" like he was the host of a game show.

"The state or the country?" James asked.

"The woman."

A girl I hadn't seen a few seconds ago melted into Tanner's side. "Sorry I'm late. I had a meeting."

On a Saturday? What was she…a stripper? She was certainly dressed like it.

"You must be Matthew," she said and stuck her hand out for me. "Tanner has been telling me all about you."

I didn't take her hand, because at the same time another girl walked up to our table.

"Oh, I'm so sorry, Tanner, am I early? I'm always early." She laughed awkwardly. "You must be Matt. I'm Stacy." She gave me a huge smile.

I turned to Tanner. "Tanner, a word?" I didn't wait for his response. I just walked over to the bar to get another drink. Since he'd stolen mine.

"What's up?" Tanner said when he joined me.

"What's up? What the hell are you doing?"

"Hanging out with the guys…"

"I don't mean that. Why do random women keep showing up saying they've heard all about me?"

"Oh, those are potential love interests. Sorry Abigail was a bust. But if you don't like Georgia or Stacy, Beatrix is coming by in ten minutes. Give Georgia a go though. She has great ratings."

"Ratings?"

"Yeah. In my binder…"

"Stop it with the binder!" I realized I'd just yelled and swallowed hard. "Man, I told you. I'm just hanging out with Penny for the sake of hanging out with her."

"Yeah, but you're going to have to start going on dates or she'll catch on to your scheme. And it's of vital importance that I'm the one that finds your match."

"I'm not finding a match."

"But…"

"Tanner, get rid of Georgia and Stacy. And call off Beatrix and whoever else is going to walk into the bar having heard all about me. I don't want to be set up tonight. I just want to drink." I lifted up my glass. "In peace. And catch up with the guys."

"Right. But there's a Jennifer due here at 10:15 that I think would really…"

I ignored him as I downed half my drink. "I don't want to be set up. Not now. Not ever."

Tanner sighed. "Very well." He pulled out his phone to shoot off a few texts. "But if you change your mind, I've got you covered."

With a whole binder full of women. Yeah, I knew that. "I'm not going to change my mind." It didn't matter that I had a stupid crush on Penny. Or if I slept with half the women in New York. I wasn't going to find someone to replace Brooklyn. I just wasn't. She wasn't replaceable. She was everything.

"Okay." He patted my shoulder. "No more lovers are stopping by. Let's go have the best damn guys' night in the history of guys' nights." He raised his glass to mine.

I tapped mine to his and we both took a drink.

"Let me get rid of Georgia and Stacy. Then please rejoin us at the table." He nodded and then walked over. Georgia blew me a kiss before looping arms with Stacy and pulling her over toward a different table filled with hopefully single men looking for what I assumed was not true love.

I took a deep breath before rejoining my table.

"Are you two finished with your lover's quarrel?" Rob asked.

I did not find that joke funny.

"Because if you really want to be set up, as your best friend, I have a few people in mind."

I cringed. First Penny. Then Tanner. Then James. Now Rob too? Was Mason also suddenly going to be a matchmaker?

"I'm his best friend," Tanner said. "And I've got this covered."

Rob laughed. "You're surely mistaken. I'm Matt's best friend. Tell him, Matt. Tell him I'm the one that's going to help set you up."

James jumped in to save me. "Enough about Matt's dating life. If he wanted any of our help, he'd ask us." He gave me a small smile. "Anyway, how are renovations on your place going?"

Thank God for the change of subject. "Good. I'm almost done."

"So are you finally going to have us over?"

I never invited anyone back to my place. Ever. None of my friends or family had ever been to my place. None of my one-night stands. I valued my privacy. And I didn't want them poking around. "I'm actually just going to sell it, so no housewarming party needed."

"You're selling it?" Mason asked. "I thought you loved that place? You went on and on about how quiet the street was when you made a bid."

Too quiet. I shrugged. "I changed my mind."

"You decided you want to live on a noisier street?"

"I just outgrew the place. I have Bill stopping by to figure out the listing price."

"Oh, so you mean like right away," Mason said. "We all have to come over before you sell then..."

"Really, it's fine. I'll have you guys over to my next place." I wouldn't. They'd ask too many questions. They wouldn't understand. Just thinking about them peeking around made me start to sweat.

"You okay?" Rob asked. "You look a little pale. Please don't tell me you're secretly a serial killer and have a bunch of dead bodies in your basement or something. Did you guys hear about all the crazy people in Penny's old neighborhood? James was just telling me about it the other day."

James laughed. "I've banned Penny from going home for a little while. There's a serial killer loose. Or maybe a few."

"Really?" I shook my head. "The world's a crazy place."

"Just imagine how crazy it was living in London while it was being bombed during World War 2," Tanner said. "All those air raids?" He closed his eyes, his eyebrows pinched together, as he took a sip from his drink. "That must have been terrifying."

"Are you a big history buff?" Rob asked.

Tanner opened his eyes again and cleared his throat. "History is a fascinating subject. As long as you don't get stuck in the past."

I felt like that was a jab at me.

"Hmm…" Rob looked back and forth between me and Tanner. "It's interesting that you have a love for history. Matt finds history very boring. Most best friends enjoy the same hobbies."

"History isn't a hobby," I said.

"Can we have a word in private, Matthew?" Rob said.

God, I was sick of all these sidebars. I followed him over to the bar. "If you called me Matthew I must be in trouble."

"I need you to tell Tanner once and for all that *I'm* your best friend. This isn't funny."

"It's a little funny," I said, smiling as I took a sip.

Rob punched my shoulder a little too hard.

"Ow."

"Who's known you the longest? Who was there for you when you had food poisoning sophomore year at Harvard and were projectile vomiting everywhere?"

That was a gross night.

"Who had sleepovers with you every weekend growing up? And acted like an idiot so girls you'd like would choose you?"

"You did that on purpose?"

"Shut up. Whose kids call you Uncle Matt?"

"James' do too..."

"This isn't about James. This is about you and me. I was your wingman. And now you have Tanner parading randos in front of you when you're supposed to be hanging out with us?"

"Right. You *were* my wingman. But you guys are all married. I needed a single friend."

"Daphne wouldn't care if you needed me to wingman for you."

"Daphne would care."

"Fine, she might care a little. But she'd understand that you needed me."

That was true. "It's not easy, you know. Being the seventh wheel."

"You're not the seventh wheel. And if you're actually looking for a girlfriend, I can help." He lowered his eyebrows as he stared at me. "I didn't realize you were ready. We've never really talked about..."

"I'm not ready." I wasn't going to have this conversation twice today. "I have no idea why Tanner brought those girls here. I'm not interested in anything but a one-night stand."

"Oh." Rob nodded. "Okay. Well, good. That makes me feel better. Well, not better for you. I'm sorry, man."

"It's fine. Really."

"If you want to talk about it…"

"I really don't," I said. "You know what would make tonight great? If no one brought up my love life again."

Rob laughed. "You know what would make tonight great for me? If you just told Tanner that you and I are besties."

"You're both my friends. Can't you try not to be jealous and get along?"

"I'm not jealous. I'm protective. That shady guy is definitely up to something on Tuesday nights. And I'm going to find out what it is."

"Until then…be nice?"

"Fine." He put his arm around my shoulders. "I'll be nice to your back-up best friend."

"Not a great start." We made our way back over to the table.

"So you and Penny are solid then?" Tanner asked. He was leaning forward a little too far on the table. It looked like he was running an interrogation. "You're absolutely sure of that?"

James frowned. "I'm positive."

What was Tanner doing? Everyone was out of control tonight.

"Interesting," Tanner said. "The last time I saw her she seemed kind of…I don't know…off."

"I don't think you've been around my wife enough to know if she's *off*."

"Who wants another round?" I asked, trying to distract my friends before we all got into a brawl like we were dumb high schoolers again.

CHAPTER 9

Sunday

I opened my eyes and blinked. The blonde hair strewn across the pillow next to me slowly came into focus. And for just a second. One stupid second. I thought it was Brooklyn. I reached out to touch her, and then my hand froze an inch away from her face. I felt like I was going to be sick.

I closed my eyes and turned away from…Georgia. *I think*. After my friends had left the bar last night, I'd gone back over to her. I wasn't looking for true love. But I didn't want to go home alone again. A fun night in a hotel with some random chick usually made me feel better.

But not when I mistook her for a ghost the next morning. My heart was beating too fast. I was having trouble catching my breath. I climbed out of bed too quickly, pulling on the sheet, startling her awake.

"Matt?" she said groggily.

Shit.

"Where are you going?" She sat up in bed, hugging the sheets to her chest.

I tried to ignore her as I pulled on my pants and looked for my shirt. *There it is.* I picked it up off a chair and finished getting dressed.

"Do you want to get breakfast or something?" she asked.

I could barely breathe. The last thing I wanted was to eat brunch and drink mimosas with her. I was never supposed to even talk to her again. I'd overslept. I should have been long gone before she woke up. "I have a meeting." My voice came out croaky. I needed to get out of this room. I needed fresh air.

"But it's Sunday. Can't you take the day off?"

I grabbed my jacket and got halfway to the door.

"Wow, okay," she said. "Tanner told me you were a nice guy."

I cringed. I wasn't a nice guy. "The room is under my card. Order whatever you want from room service."

She sighed. "That's not what I meant, asshole."

But I didn't care what she meant. I was already out the door.

The air outside the hotel was chilly, the temperatures feeling more fall-like every day. But the air was hardly fresh.

Breathe in. Breathe out.

I hailed a taxi and slammed the door behind me, blocking out the cold. I hated when my mind played tricks on me. Like fucking with me was some fun, cruel joke.

Breathe in. Breathe out.

Dreaming of waking up to Brooklyn was a regular occurrence. But opening up my eyes and actually thinking I saw her?

Breathe in. Breathe out.

"We're here," the taxi driver said far too soon.

My heartbeat had evened out and my breathing was almost back to normal. I looked out the window of the cab. Bill was sitting on the front steps. I wished I'd had time to hop in the shower real quick to wash off this morning. And last night. "Sorry I'm late," I said as I climbed out of the taxi.

"Long night?" Bill asked.

"Something like that." I pulled out my keys and let him in. I needed a glass of water. And a shower. And maybe some aspirin. I took off my jacket and hung it on one of the hooks in the entrance.

Bill whistled. "Are these new floors?"

"Just refinished."

"They're impeccable. And the molding." He ran his hand along the molding of the archway that led to the kitchen. "This is impressive work."

"Thanks." I went into the kitchen and grabbed a glass from one of the brand new kitchen cabinets. "Want something to drink?"

"I'm good." He tapped his knuckles against the countertop. "Granite?"

I nodded and downed half the glass. It felt like I'd just run for miles instead of panicking in the back seat of a cab. My heart had been racing faster than when I did sprints.

Bill shook his head. "You're really sure you want to sell the place?" He was staring at the custom stone mantle above the refurbished fireplace. "It's gonna go quick. So if you're not sure..."

"I'm sure."

"Let me just check out the bathrooms." He walked out of the kitchen, but I didn't follow him. Bill knew his way around and he knew what he was doing. He didn't need me breathing down his neck.

My phone buzzed in my pocket. I pulled it out to see a text from Tanner.

"Georgia? Good choice. But I checked, and it wasn't true love. Sorry, man. Maybe next time."

Rob was right. Sometimes Tanner was really freaking weird. "I know it wasn't true love," I texted back. "That's why I fucked her instead of asking her on a date."

"Interesting. Well, it was worth a shot."

I went to slide my phone back into my pocket when another text came through.

"Also, I called Penny and let her know I wasn't feeling well enough today to hang out. I did the whole fake cough thing to really seal the deal. She believed me. So it'll just be the two of you."

That was nice of him to bow out like he'd promised. But I wasn't really feeling up to anything today. *Maybe I should just cancel my plans with Penny too.* I pulled up her name on my phone, but my thumb paused. Would hanging out with her make me feel better? Or worse?

Another text from Tanner popped up. "And I have another surprise for you. You're welcome."

I waited a few seconds. But of course he wasn't just going to tell me without me asking. I wasn't falling for that again. "What exactly am I grateful for?"

"You'll see. It's a surprise. But you'll know it when you see it."

I shook my head. "Does it make up for the fact that you purposely pissed off James last night?"

"When did I piss him off?"

"When you kept asking him all those questions about Penny."

"Oh. That. I don't think he minded."

James definitely minded. "Just for future reference, when he does that whole thing where he lowers his eyebrows? It means he's pissed."

"I don't think so. It means we're having an engaging, intellectual conversation."

About his wife's happiness?

"Your friends are a hoot."

A hoot? I would have called him out for using such a weird word. But he said stuff like that all the time. I heard Bill's feet on the stairs and put my phone back in my pocket.

"Did you do anything to update the room that's locked upstairs?" Bill asked.

My fingers tightened around my phone. "It's the same as the other spare bedroom."

"Do you mind if I take a peek?"

I patted down my pockets, pretending to look for a key. "I think I left the key at the office," I lied. "But really, it's almost identical to the other. Even the same crown molding as the master."

He nodded. "Well, I'll definitely be able to turn a nice profit on this place for you. Not a problem at all. And what are you looking for next? Besides four bedrooms?"

I didn't really know. Did I want another fixer upper? Or some empty apartment? None of it sounded great. "I don't know. I'll need to think about it."

"You'll need to think fast. This is going to be a hot home for a family. I'll pull some ideas for you in the meantime. Maybe we'll be able to pinpoint your next investment. Or where you'll settle down."

Settling down. I wasn't sure that was something I was interested in. But I nodded anyway.

"Great. I'll work on the listing." He took a peek into the family room. "And we'll need some stagers asap."

I didn't see why there was anything wrong with my furniture. Maybe families preferred less leather and more...throw pillows? I had no idea. "Whatever you think it needs."

He snapped a few pictures with his phone. "And I'll get some photographers out here to take pictures once everything is ready." He pushed an end table two inches to the left and I laughed. "It was blocking the natural flow," he said.

"Sure."

Bill chuckled. "I'm not going to pretend I know about interior decorating, but I'd definitely run into this thing all the time if it was at my house."

He wasn't wrong. I'd hit my shin on it a few times, but didn't care enough to move it. I'd needed a place for whatever I was drinking when I was stretched out on the couch. And as far as I was concerned, an end table went by the end of the couch.

"Does all that sound good?" he asked. "I'll text you the times for the stagers and photographers."

"Sounds great, Bill." I shook his hand and watched him leave before heading up the stairs. I needed a shower before I met up with Penny. But instead of heading toward the master, I pulled out the key that was very much in my pocket, and unlocked the door to the third bedroom.

I pushed it open and smelled the calming aroma of paint and sunshine.

The floor was covered in tarp and there was an easel in the center of the room with a half-finished portrait.

Another thing I did when I was missing Brooklyn? I painted her. I stepped into the room and looked at the canvases stacked along the wall. Dozens of them. Everywhere. They almost filled up the whole room.

If I could paint anything else, I would. But I only ever came into this room when I wanted to think about her.

Some days I couldn't look at pictures of her without falling apart. Other days? I felt like I couldn't remember her face. On those days, I'd come in here and look at old photos. And sometimes I'd paint her face from them. It was all I had. An old photo album and some memories. This room was the main reason I didn't have anyone over. Because if any of my friends or family saw this, they'd look at me the way they did after Brooklyn died. Like I was broken. I hated when people looked at me like that. Even if it was true.

I stared at the painting on the easel. I was best at capturing Brooklyn's eyes. Sad yet full of warmth. Full of love. For me.

She'd given me paints, brushes, and an easel as an early Christmas present the day before she passed away. I'd told her I used to love to paint with my aunt. She'd been worried about how stressed out I was and thought painting would help. It was the sweetest present I'd ever received. And I'd promised her I'd use it. I tried my best to keep all my promises to her. Even when they killed me.

But she was right. Painting was a great escape from stress. I wasn't sure I was ever as calm as I was when I painted. Until grief took over. I'd slept on that tarp. I'd fallen apart on that tarp. This room was the most lived in. Because it held all the memories of her.

I looked down at the photo album opened next to the easel. Brooklyn's best friend, Kennedy, had given it to me. It was meant to be a present for our wedding. Instead, she'd given it to me on the day of Brooklyn's funeral. The photos inside were the only pictures of her I had.

It was one thing to stare at my paintings. It was another to see her actual face smiling at the camera. It felt like a knife in my chest. She'd been so happy. We were supposed to be so happy together.

Fuck. I pressed the heels of my hands to my eyes and turned away from the image of her. I needed to go pretend everything was fine for the rest of the afternoon. Pretend I wanted to be on some stupid dating app. Pretend that hanging out with Penny was anything like hanging out with Brooklyn.

My phone buzzed as I closed the door behind me. It was another text from Tanner.

"And make sure to wash last night's failure off. Or your surprise won't be impressed."

God no. My surprise was a person? If Tanner was sending over another round of women to my place, I wasn't freaking answering the door.

CHAPTER 10

Sunday

Penny and I were meeting at some little coffee shop near her place. She loved coffee shops. Which was weird, because I'd only ever seen her drink tea. I think it had something to do with how she and James met. But none of that mattered. What mattered was that she was waiting for me, and I was going to be late. Again. I knew how much she hated sitting alone. And how much she hated thinking I'd stood her up. I ran my fingers through my wet hair and grabbed my car keys.

I closed my front door and when I turned around, I almost ran straight into someone. I grabbed the person before I knocked them down the front steps.

"Sorry," I said. And then my voice caught in my throat. Penny. I'd wanted fresh air this morning. Penny smelled just like fresh air. Like a bouquet of spring flowers. And for the first time all morning, it felt like I could actually breathe.

"Hi," she said. "Sorry, I didn't mean to startle you. I was just about to knock."

I let my hands drop from her arms when I realized that she was *here*. At the one place she should never, ever be. The one place where I didn't want to hang out with her. "What are you doing here?"

"Tanner called me this morning. He mentioned that you were sad that no one threw you a housewarming party." She raised both her eyebrows at me. "Do you not remember when I asked you a dozen times about that very thing?"

I remembered. I nodded.

"He made me feel like a monster. He said you were super insulted that none of your friends had even come by. I've tried so many times and you've always turned me down."

"Penny..."

"And he hinted around that you'd be really happy if we hung out here for our matchmaking session today."

Fucking Tanner. So this was my surprise? Penny showing up on my doorstep? "Oh...um..."

"You know I would have thrown you one. We've all been dying to see your place. What does a girl have to do to get an invitation? Get down on my hands and knees and beg you?"

I could picture her doing a lot of things on her knees. *Stop.* "Great. You can throw me a housewarming party at my *new* place. I'm selling this one. So there's no reason to warm it. You said you loved that coffee shop, though. Let's hang out there like we'd planned."

"You're seriously not going to invite me in?"

"Nope." I tried to step around her but she blocked me on the steps.

"But I had Ian drive me all the way here. I can't just call him and make him drive me back across town. That would be so rude."

"Penny, it's his job to drive you wherever you want to go."

She waved her hand through the air. "Ian's family."

"Hardly."

"What do you mean *hardly*? He's engaged to Jen. He's going to be my brother-in-law."

Jen was James and Rob's sister. And one of the many women in New York whose body I'd used to try to numb my pain. It hadn't worked. I still wasn't sure how James and Rob had forgiven me for that one. I guess I had a get out of jail free card for everything after Brooklyn died. "Well, it's Ian's fault for being awkward and insisting he still works for you when he's shacking up with Jen."

Penny raised her eyebrows. "Are you jealous?"

"Excuse me?"

"Oh my God, Matt. You're jealous. That Ian's with Jen. Is that it?"

What? "No."

"Don't even pretend to deny it. I know that the two of you hooked up years ago. Jen told me."

"Then Jen also told you that it was just a casual summer fling that meant nothing."

"To her."

"To either of us."

Penny stared up at me. "You sound awfully defensive."

"Come on, I could really use a cup of coffee."

"I can do you one better." She lifted up a wrapped box that I hadn't seen in her arms. "A housewarming present."

"You bought me a present?"

"Mhm."

I reached for it but she pulled it away. "It's a present that someone gives to someone while touring their new house."

"You're not going to move from this step, are you?"

She smiled. "I'm really not. At least not for another two hours when Ian's supposed to pick me up."

I didn't really have a choice. It wasn't like I was going to make her sit out here. We both knew it. I sighed and grabbed the box. "Fine." My mind was filled with everything that could go wrong as I turned around and unlocked my front door. We could accidentally fuck on the couch. She could find the room filled with paintings of Brooklyn. There could be something besides coffee in the stupid box.

But it was easy to forget about all the reasons why she shouldn't come in when I saw her face light up.

"Wow." She spun in a circle in the small foyer, her skirt lifting higher on her thighs, as she took in the family room and kitchen. "Matt, this place is so..." she looked up at me.

"So what?"

"So not what I expected." Her smile grew as she stared at me.

I laughed. "What did you expect?"

"A bachelor pad of course." She walked into the kitchen.

"And that's not what this is?"

She shook her head as she looked at the dishes in the drying rack. "Nope." She turned back around. "It's a home."

Something twisted in my gut. "Well, not a home for me."

"Really? I can't understand why you'd want to sell it. The street is so peaceful. It almost feels like you're not even in the city. It's like an escape from all the chaos."

Is that why she was here? To escape from the chaos? From James? I made myself stay on the opposite side of the kitchen island from her. "I like the chaos."

She rolled her eyes. "What is it with you guys? I love New York, but only because it's where everyone I care about is. If we could all pick up and move literally anywhere else together, I'd do it in a heartbeat. The suburbs are..."

"Boring."

She laughed. "Fair point. Here." She slid the present across the counter at me.

I caught it and just stared back at her.

"Open it."

I pulled the bow on the top and ripped the paper. The box staring back at me was absolutely not coffee. "You brought me a teapot?"

"It's a kettle. I figured you didn't have one."

"Yeah, because I don't drink tea."

"It's for guests, Matt. Like me. And maybe for a special someone in your life after I set you up. Here, I'll show you how to use it." She opened the box and started washing the teakettle. She moved around the kitchen with ease, humming some tune I didn't recognize.

And as I watched her, I felt the strangest sensation. Familiarity, maybe. My mom always hummed in the kitchen too. But it wasn't really that. Maybe it was more of a…longing. Because I could get used to this. A woman in my kitchen. A woman in my house. It felt warmer with her here.

Penny placed the pot on the stove and turned back to me. "I figured you didn't have any tea bags either, so I brought some." She pulled out some more boxes from her purse and put them on the counter.

"You promised me coffee," I said.

"Coffee is for people who don't lie to their Tanners about their friends being rude and not wanting to see their place."

"Please stop calling him my Tanner. It's just Tanner."

She laughed. "But it's so fun to mess with you."

I was the one that was supposed to be messing with her. That was our thing. I didn't like when the tables were turned.

"It'll whistle when it's ready." She walked around the island. "Give me a tour?"

It was actually cute that she didn't realize how suggestive she always sounded. A tour usually meant straight to the bedroom. *Or is that what she meant?* I tried to shake off the thought as I showed her the family room and downstairs bathroom.

She peered out the window to the back yard. "You have grass?" She opened up the door before I could stop her. She laughed as she spun around in a circle, her hands lifting in the air. "It's like a little slice of Central Park!"

It was such a small yard that I couldn't help but laugh. But I'd made it look nice. There was a small stone patio with a grill and some chairs. And some flowerbeds along the back fence.

"Scarlett would love this," she said.

"You can bring her next time if you want."

Next time? Bring another person? What the fuck was I doing? I didn't want anyone here.

"You're inviting me back?" She looked so happy.

"I don't know how to say no to you."

She laughed. "Show me the rest."

I didn't know how to feel as I showed her up the stairs. She peered into my office and into the hallway bathroom.

"What's in there?" she asked, pointing to the closed door.

I stepped in front of her. "The only room that's still a work in progress."

"You can show me next time then." She wandered down the hall and into the master bedroom. "Wow, it's so much bigger than I expected."

"That's what she said."

She laughed. "Perve."

"The first thing you said when you stepped foot in my bedroom was that it was bigger than you expected. You walked right into that one."

"Fair enough. I can't believe you make your bed. I absolutely hate making my bed, knowing I'm just going to mess it up at night. But James always does it or has Ellen do it. Is that like a rich person thing?"

"Penny, you're rich too now."

"Not like you guys."

"Exactly like us. You're one of us." I made a point to make sure all my friends' wives felt like they were a part of this world. Because I'd failed on that before. I wasn't naïve. I knew we weren't untouchable. But I wanted them to know that they belonged. Especially Penny.

Her smile suddenly looked shier. "Thanks, Matt." She peered into the bathroom. "You're very…neat."

"That's probably the worst description after nice."

"Too bad. Because you're also nice."

Maybe it was just me, but it felt like the air crackled between us. The bed was literally four feet away. What would she do if I backed her up until her thighs hit the mattress? Or if I pushed up her skirt? Or if I kissed that shy smile right off her face? Would she tell me to stop? Beg me for more? Because I couldn't stop picturing her on her knees begging ever since she'd graciously put the image in my head outside.

The damned teakettle started whistling.

"Which is why I'm going to find you a nice girl." She patted my chest as she walked by. "Come on, we have teatime and plans to discuss."

That sounded like the gayest thing ever. What were we, two women at a 1900s luncheon? But I followed her out of the bedroom anyway. I wasn't sure why. But I'd follow Penny anywhere. Maybe it was the smell of her perfume. Or her subtle Delawarean accent that reminded me of Brooklyn. Or maybe something else entirely.

I watched her pour the boiling water into mugs and place tea bags into each.

"Do you have any honey?" she asked.

I shook my head.

"Oh, first time tea drinkers should really have honey. What about sugar?"

I shook my head again.

"I guess I was wrong before. This is a bachelor pad. You'll just have to tolerate it without any sweetness." She sat down on one of the stools at the kitchen island and blew at the steam coming off her mug.

God, those lips. My cock twitched to life.

"Matt?"

"Sorry?" I hadn't realized she'd said anything.

"Do you want to see some of your matches?"

"What? How can there be matches already? I barely told you anything the other night."

"But I already know you. So I typed up the rest of your profile and filled out all the necessary info. Minus the fact that you suddenly love redheads," she said with a laugh.

I'd teased her enough about that the last time we'd talked about this stupid app.

She tapped the stool next to her so I'd sit down. "Here. You just swipe when you see someone you like. Oooh, this girl is pretty."

"She doesn't have red hair." I tried to hide my smile.

Penny hit me in the ribs with her elbow as she swiped past the girl. And the next girl who looked like her face was half human half horse. She paused on another woman who looked fully human. "What about her? She looks really sweet. And lots of the women I've seen you with have blonde hair."

It felt like she'd elbowed me in the stomach. I didn't think I'd made a habit of dating blondes. But maybe I had. Brooklyn was blonde.

Penny passed by a few more girls. And by a few I mean…dozens. And I never said a word. Because I didn't want to date any of them.

I tilted my head so I could stare at her instead of at the screen.

"Yes or no?" Penny asked.

I didn't bother looking. "Pass."

This kept going for a while. Penny was super patient. She didn't seem to care that I literally hadn't liked one match. I was pretty sure I'd said the word "no" more than I ever had in my life over the next hour.

"Oh." She stopped. "She sounds perfect. Her profile is cute. She seems really fun."

"Then why don't you date her?"

Penny looked up at me. "Why are you suddenly acting so hostile? This is supposed to be fun."

"How would you feel if I forced you to look at a bunch of men you weren't interested in?"

"Confused. Because I'm married." She smiled, waiting for me to laugh, but I didn't. "Matt, you asked for my help. Why do you always get so mad whenever I follow through?"

Because I don't want any of this. I hadn't expected her to have already finished creating my dating profile. I thought we'd spend today joking about ways to describe me. And telling her things she didn't know about me. Fuck, I didn't know what I expected. But I didn't feel like swiping through a bunch of blondes that I wanted nothing to do with. "Can I at least see the profile you made for me?"

Penny pressed her lips together. "But it's more fun to look at the matches…"

"You did something weird."

"What?" She looked shocked. But in an over the top way. She was definitely lying.

"You put something weird in my profile, didn't you?"

"I did no such thing."

I grabbed the phone from her and she squealed. I clicked through to my profile and laughed. "The most eligible bachelor in the city?" I looked up from the screen. "That's the corniest thing I've ever heard in my life."

"You're a Caldwell. Everyone's going to recognize you from your picture anyway. I thought we might as well lean into it."

I shook my head as I read through all the nonsense. "Great with kids? Are you kidding me?"

"You are great with kids. Scarlett freaking loves you."

"But you made it sound like I'm looking for divorcées with children."

"Well you are over thirty…"

I glared at her.

"Would that be so bad? To have a family?"

Yes. Yes, it would be. I couldn't have a family. I couldn't have a wife. I'd promised Brooklyn it would only ever be her. I'd promised. "I'm good with your kids. Not with my own. Take that part out. And also get rid of the part about me volunteering at Empire High."

"But you do volunteer at Empire High."

I thought about the woman in the hotel room this morning. Tanner had told her I was a nice guy. I needed to lower expectations here. "It makes me sound like too much of a nice guy."

"Matt, you are a nice guy. What do you want it to say in your profile? That you're looking for a one-night stand?"

Yeah, kind of. But that didn't exactly work with the false pretense of why we were hanging out. "Get rid of all that crap. And take down my picture too. I don't want people to say yes to a date with me because they know who I am."

"I think the picture might be required."

I snapped a photo of the tea that I hadn't even tried and handed her phone back to her. "Just use that picture."

"You want a photo of cold tea to be your profile picture on your dating profile?" She shook her head.

"And tell them that I'm poor."

"That's just lying."

"It's all about low expectations, Penny."

"Why? Wouldn't you rather a girl be super nervous and excited to go on a date with you? Looking forward to something is pretty great." She immediately looked back down at her phone. And I swore she was blinking a little faster. "You know what? I'm just going to find you someone and let you know when your first date is."

Well, that sounded terrible. But I was a little more concerned about the fact that it looked like I'd almost made her cry.

"Ian just pulled up. See you for the Giants game?"

I didn't exactly feel like hanging out with everyone tonight. I shook my head.

But I wasn't sure she'd seen because she was already walking toward the door. "Bye, Matt," she said without looking back.

Great. I ran my hand down my face. Penny was setting me up with someone I couldn't even veto now. And I'd made her cry.

CHAPTER 11

Monday

"Here you go," said my administrative assistant as she placed a hot cup of coffee down on my desk.

"Thanks, Mary." I'd come back to the office after football practice to get some more work done. And I desperately needed some caffeine.

"Your mother left another message about getting together with you for lunch. What do you want me to say to her?"

My mom always bugged my assistant when I didn't answer her texts. She got overly concerned about me every fall. And I tried my best to avoid her until the holidays. I didn't want to talk about Brooklyn. I just wanted peace. "Don't worry about it, I'll call her." *Eventually.*

"Okay. Is there anything else I can get you before I head out?"

I looked down at my watch. I hadn't realized it was after six. "No, have a nice evening."

She didn't move to leave. "You know, I heard a rumor the other day. It was something about…" She lightly tapped her chin and pretended like she was trying to remember something. "Oh, right. Sleep is actually really important. Who would have thought?"

I laughed. "Mary, I've been sleeping."

"Tell your face that. And you forgot to change after practice."

I scowled at her, but only in jest. I usually did change back into a suit after practice. But over the last few weeks, I'd stopped. No one else was here this late anyway.

"Maybe try some chamomile tea."

What was with women forcing me to drink tea? But I didn't know how to say no to her. "I'll give it a try." Penny may have left some of that.

"You have a good evening, Matthew."

I'd been telling her for years to call me Matt. But she refused. She said businessmen didn't have nicknames. It was the only thing we ever bickered about. Mary was the best administrative assistant ever. And even though she did flirt with me sometimes, it was all in fun. Because she was 67. She kept threatening to retire, so I kept raising her salary. Soon she'd be making more than most of upper management. But they didn't need to know that.

Mary closed the door behind her as I stared at another set of spreadsheets. The lines kept blurring together. I pinched the bridge of my nose and leaned back in my chair. I was exhausted. Mary was right, I'd barely slept at all last night. All I could think about was Penny's face when she'd left. Why did she always seem so sad recently? How could I make it better?

There was a knock on the door.

"Really, Mary, I'm fine," I said.

The door opened. But it wasn't Mary standing there.

I immediately stood up. "Poppy." I hadn't seen her in years. But she hadn't changed at all. Probably because her face was more Botox than skin. It was like seeing another ghost. But not a sweet innocent one like Brooklyn. Poppy was almost the spitting image of her cousin, Isabella. The brunette hair. The way she stared at people with disdain. The way she made my skin crawl. I was lucky enough to not know Poppy very well. Unlike her un-dearly departed cousin. There wasn't a day that went by that I wasn't grateful that Isabella was dead. As entertaining as that story was, it wasn't mine to tell. That honor belonged to James and Penny.

But standing here now, it felt like Isabella was staring back at me. And if she wasn't already dead, I would have killed her.

Poppy's lips curled up on the edges, but I wouldn't call it a smile. People like Poppy didn't smile. "Matthew Caldwell. How many years has it been?" She shook her head. "Far too many," she said without waiting for a response. She walked into my office uninvited and started looking around.

"Poppy, what are you doing here?"

She ran her finger along the edge of my desk like she was looking for dust. "You didn't respond to Uncle Richard's texts."

Richard Pruitt had been sending me texts for years. And I never answered. That was our thing. Every time it happened, it felt like a punch in the gut. But I did my best to forget about it and move on. Those texts were no reason for Poppy to show up after-hours at my office without an appointment.

She cocked her head to the side and her eyes ran from the baseball cap on my head to my sneakers.

A chill ran down my spine, like her gaze was ice cold.

"Interesting attire. Very rugged." She bit her lower lip and I tried not to make a gagging noise.

"I came from football practice."

"Ah yes. Uncle Richard mentioned that you were coaching at Empire High. How…quaint." She smiled again, but the skin around her lips didn't move at all.

I wasn't sure which was worse. Her fake smile. Or the fact that Mr. Pruitt was keeping tabs on me. "Poppy, it's late. If you want to schedule a meeting…"

"I'm not here for a meeting." She laughed. "Why would my family come to yours for financial advice?" She put her hand to her silicone chest. "We have more money than you."

Dirty money. Everyone in the city knew that Mr. Pruitt was into some shady shit. The guilt felt like bile stirring in my stomach. I'd left Brooklyn with him. It was my fault that she was dead.

Poppy took a step closer. "We both know you wanted to marry into the family."

I didn't want to marry into her horrid family. I loved Brooklyn *despite* the fact that Mr. Pruitt was her birth father. Not because of it.

But for several years, I'd wondered about the contracts I signed when I was dating Brooklyn. Mr. Pruitt had called them relationship contracts. I'd never read the fine print. But I knew he loved to sneak sketchy, unrelated stuff into all his contracts. That had haunted me. And as Poppy took yet another step closer, I felt like I was going to be sick. What if there was some clause about…*death*? What if I had signed something about being promised to a member of their horrible family?

Poppy stopped right in front of me. "I've always loved a man who craves power. You know…" she reached out and straightened my baseball cap. "…I'm the last living heir to great granddaddy's fortune. Think of all we could do together. I have the power. And you know how to handle the money."

She meant hide the money in offshore accounts. I clenched my hands into fists. I wasn't going to hit her. But I was about to hit something if she touched me again.

She licked her bottom lip, probably mistaking my disgust for admiration. Because she was every bit as delusional as Isabella. "I actually kind of like the grunge look. I can work with that. But a suit and tie never hurt anyone. Next time we meet, maybe dress up a tad?"

I was definitely going to be sick. "Get out of my office, Poppy."

She pouted. "Uncle Richard won't be happy to hear that you didn't receive me graciously."

"I don't give a shit about what your uncle thinks."

"Hmm. Is that so?" She lifted a picture frame off my desk.

It was a framed one of me with all my friends. Their wives. Their children.

"Uncle Richard has allowed certain allowances in the past years. He still thinks of you as family, you know."

I shook my head. That man was no family of mine.

"You're going to want to talk to him. Or he might start being less…forgiving."

"What the hell does that mean?" My heart started racing. Because I knew what it meant.

"We both know what Uncle Richard is capable of."

Terrible things. He'd fucking killed my wife-to-be. He was heartless. He was a monster. And there had been things that happened that I thought for sure would have resulted in retaliation. Like when Isabella met her untimely end. For some reason, there hadn't been any repercussions.

"Aw, isn't she cute," Poppy said and pointed to Scarlett in the photo. "I heard she really likes to open doors for strangers."

"Poppy, I swear to God…"

"It's not polite to swear, Matthew. You know Uncle Richard's rules. After all, you've signed a contract agreeing to abide by them."

"If you touch one hair on Scarlett's head…"

"Me?" She laughed. "God no. Whatever makes you think I'd touch a stranger's hair? Gross. I'm not a peasant. I have people for that."

I swallowed hard.

"So call my uncle back, yes?"

I didn't respond.

"If you don't, I think we both know what will happen."

Yeah, I'd gotten the hint. But she and her minions would never get close enough to Scarlett to make good on a veiled threat. James had the best security money could buy. And I wouldn't let it happen. "Get out of my office."

"Oh." She shook her shoulders. "I like when you get stern with me. You know…I saw your dating profile. It was very endearing."

"Out. Now."

"You should just cancel that. You won't be needing it. I think there's a different future laid out for you already. Oh, and I almost forgot." Poppy pulled out an envelope from her purse. "This is from Uncle Richard." She placed the envelope on my desk, the fake nail on her pointer finger practically poking a hole through the paper. "Would you like to read this now? You can write a response and I can take it to him. I'll wait."

"I'm not going to ask you again to leave, Poppy." I grabbed my desk phone. "I'm calling security."

"You're no fun, Matthew. We'll change that, I'm sure. See you soon." She blew me a kiss, turned on her heel, and walked out of my office, taking the ice-cold air with her.

I stared at the envelope with my name written across the front. There was no use reading it. Surely it would be the same as the countless texts Mr. Pruitt had sent me over the years. Yet, I found myself ripping it open anyway.

I understand why you're angry with me. But I've been protecting you for years now. And for years you have returned my kindness by ignoring me. This is a matter of life or death now, Matthew. Call me back immediately.

I crumpled the paper in my fist and threw it in the trash. Life or death? He didn't value life. And protecting me? What the fuck was he talking about? He'd never protected me from anything. And he certainly didn't care about me. Or else he wouldn't have sent Poppy here to flirt with me. Or threaten me. Or whatever the fuck had just happened.

I picked up my phone. I'd had enough. It was one thing to harass me once a year. It was another thing to threaten one of my best friends' daughters. I'd had enough of this family of psychopaths. I pulled up his contact info, but my thumb paused above the call button.

Tanner thought I should just talk to him and get it over with. I knew most people would give me the same advice. But I didn't want to talk to Mr. Pruitt. That was what he wanted. And I didn't want to do anything that Mr. Pruitt wanted me to do. He'd find some way to twist something I said and get me stuck doing something for his muddied name. And I wasn't having any part of it. I set down the phone and walked over to the floor to ceiling windows, overlooking Manhattan. I didn't want to talk to him. I didn't want to step foot back into his haunted apartment. I wanted nothing to do with him or his evil niece.

I took a deep breath as I watched the cars speeding down below. I needed to put a stop to him trying to insert himself into my life. And the answer was right at my fingertips.

It was my job to sort out financial messes. Which meant I knew exactly what to look for if I needed to…oh, I don't know…find proof that someone was laundering money. And Mr. Pruitt was definitely laundering money. He had to be. He had a few legitimate businesses, but not enough to make him one of the wealthiest men in New York.

I was just a kid when Brooklyn died. Back then, I couldn't do anything about it. But I could now. And I didn't care what I needed to dig up. Richard Pruitt deserved to rot in prison for the rest of his life. I didn't care what the cops and private investigators said. He was a murderer. And I'd find a way to make him pay.

CHAPTER 12

Friday

I cringed as Jefferson kicked the extra point and actually fell over. It wasn't even muddy. How was this kid capable of slipping on dirt? The football flew in the air and for just a second I held my breath. But then the ball fell like it had gotten struck down by lightning, landing short from the uprights. Super short. Like 15 feet away. Jefferson gave me thumbs up as he got to his feet. I tried not to grimace and gave him what I hoped was an encouraging thumbs up in return.

Every piece of advice I gave him somehow made it worse. But honestly? I hadn't been the best coach this week. I'd been late to practice. My mind had been a little preoccupied trying to dig up dirt on Mr. Pruitt, only to find...nothing.

And that wasn't the only thing weighing on me. My stalker was back in the stands tonight. And after my visit from Poppy on Monday, I was worried she had been sent by her. Or maybe even Mr. Pruitt. Either way, I could actually feel the hairs on the back of my neck rise whenever she looked at me. What the hell was she doing here again? What did she want?

I turned around to see her in the stands, but she was gone. I shook my head. I hadn't been sleeping either. I'd tried the freaking chamomile tea and it didn't work. Maybe I was imagining the whole thing.

But the worst part about this shitty week? Penny hadn't spoken to me since leaving my place. My eyes traveled up the stands. She'd shown up tonight with James and everyone else though. Mason had his arm around Bee. I'm pretty sure they were laughing about that awful kick. Rob had just pulled Daphne onto his lap and was tickling her side. And Penny was staring up at James with the biggest smile I'd seen on her face recently. For him. Not for me.

Tanner waved at me. He was sitting with them too. It was great that they were all here. Supporting me. It should have felt nice. But them being here made my skin crawl. Like they were evaluating me or something.

I turned back to the field. I needed to talk to James about Poppy's threat. I knew that. But I was hoping to have a solution first. I'd already waited a week though. A week too long. If something happened to Scarlett before I could tell James, I'd never be able to forgive myself.

"Coach Caldwell?"

I looked down at Jefferson. "What's up?" We were up by three touchdowns, minus the three extra points he'd missed. And I knew he felt the embarrassment of those misses more than the joy of our victory.

"Do you think maybe we should start going for two-point conversions instead of extra points?" He looked so defeated.

And it broke me. I was supposed to be present enough to figure out how to help him. And all I was doing was worrying about literally everything else possible. "Absolutely not." I slapped his back and his glasses slid down his nose. "We're going to figure out how to make you the greatest kicker Empire High has ever seen."

He smiled. "Thanks, Coach Caldwell."

Now I just needed to make good on my promise. There had to be a way to get through to him. But as the game ended, I was no closer to a solution.

And all the high-fives in the world didn't pull me out of my head. I felt the little hairs on the back of my neck rise again and turned around. My stalker was standing on the edge of the field just…staring. As soon as our eyes met, she quickly walked away.

She was definitely up to something. I tried to remember the night we spent together, but it was a little fuzzy. Why had she slept with me in the first place? Did she have some kind of ulterior motive? Had Mr. Pruitt actually sent her? Had she stolen something from me? Or copied my keys or something? *I don't know.* I just had a really bad feeling. All I wanted to do was go home and take some sleeping pills.

But my brother and friends were making their way over from the stands.

Tanner waved and then pointed to his watch.

I waved back, knowing that meant he probably had a date or a late meeting. And it was probably best that he was in a hurry to leave. Because I didn't need any more "my Tanner" jokes right now.

"Just like old times," Mason said. But he wasn't really talking to me. He was staring out at the field. I couldn't tell if he looked sentimental or just…sad.

"You were great," his wife, Bee, added and gave me a hug. "I can't believe I didn't know you coached at Mason's old school. I would have gotten Mason out here way sooner."

I didn't really have anything to say to that. Because no one outside of Mason, Rob, James, and I knew why none of us wanted to step foot back on this campus. Maybe reminiscing about high school was fun for some people. I wasn't one of them. And judging from the look on Mason's face, I wasn't the only one.

"This school is unbelievable," Daphne cut in, and slapped Rob's hands away so she could give me a hug too.

"It looks more like a museum than a high school. Rob said we might get a tour?"

"Mhm." I really didn't want to walk through those doors. I'd somehow avoided doing that very thing. I wasn't the gym teacher, so there was no reason to go inside. I even bought all our practice equipment and donated a shed to keep it in. Thinking about walking into the school made my heart start to race.

"Where are all your kids?" I asked. If someone could put a smile on my face, it was Scarlett. Or Rob and Daphne's daughter, Sophie. She was just as funny as her dad.

"Ellen's watching them," James said. "Great game."

"Thanks." I looked over to the school. "The side doors are unlocked if you guys want to head in. I have a few things to clean up."

Mason grabbed Bee's hand and guided her away from the stadium, like he couldn't wait to get out of here. The school brought back more memories, though. He'd figure that out soon enough.

Penny gave me a small wave before James put his arm around her shoulders and pulled her away.

"I'm going to stay and help Matt clean up," Daphne said. "You go ahead."

Penny was easy to talk to and we always laughed together. Bee was encouraging. It was hard to leave a conversation with her without feeling motivated. And Daphne? It was like she could somehow sense pain from a mile away. She always wanted to help. And she was normally really good at it. But I think I was like a puzzle she couldn't solve. Like she knew that I needed her, but I'd never tell her why.

Rob kissed her cheek. "Hey, wait up!" he called to the others as he ran after them.

I didn't really have anything to pick up. There were no practice balls, and Jefferson hadn't brought snacks again this week. Because they hadn't been well received. Another thing to add to my list of recent failures. I busied myself by looking at my clipboard even though I had all the plays memorized.

"All the guys were quiet on the drive over here," Daphne said.

I nodded but didn't look up.

"I've looked at Rob's old yearbook from senior year. He got Class Clown. And you got Most Likely to Succeed."

I remembered trying to get out of taking pictures for the superlative. I didn't want to be Most Likely to Succeed. It felt like a sick joke. Being nominated for something pertaining to my future was meaningless when my real future, the only future that mattered, had been cut short the second Brooklyn took her last breath.

"You were all popular. So why does Rob never talk about his time here? Why don't any of you guys?"

I sighed. "Because high school sucks for everyone."

She laughed. "For people like me. Not for people like you."

Penny had said something similar to me the other day. And I hated when any of my friends' wives said shit like that. "You're one of us." I'd never gotten a chance to make Brooklyn my wife. But Daphne got to marry Rob. Bee got to marry Mason. Penny got to marry James.

"You know what I mean. I was a nerd in school, Matt. I didn't get any superlatives. But I still have good memories of high school. It's like none of you do."

That was a lie. Because for just a few months somewhere lost in those years…I'd had everything I'd ever wanted. Before it was taken away.

"I know Rob's always joking around. But he worries about you."

I froze, even though I wasn't doing anything. *He'd told her?* My heart started racing even faster. *He'd fucking told her?*

Daphne held up her hands like she knew what conclusion I'd come to. "He didn't want to come tonight. He never talks about Empire High. And I have no idea why. He just brushes it off. And I've asked James about it too. I know they both had a rough childhood. My mother-in-law has taken…some time to get used to."

I couldn't help but laugh at that. Mrs. Hunter was the worst.

"But Rob and James always speak so highly of your parents. Your mom told me she felt like she helped raise the Hunter boys. So I don't really get why you and Mason don't like talking about your childhood. It sounded like it was really great."

"It was great." Besides for that one thing. That one momentous thing that haunted me every day. That one thing I'd never get over.

"So why does it seem like you're scared to go into the school?"

"I'm not scared."

She smiled. "Fine. Apprehensive."

I took a deep breath. "There are just a lot of memories I don't feel like reliving."

"Okay." She seemed to sense that she wasn't going to get anything out of me. "But if you ever do want to relive them? I'm here, you know."

I knew she was. And I stupidly felt my eyes water. I blinked fast and pretended to cough. Daphne understood loss better than anyone else I knew. She'd understand. She was someone that would be so easy to open up to. But if I told someone…they'd want to help me move on. I didn't want to move on. That was the whole point. And no one would ever understand that.

I looked over at the school and sighed. I hadn't stepped foot into Empire High ever since graduation. Maybe walking around would help. Somehow. There were really only two things that could happen. It could make me feel farther away from Brooklyn than ever before. But I already felt her loss every day. I was more scared of the other option. That it would make me feel closer to her. If I walked through those doors and felt her presence? I'd be more stuck than ever. I'd never get away from this fucking school.

Daphne looped her arm through mine. "Come on. You promised me a tour." She said it with a weird British accent for some reason. Probably just to make me smile.

I laughed and let her guide us up the path to the school. I ignored the way my laugh died in my throat. And how I felt physically cold as I walked up toward the school.

Going back through those doors after Brooklyn had died was hell. For two and a half years I'd had to walk around those halls and pretend she'd never occupied them. Pretend I'd never kissed her against her locker. Or pulled her into an empty classroom. I could hear her laughter ringing in my ears.

If Daphne hadn't been holding on to my arm, I would have turned around. But there was something comforting about not having to do this alone. I wasn't trying to move on. I swear I wasn't. But I needed those empty hallways to make Brooklyn slip farther away. Because I wasn't sure how much longer I could breathe when the past felt so damn heavy. The weight of it on my chest felt stifling. At least, that's what I told myself. Because the fact that I was slowly dying of a broken heart somehow felt worse.

CHAPTER 13

Friday

The hallways of Empire High looked exactly the same as they always had. Shiny floors, dark wood, posters about school spirit. It even smelled the same. I swallowed the lump in my throat.

I couldn't really place the smell. It just reminded me of…being young. And alive. I closed my eyes. God, it reminded me of Brooklyn.

"You okay?" Daphne asked.

I opened my eyes and tried to focus on anything other than that damned smell. "I'm fine. We should catch up with the others." The last thing I needed was for one of them to break something. I was already on thin ice with the principal.

Daphne was quiet as we made our way through the empty halls. Past classrooms I remembered joking around in with Rob. Past the chem lab where Rob and I had made something explode that definitely shouldn't have. We'd kept finding beaker glass for weeks after that. For just a second I actually smiled. I'd only had one class with Brooklyn. But pretty much every single one with Rob. And I couldn't deny that there weren't good memories in this school.

We found the rest of our friends in the cafeteria.

"Remember when James broke this window?" Rob asked with a laugh.

My smile vanished. Yeah, I remembered.

"What did you break it with?" Bee asked. "A football or something?"

"His fist," Rob said. He pretended to box with the window, throwing a punch dangerously close to the glass.

Penny turned to James. "And why exactly did you punch a window?"

James pressed his lips together.

Rob didn't seem to notice that he was opening old wounds. "He thought Matt had slept with his high school girlfriend. But Matt hadn't done it. Or so he claims. No one knows for sure."

"We know for sure," I said. "I didn't sleep with Rachel. It was just a kiss. And she was the one that threw herself at me." But Isabella had gotten a picture of it. And then James had believed her over me. I still fucking hated James for not believing me over that witch. I hated him for making my life a living hell when I should have been focusing on my last days with Brooklyn.

Penny was staring at me, but then she looked back at James. "Why did you never tell me about all that?" she asked.

"Because it's ancient history." James put his hand protectively on her waist.

It wasn't ancient history to me. My whole fucking life had stopped right here. And I was pretty sure they all knew it.

"It was crazy," Rob said. "I took James' side of course. And Mason took Matt's side. It was an epic Hunter Caldwell feud." He laughed. "God and homecoming? That was the craziest night."

"I'm scared to ask, but what happened at homecoming?" Daphne asked.

"James retaliated by kissing Matt's girlfriend. And then we all got into this huge fist fight. We almost got kicked out of school."

Daphne shook her head.

"I can't believe you did that," Penny said to James. But she didn't push him away from her for literally being the worst. She didn't move at all. She let him keep his arm around her.

"I wasn't in a good place," he said.

Mason cleared his throat. "I wonder if the principal's office looks the same."

I knew he was trying to get our group to drop the subject and move along, but no one moved. I really wished Tanner had stuck around. He'd be able to ease the tension in some way.

"That's awful," Penny said. "What made you guys make up?"

Brooklyn's death.

Rob finally closed his big mouth. He wasn't going to say it. No one was going to say it.

But my fiancée had died. And they'd felt bad for making my life any shittier than it already was. They felt sorry for me. Not because they believed me. Not because they cared.

The cafeteria was filled with complete and utter silence. I looked over at the tables. They were still organized the same way they were back then. The Untouchables' table. And then the one that Brooklyn always sat at. Before we were an us. Before I stopped sitting at the stupid Untouchables' table for good and joined her where I should have always been.

"Because we're family," James said. "You don't turn your back on family."

I looked over at him. *You just stab your family in the back?* I should have been over it. And maybe I would have been if things had gone down differently. If I had Brooklyn wrapped in my arms like they all had their wives in theirs? Yeah, maybe I would have been more forgiving then.

"Well, I'm glad you all made up," Penny said. She looked over at the window that James had punched like she was lost in thought.

There wasn't much to think about. She was married to an asshole.

"I actually need to go check on something," I said. "I'll be back." I walked away before I had to add something to my lie. I didn't need to look at anything. And I wouldn't be back. I needed to get the fuck out of this school. But before I could reach the front doors, my feet seemed to guide me to the auditorium.

I looked over my shoulder, like I was scared someone was going to catch me going in. But no one was following me. I pushed the door in and let it close behind me with a thud, bathing me in darkness.

Brooklyn and I had kissed for the first time right here. She said I'd stolen the kiss. So I promised her I'd steal all her firsts.

I closed my eyes, trying to remember what it felt like to have her beside me. But all I felt was...cold.

First kiss. First time. First love. She'd died before I could make good on my promise of all her firsts. I was supposed to marry that girl. She was supposed to have my children. She was supposed to be my family. My whole world.

I put my hand down on one of the chairs. Why had I come in here? Just to torture myself? I closed my eyes even tighter. *No.* I wanted to remember. I wanted to remember what it was like to be happy. I needed to remember what it was like to be okay. Because I wasn't fucking okay.

And if I closed my eyes tight enough, I could almost hear Brooklyn's laughter. Almost feel her breath whispering in my ear.

I opened my eyes and saw the darkness all around me. All alone. Yeah, I really wasn't fucking okay.

I heard the auditorium doors open. I turned to see Penny standing there. Her hip kept the door ajar and let the light stream in. "Did you find that thing you needed to check on?"

I nodded. I was surprised she'd come after me. We hadn't spoken since Sunday. I figured I'd done something to upset her. And it was better if I just apologized so we could move on. "I'm sorry about Sunday," I said.

"Why are you sorry? I'm the one that practically ran out of your house." She laughed. "I should be the one apologizing to you."

We were both silent for a few moments. I wanted to ask her why she'd run. But I didn't want to push her.

She looked down at her shoes. "I know James wasn't in the best headspace in high school."

That was an understatement. Half the time he had been drunk or high off his mind.

"But…" her voice trailed off. "I also know he meant what he said about not turning your back on family. I can't believe he kissed one of your old girlfriends." She shook her head. "But he's sorry. I can tell. You can't tell me you're still mad at him about that after all these years?" She cracked a smile.

She'd never understand. Because I'd never tell her. "I'm not still mad at him." I didn't even really know if it was a lie. No matter what, I was most mad at myself. I was the one that had let Brooklyn down. Not him.

Penny stared at me like she was waiting for me to add something. But I didn't have anything to add.

"Don't tell me you broke up with that girl because of what James did."

"No." I never broke up with Brooklyn. And she still owned my heart. I'd always be hers.

"Well that's good." Penny smiled.

She probably just thought that meant my high school girlfriend and I broke up for some other reason. It was an easy mistake to make. Because Brooklyn wasn't standing beside me. It was the only reasonable conclusion to jump to. And God I wished it was true. That she was still alive. It would have killed me for her to be with someone else. But it would be a little easier to breathe knowing that she was breathing too.

"And speaking of girls..." said Penny. "You have a date tomorrow night."

I blinked. "What?" The last thing I wanted to do was go on some stupid date with some woman who wasn't Brooklyn. Not after tonight. Not ever. Penny wasn't an idiot. She could tell I was hurting. But she was way off base for thinking this was going to help. "I'm not going on some random date."

"Actually, you are. Because I already made a reservation under your name at Giordano's."

"Then cancel."

"But I think she's exactly what you're looking for."

"What does that even mean?" She had no idea what I was looking for. Because despite her asking repeatedly while swiping through random chicks for hours, I hadn't ever answered her seriously.

"You told me what you wanted. I found her."

I'd only joked about wanting Penny. No one else. I didn't want any of this. "Penny..."

"I know. You're welcome. You can thank me when you two hit it off."

That was not at all what I was about to say.

"And before you ask any more questions, I'm not telling you anything about her. No stalking her before the date and backing out. And she doesn't know what you look like either, because I used that picture of the tea you swore you wanted for your profile." She looked happier and happier as she talked. "It's the perfect blind date. I swear I have a really good feeling about this. I just need you to trust me."

Damn it. I did trust her. Which made my stomach churn. Because she probably found someone really great. Someone in another life that might have been a perfect match for me. But there was no way in hell it could work.

"She'll meet you there at 8."

I found myself nodding. I couldn't say no to Penny. Not when she looked so happy.

"And what are you doing in here in the dark anyway? Come on, we're all going out to celebrate your win."

I was just exhausted. I didn't want to go out drinking with my friends. But as I rejoined everyone in the hall, I realized maybe we all needed this.

Sixteen years ago, we'd ruled this school. We were all happy. We were fucking untouchable. And now? Rob was staring at me seriously and had abandoned his jokes. Mason looked like he literally wanted to run out of the school. And James was staring off in the distance, looking almost as depressed as me.

Coming here was like stepping into a time capsule. And yes, there were a lot of good memories at Empire High. But they were tainted with what had happened. And the secret I'd made them keep. They'd promised not to ever talk about Brooklyn again. Not until I was ready. And they'd kept their promise. They'd kept the secret from all their wives. And I was pretty sure it was eating away at them almost as much as it was eating away at me.

And the worst part? Brooklyn would have hated seeing us like this. She would have wanted all of us to be happy. I took a deep breath. "The first round is on me."

CHAPTER 14

Friday

I took another sip of my beer. I needed to talk to James in private. It was bad enough that I'd waited this long after Poppy's threat. But now everyone was having so much fun. Even I was enjoying some of the stories about us in high school. I hated to break up the party when everyone was smiling and laughing so hard. And I was pretty sure Bee was more than tipsy. Which was hilarious because she always laughed at everything when she was drunk.

But as tempting as it was to just crack jokes all night for her…this Poppy thing was serious. I was just about to ask James if we could talk for a second, when Tanner slid into the empty stool beside me.

"Sorry I'm late," he said. "What did I miss?" He somehow already had a beer in his hand.

Had he been here for a while? "I didn't realize you were coming," I said.

"Yeah, the gang invited me."

The gang? I looked over at my friends. Honestly, a gang would be the least likely phrase I'd used to describe this bunch.

"Robert," Tanner said and nodded to him.

Rob sat up a little straighter. "Tanner."

I cleared my throat before they could start making jabs at each other. "We were just talking about the four of us in high school."

"Ah," Tanner said. "All the fighting?"

Bee laughed.

"No, we were actually talking about all the good times," I said.

"Interesting." Tanner took a sip of his beer. "From a slightly outside perspective, maybe it would be better if we did dive into all the fighting though, yes? In order to move on?"

"We have moved on," Rob said. "Or else we wouldn't all be sitting here right now hanging out."

"Have you though?"

Rob stared at him. "Yes, I just said that."

"But haaaaave you though?"

"We have," James said. He looked over at me.

I pressed my lips together. I knew James wasn't really a dick. Yes, he'd acted like one when we were teenagers. But he'd had my back ever since. It was fall though. And I was always more likely to snap on him in the fall. Because it reminded me so much of Brooklyn. So yes, we'd moved on as best I was able to. I couldn't offer any more.

"Hmm." Tanner put his glass down on the table. "If you were all really over it, why did Matt drug you during your bachelor party, James?"

Bee started laughing harder.

"You what?" Penny said.

"It's not a big deal..." James started.

But Penny cut him off. "Yes it is a big deal. Why the hell would you do that, Matt?" She was using her authoritative mom voice that always made me feel in trouble but also slightly aroused.

I opened my mouth and closed it again. I wanted to say I didn't know why. But I did. It was because James had been about to get married. And I was jealous. I felt like he'd robbed me of that with Brooklyn. Like he had the life I was supposed to have. And I had been drunk myself that night. And maybe a little high. And maybe a lot an idiot.

"Did he really?" Penny asked Daphne.

Daphne had been at the same resort as us during James' bachelor party. It's where she and Rob had officially met. So she'd unfortunately seen all the shenanigans first hand.

I winced when Daphne slowly nodded.

"Look, we all went a little overboard that weekend," Mason said.

Bee tried to glare at him through her laughter. "What does that mean?" I couldn't tell if she was actually upset or she was doing an overexaggerated glare because of her intoxication.

Mason laughed. "It was a bachelor party."

She continued to stare at him. And even though it looked like she was seconds away from exploding with laughter again, the last thing I wanted was for Bee to be upset with Mason because he was trying to cover for me. The bachelor party had actually been very tame and very lame.

"I'm sorry, okay you guys?" I said.

Tanner clapped me on the back. "That's a good start, Matt. But I have an idea. James, you should just get him back. It's best to just get even. Who has some drugs?"

James shook his head. "I'm not going to drug Matt."

"Leave it to me then," Tanner said.

"I don't want you to drug him either."

"Noted. I'll think of something better." Tanner snapped his fingers. "Revenge is a dish best served hard, if you know what I mean." He raised his glass.

I literally had no idea what he meant. *Served hard?*

Bee giggled.

"You mean cold?" Rob said.

Tanner looked confused.

"The phrase is revenge is a dish best served cold," Rob said.

Tanner shook his head. "I don't think that's how it goes."

"That's definitely how it goes. Who serves a hard dish?"

"Dishes are made from glass. They're all quite hard, Young Robert. Have you never been hit by one?" He started to wave down a waitress, as if he was going to order a plate to break over Rob's head.

I grabbed Tanner's hand to lower it. We didn't need a waitress to bring over any plates for him to throw at Rob.

"I'm trying to help," he whispered back.

"By offering to beat Rob with plates?"

"By fixing your friendships. And yes, possibly teaching Robert a lesson along the way."

I looked over to see everyone staring at us. I cleared my throat and removed my hand from Tanner's arm. This conversation was ridiculous. We were all fine. Tanner was pushing buttons unnecessarily. And I still needed to have that conversation with James before it got any later. "James, can I talk to you for a second?"

"Yeah, sure." He went to stand up, but paused when his phone started ringing. "One second," he said.

"Hi Ellen, is everything okay?"

There was silence as he listened to her.

"Pumpkin, did you steal Ellen's phone again?"

Penny shook her head with a smile.

"Mommy and I are out right now. Be a good girl and let Ellen tell you a bedtime story."

He listened to Scarlett intently.

"She does do the voices. I've heard her do them."

He smiled at whatever her response was.

"Is everything okay?" Penny mouthed silently.

James nodded. "Okay, pumpkin. We'll be home in a few minutes. Love you too." He hung up. "She's refusing to go to bed without us reading her bedtime story. And she's keeping everyone else up too. I think Ellen might have a revolt on her hands."

Rob laughed. "Sophie and Scarlett are going to be such a handful when they're older."

Rob was right about that. Scarlett was a little baller for refusing to go to bed without a proper bedtime story. And Sophie seemed like she enjoyed a good revolt too. It was possible she was the one leading the troops.

"We should probably go get Sophie and RJ too," Daphne said. "It's getting late." She grabbed her coat off the back of her chair.

"Is it okay if we have that chat another time?" James asked.

No. Not really. But I just nodded. They were going home to Scarlett right now. Nothing bad could happen to her tonight.

Rob, Daphne, James, and Penny said their goodbyes.

"Have fun on your date tomorrow," Penny whispered and gave me a quick hug. I watched her duck under James' arm and giggle at something he whispered in her ear.

"You okay?" Tanner asked.

Now he was concerned about me? Moments after trying to get James to drug me?

Luckily I didn't have to answer him, because Bee was laughing harder than ever, drawing everyone's attention to her.

"So just me?" Bee said, but I could barely make out the words through her laughter.

I hadn't caught the start of her conversation with Mason, but it looked like the two of them were having the time of their lives.

"Yeah, our mom definitely didn't walk us to the bus stop in high school," Mason said. "We usually rode with James. Or I drove myself."

Bee finally stopped laughing long enough to breathe. "Not all of high school. Just until junior year when I finally snapped."

Mason was staring at her with stars in his eyes. "Your mom is amazing."

"More like mortifying," Bee said and covered her face.

Mason lowered her hand and kissed her temple.

I turned away and took another sip of my scotch. Out of all my friends, Bee looked the most like Brooklyn. Sometimes it was hard to look at her for too long. I wondered if Mason saw it. But I didn't think so. Unlike James, he hadn't had a crush on Brooklyn. And I wasn't even sure if James really had either. I was pretty sure he had only pretended to like her to mess with me. But I'd never know. Because I'd never bring her up.

I swirled the ice around in my glass. At least I wasn't the third wheel tonight. Because Tanner was here too. I actually preferred hanging out with Bee and Mason the most because they didn't have any kids. It was just adults talking. I loved my friends' kids, but I didn't need to talk about them nonstop like parents always seemed to.

"What was Mason like in high school?" Bee asked me.

I shrugged. "The same."

Bee laughed. "I'm pretty sure I had an awkward stage between first and twelfth grade. Unlike you guys with your amazing Caldwell genes. I hope our kids get them."

I was pretty sure my fingers tightened on my glass. *Not you guys too.* It was hard enough being the only single one. I didn't want to be the only one without kids too.

Mason laughed. "You should see your face right now. I promise Bee's not pregnant."

I breathed a loud sigh of relief, which made Bee laugh harder.

She lifted up her glass. "I've had like three glasses of wine. Definitely not pregnant, Matt. But really, would it be so bad to be an uncle?"

"I am an uncle."

"I mean like a real one. A blood one."

It didn't matter that I wasn't a blood relation to James and Robs' kids. I still loved those little brats. "Are you guys really thinking about it?"

"Maybe next year," Bee said and looked over at Mason.

A few years ago he would have looked as shocked as me. Instead, he just shrugged.

I silently cursed. They were definitely about to pop out a dozen babies and leave me behind.

"To be young and in love again," Tanner sighed.

He was still young. And had plenty of time to find love. He was being such a diva tonight.

"Ah, to being young and in love." Bee lifted up her wine glass and a little sloshed out the side. She was so drunk. Adorably so. Which was my fault since I kept buying everyone more rounds.

"Matt." She reached out and grabbed my hand. "What's going on with you? You keep doing that thing with your face." She pulled her lips into an exaggerated frown.

"I'm fine." I patted her hand.

"Only people who aren't fine say that they're fine. You can tell us anything, you know."

I glanced at Mason. I was pretty sure he'd been hoping I'd talk about Brooklyn for years. But I wasn't going to start tonight. "There's nothing to tell."

"You're a terrible liar. Tell me right now or you…you'll have to pay for all the drinks."

"All the drinks are already on my tab."

"Oh, crap." She stared at me. "I knew that. And I had three glasses to make up for Penny and Daphne not drinking. Because they were being lame with mom duties."

"Because they're breastfeeding, yeah."

She waved her hand through the air. "That's what I said. So you'll have to pay for the drinks."

I laughed. "I just told you. The drinks are all on my tab anyway."

She nodded. "Right. So tell me the truth or I'll…" she looked down at her glass of wine like she was about to say I'd have to pay for drinks again. But then her head snapped back up. "Or I'll do something terrible to you in your sleep."

"What the hell does that mean? When have you ever even been near me while I'm sleeping?"

She shrugged. "Wouldn't it be scary to find out?"

Yeah, she was definitely drunk.

"If something is bothering you, we are here to listen," Mason said.

I pressed my lips together. I actually did need some advice. I looked back at Bee. There was a 50-50 chance she wouldn't remember any of this anyway. I cleared my throat. It would feel better to get this off my chest. "Poppy visited my office this week."

Mason raised his eyebrow. "Poppy? As in…Isabella's cousin?"

"Yup, that one."

"Isabella has a cousin?" Bee said way too loudly. "Oh God, is she as awful as Isabella?"

I hadn't thought so until this week. Now I was worried she was somehow worse.

"I didn't even know that Richard Pruitt had a niece," Tanner said. "Why didn't I know that?"

"Because she wasn't important. I hadn't seen her in over a decade."

"Wait." Tanner slammed his hand down on the table. "*Wasn't* important? That implies that she is now. Did you sleep with her?"

"Ew. No. She's freaking devil spawn."

"Phew. You had me worried there for a second. Remember, you have to introduce me to any lucky lady you're planning to bed."

"Why does Matt have to introduce you to women he's…to bed with?" Bee asked.

"So I can…approve of them."

Bee laughed. "You're so funny, Tanner."

That was one way to put it.

"Really everything you say is so so funny. And…" her voice trailed off. "God I have the perfect word, it's on the tip of my tongue. Why can't I think of it?"

Mason put his arm around Bee's shoulders. "I think we should probably head out before Bee remembers that other word."

"Hey." She elbowed him in his side. "But yes. Take me home. I'm tired."

He smiled down at her. "Your wish is my command." He grabbed her coat and draped it over her shoulders. He was about to lead her out of the bar when he turned back to me. "Sorry, Matt. What was your story about Poppy? Why did she stop by?"

I didn't know why I'd brought it up. I didn't want to worry him. "No reason. It was really random."

"Huh." He shrugged his shoulders. "Well, have a good night, you two."

Bee blew Tanner and me each a kiss.

I pretended to choke on it and she laughed.

"That went really well," Tanner said.

I ran my fingers through my hair. "You tried to get James to drug me. And you fought with Rob again."

"Robert argued with me. And James does owe you a drugged drink, if I do recall correctly. I thought everything went great. So tell me about Poppy. Is she hot?"

"No."

"No she's not hot? Or no you're not going to tell me about her?"

"Both."

"Hm. Sounds like something you need to talk about."

I sighed. He knew me too well. "Mr. Pruitt sent her. Because I didn't respond to his texts."

"Well, he did say it was urgent this time. I have an idea. How about I come with you when you go see him. That way nothing bad can happen."

"That would just ensure that bad things would happen to both of us."

He shook his head. "Nonsense. He wouldn't mess with me."

"Mr. Pruitt messes with everyone."

"But no one messes with me."

I stared at him. He looked dead serious. Yes, Tanner had more money than anyone else I knew. Including the Pruitts. But I knew that money didn't make him untouchable. And it certainly couldn't protect him from Mr. Pruitt's line of work.

"Just think about it," Tanner said. "Like I told you before, it would probably be best just to get it over with. And this way you wouldn't have to do it alone. You'd have me."

"Yeah, maybe." That was actually really nice of him to have my back. Even if I didn't plan on taking him up on his offer. "Thanks, man."

"That's what best friends are for."

I laughed. "You're just trying to one up Rob?"

Tanner shrugged. "Well, I don't see him offering to go visit your almost father-in-law with you. Classic best friend duty if you ask me." He shook his head like he thought Rob was the most ridiculous person he'd ever met.

Which was funny. Because they were both ridiculous. It was probably why they didn't get along.

I wanted to just drop the Mr. Pruitt thing. But it was still weighing on me. I needed to talk to James about Poppy's threat. But that didn't mean I couldn't talk to Tanner about my plans. "I actually have a better idea than going to see him. I've been trying to dig up dirt on his business dealings. If I could just have some leverage…"

"Consider it done," Tanner said. He slid off his stool and pulled on his coat. "All you had to do was ask."

Wait, what?

"I'll call you with the details." He turned to walk away.

Where was he going? What details? "Tanner!" I called after him.

But he was already gone.

CHAPTER 15

Saturday

Those big blue eyes. I could drown in those eyes. But no matter what I did today, I couldn't capture the color. The size, the shape, the love they held…everything else was right. But not the color. It wasn't quite her. I was usually good at painting Brooklyn's eyes. But it was like the memory of her was drifting away.

I swirled more green into the paint and tried again. *No, that isn't right either.* I closed my eyes and tried to remember. I pictured her laughing, the cool autumn breeze blowing a strand of hair into her face. I reached out to brush it away and the back of my hand collided with wet paint.

My eyes flew open. *Crap.* I grabbed a paper towel off the roll and wiped off my hand as I stared at the smeared paint. It looked like some kind of abstract portrait of Brooklyn crying. My fingers paused on the paper towel. How many times had I made her cry versus smile? Was it weighted in the wrong direction? Because this picture looked more like her than my others now. Brooklyn crying. I tried to swallow down the lump in my throat.

I just wanted to go back and do everything differently. I wanted to meet her when I wasn't a dumb kid. I wanted another chance. Just one more freaking chance.

My cell phone buzzed, pulling my attention away from the canvas. I grabbed my phone with my hand that wasn't covered in paint. There was a text from Penny wishing me luck on my date.

My date? I looked at the time. *Shit!* I'd completely forgotten about the stupid blind date.

I hurried out of the room and closed the door behind me. I tried to scrub the stupid paint off my hand but it wouldn't come off. *Shit, shit, shit.* I didn't have time for this. I was going to be late. Being late for any kind of meeting was rude. And it seemed especially rude for a date. Not that I cared about making a good impression. I was only doing this so I could keep hanging out with Penny.

Another text came through from Penny: "I really think you're going to like her. Okay, I'll leave you to it. Good luck!"

I looked at the time again. I only had 15 minutes to get across town. Which wasn't possible. I didn't bother responding to Penny as I changed into a pair of dress pants and a white button-down. I was out the door in a matter of minutes, without having bothered to shower or get the rest of the paint off the back of my hand.

***

I had no idea what my date looked like. I didn't even know her name. But I still found myself looking around the restaurant instead of going to the hostess stand. There was a brunette in the far corner that was alone...*nope.* A man had just joined her with a kiss. If that was my date, we weren't off to a great start.

My eyes kept scanning the restaurant. Everyone was paired off. It was like flourishing couples came here in droves. There were candles on each white-tableclothed table, giving the restaurant a romantic glow. Why had Penny chosen such an intimate restaurant for a first date? Or maybe my blind date had chosen it.

Either way, I didn't see anyone else seated alone. *Wait.* I leaned forward to see a girl with mousey brown hair reading at a table. That had to be her. Penny loved reading.

It would make sense for her to choose someone else who enjoyed it too. But I didn't want to walk over, just in case I was wrong. I walked up to the hostess stand. "Hi. I have a reservation under Matthew…"

"Matthew Caldwell," the hostess said. "Yes, I know." She gave me a smile that I could only describe as seductive.

I smiled back. She was exactly the kind of girl I'd invite to spend the night in a hotel. She knew who I was. Or had at least heard about me. It was an easy win. An easy distraction. Part of me wanted to just steal her away now and skip this date that would most likely be terrible. I didn't date. I flirted and hooked up. There was a huge difference. One that Penny definitely wouldn't understand. I doubted the woman with mousey brown hair would understand either.

"I'm Tamara," the hostess said. "And if there's anything at all you need tonight, I'm your girl."

I bet you are. Tamara got me.

Her smile quickly turned into a frown when she looked down at her chart. "Oh, it says you reserved a table for two." She cleared her throat. "Your other party isn't here yet, would you like to wait at the bar or be seated?"

I looked over my shoulder at the girl with brown hair. So that wasn't her? I glanced down at my watch. I was 15 minutes late. Where the heck was my date? "Are you sure about that?" I asked. I wanted to ask her about the girl sitting alone reading, but I felt like it wouldn't be well received. If she was my date, Tamara would have taken me over there.

"Positive."

Huh. "I'll just sit at the table to wait."

"Very well. Right this way."

I followed her to the table and she handed me a menu. She took a step back and then took a step forward. Her cheeks turned rosy like she was embarrassed. "If your date ends up being a no-show, you know where to find me." And with that, she turned on her heel and walked away.

Not embarrassed. Bold. My eyes landed on her ass as she walked back to the hostess stand. All I had to do was get through this terrible date and then I could take Tamara up on her offer.

I ordered a scotch. And then another. I checked my watch one more time. Maybe my date had come, scoped the place out, and left already. Or she was just a no-show. I looked over at the girl who had been reading. She'd been joined by her date. I was the last one alone in this restaurant, looking like a damned idiot.

And I wasn't going to tell the waiter to wait any longer. I was about to wave him down to pay for my drinks when I saw someone running through the restaurant. She had bright, wavy red hair, and her face was bright red too. She looked around the restaurant feverishly. And for just a second, I was worried she was going to try to rob the place or something. Or burst into tears. Or...do something else that she really shouldn't.

Tamara went up to her and they started talking. The redhead waved her hands around as she talked, still trying to peer around the restaurant. And then they both turned to me.

Oh no. God no. Penny, you have to be kidding me right now.

But instead of the hostess showing the redhead toward my table, she tried to show her out the door. I was about to breathe a sigh of relief when the redhead sidestepped Tamara and ran into the restaurant. She almost collided with a waiter, but somehow managed to reach my table unscathed.

"I'm so so sorry that I'm late," she said. She was completely out of breath. "The subway broke down. I had to run. Luckily I wore sneakers."

I looked down. Sure enough, she was sporting a pair of sneakers in a five-star restaurant. Which I actually found endearing. Brooklyn had this pair of beat-up Keds she used to wear everywhere. She even wore them with her homecoming dress.

"I really am sorry. I hate being late. Lateness is one of my greatest fears." She sat down, still out of breath and red in the face.

"Are you thirsty?" I asked and pushed my glass of water toward her.

"So thirsty. But um...have you already put your lips on that? Because I really don't like germs. I'm not like a germophobe or anything like that. I'm not actually scared of germs. But I am scared of dying from some kind of contracted virus. Okay, yeah, I'm a little scared of germs. But it's a lot lower on my list of fears than lateness. And I don't know why I'm telling you all this. I'm just really really nervous and when I'm nervous I tend to ramble. And I think being late is making everything worse."

I can tell.

She eyed the glass of water longingly.

"Sorry, I forgot to answer your question. No, I haven't gotten any virus germs on it. I only touched it to push it over to you," I said.

"Oh thank God." She grabbed it and downed half of it in one gulp.

I stared at her as she drank water like an Olympic athlete. Penny said this girl was exactly what I was looking for. I'd joked around with Penny about liking petite redheads like her. And she'd delivered one...

"Is it like a thousand degrees in here?" My date said as she fanned her face.

I probably should have given Penny a few more details about my dating preferences. Because the girl not being an insane person was pretty high on my list. And I was pretty sure this girl didn't fit that criteria. "You're probably just overheated from running. And the heat is on full blast in here. Do you want to take off your jacket?"

Her eyes grew round. "No, I'm good."

"But you just said you were hot."

"I'm okay now." She pulled the jacket tighter around herself.

Was she topless under there or something?

She finished the rest of the water and looked slightly less flushed. "It's really nice to finally meet you, Matt."

I stared at her. So she knew my name? What else did she know about me? Had Penny actually spoken to her about me? Or had Penny pretended to be me in some weird catfishing scheme? I cleared my throat. "Nice to meet you too. I'm sorry, I didn't catch your name?"

She laughed like I was joking. But then immediately frowned. "You don't know my name? How many dates on this crazy app do you go on a week?"

I smiled. "This is my first one. Full disclosure: my friend actually made my profile for me and set up this date."

"Oh. *Oh.* Wait…so who have I been talking to exactly? I thought I'd been texting you."

"You've been chatting with my friend Penny."

"Your friend that's a woman?"

"Yes?" I don't know why my response sounded like a question. It just seemed like this girl didn't want that answer.

"Hmm. Interesting." She eyed her empty water glass and fidgeted in her seat, like she was debating whether to start eating the ice.

I should have called over the waiter to ask for more water. But I had something more pressing on my mind. "Why is that interesting?"

"Because in my experience, boys and girls can't really just be friends."

"In this case we are." *Unfortunately.* "She's married to one of my other friends."

"Ah. Okay. I get it now. You've been feeling like a bit of a third wheel and are trying to find someone to go on double dates with?"

"Something like that."

She nodded, seemingly content with my response. "Well, Matt, it's nice to actually meet you. I'm Ash, by the way. Well, Ashley, but Ash for short. Ashley Dickson." She cringed at her own name.

Which was fair. It was a pretty terrible last name. I used to know a kid with that last name. Joe "Cupcake" Dickson. That stupid son of a bitch. He'd dated Isabella. Tormented Brooklyn. Cupcake was at the top of my shit list. When did I start listing things? This girl was already rubbing off on me in a really weird way.

"Nice to meet you, Ash," I said.

"God, now I'm trying to remember if I said anything weird to your friend while I thought it was you."

Judging by how the date had started? I'd say that was very likely. But I was curious too. What had Penny said to this woman while pretending to be me? I thought back to my horrible profile she'd made. For all I knew, she'd told her about how I was the most eligible bachelor in the city. I needed to change the topic. "Are you ready to order?"

"Yes. Well, no. I don't even have a menu. The hostess was really quite rude to me. She tried to kick me out of the restaurant."

I tried not to laugh. Probably because Tamara was jealous that she wasn't my date. I glanced over at the hostess stand. Tamara had been staring, but she quickly looked away.

"But it's fine, you can just choose for me," Ash said and pointed at my menu.

"You want me to pick what meal you're having?"

"Yeah, sure."

"But I don't know anything that you like. Or if you're a vegetarian or a vegan. Or what is it when you only eat fish?"

She laughed. "I don't think that's a thing. And I'm just a normal person."

I really wasn't sure about that. "What about allergies? Do you have any allergies?"

"No. Just order me something a normal person would order and I'll be happy."

Where did Penny find this chick? "Here, just look at the menu," I said, trying to hand it to her.

At first she pushed it back, but she finally conceded. As she looked over the menu, an awkward silence enveloped the table.

I could have easily stopped it. I was quite good at small talk. But it was fun watching her literally squirm. It was like silence was driving her bonkers. Even though I was pretty sure she was crazy already.

The silence kept stretching until it looked like Ash was about to explode.

"Wow this place is fancy," she finally said and closed the menu. "I don't usually eat in places with tablecloths."

"Mhm."

She stared at me like she couldn't believe that was the only thing I had to say. "I wish someone had told me it was fancy."

"Didn't you pick the place?" I asked. Was that what Penny had said? Or had Penny picked this place while pretending to be me?

"Oh. Um. No. Well, maybe it was my fault. I have a confession too and if I don't tell you I'm going to start acting weird."

She hadn't started acting weird yet? Good God.

"My best friend Chastity made my dating profile. I told her not to. Actually, I begged her not to. But she insisted and...she was on the thing just as much as I was because she had access to my password. She intercepted several of the messages."

I laughed. "You just gave me shit for my friend talking to you. When she was really probably just talking to your friend."

"I know. I'm sorry. I was just surprised and I have no idea why my first instinct was to lie. But it was and here we are. Getting caught in a lie is on my list of fears too. So it's better to just get ahead of it, don't you think? Besides, it was me on the app half the time. And I saw all the messages. So it was kind of like it was me. Since I observed all of it after the fact."

"Right."

"Exactly." She smiled.

This girl was so strange.

"But the restaurant was Chastity's idea. In her defense, she told me to dress up. But she dresses up for everything so I thought she was kind of overstating it. But apparently she wasn't. I would have looked it up ahead of time, but she told me I was being paranoid and that it would be more fun to just go in blind, you know? Since it was kind of already a blind date since your profile was weirdly a cup of tea. I kind of thought you'd look like a monster. But you're not at all what I expected. And I'm super underdressed."

I was pretty sure there was a compliment in there somewhere. "I actually really like the sneakers."

She smiled. "Really?"

I nodded.

"Thank you."

"So now that I know that you're underdressed, why don't you go ahead and take your jacket off before you faint?"

"I'm wearing an old sweatshirt and jeans. And I ran miles to get here. So now I'm not only underdressed, but I'm super sweaty too. Just for the record, I had on a nicer shirt. But I spilled coffee all over it just when I was about to walk out the door for our date. And it's laundry day. And this sweatshirt happens to be really comfy."

I laughed. "It's fine. Take it off before we have to call an ambulance."

She laughed too and finally pulled off her jacket. It was indeed an old sweatshirt. There was even a hole on one of the elbows. But I was most distracted by the huge sweat stains under her arms. The light gray sweatshirt did nothing to hide them. If anything, it accentuated them.

"Oh God," she said. "I need to use the restroom. I'll be right back." She got up and ran, almost knocking into another waiter.

I held in my laughter as best I could until she disappeared into the bathroom. She was adorable. *Adorable?* I shook the thought away. She was a walking disaster. The waiter came over to ask for our order, but I sent him away. After all that, Ash hadn't even told me what she wanted.

I looked at my watch. Ordered another drink. Started fidgeting in my seat. What the hell was she doing in there? She'd been gone for over ten minutes.

I pulled out my phone and sent Penny a text. "Who the hell is this person?"

Penny's reply came almost immediately. "Isn't she cute? And she's exactly what you're looking for!"

I wasn't sure why she was so sure about that. "How is she exactly what I'm looking for?"

"You described your ideal girl, and I found her for you. You're welcome. Are you being nice?"

"Yes, I'm being nice."

"Good. Now stop texting during your date. It's rude."

I ran my hand down my face. And waited a few more minutes. Had Ash left? I pictured her climbing out of the window and running away. Honestly, it seemed exactly like something this Ash person would do. I just didn't know whether to check the restroom or the alleyway first.

CHAPTER 16

Saturday

After a few more minutes passed without Ash returning, I threw my napkin down on the table and went toward the restrooms. It was better to check there first. If she was planning a great escape, she was probably already gone. There was no reason to look outside for her. But if she was stuck in a stall or something and needed help? It was at least polite to check. "Ash?" I said and knocked on the door to the women's restroom.

No response.

"Ash?" I said a little louder.

No response.

For fuck's sake. Did she really ditch me? I opened up the door just to check and saw Ash standing in the middle of the restroom with her sweatshirt off. Just standing in a public restroom with nothing on but a bra and her jeans. She was trying to dry the sweatshirt underneath the hand drier, while at the same time blotting it with paper towels.

"No, he's gorgeous!" Ash said to no one at all.

She talks to herself too?

"Why didn't you tell me he was gorgeous?!" Ash practically cried as she hit the hand drier button again.

"Then stop hiding in the bathroom and get out there!" said someone else.

I looked over to see where the other voice had come from. Ash's phone was balancing precariously on the edge of the sink. I'm assuming this was her friend Chastity encouraging her through the speaker.

"I can't go back out there! I look like a homeless person!"

I couldn't help the smile that spread across my face.

"I'm sure you don't look homeless," replied Chastity.

"I do. I'm wearing my binge-watching sweatshirt."

"You are not," gasped Chastity. "I told you to dress up! What is wrong with you?!"

"I don't know!" Ash blotted the pit stains with more paper towels. "Seriously though, who is this guy, Chastity? He looks like he walked out of the pages of a magazine! You told me he wasn't going to be cute. That this was just a practice run for getting back out there. You're a dirty liar! Because he's the definition of perfection and now he thinks I have some sort of explosive diarrhea because I've been in here for..."

"Fourteen minutes," offered her friend. "He definitely thinks you shat your pants."

"No!" Ash said and slammed her fist against the hand drier again. "Chastity, tell me how I can undo this?"

I cleared my throat.

Ash's eyes grew round when she saw me. She slapped her phone off the counter instead of simply ending the call. Then for some reason she threw the sweatshirt on the ground like it was contraband. And then she yelped and put her hands directly onto her breasts to hide her bra.

I burst out laughing. I couldn't help it.

For a second I thought she was going to cry. Or scream. Instead she started laughing too. "This is the worst date in the history of dates," she said, half sobbing through her laughter.

I couldn't deny that fact. "It's not off to a great start."

"God, what is wrong with me? I'm half naked in a public restroom. I should be arrested."

"Your secret is safe with me. How about you put your sweatshirt back on and meet me back out there?"

She laughed again. "Are you serious? You're not going to report me?"

"I'm not going to report you. But I might report this place for pests. Did you just see that centipede run under the sink?"

Ash screamed at the top of her lungs and threw herself at me. "Save me!"

She almost knocked me over, but I somehow managed to catch her without slipping on the tiled floor.

She was half naked and pressed against me. Her breasts practically shoved in my face and somehow my hands had wound up on her ass.

"Is it gone?!" she shrieked.

"Um." I tried to tilt my head to see. "I don't see him." Although I was very distracted by her breasts in my face.

"He could be anywhere by now. Centipedes are at the very top of my list of greatest fears. Why do they have so many legs? No bug should need so many legs when four or six are plenty."

I laughed. "It's fine, Ash. I don't think he's coming back out."

"Okay." But she didn't let go of me. If anything, she gripped my shoulders even tighter.

It had been a long time since someone had needed me like this. I swallowed hard and put her down before I did something stupid like kiss this maniac.

"I'm so sorry that this date is such a disaster," she said. "There is literally no way to come back from this unless I drop to my knees right now." Her eyes grew huge. "Which I'm not going to do. Because I don't even know you. I don't blow strangers in bathrooms. I swear. I'm not that kind of girl. Unless that's something you…nope. Pretend I didn't offer to do that. Oh my God please say something so I can stop talking!" She put her hand on her forehead.

And that's when I noticed the engagement and wedding rings on her freaking ring finger. "You're married?" I said. What in the hell was happening right now?

"No! I mean, yes. God." She threw her hands up. "I'm separated from my asshole soon-to-be ex-husband. This is the first first-date I've been on since college. I'm a little out of practice. And a lot a bit of a walking disaster, okay? Happy?"

There was a knock on the door. "Is everything okay in there?" said a male voice. The door started to open and Ash threw her half naked self against it, blocking whoever was on the other side from coming in.

"I need some privacy!" she yelled.

"Are you okay, miss? I heard yelling…"

"Diarrhea!" she shouted and then cringed as she looked at me. "You better stay away for your own sake!"

"Um. Okay. If you need anything…"

"No, we're good! I mean, I'm good. Because I'm all alone in here."

"Alrighty then," said the person on the other side of the door.

"I'm definitely going to prison," she mumbled. "Do you think they have cameras in here?"

No. "I'm sorry, can we circle back real quick to what was happening before you yelled diarrhea at a complete stranger?"

She pressed her lips together.

"So you're getting divorced soon?"

"The lawyers are working on it. We no longer live together. And we definitely no longer speak. Trust me, if I could speed the whole thing along I would. I fucking hate Joe Dickson with a fiery passion."

"Joe Dickson?" She couldn't possibly be talking about the same prick I went to high school with. "Cupcake Joe Dickson?"

She lowered her eyebrows. "I mean he sells cupcakes. But no one calls him Cupcake Joe Dickson. Wait, do you know Joe?"

"Does his dad own Dickson and Son's Sugarcakes?"

"Joe owns it now." She shook her head. "Please God, tell me you're not friends with my ex? What the actual hell is this date?!"

I laughed. "No, I'm not friends with him. I hate that guy."

She looked significantly calmer. "*I* hate that guy. So freaking much."

I smiled. This poor girl had clearly been through enough crap if she'd been married to Cupcake. The least I could do was buy her dinner. "How about we go back out there and you can tell me all about what happened between you two?"

She laughed. "How have you not run away from this train wreck of a night yet?"

I shrugged. "I'm actually having a great time. I got to see you without a shirt and almost got head in a bathroom full of centipedes. Plus you said I was gorgeous multiple times, and I'm very flattered."

Her face started to turn red again.

"I think you said, and I quote, that I'm the definition of perfection."

"How long were you eavesdropping on me? You're a horrible human." She shook her head. "Am I drunk or something?"

"I don't know." Honestly, I wouldn't be at all surprised if she was.

"Well, I need to be. Stat."

"Here's what we're going to do. You're going to put your sweatshirt back on. And I'm going to go back out there and order you some..."

"Wine. Any wine. I usually drink it out of a box so seriously just order the cheapest thing on the list."

I laughed. "Okay, you got it. See you in a few."

"Nice to meet you!" screeched the phone.

"Damn it, Chastity" Ash said and lifted it up off the floor. "Why is everyone eavesdropping tonight?"

"You didn't hang up. I thought I was supposed to stay on the phone in case he was a murderer or something. Are you a murderer?" yelled her friend to me.

"Um. No," I said.

"That honestly wasn't very convincing," Ash said.

I shook my head. "I promise I'm not. I'll let you two finish up..." I waved my hand around the bathroom. Gossiping? Getting dressed? Screaming about centipedes? I honestly had no idea what I'd just witnessed.

Ash gave me a small smile as I left.

I figured there was a good chance she'd still climb out the bathroom window and run away. But if she didn't? I really needed to hear about how the hell she'd married an asshole like Joe Dickson.

I went back to the table and sat down. The waiter came over and I ordered a bottle of white that wasn't the cheapest one on the list, because I actually could be a nice guy. And I went ahead and ordered us some food too. Because I was starving. And she'd told me to order something a normal person would eat. I could handle that request.

A few minutes later, there was a glass of wine but still no Ash.

I glanced towards the bathroom. Her sweatshirt had seemed mostly dry. Maybe she was still trying to get advice from her friend. This had to be the craziest date I'd ever been on. I was almost positive that Ash was nuts. But I actually was having fun. Or else I would have walked out already. I needed to hear her whole story. Plus it would be great to relay this whole disaster to Penny. The more details the better.

Several minutes later Ash sat down across from me fully clothed again. "I really wish I could say that I was drunk right now, but I am decidedly not. Give me a few minutes and we can pretend I was drunk the whole time." She took a huge sip from her glass of wine. Then shimmied her shoulders slightly and took a deep breath. "Okay. Try two. Sorry about that," she said very seriously. "Now, where were we?"

I just blinked. "You were telling me about your husband."

"Soon-to-be ex-husband."

"Right. Whatever possessed you to marry a guy like Joe?"

She sighed and took another sip of wine. "It's a long story."

"I have some time."

"You are so weird," she said.

"Me?" I raised my eyebrows. She had to be kidding me right now.

"Yeah. What are you still doing here? I basically just sexually assaulted you in the bathroom. I should have been arrested ten minutes ago. I was waiting for the cops in there…"

"I told you I wasn't going to report you."

"Oh." She nodded. "I thought that maybe you were joking."

I shook my head. Honestly I'd just found the whole scene hilarious. I would never call the cops on her.

"Well, in that case…can we just start over and pretend the last few minutes didn't happen? Let's pretend I just walked in and sat down. And pretend I'm wearing a nice dress too. Use your imagination." She cleared her throat. "Hi. I'm Ash." She offered me her hand.

At least the pit stains on her sweatshirt were gone. I reached out my hand and shook hers. "Nice to meet you. I'm Matt."

Her smile was so big that I couldn't help but smile too.

"So, Matt. Tell me all about yourself."

I really wanted to talk about Joe instead. But it wouldn't hurt to play along. I had all night.

CHAPTER 17

Saturday

It sounded like Cupcake hadn't changed at all. And the innocent, yet slightly crazy, woman in front of me definitely deserved better. She'd told me the whole story of how they met and how he'd proposed. But never in her story had she said she was in love. Because it was Cupcake. How could she be? "So you married him?" I asked and shook my head.

"What was I supposed to say? No?" She tore off a piece of the complimentary bread and dipped it into the olive oil. Her eyes lit up when she took a bite and she immediately tore off another piece.

"Yes. That's exactly what you were supposed to say."

Ash laughed as she finished her second glass of wine and her second roll. "In hindsight, I really wish I had. But he was my first boyfriend and I used to suffer from a severe lack of self-confidence." She seemed to sit up a little straighter to prove that was no longer the case.

But I wasn't so sure. Most self-assured women didn't get naked in a public restroom and offer to blow a stranger a few minutes after meeting them. I wasn't complaining though. Ash was freaking hilarious. I was having a really great night. Just not in the way that Penny had hoped. Ash and I could be really great friends. But…nothing more. And I was pretty sure she felt the same way. Our conversation flowed easily. But there wasn't any sexual chemistry. I was simply curious about her.

She laughed. "Matt, I take back what I said earlier, you're an amazing human."

"Hmm?"

She gestured to the waiter who was carrying over two trays filled to the brim. "You ordered food for me."

"Yeah, you were taking forever in the bathroom."

She put her hands up to her ears. "Stop. No, that didn't happen. We started over, remember?"

I laughed and grabbed her hands, lowering them from her ears. Her eyes locked with mine for a beat. A piece of me wanted to feel some kind of spark. Some draw to her. I felt nothing. I immediately let go of her so that the waiter could serve us our dinner.

"I love when people order food for me," Ash said as the waiter walked away. "But what the heck is all this?"

"You never told me what you wanted. And you said to just order something a normal person would like. So I ordered a whole bunch of stuff a normal person might like."

She looked around at all the food that had just been put down on our table. Plate after plate after plate. She abandoned the free bread, reached toward the middle, and grabbed a chicken finger from what I was pretty sure was a kid's meal. "I think this is the best date of my life."

I raised my eyebrows.

She held up her hand with a laugh. "Don't freak out. I know this terrible date has been one for the books. But this food?" She groaned. "So freaking good. I could get lost knee deep in a basket of these chicken fingers."

I laughed. She was adorable like I'd assessed earlier. And also smart and funny. And pretty. But…she wasn't Brooklyn. I wanted to feel something. I really did. But I just…didn't. I was very aware of the fact that my heart had stopped working years ago. I never seemed to feel anything. "So what happened between you and Joe? How did it go from sort of happy to divorce?"

Ash picked up a French fry. "Sort of happy." She sighed. "That's the funniest part. I thought I was happy. But looking back? And hearing my friends' analysis of him. And yours? I don't know what I ever saw in him. I just want to be loved, you know?"

I pressed my lips together. Yeah, I knew.

"I don't need to go into specifics about how our relationship imploded. The gist is, Joe cheated on me with an Instamodel. And even though I totally fixed his family business for him and made us a small fortune in the process, he's trying to leave me with nothing."

"Have you hired a good lawyer?"

"Yes but there are…extenuating circumstances." Ash cleared her throat and took another sip of wine. A big, healthy sip that had her reaching for the bottle for a refill.

That was a very weird answer. But honestly, half the stuff that came out of her mouth was weird. Before I could ask what she meant by extenuating circumstances, she changed the topic.

"So how do you know Joe exactly? I've just been blabbering on and on about him. But I'm so curious about how a guy like you could possibly be an acquaintance of Joe's."

"I went to high school with him."

"And what was my ex like in high school?"

"A complete asshole, much like he seems to be now. He was hellbent on causing chaos and backstabbing everyone at every turn."

"That sounds about right." She paused as she took another bite of a chicken finger. "Something about the fact that I might be the first person he's ever cheated on… makes me feel terrible. Somehow I want to be one of many? If that makes any sense. I've always wanted to ask someone that knew him. Was he always a cheater? I hear that phrase a lot. Once a cheater, always a cheater."

"I have no idea."

"Oh." She looked down at her chicken finger as she doused it with ketchup.

"But any guy that cheated on you is an idiot, Ash."

I could see her smile even though she was still concentrating on covering her chicken finger with way too much ketchup.

"If it makes you feel any better, Joe sold drugs and even planted some in my friend's locker to get him arrested." I wondered what had happened to Felix. I hadn't heard from him in years. "Joe was a piece of work."

"He sold drugs? Are you serious?"

"Yeah, he put them in the cupcakes."

Her jaw literally dropped. "You don't think he still..." her voice died away and she shook her head. "He couldn't be. I oversaw the production." But she didn't look entirely convinced.

"Well, you don't have to worry about it now," I said. "If he's still selling, it's on his hands. Not yours."

"You're right. And Joe would not do well in prison. I doubt a prison commissary would sell the fancy hand moisturizer he insists on using. It costs more than my shoes."

I laughed.

"But his hands are very soft." She pretended to gag.

I laughed. "So why do you still wear the rings if you're divorcing that soft-handed prick?"

Ash looked down at her left hand. "I don't know. Because taking them off means starting over? And I'm too old to start over."

I didn't know how old she was. But she looked like she was still in her twenties. If she was too old to start over, then I was doomed. Not that I wanted to start over anyway.

She pulled a plate of lasagna in front of her. "Can I ask you a question?"

I nodded. I didn't really want to talk about me. Honestly making fun of Cupcake all night sounded a lot better. I looked at the plates and grabbed some ravioli.

"I've been dying to know all night. And I don't want to make you feel weird or anything. But I can't stand it anymore. Why is your hand blue?"

I looked down at the paint on the back of my hand. And I panicked and said the first thing that popped into my head. "It's not."

She laughed. "Um…yes it is. It's bright blue. Like you dipped it into a bucket of paint or something."

I shoved a ravioli in my mouth to stall and tried not to choke on it. I took a huge gulp of water. "I don't know what you're talking about."

She nodded knowingly. "Oh. I get it. Is it like…some kind of kinky sex thing?"

"What? No." I looked at my hand. She wasn't accusing me of being a freak and painting my dead fiancée. And she didn't know any of my friends. This would in no way result in me being locked up in a loony bin. I wasn't sure why my first instinct was to lie. But I didn't need to lie to this girl. "I was painting earlier. I paint portraits."

"You're an artist? Wow. That's so incredible. It's so hard to make it in the arts these days."

I laughed. "No. I'm not an artist. I'm the CEO of the city's largest financial firm. Painting is a hobby."

Her fork clattered against her plate. "Oh my God. You're…you're…"

I could see the moment of recognition before she even said my name. And it felt like the end of the night had come. One of the only reasons I'd put up with this crazy night was because she didn't know who I was.

"You're Matthew Caldwell? The CEO of MAC International?"

"Yup." I tried to finish up my raviolis. As much as I wanted to get the hell out of this restaurant, I was still hungry.

"So you're friends with James Hunter?" She gasped. "And Penny Hunter? I seriously idolize her. I want to be her when I grow up. I mean, she's only a few years older than me. But she's a redhead from Delaware. I'm so much like her and yet she married James Hunter and I married Joe Dickson. Such a different terrible life choice."

I smiled. "So you read tabloids?"

"No. I mean, yes. I thought you looked familiar." She threw her hand over her mouth. "Wait, your friend that set up the dating profile for you? That was Penny? Penny Penny?"

"Yup."

"Oh my God, I casually flirted with her because I thought it was you. Chastity is never going to believe this."

I had a sinking feeling in my stomach. No, she didn't know my friends. But she knew *of* them. What if the painting thing somehow got back to them? They'd have a million questions. They'd want to see the portraits. They'd think I was crazy.

"Do you think you could introduce me to them?" she asked.

Shit. "No." It came out way faster and harsher than I meant for it to.

She bit her lower lip and looked down at the smorgasbord of food on the table. "Right. Sorry. Date from hell and all that?"

"That's not it." But honestly, it kind of was.

"Was it because of the bathroom incident? Because I really didn't mean for you to see me with my shirt off until at least the third date. That's like some kind of rule, right? I've heard that somewhere. Honestly I'm a little shaky on dating rules these days. When is nudity allowed?"

"Um..."

"And we started over. I don't even think I've done anything that weird since coming back out here. Except for the whole admitting that I'm obsessed with your friends thing. I mean, don't get me wrong, I like you too. But I read all about that huge scandal with James and Penny a few years ago. It was all over the news. And then their wedding night? Oh my freaking God! I couldn't stop watching the news..."

"Yeah, I get it," I said. "They're famous."

She was silent for a moment. "Are you jealous of them or something?"

I laughed. "No."

"It kinda seems like you're jealous."

"I'm not jealous." Again, my words came out icier than I meant for them to.

"You're famous too," she said. "Matthew Caldwell." She smiled to herself. "I can't believe I went on a blind date with you. Such a crazy world. And there's no need to be jealous of your friends. You're great too."

I'm not jealous. Fine, I kind of was. But not of them. Of what they have.

We ate in silence as Ash slowly chewed another chicken finger. Until she started squirming and looked like she couldn't stand it anymore. "So what do you do at MAC International?" She shook her head. "Sorry, you already said. You're the CEO. I'm sorry about earlier, but please stop with the silent treatment. It's driving me crazy."

I laughed because it had literally been quiet for five seconds tops before she started talking again. "I'm not mad at you. And you're right. I am a little jealous of them. Of what they have, you know?" This girl was a stranger to me. And I found myself wanting to get all this shit off my chest. I didn't care if she judged me. I'd probably never see her again. And she'd certainly never meet any of my friends in person.

"Yeah, I get that. Their lives seem so perfect. True love and all that."

She sounded like Tanner.

"I hope that one day I can experience that." She sighed and dropped her chin in her hand. "Don't you?"

"I have." I wasn't sure why I said it. I hadn't gone on a blind date to talk about Brooklyn. Honestly, I don't know why the hell I was on a blind date.

"You have? What happened?"

I took a deep breath. What was the worst that could happen if I told her? I might feel better. Maybe worse. Maybe this was just what I needed. A stranger to talk about Brooklyn with. "She passed away."

"Oh my God, Matt." She reached across the table to grab my hand. But before she reached me, she knocked over the candle in the center of the table with her elbow. It fell into the olive oil and the whole plate burst into flames. Ash screamed at the top of her lungs. Before I could throw water on the fire, she grabbed the side of the tablecloth, I think to smother the fire. But she pulled too aggressively and flung the fiery oil directly onto my dick.

I don't know if it was her screaming again or a high-pitched scream came out of my own mouth. I stood up as my pants lit up like a Christmas tree.

Ash grabbed her glass of wine.

"Ash don't..."

She flung the contents at me. Luckily she missed completely because she would have made the fire way worse. But the wine somehow went right into my face. *Fuck.*

"Ash!" I screamed as I blindly reached for the tablecloth to smother the fire.

She finally seemed to understand and started whacking the front of my pants with the tablecloth as I wiped the wine out of my eyes.

Oof. It felt like I was about to barf as her hand collided with my nuts. Hard. I looked down as she continued to slap my junk with the tablecloth.

"I'm so so sorry," she said when the fire was finally out. "I think it's okay." She moved the burnt up flap of my dress pants to the side to see my barely singed boxer briefs. "It feels like it's okay. I think your pants took the worst of it." She patted the front of my boxers and then seemed to realize what she was doing. She froze with her hand pressed against me.

And we both just stood there. Me with wine dripping from my eyelashes and half singed off pants. The whole restaurant could see my boxers and her hand on me.

"I'm just going to…" she removed her hand from my cock and pointed over her shoulder. And then she ran away as fast as she could.

I didn't call after her. She'd just tried to set my fucking dick on fire. This was why I didn't tell people about Brooklyn.

CHAPTER 18

Sunday

All our friends were here to watch the big Giants/Eagles game. All paired up in couples. Today I was lucky to be the eleventh wheel. *Eleventh.* I wish I was kidding. But the games at James and Penny's place always included all my friends, plus Penny's old college friends Tyler and Melissa and their significant others. At least James and Rob's sister, Jen, wasn't here with Ian. Then I would have been the thirteenth wheel.

I'd extended the invite to Tanner but he was busy today. Something about a Club Onyx emergency. I was pretty sure he was just trying to get me to offer to come help. He'd been trying to get me to join Club Onyx for ages, but I wasn't really interested. If that club really was about trying to find *true love*, then it wasn't the place for me. And some fake emergency wasn't going to get me through the doors.

So yeah, eleventh wheel. At least all the kids were here, and that gave me some little people to hang out with. I was sitting on the floor doing a puzzle with Scarlett. She loved puzzles. And honestly she was better at them than me. But I didn't mind helping her.

"Uncle Matt, why is your hand blue?" She poked a splotch of paint by my watch that I hadn't been able to get out.

I adjusted my watch to help hide the mark. "An accident with some blueberries."

She giggled and stole the puzzle piece in my hand that I'd been holding a few seconds too long apparently. She plopped it in the right place and looked up at me. "Please don't get paint on my puzzle. You can play with Sophie's puzzle instead. Hers has a sky so it's okay if you get blue on it."

That was a very good reason. But I think her actual reasoning was that it was Sophie's puzzle that would get ruined and not hers. Sneaky little devil. "I'm not going to get paint on your puzzle, kiddo."

She looked like she was scrutinizing me. "Promise?"

"Pinky promise." I held out my pinky to her.

She wrapped her pinky around mine, we shook, and the promise was made. For a few more minutes she seemed content, silently putting a few more pieces in for every one of mine. "Could you get me a snackie?" she asked.

I looked over at the coffee table that was covered in game day snacks. All of which she could reach. What was I, her man servant? But instead of complaining, I just asked her what she wanted.

"Two juice boxes, please," she said.

"Two?"

"Mhm." She didn't look at me as she put some more puzzle pieces in the appropriate spots.

"Why two?"

"Because I neeeeeed two."

Whatever you want, kiddo. It wasn't like I had to deal with her getting all hyped up for the rest of the day. Besides, I was pretty sure one of them was supposed to be for me. I got up off the floor and wandered over to the coffee table. I'd actually been avoiding the grownups. The last thing I wanted was to talk about my disaster of a date in front of all these happy couples. Luckily no one was paying me much attention as I grabbed two juice boxes.

I turned around and saw that Tyler's son, Axel, had stolen my seat beside Scarlett. I sighed. Apparently the kids were starting to pair off too. Well, at least those two. Axel had always seemed smitten with Scarlett. And vice versa. I glanced over to James, who was watching his daughter and Axel playing. He had a scowl on his face. At least Scarlett hadn't ditched him for Axel like she'd just ditched me. I looked at the two juice boxes in my hand, now certain one of them wasn't for me. Scarlett had literally sent me away to fetch the two of them a beverage. She'd conned me.

I shook my head and walked back over to them. "Your juice boxes, madam," I said with a slight bow.

She giggled. "Thank you." She grabbed both and then handed one to Axel.

Ouch. I wasn't really offended. It was actually cute. Even though she was a manipulative little thing. She'd probably waved him over as soon as I stood up.

"Let me know if you two need anything else," I said.

I sat down next to Rob's daughter, Sophie, instead. "Hey, Soph."

She'd abandoned her puzzle. Well, kind of. She was building a 3D house with the pieces instead. I lifted up a piece to help.

She grabbed my hand. "Uncle Matt, don't. You'll make it fall."

I laughed. "I'm not going to make it fall, Soph. Look." I gently placed a piece on top of her makeshift house. And the whole thing fell over. *Shit.* "Sorry, let me..." I reached for a piece to start the building over.

But instead of letting me take one, she reached both her arms out and raked the pieces back toward her. "No thank you," she said.

"Come on, I won't make it fall again. I was just getting used to it."

"Go play with my daddy instead. He's bad at houses too."

I couldn't help but laugh. I knew when I'd been dismissed. Soph and Scarlett had both refused to entertain me today. Apparently I was the outcast in this social group too.

"Later, Soph," I said and patted her head.

She ignored me, her little tongue sticking out of the corner of her mouth as she concentrated on her construction.

I walked over to my friends and sat down in an empty spot next to Tyler. Probably because out of everyone here, he was the only one who wouldn't ask me how my dating life was going. "Hey," I said.

Tyler cursed under his breath as the Eagles fumbled. He was an Eagles fan like Penny since they both grew up close to Philly. "Hey, Matt," he said when he calmed down. "The kids giving you a hard time?"

I laughed. "Just the usual."

Tyler turned his head to glance over at Axel and Scarlett silently doing the puzzle. "I always wonder if they're up to no good when they're quiet."

"Just drinking too many juice boxes and being controlling over puzzle pieces."

Tyler laughed. "Axel hates puzzles. I don't even know what he's doing right now."

Flirting. The kid was already a pro. Although, I couldn't actually see Axel and Scarlett being together one day. They weren't related, but they called each other's parents aunt and uncle. It would just be...weird. They were pretty much cousins.

"What have you been up to recently?" Tyler asked. "You haven't been to the last few game days."

Seriously? Even he was going to question me? *Come on, Tyler, I sat here for a reason.* "Just been busy with work and stuff."

"And stuff. Right. It wouldn't have anything to do with that app that Penny's constantly on?"

What the hell? I looked over at Penny and she was laughing at something on her phone, not even paying attention to the game or anyone around her.

Did everyone know that I was on a stupid dating app? "She told you about that?"

Tyler laughed. "No. I happened to see her screen when I was grabbing a drink. And she was texting some girl and they were talking about you. I think it was safe to assume Penny is not on a dating app as herself hitting on other women."

"Fair." If Penny was looking to date someone that wasn't her husband…it would be me.

"I thought you didn't really date," Tyler said.

"I don't."

"So the dating app thing…"

I sighed. "All Penny's idea."

"That woman is relentless," he said with a smile.

Yes, yes she is. "If you'll excuse me for a second." Penny had just gone into the kitchen and I needed a word with her. In freaking private. I followed her through the archway. She was laughing quietly again as she texted. She was completely oblivious to the world around her. For just a few seconds I watched her smiling down at her phone. Her red hair fell like a curtain over one of her eyes. God she was beautiful.

And I shouldn't be staring at her like this. "Penny."

She jumped and slammed her phone down on the counter. "Hi, Matt. What's up?" She pressed her lips together like she was about to burst out laughing.

"What's up? What are you doing?"

She pressed her lips harder together.

"Give me your phone."

"What? No." She pulled it away from me.

I tried to grab it but she ducked under my arm. "I'm talking to Ashley, okay?" She held the phone tightly to her chest.

"The girl from my date last night?"

"Yeah, she rated your date and I needed to know why it was such a low number."

"*She* rated *me* poorly?"

"Mhm."

"I didn't even realize you could rate a date. Give her a zero then." I tried to reach for Penny's phone again but she sidestepped me.

"I'm not giving her a zero, Matt. That's not very nice."

"If anything, she wasn't very nice. She literally ran away halfway through the date."

"Probably because of something you did."

Wow. Okay. "Did she not tell you what happened?"

"We were just getting to that. She said she was late and things were a little awkward the whole night. I don't get it. You're great at small talk. Why was your date so awkward?"

"Because she was freaking awkward." How dare Ash call *me* awkward? I wasn't awkward in the slightest.

"I'm just trying to figure out what happened," Penny said. "This low rating is going to make finding a good candidate for your next date super hard. Unless you're planning on going out with Ash again."

"I am definitely not planning on doing that."

"Why?"

"Because it was a train wreck."

"But she's exactly what you're looking for." She smiled because she knew I'd just been messing with her. "You requested a petite redhead, so..."

"It's not just about looks, Penny."

"I know that. So tell me what happened. Regardless of her appearance, I thought she was perfect for you. She seemed funny and sweet."

"It was just a bad date."

"I need more than that," Penny said. "We can file a request to get this one-star rating removed."

"One-star?" *Fuck that.*

"Just tell me what happened."

"She tried to set my dick on fire!"

I heard Rob laugh and turned around. All our friends were standing in the archway staring at us.

"So we only caught the last bit of that, and we're all going to need this whole story," Rob said. "Who did what to your dick?"

For fuck's sake. "Penny sent me on a blind date from hell and the girl knocked over a candle into that complimentary oil you dip bread into. It burst into flames. Then she proceeded to fling the flaming oil right onto the front of my pants."

"On purpose?" James asked with a straight face.

"No." I laughed. *Huh.* "Maybe."

Mason slapped me on the back. "We've all been there, man."

"I've never set your dick on fire," Bee said.

"I just meant going on a blind date from hell."

Bee slapped his arm. The two of them met on a blind date. As their story went, it wasn't a perfect start. But in no part of their blind date had Mason's dick been set on fire. Not sure they would have gotten married if that was the case. Unless they were into some weird shit I didn't know about.

"Maybe your second date will be better," Mason said.

Oh God. Was he seriously insinuating that Ash and I were meant to be, just like him and Bee? He couldn't be more wrong. Bee was a sane person.

"So let me get this straight," Rob said. "This girl *accidentally* tried to set fire to your cock?" He put accidentally in air quotes. "What the hell happened before that? I feel like there had to be a reason."

I shrugged. "She showed up super late in a sweaty sweatshirt. Then was embarrassed about her outfit and started stripping in the bathroom..."

"And why do you know she was stripping in the bathroom?" Penny asked.

"Because she was taking forever so I followed her in."

"Of course," she said, resting her chin in her hand. "Please continue."

"She was drying the sweat off her sweatshirt with the hand dryer." I held up my hand. "It's not important. I would have freaking walked out right then. But she dropped the bomb that she was going through a divorce with...Cupcake."

"Cupcake?" Rob said. "No flipping way."

"Who's Cupcake?" Penny asked.

"This dick we went to high school with," I said. "Anyway, I felt bad about how the date started out and the fact that she'd been married to that idiot, so I decided not to walk out. And we were having an okay discussion until she figured out who I was. She was super interested in the two of you." I gestured toward Penny and James. "I wouldn't be surprised if she was stalking you guys."

Penny laughed. "Yeah right. So your date set you on fire because of me and James?"

"It was an accident." *I think.*

"Mhm. What happened right before she set you on fire?"

"I was telling her about…" I cleared my throat. "Past relationships." I'd almost let it slip. I'd almost just talked about Brooklyn. My stomach churned. And suddenly I felt like I was going to be sick.

"So you're letting Penny set you up on dates now?" Rob asked. "Why? I just offered to be your wingman again."

I waited for Penny to blab to everyone that I was on a dating app. Or James. Or Tyler, because apparently he knew too. But everyone stayed eerily quiet. "It was a one-time thing," I said. "And I'm never doing it again."

The smile on Penny's face faded.

"I actually have a meeting," I said. "Have fun watching the rest of the game." I turned away before any of them could ask me to stay.

"Matt!" Penny called after me.

But I was already out the door. I was done with that stupid dating app. And I was done pretending I even wanted to date.

CHAPTER 19

Sunday

There was one more thing I did when I missed Brooklyn. Only when I missed her so badly that it hurt. At my lowest moments. And I hit those lows more often than I wished to admit.

"Hey," I said into the cool night air. I blinked fast, the gravestone in front of me blurring slightly.

The flowers I'd brought by last time were dried and browned. I cleared them away before sitting down. I leaned my back against her tombstone and closed my eyes. Sometimes in the middle of this graveyard on a night like this, you could barely hear the city traffic. And it was like I could feel her in the silence. Like she was still here. She haunted me the most in the silence.

"I had a bad day," I said out loud and opened my eyes again. I ran my fingers along the grass that had been recently mowed. One of the worst things about those early days after I lost her was the grass on top of her grave, slowly growing in until it looked like she'd been buried here forever. I hated that fucking grass.

There were a million things I wanted to say to her. And the fact that she'd never hear them killed me every day.

"Is it just me, or does the fall really fucking suck?" I ran the back of my hand under my nose.

Silence.

"I thought I saw you the other day. I almost got in a car accident because I got so distracted. I don't know what I was thinking actually. You're gone and I'm just…stuck."

Silence.

"It's hard to breathe when I think I see you in the city."

Silence.

"I feel like I'm drowning." Brooklyn had said that to me once. I'd added to that feeling for her. I'd never been enough. She'd deserved more than me. I'd let her down. Or else she'd still be here with me.

The silence was tearing me in two.

"What am I supposed to do, Brooklyn?"

Fucking silence.

"I'm worried that you'd hate what I've become. I think I hate what I've become."

I sniffed.

"This wasn't supposed to be how my life turned out. You were supposed to be here. You were supposed to be here with me, making me feel like I wasn't drowning."

I looked down at the grass. I felt like an idiot. Talking to the silence. But it was impossible not to talk to her when I came here.

"I tried drinking chamomile tea. I don't even remember what it was for. But it clearly didn't work because I'm here."

Silence.

"Your dad texted me again." I slowly exhaled. "I can't forgive him for what he did to you. You'd probably want me to, right? You were all about second chances. And thirds. Your heart was so big."

I stared off into the distance. "I'm going to make him pay, Brooklyn. I'm going to destroy him." I should have tried to get him put away years ago. I owed it to her. And instead I'd just been…screwing around. Trying not to drown.

"I just miss you so much."

The silence was going to kill me, I knew it.

I knew why I was here though. It wasn't to talk about missing her, or to talk about how her dad was a dick. She knew all that. I was here because I felt like I needed to make a confession. And I'd feel better once I got it out. *Please let me feel better.* "Penny set me up on a dating app."

Silence.

I looked toward the spot where I was pretty sure I'd buried her engagement ring. "I wanted a family with you. It's all I wanted. I don't want that with anyone else." I took a deep breath. "I promise, Brooklyn. I promised you then and I'll make good on it now."

I wasn't sure how many times I'd come here, trying to feel better about the shitty life I was leading. But this was different. One-night stands and random hookups were meaningless. It's why I did them. Because it wasn't a betrayal. But the dating app made me feel guilty. Even though I knew I wasn't taking it seriously.

"I promise," I said again. "But…I think maybe, a little part of me still wants all that stupid stuff. A family. A home. And I'm sorry that I want it. I'm so fucking sorry." I didn't have to say anything else. We both knew I wouldn't act on those feelings. We both knew I could never move on. I'd never do that to her. I couldn't.

"It just hurts more in the fall," I said into the silence. "You get it. You get what it feels like to have no one."

I looked over to her uncle's gravestone. I knew how terribly alone she'd felt after his death. She never deserved to go through so much pain. She never deserved to die feeling like she had no one by her side. No one deserved that. "I'm sorry."

I always came here when I missed her the most. When I felt like I had other things to apologize for. But it always came back to that one moment. Of letting her down right before she passed away. Of letting her feel like she was alone. "You weren't alone. You always had me."

All I wanted to do was lie down and close my eyes. I'd done that a lot the first few months after she'd passed too. I'd slept right here. To make sure she knew she wasn't alone. I shifted so that I could lie down on top of the grass. I just needed her to know that I was here.

"It's hard this time of year, Brooklyn. And I always wonder what we would have been doing if you were here." I swallowed hard and looked up at the starless sky. I didn't have enough memories of her to fill 16 years of missing her. So I just replayed all of them. Even the ones that hurt like hell. Especially the ones that hurt like hell.

"It feels like you're disappearing on me. And I don't know how to live without you."

I didn't want to. I couldn't. "I don't know why I asked what we'd be doing if you were here. I know what we'd be doing. We'd have a family. We'd be happy in our home. We'd have each other. That's all I ever wanted."

I felt tears trickle down the corners of my eyes and into my hairline. "I don't want to do this without you anymore. I feel guilty all the time. I feel like fucking shit every day, Brooklyn."

I was tired. I'd been so fucking tired for years. I just needed something. A sign to keep going. Anything. Because I couldn't do this anymore.

I heard the sound of leaves crunching. I tried to mind my own business. There were more people buried here than just Brooklyn. More mourners than just me. But I kept my mouth closed, because I was pretty sure I was the only crazy one that talked to the dead.

Another crunch. And another. Getting closer and closer. It was like whoever was walking through the cemetery was coming toward me. Or rather, toward Brooklyn's grave.

The first person that popped into my mind was Kennedy. Brooklyn's best friend. I sat up and turned toward the sound, but could barely make out the person in the darkness. They kept walking closer and closer.

I hadn't spoken to Kennedy in years. Not since senior year of high school, actually. We'd gone to different colleges and lost touch. It was hard to keep up a friendship when all we really had in common was someone we lost. I wasn't even sure she was still in the city.

I squinted into the darkness. And I stupidly felt this tiny bit of hope. I'd asked for a sign. Was Kennedy that sign? She understood my pain better than anyone else. Maybe she could help me.

The person finally stepped underneath one of the lights sprinkled around the graveyard. But it wasn't Kennedy. It was the woman stalking me from my football games standing several gravestones away, holding a bouquet of flowers. She stared at the grave I was sitting on and then back at me.

There was no doubt in my mind now. She was following me. And I just knew Mr. Pruitt was involved. First Poppy and now this person. It was one thing for Mr. Pruitt to send her to my games. It was another thing entirely to have her follow me here. She had no right to be anywhere near Brooklyn's grave. She had no right to disturb me while I was here. And this stopped right now.

"Did Mr. Pruitt send you?" I said. The words felt like acid in my throat. When would he stop trying to ruin my life? When would he leave me alone in my misery?

She didn't say a word. She just stared at me.

"Answer me."

She took a step back, the leaves crunching under her feet.

Fuck this. I started to stand up.

The woman dropped the flowers and…ran. Faster than I expected her to in high heeled boots. She was a freaking sprinting ninja in disguise.

"Hey!" I called. But she was already halfway toward an SUV parked on the path. "Tell me who you are!" I yelled as I sprinted after her. "Who sent you?"

She jumped into the car and the engine roared to life. It started moving just as I reached the path.

"Answer me!" I yelled. I slammed the back of her SUV with my hand. An SUV just like the ones Mr. Pruitt used to make Brooklyn drive around in. When he'd been worried about her safety.

The SUV sped off, leaving me alone in the darkness of the graveyard.

My chest rose and fell as I tried to catch my breath. I had no idea what Mr. Pruitt was up to. But I knew that anything involving him had to be bad.

I pulled out my phone and shot Tanner a text: "Have you dug up any dirt on Mr. Pruitt?"

His text came back immediately. "You mean Richard Reginald Pruitt?"

"I don't know what his middle name is."

"It's Reginald."

Damn it, Tanner get to the point. "Is that a yes?"

"It's a yes."

"So what is it?"

"This is more of an in-person kind of reveal. Meet up for dinner tomorrow night?"

"Mr. Pruitt is having me tailed. I need to end this now." I didn't bother adding that I was at Brooklyn's grave. Tanner thought it was unhealthy that I visited so often. He was probably right. And I didn't need a lecture right now. Today had been shitty enough.

"Trust me, Matt. This is the kind of stuff you reveal in person, not over the phone."

"Would you just text me? It can't wait until tomorrow night." Sometimes Tanner drove me insane. Texting was a perfectly suitable form of communication. I wasn't sure why he always insisted on doing things in person.

"It's called a reveal, you fat head. Tomorrow night."

I sighed. I knew when Tanner wouldn't budge. And it was usually after he spewed off some weird insult like calling me a fat head. "Fine. See you tomorrow."

"Ciao."

Ciao? Tanner needed to learn how to read the room. This wasn't a lighthearted *ciao* moment. For all I knew, Mr. Pruitt was trying to off me. I shook my head and shoved my phone back in my pocket. Tanner's news better be good.

CHAPTER 20

Monday

I was just putting away the practice footballs when my phone vibrated in my pocket.

I pulled it out, expecting a text from Tanner. But it was Penny's name on my screen. I clicked on the message: "I'm sorry about the other night."

Which night? Yesterday when she'd almost made everyone aware that I was on a stupid dating app? Or the night before when she'd sent me on a date from hell? "It's fine," I texted back.

"Please just let me make it up to you."

I shook my head. I had better things to focus on right now than pretending to date. Like who the hell was stalking me. But instead of saying any of that, I texted back: "What did you have in mind?" I really didn't know why I couldn't say no to this girl.

"It's a surprise."

The last surprise I'd gotten was her showing up on my doorstep. But that had been Tanner's idea. Not hers. Surely Penny was better at surprises than Tanner. "It's not another teapot, is it?"

"That's a terrible way to say thank you, Matt. But no, it's not another teapot. Clear your calendar for tomorrow night. I'll text you more details."

That was super vague. But I found myself typing back okay. Hopefully I wouldn't regret it. I made my way to the parking lot and my feet froze when I heard the squeal of tires. I looked up to see an SUV speeding out of the parking lot. I swore it was the same SUV from the graveyard last night. *What the hell Mr. Pruitt?*

I climbed into my car. Tanner better have good news for me.

***

Tanner had texted me the address of the restaurant. It was some swanky new place he wanted to try. When I pulled up outside, I sighed. The name of the place was literally in the middle of a neon heart. This was a restaurant for couples. Tanner loved trying all the newest places as he scoped out appropriate dating sights for his club. But I was seriously sick of being the guinea pig. If we got mistaken for a gay couple one more time I was going to lose it. He knew I hated this shit.

I gave the valet the keys to my car.

"Enjoy your date," he said.

Kill me now.

I walked into the restaurant and looked around for Tanner. I spotted him at the same time he saw me. He waved me over with a smile on his face, completely oblivious to the fact that I was annoyed.

"Another place to check out for the club?" I asked when I reached his table.

"I like to kill two birds with one stone, you know this."

"What I know is that I told you to stop taking me to places obviously designed for couples. The valet told me to enjoy my date."

Tanner tried and failed to hide his amusement. "If I recall, I just did you an immense favor. So you'll be a good date and eat your lobster and steak and say no more, or I'll have to give you a one-star rating."

I laughed. "You talked to Penny about my date huh?"

"She said your date set your dick on fire." He chuckled. "If only."

I didn't get his joke. Ash *had* set my dick on fire. Penny must have told the story wrong.

"Sit down," Tanner said. "I already ordered their most popular apps and we'll be doing a wine sampling as well."

There was no use arguing with him. I knew for a fact that the only reason I was here with him was because he didn't really like to eat alone. Neither did I. It was a win for both of us. And honestly, the lobster and steak on the table next to ours looked delicious. I sat down without another word.

"So let's start with the issue at hand." Tanner put his menu aside.

Good. I'd been dying to hear the dirt he'd dug up on Mr. Pruitt. Poppy showing up had shaken me. I needed to put an end to her threats. And being followed wasn't making it any easier to sleep at night.

Tanner took a deep breath. "Whatever possessed you to go on a date without telling me?"

"What? Tanner, we need to talk about Mr. Pruitt. You swore you'd tell me in person when you refused to do it over text."

"We can talk about Richard in a minute. I thought we had agreed that you'd tell me about all your dates on the app ahead of time so I could properly scope them out. And I don't recall getting any notice about this one."

"I thought you were joking." Honestly, I didn't think he was joking. But it was a really weird request so I'd chosen to ignore it.

"Well, what happened after she set you on fire?"

"She threw a glass of wine in my face and then took pity on me and helped put the fire out before running out of the restaurant."

Tanner kept a completely straight face. "So you didn't sleep with her?"

"No, she was an insane person."

He nodded. "Do you think you'll have another date? Because I really think the two of us need to meet if…"

"Did you not hear what I just said?"

"It's a yes or no question, Matt."

"No, I'm not going on a date with her again. She set me on fire!"

Tanner nodded. "Alright then. But for your next date, you need to tell me all the details before you go. Agreed?"

"I'm not going to do that. And I couldn't even if I wanted to. Penny is catfishing people as me. I didn't even know the girl's name or what she looked like until I showed up for the blind date."

"Interesting. I'll coordinate with Penny and then stage random bump ins with your suitresses."

"Please don't do that."

"But this way you can still be surprised for a blind date. And I can keep tabs on the situation."

Our waiter cleared his throat as he set down a few bottles of wine. "Should I give the two of you a minute?" He looked shocked by our conversation.

"Yes," I said at the exact same time that Tanner said, "No need."

He laughed. "Lovers quarrel?"

For fuck's sake. What had we just been talking about? He probably thought we were in some weird open relationship. "We're just friends," I said.

"No need to explain. We're very discreet. I'll give you two gentlemen a minute." He winked at us and walked away.

Tanner pulled out a notebook that I hadn't seen a minute ago. "Good to know that they're discreet." He jotted down the note. "That's definitely a plus."

"Tanner, you let the waiter think that we were dating."

"Of course. We need the full couple's experience. I need to know what it's like to go on a date here."

I sighed.

He made an overexaggerated sigh to mimic me. "If I recall correctly, you owe me," he said.

"For finding dirt on Mr. Pruitt? Because as far as I can tell you have nothing. Besides, you made it seem like you were doing me a favor because we're best friends."

"Best friends? Ha. Wait until Robert hears about this confession."

Before I could say anything, Tanner kept talking.

"And as my best friend, you can also do favors for me. And tonight I need you to pretend to be my gay date so we can figure out if this is a suitable place to send couples from the club."

"I don't understand why these *couples* aren't just going on dates at the club."

"If you'd attend an event, you'd understand."

"I'm not interested in finding true love."

"Oh yes, dear," he said really loudly. "Because you've already found it."

The waiter appeared next to our table with a tray full of appetizers.

I forced myself not to roll my eyes. It didn't hurt me to be his gay date for restaurant scouting purposes. It wasn't the first time Tanner had asked me to do this and it wouldn't be the last. And it's not like he was going to go over the top with the acting and kiss me or something. He was as straight as me. He only ever greeted strangers with mouth kisses if he got super drunk and started talking in a weird accent. Something about his schooling overseas. I think it was a French thing. I knew all this, yet tonight my patience was wearing thin.

Tanner silently started to taste test the appetizers when the waiter walked away.

"Are you seriously just going to sit there and eat?" I asked.

"They'll get cold." He pushed the sampling tray closer to me.

"Tanner, tell me what you found out about Mr. Pruitt. You said it was good. Tell me."

He patted a napkin against his lips. "Oh, it's good. I feel like we need a drumroll." He looked around like he was expecting a drummer to magically appear for his whim. And when it didn't happen, he jotted another note down in his notebook. "Well, you won't believe what I found."

Just freaking tell me! "What is it?"

"It's so good."

"Tanner I swear to God."

He put his elbows on the table and leaned forward slightly. "You're going to laugh so hard."

"Wait, what?" *I wanted dirt, not to laugh.*

"So get this. I was following him…"

"Did he see you?" For some reason my heart had started racing. If I got Tanner tangled up in this mess too, I'd never forgive myself.

"Of course not. I'm as discreet as our waiter. I followed him into this old timey theater that shows classics during the day. And in my humble opinion, Titanic is pushing the whole classics thing since it feels like that barely happened a year ago. But this theater is particularly lenient in their classifications. I think they were even airing..."

"Tanner, focus."

"Right. The theater doesn't matter. But what happened at that theater?" He shook his head with a laugh. "I saw the unthinkable. I mean, I'd been trailing the guy all day. He's a little rough around the edges. But as he watched Leonardo DiCaprio let go of that wooden door? He started bawling."

I blinked. "That's the dirt you dug up? That he cried during the Titanic movie?"

"Like a baby. Buckets of tears." He waved his hands in front of his eyes to show me like I didn't understand.

"Yeah, I got you. But how does that help me out of this mess?"

"It doesn't. But it's hilarious. Come on. Picture Richard in his crisp little suit all stoic watching a romantic movie. And then crying at the end when everyone I've ever known is sensible enough not to go on a floating death ship. The propaganda around that boat. I don't know why anyone bought into it. I still don't trust cruise ships." He shook his head. "Regardless, Richard was clearly embarrassed about the whole ordeal. And I got a firsthand witness of the events."

"How the hell am I going to use Mr. Pruitt crying during the Titanic against him?"

"Well, I'm sure he's embarrassed, or else he wouldn't have been all alone in the middle of the day in a theater so far away from his apartment."

"Tanner, I have a freaking woman following me everywhere. And Poppy threatened Scarlett. I need leverage. Or answers. Not...whatever that is."

"You have to admit it's funny." He popped an appetizer into his mouth. "Almost as funny as this poor excuse for foie gras." He started writing in his notebook again. "Titanic." He laughed to himself. "You should have seen it."

I tried to picture Mr. Pruitt crying during a movie. And I…couldn't. Mr. Pruitt was heartless.

"Buckets," Tanner said with a giggle.

And I couldn't help it. I started laughing too. Not just at the thought of him crying over a romantic movie. But also just over the whole situation. Should I really be so worried about Mr. Pruitt? He'd had years to do something to me and he hadn't. Why was I still scared of him? The man cried over Titanic for God's sake.

"See," Tanner said. "Hilarious. Now I have an important question for you. What do you think this restaurant's nudity policy is?" He looked around like he thought a streaker was about to run by.

What? "I'm assuming they don't allow it. It's a restaurant."

"That's a darn shame."

"Tanner, is that really it?" I asked, hoping to steer the conversation back to whatever he found out about Mr. Pruitt.

He looked down at his notebook. "Well, I have a few more questions, but the nudity thing really is a bummer. The food is really going to have to make up for that deficit."

"I'm not talking about the restaurant's nudity policies. I'm talking about Mr. Pruitt. Is that really all you found? There has to be something else."

"Oh. Well, yes. But the rest isn't quite as funny though. I think it's more of an after-dessert kind of discussion, if you know what I mean."

"If you don't tell me right now I'm going to leave before we even eat."

Tanner sighed. "As you wish. But I did warn you. This might ruin your appetite altogether." He pulled out a few pictures from his notebook. "Before Richard went to the theater, he had some sketchy meeting. I couldn't get inside the old warehouse to see what was going on. But I did see one of the men that came out afterward." He poked the top image.

I stared at the image of a guy with a deep scar under one of his green eyes.

"I did some digging. His name is Isaac Russo. He's a known hitman. Richard recently paid Isaac a large sum and there was another equal amount that popped up." He moved the picture of Isaac to the side to show another intimidating hitman. "This is Isaac's brother, Antonio. He's been in and out of prison over the last two decades but no verdict ever sticks if you know what I mean. I'm pretty sure he's killed at least eight people. I think Richard hired him too."

My heart was racing. But this was good news, right? Bad news for whoever the hit was against. But good news for me. The person trailing me was a woman. "Well at least Scarlett isn't really in danger. Or me. Maybe we can use that money trail to pin a few murders on Mr. Pruitt?"

"Yeah, maybe. Although, I got all this information illegally, so probably not. And I wouldn't say you and Scarlett are in the clear yet. The Russo brothers are good at what they do. But not great. Or else Antonio never would have even stepped foot in a prison. The real problem is that there's one more hire. The worst hitman of all. Or should I say hitwoman. You know…because she's a woman."

I swallowed hard. "Where's the picture of her?" I pushed the picture of Antonio to the side but there was no other printout.

"No known images of her I'm afraid. But she was paid recently too. So she's definitely going through with a hit soon. And I'm assuming she's really good because Richard dropped double the amount on her."

"The woman that's following me? Do you think that could be her?"

"All I know is that she's a woman. And she's good at her job. That's probably why I couldn't find a picture."

Shit. "Why the hell didn't you tell me this last night? I could have been killed."

"Richard's been pretty insistent that he wants to speak with you. I doubt he'll go through with your hit before you've given him the last word."

Maybe that was true. But that had nothing to do with Scarlett. "I have to go."

"We haven't even gotten to the main. I heard the lobster really is quite lovely. I still can't believe I wasted so many years of my life not eating lobster." He shook his head.

I didn't have time for Tanner to tell me for the tenth time that lobster had only recently become a delicacy and that he was making up for lost time by eating loads of it. He never made any sense. My parents had served lobster for years. It hadn't just recently become a delicacy. "I need to tell James everything." I stood up and pulled on my coat.

"It's about time you told him you're still upset about what happened with Brooklyn. I'm surprised it's taken you this long. I really think harboring all these feelings of resentment and bitterness aren't doing you any favors."

"Not that. I'm talking about Poppy's threat regarding Scarlett. I should have told him right after it happened. I don't know what I was thinking."

"Oh, yeah. You should really get on that. Let's just finish up here..."

This was a little more important than a fake date night. "I'm sorry Tanner, but I have to go. We'll do dinner another night." I was already hurrying out of the restaurant before he could respond.

The valet looked up at me.

"I'm in a hurry," I said.

"Bad date?" he asked as he looked for my keys.

Something like that. Why was he taking forever? I could see my keys from here. "Top right, one row down."

"Ah, here we are. Let me just go..."

I grabbed the keys from his hand. "I can get it." I pressed the button and heard a beep somewhere to the left. I took off running. It didn't take me long to find my car and hop in. I started the engine, pulled out onto the street, and almost ran right into a pedestrian.

My foot slammed onto the brakes just before my car collided with...Tanner? Where the hell had he even come from so quickly? Had he jilted the waiter with the check instead of me?

Tanner patted the front of the car and shook his head. He ran his fingers down the front of his peacoat and straightened the to-go containers in his hands that somehow hadn't ended up on my windshield.

He walked around and opened the passenger's side door. "Mechanical beasts," he huffed. "I got our food to-go. Very fast service."

Crazy fast. Our main courses hadn't even arrived at the table yet. But I guess maybe that had saved them time.

"We can warm it up after we go air out all our dirty laundry with James. If he's well behaved I'll let him eat some of your lobster."

"I'm not talking to him about Brooklyn."

"We'll just see how the night progresses."

"You don't need to come," I said.

"I'm already committed to this." Tanner pulled on his seat belt. "What are you waiting for? Gun it."

CHAPTER 21

Monday

As each minute ticked by, I started to panic more and more. What if I was too late? What if something had happened to Scarlett? Why the fuck had I taken so long to tell James about Poppy's visit?

"It's going to be fine," Tanner said as the elevator doors closed. "I'm pretty sure you would have heard if Scarlett had been abducted by one of Richard's crazed relatives."

"I wouldn't exactly be the first person James called if something went wrong."

Tanner frowned. "Of course you would be. You've been friends for forever."

Fine. If *I* was in trouble *I* wouldn't go to James first. Which is how I wound up not telling him this very important information for a week. What was wrong with me? First I'd been flirting with his wife. Now I was trying to get his children offed? And how long did this elevator take to get to the top floor? I hit the button again.

"This is exactly why I think it would be good for you to talk to James about Brooklyn. Secrets have a way of festering until they tear one apart."

I didn't need pretend-psychologist Tanner right now. He was making me feel worse not better. "I should have told him right after Poppy stopped by my office."

"You really should have."

"You're not helping!"

"Hm. Maybe you'll be singing a different tune when James tries to kill you and I make sure that doesn't happen. You're welcome."

I winced. "He's going to try to kill me, isn't he?"

Tanner shrugged.

The doors dinged open on James and Penny's floor. I ran over to their door and banged on it with my fist. Again and again until it opened. But no one was there. A chill ran down my spine. Why the hell was their door just open like that? *Fuck, I was too late.*

"Hi, Uncle Matt! Hi, Mr. Tanner."

I looked down and saw Scarlett smiling up at us. *Oh thank God.* "Kiddo, you're not supposed to answer the door. How many times do your parents have to tell you that?" What if I'd been Poppy? Or my stalker? Or Mr. Pruitt himself? Scarlett could have easily been snatched. Or worse.

She pressed her lips together. "Maybe they need to tell me one more time." She smiled but the corners of her lips instantly fell when I didn't smile back. "Please don't tell them, Uncle Matt. I didn't mean to do it. But you knocked. So I answered the door."

How was that not meaning to do it? "Where are your parents?"

"Mommy's putting Liam to bed and Daddy's in his office."

I sighed and ran my hand down my face. Scarlett was okay. That was the important thing. But she was going to give me a heart attack at this rate.

"Am I in trouble?" she asked.

"Nonsense, why would you be?" Tanner said.

I glared at him. We weren't playing good cop, bad cop here. And even if we were, I didn't want to be the bad cop. "You're a little in trouble."

"I am?" She blinked up at me.

"That depends." I crouched down to look her in the eyes. "Do you promise not to answer the door again?"

"Yes?"

"Scarlett, you're going to have to sound a little more affirmative than that."

"But I don't know what affima...formitative...I don't know what that word means."

"Say it with conviction," Tanner said.

She shook her head, not knowing what that word meant either.

"Kiddo, I just need you to promise me. For real this time. Promise me you won't answer the door by yourself ever again."

She looked down at her socks. "Okay. I'm sorry." She sounded like she was going to cry. "I didn't mean to, Uncle Matt. It was an accident."

She was such a dirty little liar. But I hated when she was upset. I put my arms out. "It's alright."

She ran into my arms and hugged me. I stood, lifting her up with me. "Where did you say your dad was?"

"In his office." She pointed toward the hall as if I'd never been here before.

The three of us walked to James' office. I knocked on the door before opening it. "Hey."

"Matt. What are you...oh, hi, Tanner. What are you guys doing here?"

James usually only wore his glasses when he wasn't getting enough sleep. He looked tired and stressed. He looked how I felt. And clearly Tanner was wrong about my friendship with James. Because something was clearly wrong and he hadn't come to me for help.

"I need to talk to you," I said.

James nodded and then his eyes fell to Scarlett in my arms. "Scarlett, you're supposed to be in bed. What are you doing down here?"

"I got thirsty."

"Give me one second," he said to me and lifted Scarlett out of my arms. "Pumpkin, it's called bedtime for a reason."

"I don't know what bedtime means," she said.

He laughed. "Yes you do." He disappeared down the hall.

Tanner stepped into James' office and started wandering around. He stopped at a picture of Mason, Rob, James, and me while we were at Harvard together. He picked it up and laughed. "That haircut is no good."

"That surfer shaggy kind of style was in."

He looked over at me. "But you're not a surfer. Have you ever even been out on a wave?"

I hadn't. And I was pretty sure he knew that.

He put the framed picture back down. "I've been through many a bad haircut as well. You wouldn't believe how frequently popular haircuts come and go. It's impossible to keep up with the times."

Okay. I was pretty sure Tanner hadn't changed his hairstyle once since I'd known him. Unless you counted the fake sightings Rob had of Tanner prancing around the city in fluorescent suits and a man bun. There was no way his hair was long enough for a man bun. *I think.* I shook my head.

"Scarlett opened the door for you guys, didn't she?" James asked as he came back into the room.

I didn't want to betray Scarlett's confidence. But her safety was more important. "Yeah, she did."

James sighed. "She's as impossible as she is adorable." He shoved his hands into his pockets. "So what's going on? I'm assuming the two of you didn't just stop by to get Scarlett in trouble?"

"She said it was an accident," Tanner said.

James laughed. "How was it an accident that she opened the door?"

"I don't know, but she's too cute not to believe."

"That's the whole problem." James sat down on the edge of his desk. "I give in to her too much. With everything that's happened over the past few months, I just want her to be happy."

James' family had been through enough devastation. And I couldn't be the reason for any more. "I need to tell you something."

"About Scarlett?"

"No. Well, yes actually. I should just start at the beginning. Ever since Brooklyn died..." my voice caught saying the words out loud. "Mr. Pruitt has been sending me texts. A few a year. Sometimes more often. He always says he needs to speak with me. And I never reply."

James pushed himself off his desk. "Why didn't you tell me about this?"

Because I was mad at you. Because you married his psychotic daughter. The list was endless. "I don't know. I didn't think it mattered. I didn't care about what he wanted. But the last few texts he's sent said it's urgent. I didn't respond to those either and I started noticing a woman following me around. At first I thought she was just some woman I'd slept with..."

"You slept with her?" James asked.

"Months ago. I think. Actually, that night's a little foggy. But she looks familiar. And that doesn't matter. What matters is that she started showing up at my games. And she was at the graveyard the other night."

James pressed his lips together. He didn't need to ask why I was at the graveyard.

"Tanner did some digging and Mr. Pruitt hired a few hitmen recently. One of them is some woman who's really good at her job. We think it might be her."

"Jesus." James shook his head. "Okay, well, we'll figure this out. No need to panic. Do you want to spend the night here? I can let my security team know about the woman if you give me a description. And maybe I can call Mr. Pruitt. I expected him to hate me after everything that happened with Isabella. But he was surprisingly understanding the last time we spoke. I can..."

"That's not everything. Poppy showed up at my office. She actually may have mentioned something about Mr. Pruitt making certain allowances with my friends because he still thinks of me as family."

James lowered his eyebrows.

I got how that sounded. I had never technically been part of Mr. Pruitt's family. James had. And he was probably insulted by that. But I didn't care how insulting Mr. Pruitt was right now. I only cared how violent he was. "Poppy said that if I didn't return his texts he wouldn't be as forgiving. She threatened Scarlett."

The color drained from James' face. "So what did Mr. Pruitt say when you called him?"

"I didn't call him."

"What? When did you say Poppy told you this?"

I hadn't said. I was really hoping he wouldn't ask. "Monday."

"Today?"

I swallowed hard. "No, last Monday."

"You didn't tell me for a week?"

"I tried to tell you after the game but you had to leave early..."

"You mean on Friday? When I had to go home early to put my daughter to bed? Matt, that was still five days after Poppy threatened Scarlett. Why the hell would you wait so long?" He pulled out his phone and sent a text. "You won't be happy until you destroy my family, will you?"

"James, that's not…"

"Don't. I'm not a fucking idiot, Matt. You think I haven't seen the way you look at Penny? I don't know how many times I have to tell you this. She's not Brooklyn."

"And you think I don't know that? Brooklyn's dead. And she died thinking I didn't love her because of you, you piece of shit."

"Hey, guys," Tanner said. "Let's all take a deep meditative breath on three, shall we?" He stepped between us. "Now I get that Matt's a disloyal little bastard on occasion, but you know he has a good heart. And James, from what I've heard, that shoe fits you as well. I think it's best that we get all the animosity out right now before anyone messes up anyone else's life."

"I've apologized for kissing Brooklyn so many times," James said. "High school sucked for me. I was drunk and high half the time. Brooklyn was my friend and I crossed the line, but I was freaking drowning. I wasn't thinking clearly. But you're thinking clearly right now, Matt. And what does that say about you?"

I wanted to yell at him. And punch him in his stupid face. But honestly? He was right. He hadn't been thinking clearly back then. I knew that. And yet… "It was me who cleaned up your mess half the time. And covered for you showing up to school hammered. It was me who was worried that you'd take it too far and fucking kill yourself."

Tanner sighed. "This isn't going well. How about we take a lobster break? It's getting cold."

James stepped around Tanner to look at me. "Kill myself? What are you talking about?"

James knew what happened to my aunt. He had been there that night when we found her. And not once had he asked if I was okay. He'd been too busy getting shit-faced while I was worried he'd do the same thing. I was the only one that cared about him, and he'd pushed me away because of a stupid rumor. He hadn't even given me a chance to tell my side. "You're a hypocrite. And a liar," I said. Those had been Brooklyn's last words to me, and I knew how deeply they could sting. I regretted them as soon as they were out of my mouth. But I wasn't going to stand here and tell him that. He'd messed up my whole life and he was too blind to see it. He'd gotten the wife, the family, the kids. He'd gotten everything I'd ever wanted. And I hated him for it.

"I've never lied," James said.

Well at least he knew better than to deny that he was a hypocrite. "Oh yeah? Because I know that the two of you weren't just friends."

Tanner gasped.

"You don't look at friends like that," I said. "You loved Brooklyn too." And I think that was the worst part. He'd betrayed me worse than I'd ever betrayed him. I had to get out of this apartment. I couldn't freaking breathe. "Don't worry about Mr. Pruitt. I'll handle it myself." I didn't need to hear anything else James had to say.

"Um, good day to you," Tanner said to James before hurrying out of the room behind me. "I guess we won't be sharing the lobster with him after all," he said to me. "That did not go well. Look out!"

I almost ran straight into Penny because I was trying to figure out what Tanner was yelling about.

She looked up at me. "Matt, what's going on?"

How much of that conversation had she heard? "Ask your husband. Maybe if he'd sobered up enough in his twenties and not married that witch we wouldn't be in this mess." I walked past her without another word. *Fuck James. Fuck everything.*

CHAPTER 22

Monday

"Are you sure this is a good idea?" Tanner asked.

No, I wasn't. But I was already knocking on Mr. Pruitt's door. "I just need to get this over with." My heart was still pounding in my chest. I was pissed at James. I was pissed at Mr. Pruitt. I was freaking pissed at everyone. I tried to take a deep breath.

"It's pretty late," Tanner said. "Doesn't Richard usually invite you over right after dinner? Around 7 if I recall correctly from his texts? He was rather specific about it."

"Yeah, I don't care if I'm inconveniencing him." Mr. Pruitt had been inconveniencing me for years. His texts had been slowly driving me insane. I could bother him for one night.

Tanner stuffed his hands in his pockets, pulled them back out, and then stuffed them in again. "You're not at all worried that you're about to upset a mobster?"

"I told you to wait in the car."

"I'm not worried about my safety. I'm worried about yours. You think Richard is having you tailed. All he has to do is make the call and you're a dead man."

"That's an even better reason for you to wait in the car. You don't want to get caught up in this."

"Do you have a freaking death wish?"

Maybe. But that didn't mean I needed to bring anyone else down with me. "Tanner, seriously, go back to the car."

"If I'd waited in the car when you went to see James, you two definitely would have brawled."

"I'm not going to brawl with Mr. Pruitt."

Tanner stared at the door. "Doesn't mean he's not going to brawl with you."

"If you're scared..."

Tanner laughed. "I'm not scared of anything." But his eyebrows were pulled together and he was just staring straight ahead.

I knew he was lying. He wasn't even really trying to hide it. But I didn't get a chance to ask him about it, because the door opened.

Mr. Pruitt was standing there in a...nightgown? I wasn't sure how else to describe it. A long men's shirt, perhaps? He was also wearing some weird little cap that I couldn't explain either. And for just a second, all that pent up anger I had for him evaporated. I just wanted to laugh. The man in front of me wasn't scary. He was wearing a nightgown and cried during the Titanic. I was going to end this right here right now.

He cleared his throat. "Matthew." His voice came out hoarse and strange despite the fact that he'd just cleared it. "What are you doing here at this hour?"

I wanted to ask him what the hell he was wearing. But that wasn't why I was here. Making fun of him didn't seem like the best approach anyway. "I need you to listen to me because I'm only going to say this once. Leave me and my friends the hell alone."

Mr. Pruitt lowered his eyebrows and glanced at Tanner. "I don't know who this man is. And I have no idea what you're referring to."

Tanner offered him his hand. "I'm Tanner Rhodes. Matt's best friend. Nice nightshirt, by the way. Very retro of you."

Why the hell had he told Mr. Pruitt his full name? Was he trying to get killed too?

Mr. Pruitt paused a beat too long before shaking Tanner's hand. "I'm sorry, I was under the impression that Robert was Matthew's best friend?"

"No, that title belongs to me," Tanner said.

Why did everyone always want to discuss who my best friend was? This wasn't relevant at all. "It doesn't matter who my best friend is." I felt stupid saying the words out loud. "I'm here to tell you that you're done messing with my life."

"Messing with your life? Matthew, I have no intention of hurting Tanner or…"

"Cut the crap, Mr. Pruitt. You sent Poppy to my office to threaten a child. What the hell is wrong with you?"

Mr. Pruitt sighed. "I told her to deliver a letter to you. That is all." He shook his head. "She doesn't love following simple directions. Now tell me, what did she say about a child?"

The nerve of this asshole. "You threatened James' daughter. Don't play dumb with me."

"Ah. Well, Poppy has her own…unique set of strengths to get what she wants. She's very good at spotting weaknesses and using them to her advantage."

I didn't believe him for a second. Threatening children could never be considered a strength. And me caring for my friend's child's safety wasn't a weakness. *Fuck him.*

"Let me guess," Mr. Pruitt said. "She also tried to seduce you?"

Who talked about their niece like that? And why was he acting like he had nothing to do with this? If he'd just wanted to send a letter, he could have sent it via FedEx. He hadn't needed to involve Poppy. "I don't know what delusional plans you have for me and Poppy, but I'm not playing any part."

"It's late, Matthew. Can we talk about this in the morning? I'm having trouble following your logic. Are you feeling quite alright?"

Son of a bitch. I wasn't the crazy one here. He was. "I know you're having me tailed. I know you hired hitmen to come after me..."

"Maybe Richard is right," Tanner said. "Why don't we come back in the morning after we've calmed down a bit?" He tilted his head in the direction of the elevators and gave me angry eyes. "You're going to get yourself killed," he mouthed silently at me.

"I'm never stepping foot back into this cursed apartment," I said.

Mr. Pruitt sighed. "Matthew..."

"Stop texting me! Don't send crazy people to my office with letters and threats. Don't contact me in any way. We're done."

"We are not done. I've been asking you for years to come speak to me and the best you can do is show up in the middle of the night half lucid. This isn't a game. You're in danger, Matthew. I'm trying to protect you. Just like I have been for years. This is a life and death..."

"You expect me to believe that you're worried about me? Where were you after Brooklyn died? You never came to her grave. You never stopped by my parents' house to talk to me. You never gave a shit about everything you took from me. So don't stand there and pretend you care now. You don't care about me. And I don't give a shit about you. So get it through your thick skull. Leave me and my friends the hell alone. "

Mr. Pruitt looked so calm. "You can't keep blaming me for Brooklyn's death. It wasn't my..."

"It wasn't your fault? You tricked her into loving you. Into trusting you. And then you murdered her."

"Murder is such a strong word," Tanner said with a grimace as he elbowed me in the ribcage.

"She agreed to the surgery," Mr. Pruitt said. "She knew the risks. It was a misunderstanding at best."

Misunderstanding? He'd murdered his daughter. "Is that how you sleep at night? Watch your back, Mr. Pruitt. Because I have resources too."

"Are you threatening me?"

Damn right. "Enjoy one of your last nights in your own bed."

Tanner was staring at me like I was insane. He turned to Mr. Pruitt. "He doesn't mean that," Tanner said. "He hasn't been getting much sleep. If you would just call off your hitmen, maybe..."

"Come at me with whatever you have," I added. "I'm going to fucking destroy you."

"Watch your own back, Matthew," Mr. Pruitt said. "I'm not having you tailed. And you're not in danger because of me. Despite what you think, I've been protecting you for years. And if you refuse to thank me, consider my protection revoked. Come back to me once you've learned reason and an ounce of respect." Mr. Pruitt slammed the door in our faces.

"I know you cry during the Titanic!" I yelled at the door. "Wait until everyone finds out about that!" I laughed.

"Why are you laughing?" Tanner said. "He's so fucking pissed. He's definitely going to off you."

"Good. Let him try."

"What?"

I grabbed Tanner's arm and pulled him away from the Pruitt's door. "I want him to try to kill me. You said you got the information about the hitmen illegally so it can't be used in court. So I'll catch him in the act and get him sent to prison where he belongs. Attempted murder isn't as bad as actual murder, but he's old. Hopefully he'll just rot in prison for the rest of his miserable life."

"Oh. Oooh. Well, that's a good idea. Minus the fact that you might die in the process."

"I'm not going to die. I have a plan."

"Well...are you going to fill me in?"

It was fitting to make Tanner wait for something for once. The only problem was that I didn't actually have more of a plan than what I'd told him. Seeing how angry Mr. Pruitt had gotten was what had given me the idea. I'd dug my heels in and gone all in by throwing more insults his way. There was no going back now. Surely Mr. Pruitt had murdered people for less. And I needed to think of something fast or else I was an idiot. I'd just threatened a mobster. Maybe I was an idiot. An idea finally popped into my head. "James has prototypes of these little undetectable cameras..."

"You're fighting with James. I doubt he'll loan expensive prototype cameras to you right now."

Damn, that was a good point. I'd basically told James to fuck off. "Well, Penny will let me borrow them."

"You really think James is going to let Penny hang out with you while you guys are in a fight? He knows you have feelings for Penny. That was part of your argument."

"Penny's her own woman. She doesn't need James' permission to hang out with me. Besides, we have plans for dinner tomorrow night. She won't cancel." *I think.* She hated when I canceled on her. I doubted she'd do it to me. But that really depended on what she and James were talking about right now. She'd definitely overheard some of our conversation earlier. Maybe James was telling her everything. The thought of Penny knowing about Brooklyn gave me a sinking feeling in my stomach.

"A dinner date?" asked Tanner. "Nice. So you're going to seduce Penny and then she'll bend to your every whim?"

"No." *Maybe. No.* "We're friends. If I tell her I need the cameras, she'll give them to me. She won't even ask any questions." That was a lie. Penny would definitely have a million questions about why I needed spy-grade cameras.

"Great. So you'll get a hitman trying to kill you on film with a tiny, undetectable Hunter Tech camera. And somehow get away with the evidence *and* your life. That's your big plan?"

"I'm open to suggestions."

"Why don't we just try to confront the hitwoman directly? Get her to confess to being hired to kill you before she actually has a chance to kill you?"

Damn, that was a much better idea. "I've tried to talk to her. But she always runs away. And she's pretty fast."

Tanner cracked his knuckles. "Not as fast as me."

I stared at him. I'd never seen Tanner run. The closest was him hurrying to my car tonight and he was so unaware that I'd almost run him over.

"Don't look at me like that. I'm quite the athlete. I've been running more years than you've been alive." He laughed because it made no sense. "As the saying goes."

"I've never heard that saying."

"You know what I mean. I'm fast. Much faster than you or a hitwoman."

"If you say so." I would have sworn I was faster than a hitwoman too. Maybe the heels on her boots were somehow powered to make her move faster or something. Or she was a retired track star.

"She shows up at your games sometimes right?" Tanner asked.

"Yeah. I think she was even at my practice today. I saw her SUV hightailing it out of the parking lot this afternoon."

"Perfect. You get the cameras tomorrow by seducing Penny. And I'll come to your practice on Wednesday for surveillance. Maybe we can even corner her right away and just get it over with. And don't worry, I'll wear a disguise so that no one is the wiser. Now let's go eat that lobster before it turns."

"It's been sitting in the car for a while. Maybe we should skip the spoiled seafood and just grab some drinks."

"You can't toss lobster! It's a delicacy now. It'll be fine. Come on, we'll go back to my place so we can reheat it and wet your whistle."

I internally groaned. Tanner had an awesome place. But his houseboy always made me feel wildly uncomfortable.

CHAPTER 23

Tuesday

The sound of bells made me cringe. I wasn't sure if it was my pounding headache that was making me hallucinate them…or if there was actually something ringing.

Ring.

I definitely wasn't imagining it. It sounded like a shit ton of bells. Where the hell was I, at the symphony? I rolled over and reached out, my fingers colliding with the softest sheets I'd ever felt. Definitely not the symphony. I blinked my eyes open to see a short little man looking at sheet music, holding a gold bell in each hand.

He lifted one of his arms. Ring.

I screamed.

He screamed and dropped the bells. "I'm sorry, Mr. Caldwell," the man said in a British accent. "Master Tanner said you wanted to wake up to a chorus of bells. I didn't have much time to practice."

It took me a second to recognize the little man as Nigel, Tanner's houseboy. I hadn't recognized him because today he was dressed in some weird lederhosen. All the other times I had been here he'd always been outfitted in a strange Victorian era butler outfit. Tanner said it was his uniform. I wondered why the sudden change since all the outfits made zero sense anyway.

During the awkward stretch of silence, Nigel looked down at my lap.

I followed his gaze to see what he was staring at. What the actual fuck? "Why am I naked?!" I grabbed the sheets and pulled them to my chest like he hadn't just seen my morning wood.

"Master Tanner said you liked to sleep that way. It appears as though he was correct." He raised his eyebrows and had a silly little grin on his face.

"So you stripped me?!"

He nodded. "Yes, Mr. Caldwell."

"What is wrong with you? Get out!"

"But Master Tanner…"

"I don't care what Tanner said. I don't want to be stripped. And the last thing I need right now is to be played a chorus of bells."

"It's actually a very peaceful way to awake from one's slumber."

"Nigel. Out."

He gave me a little bow and scurried out the bedroom door.

I rubbed my forehead. Fuck. How much had I had to drink last night? It felt like there was a freight train careening around in my head.

There was a knock on the door and Nigel poked his head back in. "Sorry to bother you, but breakfast is being served in 15 minutes and Master Tanner wanted to extend you an invitation."

I just glared at him.

"Your clothes are also freshly pressed and hanging in the closet."

I looked over at the open closet doors. Even my socks were hung up. I was pretty sure he'd ironed them too.

"Would you like me to draw you a bath?"

"I think I can manage, Nigel."

He nodded. "I'll come check on you in a few minutes."

"Please don't."

"Just in case there's anything else you need. You never know when something will come up. See you shortly." He closed the door.

Why did it seem like Nigel just wanted to see me naked again? I'd grown up with a staff, but none of them were as weird as Nigel. Where had Tanner found this guy?

I pushed the sheets off of me and practically ran to the bathroom. I showered as fast as I could and somehow managed to have a towel wrapped around my waist before Nigel came into the guest bathroom.

"Ah, you're finished." He sounded disappointed. "Shall I help you into your little outfit?"

Had he seriously just called my expensive suit a little outfit when he was dressed in what had to be costume lederhosen? "No, I'm good."

"It's no trouble, Mr. Caldwell."

"I swear to God." I took a deep breath, which somehow made my headache worse. "I just need a minute."

He did a weird little bow and hurried out of the room.

I quickly changed before Nigel could get a dick pic or whatever the hell he was after. I wandered out into the hall. Just like every time I'd been here before, there were white sheets covering most of the furniture and there were even some cloths draped over what I assumed were paintings on the walls. If the décor wasn't all so modern, it would have seemed like I was walking around in a haunted house.

Tanner had been renovating the place for years. Which was crazy because I'd completely renovated a whole house in less time. Although, this place may have had just as much square footage as my house. I walked by one of the many doors in the hall. Maybe this penthouse was even bigger than my place, because I'd just taken yet another turn in the hallway and I still hadn't found the great room. Huh.

I looked over my shoulder to make sure that I was alone and reached out to grab one of the doorknobs so I could see just how much space Tanner had here. All I saw was a blinding white light before Nigel came out of nowhere and slammed the door closed.

He seemed completely out of breath like he'd just sprinted over to stop me. "Mr. Caldwell, you mustn't go in there. Are you trying to get burned?"

What? "Burned?"

Nigel's eyes bulged. "Snoopers get burned by fire. Lit up like a spark. As the old saying goes."

Nigel's sayings were as strange as Tanner's. I laughed. "I was just trying to get a read on the square footage of this place."

"It depends on the day. Now if you please, sir, the dining room is right this way." He gestured down the hall.

"What do you mean it depends on the day?"

"Expansions."

Was he high? I looked down at him as we made our way through the impossibly long hallway. We were on the 89th floor. The top floor of One57. Logistically it would be really hard to expand this property. And why did Tanner even need to expand? He hadn't even properly moved in yet.

We were almost at the dining room when I had to sidestep a white sheet that was blanketing something tall and wide. Was it a tree or something? How the heck did Tanner even get something so large up here?

I reached out to push the fabric aside and Nigel slapped my hand.

"Ow." I pulled my hand away from the cloth.

"Off-limits," Nigel said. "Now please, Mr. Caldwell, go eat before you accidentally catch fire."

"Nigel, I just…"

"Master Tanner, your guest has arrived for breakfast," Nigel said super loudly.

Normally I'd be distracted by the amazing view of Central Park from Tanner's open floor plan. But it was rather hard to look at the view when Tanner was sitting at the far end of a long dining room table being fed grapes by two topless women. His silk robe didn't look like it had been closed properly and I wouldn't have been at all surprised if one of those women had just had something other than a grape in her mouth.

One of them giggled as she plopped another grape in Tanner's mouth.

It honestly wasn't the strangest thing I'd ever walked in on Tanner doing. It didn't even make the top ten list. I was just surprised the women weren't decked out in weird lederhosen like Nigel.

"Good morning, Matt," Tanner said. "Did you sleep alright?" The stupid grin on his face made me think that Tanner probably had a hand in Nigel's antics this morning. The blonde to his left ceremoniously plopped another grape into his mouth.

"That depends on if you think waking up to a terrible chorus of bells and finding out a houseboy stripped you in the middle of the night…"

Tanner started laughing. "I thought you'd find that funny."

"My headache begs to differ."

"Well, I didn't give him much time to practice." He turned to his houseboy. "Good heavens, Nigel, what are you wearing?"

Nigel looked down at his ridiculous costume. "I'm wearing what I always wear. Just like you insisted last night when you and Mr. Caldwell got lost in the wine cellar."

"No, you're supposed to wear the other costume when Matt..." Tanner's voice trailed off.

Nigel and Tanner both looked like they'd been caught in some weird lie.

"How many costumes does he have?" I asked.

Tanner cleared his throat. "Just that one. Like Nigel said. He's always wearing that."

"No, he's usually wearing that weird Victorian butler outfit..."

"Nonsense," Tanner said. "Nigel always wears lederhosen. Don't you Nigel?"

"Why, yes, Master Tanner. These are my favorite...pant. Pants? Shorts? I don't really know what this is. And it's rather itchy."

"That's quite enough, Nigel. Please leave us to eat."

Nigel hurried off.

"And girls, would you wait for me in my room?" Tanner said. "I need a word with Matt in private before he goes to work." He whispered something in one of their ears as he slapped the other girl on the butt. They both giggled and went off down the hall I'd just come from.

Tanner stabbed his fork into some strange looking sausage. "Help yourself to whatever you'd like."

I looked at the huge spread of food on the table. Did he have ten more women waiting for him in his bedroom? Because this was way too much for just the two of us. But there were only two chairs. The one where Tanner was sitting at the other end of the table and the one at this end which I assumed was for me. Why were we so spread out? We were going to have to shout at each other.

"Sit, sit," Tanner said. "I've been cooking all morning."

"You made all this?"

Tanner laughed. "Gotcha. No. Of course not. Nigel's been up for hours. He insisted that he knew all your favorites and wanted to cater to you."

How on earth would Nigel know all my favorites? And why did this weird little man seem hellbent on catering to me?

"He even made protein pancakes." Tanner pointed to a plate full of them.

I did love protein pancakes. I grabbed a plate and started to fill it up.

"And make sure to drink that green juice. It has a few secret ingredients to cure hangovers. Nigel's top-secret elixir."

I couldn't argue with that. I grabbed one of the glasses of green juice too and sat down. One bite of pancakes and I was a little less pissed at Nigel. These were amazing. "You'll have to let Nigel know these are great. What kind of plant protein is this?"

"I'm not sure, I'll have to ask him. But he'll be happy to hear that you enjoyed them. Speaking of Nigel. About his uniform. Forgive him, he's forgetful."

"Or maybe you are. He's definitely never worn that before."

"Of course he has. Because it's what he always wears. Regardless, are you excited to execute the plan?"

"The plan?" Honestly, I'd had too much to drink last night. Nigel had said something about getting lost in Tanner's wine cellar. Had we drank our way out of it? And how did he have a wine cellar? There were no basements in penthouses.

"Yes, the plan." Tanner abandoned his sausage and stood up. He pulled a cloth off a whiteboard that was filled with pictures and yarn connecting them and I was pretty sure there were even words in a different language linking everything together. Chinese maybe?

I opened my mouth and then closed it again. "What the hell is all this?"

"Our plan to take down Richard of course. We spent all night on it."

"Did we? Could you maybe just explain what it means to me? I can't read whatever that is."

"Oh it says…" Tanner started coughing. "I mean. Huh. I don't know. What language is that? Maybe Nigel came in here and messed with it. I'm pretty sure he speaks whatever tongue that is. That sneaky little bastard. I told him to stop touching my things. Let's circle back to this tonight." He quickly covered the weird diagram back up.

"I can't tonight. I have dinner plans with Penny, remember?"

"Right, I mean after that."

"I have a feeling this headache isn't going away any time soon. I'm just going to call it an early night after hanging out with Penny."

"Right. Here."

"No, at my house."

"Matt, we talked about this last night. You'll be staying here until this nonsense with Richard is sorted. Sleeping at your own home is like being asked to be murdered by a hitwoman. Trust me, this is for the best."

"I can't stay here…"

"Of course you can. It's no bother. And Nigel rather likes when you're around."

I looked around to make sure Nigel wasn't nearby. "Yeah, about that. Why the heck won't he leave me alone?"

"You're engaging with him too much. He's a houseboy, not a friend. Just think of him like a piece of furniture. He's there to assist when needed but invisible when not."

"But he keeps talking to me. And trying to see me naked."

Tanner laughed. "No, no. The stripping you thing was a prank I was playing on you. I just made him do it."

I sighed. "That doesn't explain him wanting to draw me a bath."

"Were you planning on standing there nude while he did it? That's not appropriate."

Oh. Well. No. "Well, what about him offering to help dress me?"

"Did he do that?"

"Yeah."

"Surely he meant for you to put on your underwear first."

"I don't know, he was staring at my penis earlier."

"Why did you have your penis out in front of Nigel?"

"Because you told him to strip me last night!"

"Oh right." Tanner laughed. "Hilarious. Well, please stop flashing the staff, will you?"

"Tanner…"

"I'm joking. I'll speak to Nigel on your behalf and tell him you're uncomfortable…"

"Don't tell him I complained." Nigel was already awkward enough around me. I didn't need awkward angry Nigel.

"Then what am I supposed to say to rectify the situation? He doesn't dress me and I rarely require him to draw a bath. As soon as I mention the situation he'll know it's about you."

"Just don't say anything then."

"Very well." Tanner glanced at his watch. "You should get going or you'll be late for work. Do you want a bag lunch? Nigel mentioned packing one up for you."

"I'm okay."

"Well make sure to eat lunch. You need to make sure you're alert just in case someone tries to murder you." Tanner loaded up a plate and stood up. A biscuit fell off the top of the plate and rolled on the polished hardwood floors.

"Aren't you going to work too?" I asked.

"I have company to attend to. Now don't forget to drink that juice before you head out. Trust me. It'll make your headache evaporate in a flash. I'll see you tonight." He disappeared down the hall with his big plate of food.

I stood up and took a quick sip of the green juice, expecting it to be bitter and gross like green juice usually was. But it was actually delicious. It tasted just like a strawberry banana smoothie. I wondered if those were the two secret ingredients. If they were, my headache wouldn't be gone in a flash like promised. I quickly downed the rest. Before I even put the glass down I took a deep breath. What the hell? I touched my forehead. My headache was gone. I blinked. Actually, I felt amazing. Like I'd just slept for days instead of a few hours. I eyed the glass. I was going to need that recipe. But not if it involved asking Nigel for it. Who knows what kind of favor he'd ask for in return.

I was about to leave the great room when a large cloth draped over something above the fireplace caught my eye. I double checked that no one was around and pushed the cloth to the side. Beneath the fabric was a portrait of Tanner in a weird Victorian outfit, similar to what he most definitely usually made Nigel wear. Someone loved history a little too much if you asked me. I looked around the room and wondered how much of the covered wall art featured Tanner playing dress up. I let the cloth fall back in place and made my way past the kitchen.

I stopped when I noticed a brown paper bag sitting on the counter with my name on it. Well, I guess if Nigel had already made me a lunch it would just be rude not to take it. I grabbed the bag and headed out the front door.

Nigel was hanging off the side of the weird little footbridge that went from the elevator to Tanner's apartment door. Nigel had a staple gun and was stapling a tarp over top of the water. He grunted as he tried to maneuver without falling in.

"What are you doing, Nigel?"

"Hiding the…" Nigel started coughing. "Nothing. What are you doing, Mr. Caldwell?" He placed one more staple and then slid back safely onto the bridge. He was completely out of breath, but he quickly wiped off his lederhosen and stood up with a bow.

"Heading to work." I lifted up the bag lunch.

"Good, good. I'm glad you found your lunch. Please don't look down."

"Nigel, I've been here before. I know Tanner somehow has water under this bridge."

"Right. Of course. Just normal everyday water and nothing more. See you tonight, Mr. Caldwell. I'll have a bath and a snifter of cognac waiting for you upon your arrival."

If that wasn't the weirdest sentence I'd ever heard. "That won't be necessary, Nigel."

"But you're Master Tanner's guest."

"Just pretend I'm not here."

"But you're also Master Tanner's best friend. Only the best for Master Tanner's best friend."

Okay. "I don't really take baths, but I appreciate the offer."

"We'll see if I can change your mind about that to-night. Good day." He hurried back inside with his staple gun.

Bath references should never sound dirty, but Nigel made it sound absolutely filthy. I sighed and looked down. And I swore I saw the tarp move. I grabbed the railing on the bridge. What the hell? Was there something under there?

Fuck it. I didn't even want to know what was in that water. It was probably another houseboy dressed in leder-hosen ready to jump out and scare me half to death. And I wanted no part in it. I'd had enough weirdness for one morning. I made my way over the footbridge and safely onto the elevator.

I just needed to focus on staying alive and convincing Penny to give me those prototypes. And for Nigel to stop trying to see me naked.

CHAPTER 24

Tuesday

I hadn't heard from Penny all day. I'd texted her this morning to see if we were still on for dinner. But she hadn't responded. I'd texted her again an hour ago asking if she had gotten my first text, and immediately wished I could have unsent it. Obviously she had gotten my other text and was just not responding.

I opened up my bag lunch, very aware of the fact that Tanner had probably made Nigel make it so I wouldn't leave the office today. Not like that mattered. Poppy had waltzed into MAC International undetected before. Certainly a hitwoman could do the same.

There was a folded note on top of the food:

Mr. Caldwell,

I'm so elated that you'll be staying with us for the foreseeable future. It is my job to make sure you are comfortable and happy during the duration of your visit. So please let me know if there's anything you need me to acquire. At your convenience, my number is below and I'll go out and fetch everything you require today. Or if you need me to get items from your home, I'm happy to do that as well.

Have a good and prosperous day at work. Remember to smile and be kind to others. And use your words not your fists.

Yours,

-Nigel

XOXO
P.S. I hope you like meat!

Gross. Well, the note was gross. The turkey sandwich piled high with lettuce and tomato on rye bread looked excellent. I took a bite and it practically melted in my mouth. What kind of cheese was that? Gruyere?

I looked at the note again. That was too many X's and O's from one man to another. And the meat comment could have been innocent. But when it came to Nigel, I had no idea. I wondered how he'd take it if I texted him that all I required was privacy. Probably not well. And then he'd also have my number. I couldn't let that happen. And what was all that weird stuff about fighting and being kind? Did he think I was a petulant child? I pushed the note to the side and tried to enjoy my sandwich.

Tanner said that Nigel didn't try to dress and bathe him. So maybe Nigel just had a weird crush on me. It wouldn't be the first time a guy had hit on me. It was flattering. But very much unreciprocated. If he was giving me attention for that reason, I needed to make sure he knew I was straight. Was it rude to just tell him flat out?

There was a knock on my door.

"Not now!" *Hm. Be kind and smile.* Maybe that was advice I needed to remember. "I mean, yes?" I called in a more upbeat voice.

My receptionist, Mary, walked in. "I'm sorry to bother you, but do you know a Ms. Cannavaro?"

Poppy Cannavaro. I swallowed down a chunk of too much turkey and cleared my throat. "Why?" Please let there be news that she died in an explosion or something and that this wasn't about her being outside my office right now. *One can hope.*

"I input all your meetings myself. And for the life of me I can't remember setting one with her. I honestly don't even remember seeing it this morning when I double checked today's schedule. But I just got an alert saying you have a 1 o'clock with her. And sure enough, I looked and there the appointment is in the system." She shook her head. "Maybe she set it up a long time ago and I just don't remember?"

I doubted that. It was a lot more likely that Poppy had someone hack into our system. *Damn it.* I looked down at my watch. Poppy would be here any minute.

"Do you want me to cancel?"

As appealing as that sounded, canceling on Poppy wouldn't make her go away. She was a pest that just kept showing up. I needed to see what she wanted now and try to squash it. "That won't be necessary. I'll handle it."

"I'm very sorry, Matthew."

"It's not your fault. I'm sure it was just a glitch."

"Yeah. Maybe." She smiled. "You look well-rested today. Did the chamomile tea work?"

More like the magical green juice. Hell, maybe chamomile was the secret ingredient. Regardless, I wanted to make Mary smile today. "It must have."

"That's wonderful. Let me know if you'd like me to bring you a cup before work ends today. And I'll ring you when Ms. Cannavaro arrives."

I nodded and looked down at my sandwich as Mary closed the door. I suddenly wasn't hungry anymore. What if Poppy wasn't stopping by to talk? I swallowed hard. Was this it? Was Poppy going to walk in here with a gun and pull the trigger? Would someone find this weird note on my desk and think I was having a gay affair with Nigel? Would my murder make the late night news? How would I be remembered?"

Fuck. James. The last words I'd said to him. I knew better than that. I knew better than anyone that life could be cut short. I didn't want those to be my last words to him. I pulled out my phone. But there were suddenly a million things I wanted to do. I needed to finally call my mom back. I didn't care that she always pestered me this time of year. I needed to tell her that I loved her. And thank Mason for always looking out for me. And I stupidly even wanted to call Rob and make sure he knew he was my best friend too. And Tanner for the same reason. It was okay to have two best friends, and I wasn't sure why the hell this was the last thing I was thinking about before I died.

But I didn't have any time to call a soul, because my intercom button was blinking. I hit the light.

"Ms. Cannavaro has arrived," Mary's voice said through the speaker.

"Let her in."

Mary opened the door and I held my breath.

But I slowly exhaled when Poppy walked in. Because she wasn't holding a gun. She was holding a toddler in her arms.

The first thing I thought of was Scarlett. But there was no cute little "Hi, Uncle Matt." And the little girl wasn't a redhead. She was brunette.

"Let me know if you need anything," Mary said and closed the door behind us.

As soon as the door was closed I stood up. "Did you steal that child?"

Poppy laughed. "No."

"I swear to God, Poppy, if you…"

"She's mine."

"Yours?" I looked down at the little girl and then back at her mother. The resemblance was uncanny. The little girl was even holding her nose slightly in the air like she was looking down at me even though she literally had to look up at me. "You have a…kid?" I couldn't imagine Poppy being a mom. A mobster? Sure. A mother? It didn't quite fit. But the little mini-her scowling back at me begged to differ.

"Funny," Poppy said. "I know everything about you and you know nothing about me. It's good that I'm here so we can rectify that." She put the child down on the ground. "Go play," she said and gestured toward my shelves that held nothing to play with. And then Poppy sat down without being invited.

I watched the little girl walk over to one of my shelves and inspect some of the framed pictures. Why did I have a feeling that she was somehow trained in surveillance even though she couldn't be older than Scarlett? The way she examined the people in the picture sent a chill down my spine.

Poppy cleared her throat. "I heard about your eventful evening." She started straightening a few things on my desk.

I just stared at her.

"Uncle Richard's angry with me. So I'm here to apologize."

I leaned forward, resting my hands on my desk. "It doesn't matter what you say. I don't believe a word that comes out of your mouth."

It was like she didn't even hear me. She just blinked and continued on with whatever she'd planned to say. "Obviously I'm not going to hurt a child. As a mother, I would never."

"So you brought your kid here as a prop?"

"I brought her here to show you that I'm a caring mother."

Well, it wasn't working. She'd barely even looked at her daughter this whole time. "I didn't know that you were married." I wasn't sure why the hell that was what came out of my mouth. I didn't care if this woman was married. For all I knew the little girl in the corner who looked like she was about to smash a paperweight was just an actress.

Poppy raised one of her penciled-in eyebrows. "Divorced, actually. I'm very much single, Matthew. For the record. But I have a feeling that's about to change."

I wasn't sure which was worse. Nigel or Poppy hitting on me.

Just as I expected, I watched as the little girl dropped the paperweight onto the ground. It shattered and for just a second a smile spread across her face.

Poppy snapped her fingers. "Behave, Gigi. Children are to be seen and not heard. How many times do I need to give you simple instructions?"

Gigi's smile immediately disappeared and she had her lips trained in a thin line, showing no shock or guilt or anything. Like a weird little demon child.

"Do we understand?" Poppy asked.

"Yes, Mother."

"Now apologize to the gentleman."

"Sorry, sir." Gigi curtseyed and then just stood there staring at the floor.

I knew she'd deliberately smashed it. But I still felt bad for her. Her mom was Poppy. Wasn't that punishment enough? She didn't need to be reprimanded any more by me. "It's alright. Just be more careful. You can keep playing."

Her eyes lit up and she turned around to touch more expensive things.

I cringed.

"So where were we?" Poppy asked. "Oh, yes, I don't hurt children. So as long as you understand, I'll just let Uncle Richard know you and I are on good terms and we can move forward from this hiccup of a misunderstanding."

"You swear you're not going to hurt Scarlett?"

"I don't recall ever saying I would *hurt* her. You're putting words in my mouth."

"Poppy."

"What I implied was more of a kidnapping situation, but alas. I won't do that either. Because I'm a mother and all that. You have my word."

"That's the whole problem. I don't trust your word."

She sighed, looking human for the first time since she'd walked back into my life. "Look, my uncle is really hard to please. As you know. I was just trying to get the results he wanted. And I mean…I did. You went to go talk to him. Or yell at him I guess. You didn't give him a chance to tell you the news."

"What news?"

She smiled. "It's not mine to share. And I'm not even sure that you'll care. For some reason he thinks you will. He's off his game." She looked over at Gigi to make sure she wasn't breaking anything else. "Which is why I'll be taking over operations soon."

Okay.

"Just me at the head of the whole business. All alone." She touched her chest and for some reason it seemed like she just did it to make me look at the tops of her breasts.

Where the hell was she going with this?

"You know what? We're going to need more time to catch up than just a 15-minute meeting made at the last second, don't you think? And maybe more privacy too. A relaxing night just the two of us. Let's do dinner to properly catch up and I can tell you all about my plans for the company."

Is that what she called her illegal dealings? A company? *Give me a break*. "I'm busy."

"Tonight? Well, let's do tomorrow night then. I'll arrange it with your secretary."

"She doesn't arrange my personal schedule."

"All good secretaries do."

"She's actually an administrative assistant. And she's fantastic at her job."

Poppy laughed. "Don't tell me you're dating her. Isn't she a little old for you? Certainly there are people in your life a little more suitable. A certain someone right under your nose, perchance?"

"Who I'm dating is none of your business."

"So you are dating someone? Well, that should make things interesting. Let her know I'll be preoccupying your evening tomorrow night. No reason for her to wait up for you."

"I'm not going out with you."

"I never said it was a date. That was all you. I've always loved a man who's forward."

I sighed. "Poppy, we're not having dinner. No matter what you want to call it."

"Then I'll just have to tell the hitmen to go forward with their plans."

I froze. Last night Mr. Pruitt said he hadn't hired hitmen to follow me around. I knew he was lying. But for her to actually sit there and admit it? Why hadn't I recorded this conversation? *Damn it.* "Mr. Pruitt said he wasn't having me followed."

"Darling, you know better than that. You don't think Uncle Richard doubled the size of our business by telling the truth? Honestly, you're so naïve. It's adorable." She smiled and her teeth were so straight and white that they almost looked fake. "You'll be perfect. I'll have a car sent for you at 7."

Perfect for what? "I won't be home."

"Yes, I'll be sending the car to Tanner Rhodes' apartment building of course. That is where you're staying, yes?"

Fuck. She knew I was staying with Tanner? "That's not..."

"Don't play coy. It was smart to not go back to your house. Staying with a friend was the safer choice given the circumstances. At least for the time being. You won't be staying there for long if I have my way though."

I thought she'd meant because I was surely about to die, but then she gave me a salacious wink and lightly bit her lower lip. *No. Good God, no.* Did she think she was going to sink her claws in me and turn me into husband number two? Because there was literally no way that was fucking happening. I'd rather the hitwoman off me.

"I won't take no for an answer." She turned to Gigi and put her hand out. "Time to go." The little girl ran over and slid her hand into her mother's.

"Ugh. Gigi, your hand is bleeding." Poppy pulled away from her daughter in disgust. "Why didn't you tell me you'd made a mess?"

The little girl didn't say anything. She just blinked even though there was blood literally dripping down her hand.

I looked over at the shattered glass. There was blood everywhere, like Gigi had been playing with the broken shards of glass, accidentally cutting her palms this whole time. How had she not screamed? I grabbed a tissue to hand to her.

Poppy snatched it from me and pressed it against one of Gigi's bloody palms. "We'll need to get that looked at.

There goes my whole day. Follow me. And don't touch anything. Especially my dress."

"Yes, Mother."

"See you tomorrow night, Matthew," Poppy said over her shoulder, avoiding her daughter like the plague. Gigi looked down at her shoes as she hurried after her mother.

Yikes. That kid was going to grow up and be a real monster at this rate. Breaking things on purpose and not even caring when she got a cut? Scarlett screamed bloody murder whenever she got boo-boos, as she called them. I'd never seen a child not cry when they got even a little hurt.

Mary walked in. "Miss Cannavaro said to set up a dinner for the two of you tomorrow night?"

"Yeah, just ignore her. There's no dinner."

"She seemed rather adamant. Oh my, what in the world happened in here?" Mary had spotted the bloody mess.

"It was just an accident. Could you call someone to clean that up?"

"Um, yes, right away." She walked over to the door, but then stopped and turned around. "It's none of my business, Matthew. But that woman?" She shook her head. "No one's ever spoken to me the way she does. I just thought you should know before your date."

I stared at Mary. I hadn't noticed that her eyes were a little glossed over like she was about to cry. "What did she say to you?"

"It wasn't what she said. It's how she said it. Like I was…nothing."

I shook my head. "I'm sorry, Mary. But you don't need to worry, I won't be having dinner with her. And about whatever she said or how she said it? Ignore her. She's the one that's nothing."

Mary smiled and nodded. "Okay. Let me know if you need anything else." She quietly closed the door behind her.

I walked over to the window and looked out at the view of the city. I really hoped I wouldn't have to have dinner with Poppy. But that depended on a few things. I needed to get those prototypes from Penny. And I needed to be able to corner the hitwoman and get a confession out of her. All without getting killed.

If I couldn't do all that? I sighed. I'd have to go to dinner with Poppy. The thought of sitting with her through a whole meal made me feel queasy. But I wouldn't have a choice. I couldn't risk my friends' safety by not going to dinner. Poppy having a child meant nothing and I knew it. She was just playing a game. If I crossed her, she wouldn't hesitate to hurt Scarlett or someone else. Or me. I had no idea what she really wanted. That was the whole problem.

I saw her and Gigi exiting the building onto the sidewalk below. They hurried over to a town car. She made the driver lift up Gigi and put her into the car. Probably so Poppy wouldn't get blood on her dress.

What the hell do you want from me? It had to be something with the contracts I signed when I was 16. I didn't know what else it could possibly be about. There were hidden clauses in them, I knew that to be true. But what did they say? What had I agreed to?

All I wanted was to be able to stand her up and not die as a consequence. But I wasn't confident in my plan. Especially because Penny still hadn't texted me back. I turned away from the window. I needed a backup plan.

CHAPTER 25

Tuesday

I climbed into my car and slammed the door closed. The hitwoman didn't show up at practice today, which I was grateful for. But it was hard to be too happy when Penny was ghosting me. I pulled out of the Empire High parking lot and turned in the opposite direction of Tanner's place.

Tanner thought I was hanging out with Penny, so he wasn't expecting me until later. I had some time to stop by my house before heading over to his place for the night. He never needed to know that I'd put myself in danger. Besides, I was pretty sure Mr. Pruitt would have already had me killed if that was his intention. He'd had plenty of opportunities. And it really seemed like Poppy wanted to wine and dine me before murdering me. I felt safe enough for now.

I'd been researching tiny cameras all afternoon. Sure, I could just use my phone to record my upcoming encounter with the hitwoman. But it would just be the audio and not the video footage I wanted. Would that be enough? *Probably not.* I hadn't found any suitable options yet. I needed to find an alternative soon though. Maybe I could just spend the rest of my night doing more research. There had to be something just as good as James' stupid prototype.

Or I could just apologize to him. But for what? He should be apologizing to me, not the other way around. And I hadn't heard anything from him either. Earlier today when I thought I might die, apologizing had been on my mind. But now that I was nowhere near Poppy? I was still mad at him. Yes, over the years he'd apologized a lot for what happened with Brooklyn. But I don't think he knew exactly what he was apologizing for. He'd fucking ruined my life.

I turned onto my street and pulled into an empty spot along the sidewalk. *Screw James.* I didn't need his stupid tiny cameras. I pulled out my phone and brought up a camera option on Amazon. Why were all of these so big? I had typed in *discreet.* I didn't have the patience for searching for stuff like this. I sighed and climbed out of my car. If Mary wasn't so nosy, I would have asked her to research them. But she would have had tons of questions. Maybe this was why all my friends had a staff. To do stuff like this. *Maybe I could ask Nigel to do it…*

"Matt."

I'd been so distracted on my phone that I didn't realize there was someone sitting on my front stoop. I looked up at Penny. Her cheeks were rosy and I could tell she'd been sitting out here in the cold for a long time. But what was worse was that her eyes were slightly red like she'd been crying.

"Hey," I said.

"Hey?" She shook her head. "That's all you have to say?"

What did she want me to say? It was pretty clear that her asshole of a husband had made her cry. But I didn't bother asking her if she'd been crying. Because I knew she'd deny it. We were both quiet for a minute. Her staring at me from the stoop. And me just standing there like an idiot.

"I should have texted you. I forgot you have practice after work and I shouldn't have just shown up…. But can I come in? Please? We need to talk and I'm freezing."

I didn't love the idea of needing to talk. That was never good. But I wouldn't make her stand out here in the cold anymore. I quickly opened the door and ushered her inside.

She sighed. "It's so nice and warm in here." She rubbed her hands together.

"Let me get you a cup of tea."

She smiled, but it looked forced. "That sounds lovely. You must have a really smart friend that thought ahead and bought you a teakettle."

"A smart and thoughtful friend, yeah."

I filled the kettle up with water and turned on the stove. When I turned back to her, she'd peeled off her coat and was sitting at the kitchen counter. I stayed on the other side of the island. I hated seeing her upset. And I knew if I was next to her I'd touch her. I wouldn't be able to stop myself.

"I tried texting you earlier," I said. "I figured you'd canceled our plans."

"Yeah. I was going to." She shook her head. "I probably should have."

That didn't really answer my question. "But you changed your mind?"

She didn't reply.

I couldn't read her tonight. Was she upset with James? Or was she upset with me? Because it kind of seemed like she was pissed at me. Had James told her about Brooklyn? I didn't know what to say. I didn't know what she knew. I wasn't even sure how much of James and my conversation she'd overheard the other night, if any. It was better to play it safe. "I'm sorry that I barged in last night," I said. "I should have just called."

"Called?" She finally made eye contact with me. "No, Matt. What you should have done was told James and me right away that someone threatened our daughter."

"Penny, I'm sorry..."

"You could have gotten her killed." She took a deep breath. "I'm sure James has already given you a piece of his mind. And you don't need to hear it from me too. But I'm really freaking mad at you, Matt."

I swallowed hard. So she was mad at me. Not James. *Fuck.*

"James is furious with you. But you know I always try to see the good in people..." her voice trailed off. "James and I got in a fight. And I...I just needed to talk to you."

So he had made her cry? It was easier to latch on to that idea instead of her being mad at me. James was such an ass. It just made me regret what I'd said to him last night even less. But why did she need to talk to me about their fight? There could only be two reasons. He either told her all about Brooklyn and she was wondering why I hadn't told her. Or she was here because she finally realized James was the worst and she was giving in to her feelings for me. Because they were definitely there. I could feel it. Couldn't she?

The teakettle started wailing. I pulled it off the stove and poured the hot water into two mugs. I handed one to her after putting a bag of chamomile tea in it.

"Oh it feels so good," she said as she wrapped her hands around the hot cup.

Just you wait. I thought about what else she could wrap her hands around to warm up. *Stop.* Her eyes were still puffy from crying. All I knew was that if she was mine, she wouldn't be crying right now. I'd fucking worship that girl. Like she deserved. It was easy to think that was true. But was it really? Because I could never actually love her. And she certainly didn't deserve to be someone's second choice. "Are you going to tell me what you two fought about?" I asked.

"Stress."

Wait, what? "Stress?"

"Yes, stress. You unloaded all this stuff on him and it's too much. He's been working on stress management. After everything he's been through…he's under enough pressure balancing work and fatherhood because he has to pick up my slack..." her voice trailed off and she pressed her lips together like she'd said too much.

"What's going on with you?"

She ran her thumb down the side of the mug. "I'm just worried about him."

"I'm not asking about James. I'm asking about you. What slack is James being forced to be pick up?"

"That doesn't matter. What matters is that James always puts the weight of the world on his shoulders. Isabella's father isn't taking his calls and he doesn't know how to make sure Scarlett is safe. We both know what the Pruitt family is capable of. James hired more security, but we're not dumb. We know it's not enough. And on top of all that, he's worried you hate him." It looked like she was going to cry again.

I swallowed hard.

"I told him that of course that wasn't true. That he's one of your best friends. But he just told me I didn't understand. What don't I understand? Why are you two fighting? Things have been weird between you two ever since we came to your game. I overheard something about loving Brooklyn last night?"

I couldn't breathe.

"I didn't even realize you ever lived outside of Manhattan. And James is focusing on your fight and he won't tell me what's going on."

So she didn't know? She thought we both loved living in Brooklyn or something? As in the place? Not my fiancée?

"James tells me everything. So if he's not telling me this, it's because you specifically asked him not to. And I don't understand. You know everything about me, Matt."

Not what it feels like to kiss you. "I don't think that's true."

"I don't keep stuff from you. Secrets are awful. God, if I learned one thing in that huge scandal with James, it's that secrets are toxic. So what aren't you telling me?"

I hated seeing her with unshed tears. I hated seeing her upset in any way. And I was pretty sure my brain short circuited, because somehow I'd gotten on the other side of the island and was standing right next to her. I didn't want to talk about her husband. I didn't want to talk about any of this. All I could think about were ways to silence her with my lips.

She looked up at me. "Just tell me, Matt. Tell me what you're keeping from me."

"You first."

She pulled her eyebrows together. "I'm not…"

"You just said how toxic secrets are. But you're hiding something too, Penny."

"This isn't about me. This is about you and James."

"Fuck James."

"That is so far from the answer that I expected. Fuck James? Seriously? How could you even say that? You're one of his best friends. And I'm not here to listen to you hurl insults at my husband. Don't you see that insulting him is essentially insulting me?" She shook her head. "That doesn't matter. Insult me all you want. I'm here because I love James and he's upset because of *you*. I'm here to try to help fix whatever the hell is going on between you two. He cares about you and I thought you cared about him."

"He doesn't care about me. He doesn't care about anyone but himself."

"Excuse me?" She pushed her stool away from the counter and stood up. "James is right. I don't know how I didn't see it before. You are trying to ruin his life. You're trying to turn me against him. And for what purpose? We're not pawns in some stupid game you're playing. This is my life. James' life. We're two of your best friends. I had your back. I told James that he was wrong. I tried to stand up for you and I came here to try to help mend whatever is broken between you. But you don't even care. So you know what?" She stood up a little taller. "Fuck you."

I'd never heard her curse before. I'd never seen her as upset as she was right now. I should have just apologized. But instead, it was easier to throw more insults. "I'm not the one making you sad all the fucking time. You showed up at my doorstep wiping tears off your cheeks. Because of *him*. And don't act like it's the first time you came crawling to me when you want to escape from him."

She opened her mouth. And then closed it again. She started blinking fast like she'd done the other day before she'd run off without explanation. "I'm not depressed because of James."

I just stared at her. I never said anything about depression. Was she actually depressed? I just thought she was a little…sad. Her words made my stomach twist into knots.

She closed her eyes like it pained her to say her next words to me. "James is the love of my life. He's my whole world. He's given me everything. A life I never even dreamed of. I love him so much that it hurts. I love his friends like they're my own family. And it hurts that I can't give him anything in return. And I just wanted to fix what's going on between you because I can't fix *me*."

What was she talking about? There wasn't anything about her that needed to be fixed. She was beautiful and smart and funny. I stared at her as her eyes locked with mine again. She was perfect exactly the way she was. "There's nothing wrong with you."

She wrapped her arms around her stomach liked she was afraid she was falling to pieces. "I'm not here to talk about me." She took a deep breath. "I don't have any siblings. But all of you guys? You're like the brothers I never had."

Ouch. I'd been worse than friend zoned. I'd been brotherized.

"And I know James thinks of you and Mason as brothers just as much as Rob. And until about ten minutes ago, I thought you considered him to be family too. I don't know what's going on between you. But I need you to fix it. If you care about him at all. Please, Matt. He can't handle any more stress. And I can't lose him. I don't know what I would do if I ever lost him."

She'd mope around searching for ghosts on the city sidewalks. Just like I did with Brooklyn. Forever stuck. I pressed my lips together. There was no way to work around what she just said. She definitely did not reciprocate my feelings. This wasn't how it was supposed to go. I was supposed to kiss her and she was supposed to tell me how unhappy she was in her marriage. I was supposed to save her. My heart ached. I'd just wanted to save her. I sat down on one of the stools. Because I couldn't save Brooklyn. I just wanted to save Brooklyn.

"Matt?"

I looked up at Penny. I was so tired of hurting everyone around me because I was so fucked up in the head. "I'll call him, okay?"

She nodded. "Thank you."

"I'm sorry, Penny. About not telling you guys about Scarlett sooner. About stressing James out."

"Are you going to tell me what all this is about? How did you get tied up with Isabella's father? Do you owe him money or something? Because I can..."

"I don't owe him money. The only thing that matters now is keeping Scarlett safe. And I think I have a way to do that. But I'm going to need one of James' prototype cameras." That was probably the worst segue ever. But I had to ask her before she walked out the door.

"The prototypes are at Hunter Tech headquarters. Why don't you just ask Rob? It's easier for him to grab them."

Rob. Of course. Why hadn't I thought of that? I could have avoided this whole thing. Well, not really. I'd made a mess of everything last night. And it was just like Penny to come try to pick up all the pieces. "Good idea."

"You really think you'll be able to get out of this alone?" asked Penny. "Because you don't have to. It's my daughter's life that's on the line. I want to help. I need to help. If you would just talk to me."

"Tanner's actually helping me."

"Oh. Well, that's good, I guess. He's a really nice guy."

"Mhm." I stared at her.

She just stared back, waiting for me to tell her how I'd gotten into this mess. Or what my problem was with James. Or maybe to talk about how nice of a guy Tanner was. Or something. Anything. But I didn't want to drag her into this.

"I should probably go," she said. "James is expecting me home for dinner. I told him our plans were canceled, even though I never told you."

I gave her a half-hearted smile.

"Call him soon, okay?" Before she could even turn around to leave, the sound of my front door opening made us both freeze.

But it didn't take me long to get moving. I grabbed Penny's hand and pulled her behind the kitchen island.

"What's going…"

I put my hand over her mouth to silence her. "Don't say a word," I whispered.

Penny looked terrified, but she nodded.

I didn't know what was going on, but it couldn't be good. No one had keys to my place. Whoever had just come in hadn't come in with good motives. It was like I could hear the seconds of my life ticking down in my head. I'd purposely upset Mr. Pruitt. I'd provoked him into action. And I'd even come to my house despite Tanner warning me not to. I had no one to blame but myself.

But instead of freaking out, all I could do was stare at the woman kneeling beside me.

I relished the way her lips felt on the palm of my hand. Her looking at me like she was relying on me. And for just a second, I forgot all about the intruder. This would have been the perfect moment to kiss her. As the seconds ticked down. To show her how I felt. All I had to do was remove my hand.

CHAPTER 26

Tuesday

A tear trickled down Penny's cheek, pulling me out of my daydream. She was terrified. Her thoughts were probably swirling with her love for her children and James. *Not me.*

I didn't want James to be right about me. I didn't want to ruin his life. Kissing Penny would be a mistake. And I was tired of making mistakes. I slowly lowered my hand from her mouth, knowing that was as close as I'd get to her lips kissing my skin. My crush on her was unrequited. But that didn't mean I wouldn't give my life to save her. She was still one of my closest friends. She was still able to make me smile when no one else seemed able to. I owed her for that. For making a few of the years after Brooklyn's death bearable.

We both sat there and listened to the footsteps in the foyer. It sounded like whoever it was had high heels on. Or high heeled boots. Which meant it was probably the hitwoman. She wasn't here to hurt Penny. She was here for me. No one else needed to get hurt.

I glanced at Penny. Another tear rolled down her cheek. We weren't going to be able to hide in here for long. I hadn't even had time to hit the lights to bathe us in darkness. We were almost completely exposed. I put my index finger to my lips to remind Penny to stay quiet. And then I crawled along the hardwood floors toward the other end of the kitchen island. I reached up and grabbed a knife out of the knife block and then sat back down.

The footsteps were coming this way. I couldn't save Brooklyn all those years ago. But I could save Penny now.

I grasped the knife tighter in my hand. All I had was the element of surprise.

Penny moved to sit next to me, then grabbed my arm and shook her head.

I reached out and ran my thumb along her cheek, removing the tears. "Tell James I forgive him," I whispered.

She looked confused. But James would understand. He'd know I was talking about Brooklyn. The least I could do was make that right. I pulled my hand away from Penny's face.

I peered around the end of the island, but I couldn't see anyone.

"Matt," Penny hissed.

The footsteps stopped. "Is someone there?"

Fuck. I made my way around the side of the counter and poked my head out. I could see high heeled boots through my vantage point beneath the kitchen stools. They weren't the high heeled black ones the hitwoman had been wearing the other day. They were shorter with a thick heel and kind of beat up in an on-purpose kind of way that I'd never understand. But it had to be her. Who else could it be? I gripped the knife tighter.

"Hello?" the hitwoman called again and made her way farther into the kitchen. Farther. Farther. Until her feet paused right next to my hiding spot. Before I could convince myself not to, I reached out, grabbed her ankle, and pulled as hard as I could.

She yelped as her feet got pulled out from beneath her and her gun clattered to the ground. I climbed on top of her, pinning her to the ground.

She screamed and started thrashing beneath me.

"Penny, get the gun!" But when I reached out to knock the gun farther away from the woman, all I saw was a high-end camera. A very broken high-end camera. I looked down at the woman beneath me. And for just a second I lost my breath.

Her dark hair was splayed out on the hardwood floors and she was staring at me like she wanted to kill me. Honestly, it wasn't the first time she'd looked at me like that. And definitely not the only time I deserved that look of disdain. It had been years since I'd seen her. I'd asked Brooklyn for a sign at the graveyard the other day. And when I'd first seen the hitwoman there, I'd thought she was Brooklyn's best friend, Kennedy. My sign was a few days late. But here she was. "Kennedy?"

Just as her name left my mouth she kneed me hard in the balls.

Fuck. I rolled off of her and tried not to start crying. Why did women keep trying to maim my member? Couldn't they just slap me or something?

"Don't move," Penny said. She'd grabbed a knife too and was holding the teakettle in her other hand like she was going to throw it at Kennedy's face. It wasn't a bad plan. The metal and boiling water would be enough to hurt her. But I didn't want Penny or Kennedy to get hurt.

"Stop," I groaned, but it was barely a whisper.

"Put your hands in the air," Penny said.

"Who the hell are you people?" Kennedy said. But she didn't try to get off the ground. She just sat there, the look of anger replaced by fear. She slowly lifted up her hands.

"Who the hell are you?!" Penny countered.

"Stop," I groaned again. I winced as I tried to sit back up.

Penny took another step forward, waving the knife around. "If you don't tell me in two seconds who you are, I'll… I'll stab you in the face," Penny said with very little conviction.

But Kennedy didn't know that Penny wouldn't hurt a fly. She looked as scared as Penny had a minute ago. There were even tears in her large brown eyes.

"Penny, put the knife down," I croaked. "I know her. Kennedy…Kennedy it's me." I gestured to my face, waiting for recognition to hit her.

Kennedy blinked, the tears still pooling in her eyes. She didn't seem to know who I was. Maybe because my face was distorted in pain.

"It's me. Matt," I said.

She searched my face. "Oh my God. Matthew freaking Caldwell? *Oh my God.*" She put her hand to her mouth. "I'm so sorry." She reached out like she was going to touch my nuts and then pulled back. "Do you need some ice or something?"

"You two know each other?" Penny asked, her arm still outstretched with the knife.

"Penny, would you put down the knife?" I asked again.

I watched as Penny put the knife down on the counter. But she was still holding the teakettle, like she was worried I was reading the situation wrong.

"I'm so sorry," I said to Kennedy. "I didn't know you were coming…wait, why are you in my house?"

"I had no idea this was your place. I'm here to take pictures for a listing." She looked over at her broken camera.

Oh. Oh! Bill had said he'd send someone over. I never asked him for details because I assumed it would be during the day when I wasn't home. Not that I was supposed to be home now either.

Kennedy tried to stand up and winced. "Ow. I think I may have twisted my ankle."

More like I had twisted it when I pulled her to the ground. She'd offered to get me ice a second ago when she was the one that was actually hurt. "Don't move. We need to get your ankle elevated before it starts to swell. Penny, get me some ice from the freezer." I bent down and lifted Kennedy into my arms.

She inhaled sharply. And I wasn't sure if it was because her ankle hurt or because for just a second she felt like she'd been transported back 16 years too.

She smelled like her mother's cooking. Mrs. Alcaraz's famous empanadas. She smelled just like Brooklyn had when she'd lived with her uncle and then with the Alcaraz's. And in the weirdest way, it smelled like home.

I held her like that in the kitchen for a beat too long.

She looked up at me, her eyes no longer filled with unshed tears. "Um…you can put me down now," she said with a smile.

"Right." I carried her into the family room and laid her down on my couch. I grabbed a few pillows to prop her ankle up. And then I unzipped her boots…boots that were perfect for Kennedy. The distressed leather was artsy and stylish on her. I let her boots fall to the ground and ran my thumb down the inside of her ankle. "Does that hurt?"

She nodded.

For a few seconds we just stared at each other. The scent of her skin made me feel at ease for the first time in years. Did she feel it too?

"Here's some ice," Penny said, rushing into the room. "I'm so sorry I threatened to stab you in the face. I thought you were someone else." She finished wrapping a towel around the ice pack and gently placed it on Kennedy's ankle, somehow knowing exactly what to do. I guess it was the mother in her.

Kennedy reached down to hold the ice in place. "Who did you think I was?"

"A murderer," Penny said at the same time I said, "no one."

Kennedy glanced back and forth between us. "I'm so sorry. I haven't even introduced myself to your wife. I'm Kennedy." She held her free hand out to Penny.

Penny looked at me and laughed. "Matt's not my husband."

It's not that funny.

"We're just friends," Penny clarified. "Matt practically grew up with my husband, James."

"James Hunter?" Kennedy's eyebrows both raised.

I knew what she was thinking. James hadn't exactly been the kind of guy to settle down in high school. He was high or drunk more than half the time.

"Mhm," Penny said. "Do you know him too?"

"Um, yeah. I mean, I used to in high school," Kennedy said.

"Wait, you all went to high school together?"

"Yeah, we were all friends because Brooklyn…"

"We used to hang out in Brooklyn," I quickly corrected. I didn't mean for it to sound so dirty though.

Kennedy opened her mouth, probably to call me out on my bullshit, but I cut her off.

"Penny, could you grab some more ice?" I asked. "We definitely need more. I think there's another pack somewhere in the back of the freezer." It was a total lie. But sending Penny on a wild goose chase was the only way I could think to buy time to bring Kennedy up to speed on everything.

"Sure thing," she said and stood up. As soon as Penny was out of earshot, I started talking.

"Penny doesn't know about Brooklyn. Please don't tell her. She's one of the only people in my life who doesn't stare at me like I'm broken. Kind of like you are right now."

Kennedy put her hand to her chest like it hurt. Maybe it did. Because mine physically ached. "I've never looked at you like you were broken. I looked at you like you were grieving." She searched my face. "You're still grieving." She didn't ask it like a question. She said it like a statement. Like I was that easy to read. Was I really that transparent?

"Matt!" Penny called from the kitchen. "I can't find it. Where did you say it was?"

"I'll be right back." I left Kennedy alone and joined Penny in the kitchen. "Sorry, Penny, I must only have the one."

She kept the freezer door open and leaned in a little closer to me. "She's pretty," Penny said. "And I didn't see a ring on her finger."

I glanced back toward the living room. "Yeah."

"Maybe it's just me, but I can practically feel the chemistry between you two. And now she's hurt and has to spend the night?" Penny shrugged her shoulders. "Seems like fate to me."

"Would you stop being a nosy matchmaker for five seconds? She's not going to spend the night."

"Why not? You're always spending the night with random women."

Exactly. Random women. Not women like Kennedy. She deserved more than that. And I couldn't give that to her. I glanced back into the other room.

"I should probably get going," Penny said loudly enough for Kennedy to hear. "I don't want to be late for dinner." She winked at me. "Ask her out." She left me alone in the kitchen and went back into the living room.

"Need anything else before I head out?" Penny asked. "Do you want me to call a doctor?"

"No, I think the ice is enough," Kennedy said. She reached down to readjust it.

"It was really nice meeting you. Hopefully I'll see you around again soon." Penny turned to me. "Don't forget to call James." She patted my chest and was out the door before I could even say goodbye.

The door closed behind her and the silence settling around me was unnerving. The last time I'd been alone with Kennedy was at Brooklyn's gravesite. It had been right before we both went off to college. And we didn't know how to say goodbye to the person that couldn't come with us.

We promised we'd keep coming back to visit Brooklyn. I'd kept my promise. But I didn't think Kennedy had. Not that I blamed her. I was the only one who seemed keen on staying stuck in the past. Losing a best friend was hard. But losing the love of your life? There was no healing from that.

And as much as I wished Kennedy understood what I was going through, she didn't. I glanced up the stairs. And it was a good thing that I was here. Because I couldn't let Kennedy see the paintings upstairs during her picture taking. She'd think I'd completely lost it.

CHAPTER 27

Tuesday

"Penny seems nice," Kennedy said as I made my way back into the family room.

"Yeah. She is." *Even if she is a dirty little meddler.* I sat down next to Kennedy on the couch. I thought the silence stretching between us would feel awkward. But it didn't.

"I'm glad James remarried. When I heard he tied the knot with Isabella?" She shook her head. "What was he thinking?"

"He wasn't." I didn't need to elaborate. Kennedy knew what James had been like when he was a teenager. He was rarely sober enough to think anything through.

"You know, sound really carries in this house," Kennedy said. "So do you often spend the night with random women? Don't tell me you've become Mason?"

I laughed. "You'll be happy to know that Mason has settled down. Rob too."

Kennedy smiled. "The woman married to Rob must have all the patience in the world."

"She does. They somehow balance each other out perfectly." Daphne also somehow never got mad when Rob was a flirtatious fool.

"So all the Untouchables are hitched? Except you."

I laughed. "No one calls us that anymore." I looked over at the TV and wished it was on to distract us. The last thing I needed was anyone else obsessed with my love life. Or lack of one. "Penny's been trying to set me up. She has a whole dating profile for me and everything."

"Wow, I cannot imagine you on a dating app. Any matches yet?"

I thought about Ash throwing a ball of fire at my dick. "No, not yet."

"I'm really surprised you're the only one who hasn't settled down. I mean, you were ready to all the way back in high school."

We were both quiet for a minute.

She rested her chin in her hand as she stared at me. "It's been 16 years, Matt. I kind of just figured…"

"Brooklyn was endgame for me, Kennedy."

It looked like Kennedy wanted to cry. "I miss her too," Kennedy said. "You expect that hole to fill up with something, anything. But she left a damn big hole."

"She really did."

Kennedy pressed her lips together. "All those things you said at her funeral. They were supposed to be your vows. Not promises to someone whose life was cut short."

"Kennedy…"

"You can't just go through the rest of your life missing her. Keeping her a secret from one of your good friends? Pretending she didn't exist, yet letting her death dictate everything you do? Matt, that's not living."

She didn't have to tell me that. I knew it wasn't living. Because I was fucking drowning. "And what about you?"

"What about me?"

"Like I'm sure you overheard Penny say in the kitchen. You don't have a ring on your finger."

"I've been focused on growing my business."

"Taking pictures?"

She frowned. "I'm a professional photographer, Matt. I'm taking these photos because I have a very lucrative partnership with one of the top real estate firms in the city. I own my own company and it's doing great, for the record. And I won't let people like you look at me like I'm nothing anymore." She sat up and shoved the ice at me.

"Kennedy, I didn't…"

"Yes you did. I'm not the same poor girl from the wrong side of the tracks that you had to hang out with just because I was friends with Brooklyn." She pulled on one of her boots. Boots that I hadn't noticed before had royal blue soles. They were Odegaards. And anyone that could afford $3,000 Odegaards was pretty well off.

"Hey." I grabbed her hand. "I didn't mean anything by it. I really didn't. I used the wrong term. I meant photographer. You followed your passion. I think that's amazing."

"Really?" Her eyes softened.

"Yes, really. You went out and did your own thing. And you're clearly killing it."

She smiled. "I'm sorry I got so defensive. I think maybe I still have a little chip on my shoulder from going to Empire High. Especially being back in the city after all this time. I almost feel like the old me, if that makes any sense. And I've tried so hard to leave that person behind."

I couldn't help the corners of my mouth rising. "I always liked that person."

Her face flushed.

"When did you move back to the city?" I asked.

"A few weeks ago. I've been wanting to expand my business for a while and there's just more opportunities here. I tried my best to stay away. But then there was this vacancy in the perfect location in Manhattan for my offices. I couldn't say no."

"Are you living in Manhattan too?"

"Actually, I moved in with my mom temporarily. Just until I have time to search for a new place."

That explained the delicious smell of empanadas. "How is your mom?"

"The same." Kennedy smiled. "It's so weird being home and having to live with her rules again." She laughed.

"I bet."

"She treats me like I'm still a kid. I could really use a night out."

Was she asking me to ask her out? I didn't know what to say. I was drawn to her, that was undeniable. But I think it had more to do with our shared past. I couldn't deny that she was attractive though. She had all the same beauty she did when she was younger, but her curves had filled out. In any other circumstance, she'd be someone I'd hit on. But she was Kennedy. My fiancée's best friend. She was older, sure. But she was still just as off-limits.

"Do you know the weirdest part about being back here?" Kennedy asked.

I shook my head.

"Every now and then, I see a blonde walking on the street and I completely freeze, thinking it's her. I so badly wish it was her. But it never is." Kennedy sighed. "It was easier to be off somewhere I never knew her, you know? God, I can't even imagine if she was still alive after all this time? What I would say to her? Honestly, I'd be so pissed. I'd probably curse up a storm and make my mom furious." She laughed. "Pull out a few of my favorite Spanish expletives."

"Sounds about right." I never let my mind venture there. To the possibility of Brooklyn still being alive. Not after all the private investigators I'd hired came back without any information. She was gone. Brooklyn was dead.

"So what have you been up to all these years?"

"Taking over MAC International."

"Really?" She smiled. "I know you wanted that. Wasn't Mason supposed to take over though?"

"He followed his passion, just like you did. He started his own marketing firm. With his wife, actually."

"That's amazing. But you followed your passion too, right? Isn't running that company what you always wanted?"

What I always wanted? No, being married to my job wasn't what I always wanted. What I wanted was Brooklyn as my wife and a house full of kids. A house full of happiness. "Yeah," I lied.

"It's amazing that the four of you guys are still friends. I wish I had a group of friends like that. I basically know no one in the entire city."

Brooklyn had been one of Kennedy's only friends in high school. She'd been kind of a loner before Brooklyn moved to town. But I hadn't let her feel that way after Brooklyn's death. I still sat with her at lunch every day. She'd been one of the Untouchables just as much as I had. But I guess we'd all lost touch with her.

"I'll let you know next time we all hang out. You're more than welcome to come." It wasn't a date. But it was the best I could do. And it would be a little while before that invite came. I needed to apologize to James first.

"That would be amazing." She reached down and finished putting on her boots. "I should probably get going. My mom's actually expecting me to be home for dinner."

"Let me grab your camera." I picked it up off the kitchen floor. "Or what's left of it. I'm sorry, Kennedy. Let me replace it for you."

"I don't need handouts anymore, remember? Besides, it's insured. Is it okay if I come back tomorrow morning to shoot the pictures?"

"Fine by me. Just let yourself in."

She laughed. "I think I'll knock next time just to be safe."

"Actually, can you hold off from taking the pictures for a few days?"

"Why? Have you changed your mind about selling the place? It really is a beautiful home."

I hadn't changed my mind. But I was worried about her safety. If I wasn't staying here because of Mr. Pruitt, she shouldn't be here either. "Yeah, I'm still thinking about it."

"No problem. I'll let Bill know you want to hold off a few more days." She stood up and winced.

I wrapped my arm around her waist. "Let me drive you home."

"It's all the way on the other side of town. I can take a taxi. I'll be fine, really." She wiggled her foot and pretended like she was fine. But I could tell she wasn't. She was in pain and she was putting on a brave face.

"I insist." I scooped her up in my arms before she had a chance to protest. She didn't say a word as I got her safely into my car and pulled out onto the city street. The silence was comfortable between us, but for some reason I still wanted to fill it. Maybe because I wanted her to fill in the gaps of her life that I'd missed. "What do you do for fun?" I asked.

"Photography is my hobby and my job. There isn't really much time for anything else. What about you?"

Penny had asked me this same question recently. But I didn't want to tell Kennedy that I worked out for fun. That seemed like a pompous answer. "I coach the Empire High football team."

"Really? Wow, I need to come to one of your games."

I caught her smile out of the corner of my eye. "I'd like that," I said.

She turned to look out the window. She was absorbing the city like it was her first time here. There was something sweet about it.

We drove on in silence until I pulled to a stop in front of her mom's old apartment building. Kennedy tried to protest again, but I carried her up the few flights of stairs. I tried not to look at Brooklyn's apartment door. It would be filled with another family now. One not aware of the people that had lived there before. Something in my chest tightened.

Mrs. Alcaraz opened up the door like she knew we were coming.

"Mi amor! What happened?"

"I'm fine, Mama," Kennedy said. "Matt's just being…Matt."

I laughed at that as I laid her down on the couch.

She smiled up at me.

"Matt." Mrs. Alcaraz looked up at me. She looked almost exactly the same, but she had a few lines around her eyes now. She put her hands on both sides of my face. "Mi amor," she called me, just like she called Kennedy. "Why do you look so sad? You're in good company now." She let her hands fall from my face. "Let's eat. Dinner is getting cold."

***

I couldn't remember the last time I'd smiled so hard. I used to eat here all the time when Brooklyn and I had dated. Mrs. Alcaraz was the only woman I knew whose cooking rivaled my mom's.

Kennedy walked me to the door. "Thanks for tonight. It was nice seeing a friendly face in this city."

"Any time." My eyes wandered to her lips. I have no fucking idea why.

"Matt?"

My eyes lifted back to hers.

"Give me your phone."

I didn't ask why she wanted it. But I handed my phone to her without protest.

She typed something in and handed it back to me. "You can text me when you're missing her. I bet I'll be missing her too." She shrugged. "Two lost souls in this crazy city could maybe feel a little less alone with a friend."

A friend. Right. I shoved my phone into my pocket. I believed that two lost souls could feel a little less alone together. In one way or another.

"You deserve to be happy," she said.

"So do you," I said.

She smiled up at me. "How is it that you look almost the same after all these years?"

"How is it that you look even more beautiful?" I shouldn't have said it. I was used to flirting. But flirting with my dead fiancée's best friend? Definitely off-limits.

"You know what? Hold on one sec." She left me alone standing at the door for only a minute. "It's vacant right now. And my mom still had this." She placed a key into my palm.

I looked over my shoulder at Brooklyn's old apartment. I couldn't even imagine going in there.

"It was the first thing I did when I got back. I think being in there gave me a little closure."

I doubted it would do that for me. But I closed my hand around the key anyway.

She leaned forward to hug me. It took me by surprise, but as soon as her arms were wrapped around me, I sighed. I took a deep breath. *Home.* God, I wanted to just hold her right here forever.

But she pulled back. "Goodnight, Matt."

"Goodnight, Kennedy."

She closed the door and I turned around and faced the door to Brooklyn's apartment. My mind screamed at me not to go in. But my feet seemed to have a mind of their own as they approached the door. And my hand as it unlocked it.

The door creaked opened and I stared at the empty kitchen. The whole place seemed so small. I stepped inside, picturing Uncle Jim's warm smile. And Brooklyn's big blue eyes. This place was filled with ghosts. I felt a tear roll down my cheek as I made my way into the small living room. It used to feel so full of love and laughter. And now it just felt…empty. I stopped outside Brooklyn's bedroom door, leaning against the doorjamb.

We'd fought in here. She'd threatened to push me off the fire escape when she was mad. And she promised to love me forever right there.

My knees must have given out, because I was somehow sitting where her bed used to be. I'd held her right here when she'd cried. I held her in my arms, hoping she'd feel whole again when she lost her uncle.

I promised her forever. Forever wasn't supposed to be only for a few months. This wasn't supposed to be what happened to us. She should have been here with me.

My fingers fumbled, pulling my phone out of my pocket. And I texted the one person who would understand. Not my high school friends. Not Tanner. "I don't want to feel alone," I texted.

Kennedy's response came almost immediately. "Are you still in her apartment?"

I didn't have time to respond before I heard the door creak. She was limping slightly, but she still showed up. She sat down next to me and put her head on my shoulder, just like she always did when we visited Brooklyn's grave. And she didn't say a word when I cried. And I didn't say a word when I heard her sniffling either.

Her right hand was resting on her thigh. I reached out, lacing her fingers with mine. How had I been surviving without her? She'd been my rock after Brooklyn died. I looked down at her tear-stained face. I'd asked Brooklyn to send me a sign. Kennedy was it. I knew it. She had to be. I closed my eyes and exhaled slowly, the smell of home surrounding me. I just didn't know what I was supposed to do with this sign.

CHAPTER 28

Wednesday

The light streaming into my room made me close my eyes tighter. My whole body ached. What was I sleeping on? Bricks?

Someone moaned.

I opened my eyes and stared down at Kennedy's head on my chest. We weren't in my room. We were still on the hardwood floor in Brooklyn's old apartment. My back ached. But for just a few minutes, I didn't move. All I could do was stare down at Kennedy.

She sniffled like she was crying in her sleep. My chest ached. But it had nothing to do with her head lying on it. It was something deeper. And it hurt more as I stared at her. Despite the ache in my chest, it had been a long time since I'd woken up feeling so…okay. Like my breaths were coming easier. And I was very aware it was because of her.

I reached out to run my fingers through her hair, but I pulled back before I made contact. She was sleeping so peacefully. Her breath slowly rising and falling.

I felt sick to my stomach. This was where Brooklyn and I had fallen asleep. I never should have come in here. I never should have asked Kennedy to come. But still, I didn't move.

Had Kennedy shown up because I needed a friend?

Or had she shown back up in my life because I just needed her?

And I did need her. I think maybe I'd needed her this whole time. She was the only one that understood. She was the only one that felt my pain so acutely. I'd always loved Kennedy as a friend. She'd been there when I'd needed her the most. I wasn't sure how I'd even pretended to be okay while she wasn't in New York.

I heard my phone vibrating on the floorboards where I'd left it last night. I wished it would stop. I wished I could freeze time.

But Kennedy yawned and slowly opened her eyes. For a second she seemed just as disoriented as I was. But when she realized I was her pillow, she sat up super fast. "I'm so sorry, we must have fallen asleep." She wiped the side of her face like she was worried there'd be drool or something.

There wasn't. She looked beautiful. Honestly, I'd never seen her look more beautiful. Her eyes rimmed with red were real. And I always loved real beauty over a made up face any day.

"Sorry," she said again, running her fingers through her hair, just like I'd wanted to do a second ago.

I wasn't sure why she was apologizing. It was more my fault than hers. "How is your ankle feeling?"

She rotated her ankle slowly and smiled. "It actually feels quite a bit better. I guess a night on a hard floor was just what it needed?" She laughed.

There was another buzzing sound. Kennedy leaned over me and grabbed my phone off the ground.

I was tempted to pull her down on top of me. To hold her like she'd held me last night.

"Is this the time?" she asked. "Shit, I have to go." She ran her fingers through her hair again and pushed herself up.

I slowly sat up. "What time is it?"

"Nearly 7. And you have like 20 missed calls." She handed me my phone.

I clicked on the screen. I also had about 50 unread texts. All from Tanner. I clicked on the top one: "Where the hell are you?! I've been waiting up all night for you!"

Oh fuck. He'd expected me back at his house. He was probably worried sick with everything going on with the hitwoman and Mr. Pruitt.

"Everything okay?" Kennedy asked.

I looked up at her. I hadn't noticed it last night. But sometime after dinner and before my text, she must have changed into a pair of flannel pajamas with little polar bears all over them. She was even wearing a pair of polar bear slippers. "Everything's fine." I slid my phone into my pocket. "I like the PJs."

"What?" She looked down.

I started laughing.

"Hey, I came over because you texted. I didn't have time to change."

I couldn't help it. I just started laughing harder. The polar bear slippers even looked like they were laughing.

"Don't laugh at me." She tore one of her slippers off and chucked it at me.

I caught it and narrowly prevented the polar bear from colliding with my face.

"Nice to see you still know how to catch. Because you've certainly lost your prep-school manners. I think, 'Thank you, Kennedy, for being wonderfully supportive,' would be a more appropriate reaction this morning. You're welcome."

"You're right." I stood up. "Thank you, Kennedy. For being wonderfully supportive."

"Was that so hard?" She snatched her slipper out of my hand. "As fun as you laughing at me is, I really do have to go."

"I'll walk you out." I have no idea why I said it. This wasn't my place to walk anyone out of. I just knew that I wasn't quite ready to say goodbye yet.

We didn't say anything as we made our way out of Brooklyn's old place.

But before Kennedy reached her mom's apartment door, I said, "I'll text you."

She turned around. She pressed her lips together and nodded. "Good."

"Good." I couldn't help the smile that spread over my face. She wanted me to text her. It felt like I was a kid again. This giddy feeling in my stomach. I felt stupid and excited all at once.

She rolled her eyes, just adding to the feeling that we were kids again. "Have a good day, Matt." She left me alone in the hallway, with my stomach feeling weird and about a million things I needed to do.

I would have called Tanner back right away. But Tanner would insist on an apology in person anyway. He was old-fashioned like that. So as I drove to his apartment, I called Rob.

"Hey," Rob said. "It's early. Is everything alright?"

"Yeah…"

"Oh, never mind," he said, cutting me off. "Everything's not okay. Because you're trying to get my niece killed, you ass face."

I cringed. "Good morning to you too."

"Good morning," Rob mumbled.

"And just for the record, Scarlett is my niece too, Rob."

"Lies. Only in the friendship way. Everyone's always trying to steal my niece and nephew away from me. I'm their one and only uncle."

Every now and then Rob got defensive about the whole *friend* uncle thing. Usually when he was mad at me about something. And if he was bringing that up, then I wasn't off to a good start for getting the camera. Angry Rob was hard to negotiate with.

"Blood isn't everything," I said.

"Did you call to tell me your other non-related niece is going to get murdered too? How long have you known that my daughter is in trouble with freaking mobsters? A week? A month? Longer?"

I would have hung up on him, but my hands were on the wheel. "I made a mistake..."

"A mistake is bringing me a burger without bacon when I specifically asked for bacon."

"That happened one time," I said.

"Best friends know best friends' burger orders."

"True. Which is why it only happened one time. I know you like your burgers without the lettuce and tomato because veggies have no right to be on top of meat. And mayo doesn't belong on hot things, which is why you always ask for extra ketchup on the side. And crispy bacon of course."

"Exactly." The laughter was back in Rob's voice.

It was now or never. "I need a favor, Rob."

Rob groaned.

"I know Hunter Tech has a prototype for an undetectable camera. Can I borrow it?"

"There's only one prototype, man. And how do you even know about that?"

"You told me."

"I never told you about it," Rob said. "It's highly classified."

I laughed. "Isn't that only for government stuff? Rob, you told me a few guys' nights ago. We were talking about sexting, remember?"

"No, I don't remember."

"Well, you did get pretty drunk," I said. "Pretty sure you even sexted me."

"I did not sext you. I only sext my wife."

"Rob you sext me all the time. I have at least a dozen texts of your left ass cheek on my phone."

"Fine, I occasionally send you pictures of myself in what some might deem compromising positions. But only because you're the only one that's seen my mole since it first showed up, so who else is supposed to tell me if it's grown?"

"A dermatologist."

"Psh. I'm not showing a stranger my left ass cheek. And by the way, you should delete those photos after I send them to you. They're also highly classified."

I laughed. "So in exchange for staring at your ass a few times a year, can I maybe borrow that camera? I'll give it back, I swear. I just need it for one night."

"Tonight?"

"Yes." There was an awkward silence.

"I'm going to need more details than that, Matt," he said. "What do you need it for?"

I didn't want to tell Rob about my mission to get the hitwoman to confess everything. He'd tell me it was too dangerous. He'd tell me not to go through with it. But I didn't really have a choice. Telling him it would help save Scarlett would guarantee me a yes. "It's to get Poppy and Mr. Pruitt off my back. And keep Scarlett safe. I have a plan to corner the hitwoman that's after me and get her to confess everything. I'm hoping the footage will be enough to get Mr. Pruitt sent to prison where he belongs."

"You're going to corner a hitwoman? All by yourself?"

"Tanner's helping me."

"Tanner? Ugh. He barely counts as help. I'll help you."

I didn't want Rob to help me. He had a wife and kids at home that relied on him. Not that something happening to Tanner wouldn't be awful too. I'd sure miss him a ton. And what would Nigel do without him? *Probably follow me around…*

"Rob, I don't think that's a good idea."

"Too late. You need me. I'm the one with the camera."

I sighed. "Fine."

"But there is one condition?"

"What's the condition?" I asked.

"You have to say that I'm your best friend in front of Tanner. Tonight. Right before this all goes down."

"Rob, I'm allowed to have two best friends."

"You are not! It's not a plural term. Accept my conditions or you can count me and my fancy camera out."

"Can't I just tell you that you're my best friend over the phone?"

"No, it has to be in person."

Geez, he was more like Tanner than he realized. Maybe that was why they butted heads so much.

"Do we have a deal?" Rob asked.

"Fine. Come to my practice today. The hitwoman has been to a few of my games and practices. We're hoping she shows up again."

"Done. See you later," he hung up the phone just as I pulled up to Tanners' apartment building.

Tanner was going to be pissed about worrying him last night, sure. But he was going to be more upset about Rob joining our secret mission tonight. And completely devastated when I said Rob was my best friend in front of him. *Fuck*.

I slowly made my way inside and onto the elevator. Why wasn't I allowed to have two best friends? Honestly, I had four. Because Mason and James were up there too. Crap, I had to apologize to James too. I'd promised Penny.

The doors dinged open and I crossed the footbridge, avoiding looking down at the moving tarp. Really, what the hell was in that water? The door was unlocked so I let myself in. Despite the fact that the sun had risen, the apartment was pitch black. And I had no idea where the light switches were.

I kept my hand on the wall and tried to make my way into the great room. Seriously, how was it so dark? Did he have blackout curtains in his main living area? And if so…why? I found the corner of the wall and knew I was turning into the great room. But I didn't have to guess where I was for long, because a light turned on in the middle of the room.

Tanner was sitting in an antique wingback chair that I'm pretty sure hadn't been in the great room last night. The small lamp lit up him and only him. He calmly folded his newspaper and set it on the end table that also hadn't been there before. It was like he'd set up this whole little scene just to make a point. "Do you have any idea what time it is, Matthew?"

Oh no. Whenever he used my full name I knew he was mad. Kind of like how he always called Rob Robert. This wasn't good. "Like, 7:30."

"7:30. In the morning! I expected you home by midnight, young man. Do you have any idea how worried I've been? I've been up all night waiting for you."

"I'm sorry…"

"You're sorry? I thought you were dead in a ditch!"

"Tanner, I really am sorry. But I didn't know I had a curfew."

"Of course you have a curfew! How else am I supposed to know if you're alive?" His voice cracked.

Tanner didn't look that angry. He looked more…sad. And I wondered if this had anything to do with him losing his girlfriend when he was young. He'd never told me much about her. But had she not come home one night? Is that what this was about? "I'm okay, Tanner," I said. "I just lost track of time. I really am sorry."

"Just don't do it again, man."

"I won't." I didn't want to see him look this upset again. I had a feeling that if Tanner suddenly started crying, I'd start crying too. And no one wanted that.

He nodded. "Where were you?"

"I spent the night with an old friend." Wow, that sounded way more sexual than I meant for it to. "A friend from high school. Kennedy. Actually, she was Brooklyn's best friend. But we were friends too. I'm pretty sure I've told you about her before."

"Did you sleep with her?" Tanner asked.

"No." I guess he thought it was as inappropriate as I was worried it was.

"Are you going to?"

Oh. He wasn't concerned about the fact that it was immoral to sleep with Kennedy. He was just concerned because he loved to meet all the women I slept with ahead of time. Because he was Tanner. "Um." I didn't know how to answer his question. Because I didn't know the answer.

"Are you going to sleep with her?" Tanner asked again.

I sat down on the sofa across from his makeshift worried-dad scene. "I mean, we're friends." *It would be wrong, right? To sleep with Kennedy? To even want to?* I ran my hand down my face. *Fuck*. Did I want to? I smiled, picturing her in her adorable pajamas.

"Penny's your friend and you want to sleep with her."

"Yeah, but I think Penny and I are better off as just friends."

"I guess your dinner to seduce her went poorly?" Tanner asked.

I nodded. "She brotherized me."

Tanner laughed. "Brotherized? What is that?"

"When someone friend zone's you in a brother way. It's even worse than a friend zone."

"Ouch. So you haven't secured the camera then?"

"No, I got it."

Tanner just stared at me. "So where is it? Wait, don't tell me." He stood up and started examining my shirt.

"I meant I will have it. Rob's bringing it by practice."

Tanner let go of the collar of my shirt. "But he can't come. It's a best friend's secret mission."

"He's my best friend too."

Tanner lowered his eyebrows. "Best friend isn't plural."

Seriously, Tanner and Rob might as well be twins. How could they not see that they had the same sense of humor? And the same obsession with singular and plural nouns? Why did they hate each other so much? It was ridiculous. "He didn't give me a choice," I said.

"Stubborn little ass. Well, that's fine. We'll get his camera and tell him to get lost."

"Why can't the two of you just get along?"

"Because there's only room for one of us in this town. And I'm not leaving. I love it here." He sat back down.

"Then why haven't you properly moved in yet?"

"I have."

I gestured to the sheet that was covering what I thought was a tree.

"Oh that?" He laughed. "Nigel already has so much to dust. It's just easier this way. Speaking of Nigel, he was worried sick too. You owe him an apology as well."

"I'll do that when I see him. But right now I need to go home and change before work." I stood up.

"No need, Nigel brought all your things."

"All my things?"

Tanner pointed to the couch I'd been sitting on.

I turned to look at the very familiar couch. "Is this my couch?"

"Yes. Nigel has a good eye for these things. As he put it, 'a leather couch has no business being in photos to sell a family home.' He let Bill know you'd need a few more things for the staging."

"So my clothes..."

"All in your room here."

Okay. "Well, I should probably go change."

"I'll be waiting. We can take my car to work. I'll just have my driver drop you off first."

I knew Tanner was trying to keep me safe. But I couldn't be in his sight all the time. I left Tanner in the great room and wandered down the hall to the room I'd stayed in the other night. I swear the room seemed bigger. And everything but my couch was in it. Really, how did this room not look more cramped?

I opened up the closet to see all my suits, perfectly organized by color. Just the way they had been at my house.

"Mr. Caldwell," Nigel said.

I jumped. "Nigel, please stop sneaking up on me like that."

"Sorry, Mr. Caldwell. I just wanted to let you know that I've removed everything from your home and brought it here."

I looked around. Actually there was one noticeable thing missing. All my paintings of Brooklyn. Probably because the room was locked.

It was like Nigel could read my mind. "Well, everything but the paintings, sir. They weren't my taste."

I looked over at him. Not his taste? Maybe he was just jealous that I'd been painting Brooklyn's face and not his. If anyone else had seen them, I would have been embarrassed. Or worried they would think I was crazy. But Nigel was staring at me like he always did. And it didn't seem like he thought I was weird or crazy. There was only love in his eyes. A little too much love. But still love. Or was that just the look of a man hoping to get a dick pic?

I cleared my throat. "Nigel, I'm going to need a minute."

"Of course." He stepped into the corner of the room and just stared at me.

"In private, Nigel."

"Of course, Mr. Caldwell. I'll be right outside the door when you need me. Don't worry about calling for me. I'll be back in exactly in one minute." He bowed and left me alone.

I sighed and sat down on the edge of my bed. Yes, *my* bed. I guess I lived with Tanner now. And Nigel. That was a lot to take in. And I should have been thinking about that and the secret mission tonight with the hitwoman. But for some reason my mind was fixated on Kennedy. And the way she'd smiled when she chucked her slipper at my face. And the way she laughed. And the way she didn't judge me when I cried.

I put my face in my hands. I shouldn't have been thinking about her at all. So why couldn't I get her out of my head?

I heard the door open and knew Nigel was staring at me. But I didn't even care. It was better than him staring at me while I was naked again.

CHAPTER 29

Wednesday

Jefferson fell over as he kicked the ball, somehow sending the ball behind him. He was closer to getting it through the other goal post than his own. How the hell was he getting worse? I'd tried everything. I'd studied videos and read tips and tried to figure out if it was some kind of mental block. But I was seriously out of ideas.

Jefferson was a terrible kicker.

I ran my hand down my face with a sigh. Jefferson might go down as the worst kicker in the history of Empire High. And no one wanted that title. But how could I fix it if nothing worked?

My phone buzzed in my pocket and I pulled it out. There was a text from Tanner: "Ready and in place."

I texted him back. "Where are you exactly?"

"At 7 o'clock."

I looked down at my watch and another text came through.

"Not the time. The direction. At 7 o'clock means behind you."

I laughed and turned around but didn't see him.

Another text: "Sorry, more like 4 o'clock."

I turned my head but only saw a homeless man sitting on the bleachers. The homeless man proceeded to stand up and wave frantically at me.

I squinted at him. Yeah, the guy in the frumpy clothes was Tanner alright. With a big fake mustache. I couldn't help but laugh. It reminded me of all the times Rob had tried to convince me that Tanner was great at disguises.

That he walked around the city in fancy suits and a man bun. If Tanner's current ensemble and the fuzzy caterpillar sitting on his upper lip was any indicator, he was freaking awful at disguises.

Tanner texted me again: "So we're both set. Only one loose thread. Where is stupid Robert?"

Super clever burn. "I told him to be here a little before practice ended. He'll be here soon."

"Practice ends in 20 min. Cutting it close if you ask me. He has no respect for top secret missions."

I shook my head and turned back to practice. Maybe Jefferson was still struggling because I couldn't ever focus anymore. At the beginning of the season, I had been day-dreaming about Penny all the time. Then I started worrying about Poppy and Mr. Pruitt. And now I was thinking about Kennedy all day. Which made no sense, because I was probably 20 minutes away from being killed by a hitwoman. Kennedy should have been the last person on my mind. She should have always been the last person on my mind in *that* way. But seeing her again had been a breath of fresh air.

"Just kick the ball!" Smith yelled at Jefferson. "It's not that hard." Smith grabbed the football off the ground, placed it in the dirt, and then proceeded to kick a perfect field goal.

Fuck. I blew my whistle. "Sprints. Now."

Smith turned to me. "But Coach…"

I blew my whistle again. I didn't want to hear what smart remark he had. The last thing Jefferson needed right now was to feel even worse. Couldn't Smith see that? "Everyone. Now."

The whole team groaned. But they started to run back and forth on the field, because they knew if they didn't, I'd just demand they do something even worse.

"What did the team do to deserve that?" Rob asked as he joined me on the sidelines.

"Roughing the kicker." *More or less.*

Rob laughed. "That scrawny little guy? What the heck is he even doing on the team?"

I looked at Rob. Honestly, I had no idea what Jefferson was doing on the team. I had been trying to make his time at Empire High easier, but all I was doing was making it worse. All of that was suddenly in the back of my mind though because Rob was also dressed like a homeless guy.

"What the hell are you wearing?" I asked.

"A disguise."

"I didn't tell you to dress up."

"Right. But it's a top secret mission. Which always require disguises." He scrutinized my sweatpants and Empire High t-shirt. "I guess we chose the same disguise."

Why did everyone keep making fun of my coaching outfit? "I'm not dressed like a homeless guy."

"Whatever you say." He patted my back. "So what's the plan? Is the hitwoman even here?"

"I haven't seen her yet."

"I guess I should go hide somewhere? Oh yeah, here's the camera." He pulled the camera out of a small case in his pocket. "Don't break it."

"I won't. But um...how does it work?"

Rob laughed and peeled it out of the case. Yes, peeled it out, like a sticker. It was clear and he stuck it next to the Eagle emblem on my t-shirt. It was completely undetectable. I even knew where it was and I could hardly see it.

"I need your phone," he said.

I handed it to him.

He pressed a few buttons and then handed it to me. "It's all linked up now. The video feed is already rolling and it's getting uploaded directly to your phone."

"That's amazing." I looked at my phone and could see what the camera was recording.

"It is pretty crazy. So where should I hide? I was going to hide in the stands, but I don't want to be next to that homeless guy."

"That's Tanner."

Rob squinted. "Are you sure?"

I laughed. "If you can't tell that's him, how do you expect me to believe you when you tell me about his other disguise?"

"I see his stupid face now. I can tell it's him. Just like I can tell it's him when he's rocking a man bun. What the hell kind of mustache is that, anyway?"

I stared at Tanner. "I have no idea."

"Well, I'm glad all three of us coordinated to dress like homeless men," Rob said.

"I'm not dressed like a homeless person."

"Whatever you say. I'll wait at the entrance instead of in the stands. I don't want to be anywhere near Tanner. And speaking of Tanner…how about you wave him down here so you can tell him that I'm your best friend right in front of his mustachioed face?"

"Let's wait until after. I don't want the hitwoman to see us all together before we try to corner her."

"Fine. But you have to tell him. In front of me."

"I will." Honestly, if I was still alive in a few minutes I'd do whatever Rob wanted. Because I wouldn't have been able to do any of this without his camera.

I watched as Rob walked over to the entrance. And that's when I saw the hitwoman coming into the stadium.

I opened up a group chat between Rob and Tanner and sent them a text. "That's her walking in now. Keep an eye on her."

"Get me out of this group chat," Rob texted back.

Tanner's message popped up next: "I concur."

"You guys, focus. I need to wrap up practice and then we can surround her."

"Fine. I've got eyes on her," Tanner said. "She sat down right in front of me on the bleachers. I can't see a gun, but it's probably under her coat."

I swallowed hard as I watched the kids do sprints. This was it. Either the end of Mr. Pruitt or the end of me.

"We need a mission name," Rob texted.

"I actually agree with Robert on this," Tanner replied. "How about Operation Robert Shouldn't Be Here?"

"Or Operation Tanner is a Liar."

"What have I ever lied about?"

I put my phone in my pocket and ignored them. Honestly, it was nice that they were here. But I didn't want to put either of them at risk. I wasn't going to tell them when I was approaching her. Hopefully she'd start moving away from Tanner soon and then I'd get there and restrain her before Rob and Tanner even reached us. That way I would be the only one in danger.

And I couldn't wait till the end of practice. I'd already made the team sprint for far too long anyway. I blew my whistle and waved them in.

I wanted to make Smith apologize, but I knew that would just make him hate Jefferson even more. "Great practice," I said instead. "I'll see you guys tomorrow."

Smith grumbled something under his breath.

I also didn't have the patience to reprimand him right now. I could feel the hitwoman staring at me.

"Coach Caldwell?" Jefferson said.

I didn't have any advice for him right now. It was back to the drawing board. "I'm sorry, Jefferson," I said. "I actually have to get going."

"Oh, okay." He looked down at his feet and started walking toward the stands.

What was he doing? "Jefferson, wait. I'll talk to you. Just let me clean up this stuff. I'll meet you by my car."

He smiled and nodded, then hurried off to the parking lot.

The hitwoman was already on the move. *Shit.* I tried not to look like I was staring at her, as I hurried towards her. But I was pretty sure she saw me because she picked up her speed. Not fast enough this time, though.

My phone buzzed in my pocket, but I ignored it as I caught her arm.

She turned around and looked up at me. "Matt." She didn't say it like she was about to kill me. She said it like she had no idea why I was touching her.

"I know you're working for Richard Pruitt."

"What?"

Rob and Tanner were coming this way. I gripped her wrist a little harder. "Tell me everything you know and no one needs to get hurt."

"I don't know what you're talking about."

I studied her face and only saw…confusion. "How much money did he pay you to kill me?" I demanded.

"Kill you? What?"

"Don't play dumb with me."

"I have no idea what you're talking about, Matt." She pulled her arm out of my grasp. "You have no right to touch me after you never called me. I waited weeks like a freaking idiot."

I lowered my eyebrows. So I was right. I had slept with her? But what the hell did that have to do with anything?

"And the whole time you were with someone else? I don't even want to know if that woman is your wife. I don't want to be pulled into your mess of a life."

"My wife?"

"I saw you with that redhead and the cute little girl."

I remembered the first time this woman had run off. Right after she saw me with Penny and Scarlett. "Wait, you've been running away from me because you think I'm married?"

"I've been avoiding you because you're a dick."

"Then what the hell are you doing here stalking me?"

"Stalking you? God, I'd rather be anywhere than talking to you. But I came to see Henry's practice."

"What?"

"My son, Henry Jefferson. The kicker."

This woman was Jefferson's mom? What the fuck was going on? "So you don't work for Mr. Pruitt?"

"I have no idea who you're even talking about."

Her being Jefferson's mom explained why she'd been to some games and practices. But it didn't explain everything. "Why did you follow me at the cemetery?"

"I didn't follow you. I was there to put flowers on my late husband's grave."

Oh fuck. It all finally hit me. I'd slept with Jefferson's mom? That was so wrong on so many levels. And not only that, but she was a widow. She was absolutely right. I was a dick.

"And you were the one literally chasing *me*," she added. "I thought you were trying to tell me to keep quiet because of the whole cheating thing."

"What the hell," Rob said, panting. "Freeze." He put out his hand like that would have stopped her from running off.

"We have you surrounded," Tanner said.

"Who are you people?" She put her hands in the air like she was worried she was part of an actual sting operation. She looked more scared of the homeless men threatening her than she had of me. She backed up until she was practically in my arms.

"It's fine," I said. "They're my friends."

She looked even more confused than before. And I didn't blame her. She was probably wondering why I was friends with two homeless guys.

"I'm just here to pick up my son," she said. "Can I please just go?"

"You're not going anywhere with Matt," Tanner said.

She shook her head. "I'm not this grown man's mother. Look, I don't know what the hell kind of weird stuff you're into, but I want no part in it. If you weren't my son's favorite teacher, I'd freaking report you. Now, stop following me."

I felt like telling her I wasn't technically a teacher wasn't the right move here. "So you're not a hitwoman?"

She laughed. "No. But you and your friends are completely insane." She started walking away.

Tanner looked like he was about to reach out and grab her, but I told him to stop. "She doesn't work for Mr. Pruitt," I said. I let her walk away. I didn't bother telling her that I wasn't married. Or that I wasn't crazy. *Fuck, am I crazy?*

"Why the hell didn't you tell us Operation Water Buffalo was a go?" Rob asked. "She could have killed you."

That was the name they'd come up with? *Why?* I shook my head. "She's not a hitwoman. What the hell am I supposed to do now?"

Rob cleared his throat. "I can think of one thing you can do." He nodded toward Tanner.

Did he really think this was the time or place to announce our best friend status? "You guys, if she's not the one Mr. Pruitt hired, then who the hell is?" The little hairs on the back of my neck stood up and I turned around, but no one was there.

"It's going to be fine," Tanner said. "We'll figure it out. I'm here for you."

"Not as much as I'm here for you," Rob said. "Tell him, Matt."

"Tell me what?" Tanner asked.

I sighed and turned around. It was better just to get this over with. "Tanner, Rob's my best friend."

Tanner laughed. "Sorry, I think you just suffered an aneurysm. What did you say?"

"Rob's my best friend."

"Knew it," Rob said and shoved Tanner's shoulder.

"Did Robert force you to say that?" Tanner asked.

"No?"

"Ha!" said Tanner. "I knew it. What is wrong with you, Robert? Matt's in distress. This isn't the time for your shenanigans."

"Matt, you have to say it like you mean it," Rob said.

"But he doesn't mean it," Tanner said.

Rob reached out and ripped Tanner's fake mustache off.

Tanner screamed at the top of his lungs.

I started laughing. Because there was nothing else I could do. And laughing. And laughing. My legs gave out and I sat down and just stared up at the stands.

"Um…are you okay?" Rob asked.

I didn't reply.

He sat down next to me, and then Tanner did the same.

I'd put everything into this plan. And now I had…no idea what to do next. There was probably a hitwoman still out there somewhere. Mr. Pruitt was still on my back. And worst of all, Scarlett was still in danger.

"It's going to be fine, man," Rob said.

"No. It's not." I had to go to dinner with Poppy now. I had to do whatever she wanted in order to keep Scarlett safe. It was worse than owing a debt to the Pruitts. Poppy Cannavaro owned me. And she knew it.

CHAPTER 30

Wednesday

I hadn't bothered changing for my dinner with Poppy. If she was forcing me to go out with her, I'd put in as little effort as possible until she got bored of me. Hopefully she'd get bored quickly. Tonight if I was lucky. But I wasn't feeling very lucky. Because Poppy had chosen the one restaurant in the city that I hated.

Before stepping into Central Park, I stopped on the sidewalk and texted Kennedy. "How's your ankle feeling tonight?" I couldn't get her out of my head. I just needed one positive thing to happen today. And maybe looking forward to her reply would somehow get me through this dinner date from hell.

But I didn't have to wait, because before I could even put my phone back in my pocket, her response came. It was a selfie of her in a chair with ice on her ankle. She was sticking her tongue out in the picture and I couldn't help but laugh even though I felt guilty as hell.

I texted her back. "I have a dinner meeting right now. But can I bring you something to eat when I'm done?"

"I'm living with my mom. And she thinks food fixes everything, so I'm literally surrounded by food. So. Much. Food."

I laughed again. That sounded about right. I pressed my lips together. I'd pretty much tried to invite myself over for the second night in a row. And she'd turned me down. I was surprised by the sinking feeling in my stomach. I wanted to pretend that I'd feel this way if any of my friends told me not to come over. But this was different.

And I didn't really know how to feel about that. My phone buzzed again.

"But if you're up for a movie, my mom goes to sleep at like 9."

I smiled. She was asking me to come watch a movie with her. Like a date. But that was the question. Was it *like* a date or was it a date?

"Unless you want to hang out with her again. In which case, come before 9. But you better come hungry, because I can't eat all of this."

That felt a little less like a date. And for some reason that made me even more confused. I loved Mrs. Alcaraz. But I didn't want to hang out with her again tonight. I just wanted to spend more time with Kennedy. "I'll be there after 9."

"Okay then."

"Okay." I shook my head and shoved my phone in my sweatpants pocket. *Okay.* The word turned around in my head as I made my way into Central Park. I'm pretty sure I just agreed to go on a date with Kennedy. And I did feel okay. I wasn't panicking. I should have been panicking, but my breaths felt easier than they had in a long time. *Okay.*

Or maybe it was just that I was in the one place in the city where the air truly felt fresh. James, Mason, and Rob all loved running through this park. But I preferred running on a treadmill. Being here always reminded me of Brooklyn. And most days I didn't purposely want to feel the knife twisting in my chest. The farther I walked into Central Park, the guiltier I felt. Had I seriously just agreed to go on a date with Kennedy? Brooklyn's best friend? What the fuck was wrong with me?

I tried to take a deep breath, but this time my lungs felt weird. I needed to calm down. I counted down slowly from ten again and again. The last thing I needed was for

Poppy to witness me having a panic attack. She'd think I'd be easy to control in whatever game she was playing. But it would have been easier if she'd chosen a different fucking restaurant.

I took a deep breath, keeping my eyes trained on the sidewalk instead of letting my gaze wander to all the places that would remind me of Brooklyn. But I kept looking up. Like I was expecting to see Brooklyn's smiling face on the path up ahead.

My feet froze on the little bridge I'd come to a million times. The corner of my mouth rose as I remembered getting down on one knee. Brooklyn had thought I was going to propose. I'd been able to tell by the expression on her face. She'd stared at me like she was excited but also like she thought I'd lost my mind. And I was pretty sure it was in that moment that I realized I wanted to marry her. That I couldn't imagine my life without her.

And she'd laughed as I pulled a hotdog out from behind my back instead of a ring. That sealed the deal. The fact that she'd seemed just as delighted with a cheap hotdog as she would have with a ring. I stared out over the water.

And that's when I saw her. I squinted at the woman with red hair coming out of the nearby restaurant. She was alone and looked upset. Most likely she had just set some other poor asshole on fire and was making a quick exit.

"Ash?" I called. It was definitely her. Although, she was better dressed than when we'd had our date.

She looked up and her eyes grew so round. A few people walked in front of her, blocking my view. I walked across the bridge and…she was gone. "Ash?" I turned in a circle. It was weird. When Kennedy had shown up, I had this gut feeling that she was supposed to be some kind of sign from Brooklyn. But what if I was wrong? What if Ash was the sign? Because she'd just shown up when I was thinking about Brooklyn.

I looked around once more. Or had Ash shown up? Because she'd literally disappeared. Had I just imagined that? Was I fucking losing my mind now? *Probably. I had thought Jefferson's mom was stalking me...*

But then I heard a splash.

I looked at the water and sure enough...Ash's head was bobbing on top of the surface.

"What the hell are you doing?" I hurried over to help her out of the water.

"Go away! Pretend you didn't see me!" she yelled, flailing her arms in the water. "Imagine this isn't happening right now! Please, I'm begging you."

I couldn't tell if she was drowning or just really upset. But I wasn't going to walk away in case it was the prior. "Did you just throw yourself in the lake to avoid me?"

"No." Her teeth chattered. "That would be crazy."

Her point? "Let me help you." I put my hand out.

"Please, Matt, just let me drown in my misery."

"I'm not going anywhere until you're out of that water."

"I'm not actually drowning! I'm just swimming recreationally." She continued to tread water. "See."

"I don't think you're supposed to swim in there."

"I know that." She looked up at the sky like she was hoping a lightning bolt would come down and just end everything.

"Then what are you doing?" I asked.

"Fine! I admit it! I was trying to avoid you. So please walk away before either of us gets hurt."

I laughed. "Let me help you out."

She stared at me like she couldn't believe I was still standing there. "You're not going to do the gentlemanly thing and walk away because I asked you to?"

"No. I'm not."

"Men." She sighed so loudly that she scared a duck swimming by. It squawked angrily. "Fine. But only because I'm a little scared of birds. Only slightly. It's not on my list or anything." Ash swam over to me, avoiding the angry duck, and took my hand.

I pulled her out and her body collided against mine. She was wet from head to toe. She'd clearly dove headfirst in the lake just to avoid walking past me. And she was shivering.

But instead of letting me run my hands up and down her arms, she pulled back. "I am so so beyond sorry, Matt."

"My dick is fine."

"Yeah, that. But also…" she waved her hand in front of me.

I looked down. She'd gotten the front of my hoody all wet and…a little slimy. "It's fine," I said. "Seriously, why did you throw yourself into the lake to avoid me?"

"Oh, I don't know." She wrapped her arms around herself. "Maybe because I was half an hour late for our date, flashed you in the bathroom, and then set your dick on fire!"

People had been already staring at us as soon as I found her in the water. Now they weren't even trying to pretend they weren't staring.

"So that wasn't a normal date for you?" I couldn't help but laugh.

"God, you were supposed to just keep walking. Not find me and pull me out of the lake. Why would you even look in there? It was such a good hiding spot. I have to go." She turned around.

I grabbed her hand. "It's okay, Ash. Bad dates happen."

"It wasn't a bad date. It was mortifying." She pulled her hand out of mine. "And in this huge city what are the odds that I'd run into you again? One in a million? Don't answer that. And if you ever do see me again and then you suddenly don't…just keep walking. Because it means I'm hiding to avoid you. So do the respectable thing and just keep walking. Because I can't relive that date ever again. My best friend already tortures me enough about it. She called me inferno dick for a whole week. Inferno dick. Like I make a habit of setting people's privates on fire. It happened one time! One time," she yelled to one of the people watching us.

The guy that had been staring quickly walked away.

"See." She pointed to the stranger. "People are literally terrified of me because of that nickname." A drop of something green and slimy fell from her arm. "What is that?! I have to go to the doctor! No, I hate doctors. But what if I just contracted something in that dirty city water? Gah, I have to! What the hell is my life?!" She ran away before I could get another word in.

"Don't jump in any more lakes because of me!" I yelled after her.

"Then don't make eye contact with me ever again!" she yelled back before sprinting over the little bridge, leaving a trail of wet footprints behind her.

She really was adorable. And a little crazy. And definitely not a sign from Brooklyn. Besides, I didn't feel drawn to her. Not the same way I felt drawn to Kennedy. I sighed. I was going to hell.

I turned to the restaurant. Even though Ash was crazy, I wished I was running in the opposite direction of this restaurant like her. Because at least she was nice crazy and not mean crazy like Poppy. I sighed and pushed through the doors of the venue Brooklyn and I had chosen for our wedding. Surely Mr. Pruitt had invited Poppy to the wedding. She knew what this place meant to me. And she was going to purposely shit all over it. Not that it mattered. I hadn't come here since Brooklyn died.

Poppy was already seated in the restaurant. She was easy to spot. She was the only one with an evil smile staring directly at me. I was probably crazy, but I would have risked another night with Ash over this any day.

"Hey," I said when I reached the table.

Her gaze scrutinized me from head to toe. "Do you have algae on your shoulder?"

I looked down at my right shoulder. There was definitely something green on there. I pulled my sweatshirt off and plopped down across from Poppy. "So what's good here?" I lifted up the menu so I didn't have to look at her.

"I thought this was one of your favorite restaurants?"

So she did bring me here to torture me? "Not anymore. And I think you know why."

She reached out and pulled the menu down so I'd look at her. "Matthew, I didn't ask you here to be spiteful. I honestly thought you liked this restaurant."

I didn't know what to say to that. Anything Poppy did was part of some bigger scheme. But she seemed different than she had in my office the other day. Her face didn't look as stiff. She almost looked…kind.

The waiter came over. "Hi, I'm…"

"Can't you see that we're in the middle of a conversation?" Poppy snapped.

Wow, okay, not kind then.

"Sorry," the waiter said. He went to walk away.

"But we'll have two glasses of champagne to start," Poppy said.

He nodded before practically fleeing.

"Champagne?" I asked. What in the hell did we have to celebrate?

"It feels like a good evening for champagne."

I had nothing to say to that.

She leaned back in her chair. "You know…both my parents passed away when I was in college."

I was starting to wonder if evil people were bad at segues because they were so socially unaware. Or did she think talking about death was a champagne kind of thing? That wouldn't have surprised me.

"It was a tragic accident," she said.

I'd heard about her parents' deaths. And I was sorry for her loss. But it was no accident. Her parents died in a shoot-out at a restaurant. I couldn't sit here and pretend they were good people. Innocent lives were lost that night. It had been all over the news.

"Uncle Richard is really the only father figure I have left."

"I'm sorry about that." And I truly was. Because having Mr. Pruitt for a father was worse than not having one at all.

She smiled. "Why do you hate him so much? He always speaks so highly of you."

"I'm sure that's not true."

"It is." Her lips pouted slightly as she stared at me. "I mean, I guess he is a little displeased with you right now."

"About that. If he wants to hurt me? Fine. But Scarlett…"

"I really don't want to talk about business tonight."

"I'm only here to talk about business."

Her eyes searched mine. "Is the thought of getting to know me that awful?"

"I fell in love with a member of your family. Mr. Pruitt killed her. And Isabella forced one of my best friends to marry her. And then after he finally divorced her, she went even more psycho and tried to have him and his wife…"

"I'm not Isabella."

"You could have fooled me."

She lowered her eyebrows. "I know my cousin had her flaws."

"It was a little more than that."

"Fine, she was crazy," Poppy said with a laugh.

And for some reason I smiled too.

"It's a lot of pressure being in this family. Uncle Richard is very hard to please. And honestly? I had no desire to take over the business. It was always supposed to be Isabella. There were even rumors in the family for a few months there when we all thought Brooklyn might be handed the reins."

That never would have happened.

"But…here I am." She shrugged. "I'm actually kind of good at it. And I enjoy the work. It's given me something to focus on after my divorce."

"You could just get a normal job."

"Now where's the fun in that? Besides, you got a legacy job. It's not that different."

"I earned my position. And it is different, Poppy. My job is legal."

"So is mine."

Did she honestly believe that? I stared at her and she smiled. It didn't look quite as evil as before, but the message was still clear. She wasn't stupid. She knew what kind of business she was about to take over.

"I'm no accountant though," Poppy said. "Uncle Richard had Isabella study the appropriate subjects in college to prepare. But I was never supposed to take over. You do accounting though, right?"

"Finance is different."

"Surely you took similar classes. All business majors do. I was going to be a teacher."

I raised my eyebrows. I really couldn't picture her teaching children. She'd been really harsh and distant with her daughter, Gigi.

"Don't look at me like that," she said with a laugh. "I actually love children. Stop, I'm serious," she said with a laugh.

I must have still been making the same face. "I'm sorry. It just seemed like Gigi…"

"Annoys me to no end? Well, sometimes. Most people see me when they look at her. But she has her father's eyes. And nose. And I can't help but see a cheating scoundrel. I'm going to therapy for that. I don't want to resent my daughter the way I resent my ex-husband."

Wow. That was…a lot. And way more insightful than I ever expected from her.

"But I do love children. And I will do my best to make sure nothing happens to Scarlett."

"Your best? The other day you said you wouldn't hurt her."

She shrugged. "Like I just said, I'll do my best. But I'm not the one in charge right now. My uncle is."

"Mr. Pruitt said he didn't know what I was talking about when I brought up Scarlett."

"And who do you believe more? Him or me?"

"Neither." I'd never trust a thing either of them said.

She smiled. "So you don't really have much of a choice to go along with this, Matthew. Speaking of which,

I'm going to need something from you in return for keeping Scarlett safe."

Of course she was going to ask for something in return. And I knew exactly what it was. She'd certainly mentioned my career enough times whenever I'd seen her.

The waiter dropped off our glasses of champagne and Poppy dismissed him with a wave of her hand.

"Perfect timing," she said and lifted up her champagne flute.

"Poppy…"

"Just hear me out. If we start dating, I think Uncle Richard will be more likely to step down."

Dating?!

"Honestly, it's suffocating with him breathing down my neck. I'm ready to take over. And if he thinks we're going steady, he'll feel more comfortable, I know it. Like I said before, he respects you. And your business is in my weak spot. We'd be the perfect couple in his eyes."

I laughed. "I'm not going to date you, Poppy."

She put down her champagne flute. "But, Matthew…" She reached out and tried to put her hand on top of mine on the table, but I quickly pulled away. "You don't have much of a choice," she said. "Unless you don't care about little Scarlett after all?"

I felt like I was holding my breath. Like I'd been holding it for years. And I had no idea if my lungs knew how to work anymore. Not in this shitty world where Brooklyn didn't exist and Poppy held all the cards.

"What do you say?" she said with a smile and lifted her champagne flute again.

My phone buzzed. I looked down at a text from Kennedy: "Actually, if you do happen to want even more food, I have a craving for ice cream. I would be 100% okay if you wanted to bring some. Something chocolatey please and thank you."

It would have made me laugh if it didn't feel like I was being suffocated.

"Matthew?" Poppy said. "Do we have a deal?"

There was nothing I could say. Maybe being close to her would give me the dirt I needed on Mr. Pruitt. My mind swirled with maybes. But none of them mattered. They didn't change what I had to do. I didn't have a choice. Because I'd do anything to keep James and Penny's daughter safe. "You swear you'll stay away from Scarlett? That no one will touch a hair on her head?"

"I promise. She'll be perfectly safe."

I lifted my glass. "Is there an end date to this charade?"

"Why? Are you seeing someone?"

I thought about Kennedy. The way it felt to wake up with her head on my chest and my arms wrapped around her. I wanted that again. It was wrong. I knew that. And yet...I wanted it again tonight. For the first time in 16 years, I felt like I was actually ready for another chance. I stared at Poppy. "No, I'm not seeing anyone." What the hell else could I say?

"Good. That would complicate things. It's all about the image, but obviously I'm hoping this becomes much more than a charade. Wouldn't that be nice?" She clinked her glass against mine.

I felt like I was going to throw up. I downed my champagne. *That did not help.*

"Speaking of which, the photographers will be here shortly so we can get our picture taken for all the tabloids. By this time tomorrow the whole city will know we're together. Let's make sure our meal is placed so it looks like we're having a romantic dinner. We have to set the scene.

Where is that dreadful waiter?" She snapped her fingers. "And next time please wear something more presentable."

CHAPTER 31

Wednesday

I'd finished the bottle of champagne before the photographers had even shown up. I could tell Poppy was mad at me. But I really didn't fucking care. I'd had a few scotches after she was done pretending to stare affectionately at me for the cameras. Anyone would have after that ordeal, especially after the awkward few seconds when Poppy had put her lips to mine while the cameras flashed. I was pretty sure I'd vomited a little in my mouth. This was a date from hell. And all that seemed to make it better was scotch. Lots and lots of scotch.

Well, maybe something else would too. Or, someone.

I hit the intercom button outside Kennedy's place. I smiled remembering all the times I'd snuck into this building back in high school. I took a few steps backwards to see if I'd still be able to jump and pull down the fire escape ladder. It was pretty high. But I totally had this. I cracked my neck and stretched my arms. But before I could leap, the door buzzed open. *Score!* I took the stairs two at a time and felt a little dizzy by the time I reached Kennedy's floor. I managed to avoid looking at Brooklyn's apartment door and headed straight for Kennedy's.

Before I could knock, Kennedy opened the door.

"You're a sight for sore eyes," I said and then laughed. I literally had no idea what that phrase meant or why I'd said it. But my eyes did like staring at her.

"Shh!" Kennedy said with a laugh. "You'll wake my mom."

"I don't want to wake your mom."

"Then lower your voice," she hissed.

I laughed. "You lower your voice."

"Oh my God, Matt. Are you drunk?"

"No," I somehow managed to say with a completely straight face. Because I was plastered.

"Are you sure about that?" She raised one of her eyebrows in a way I could only describe as overtly sexual. Yep. That was it. Overtly sexual.

"Absolutely positively not drunk," I said. "Here's your ice cream." I shoved the bag into her hands. "They had your favorite." I knew her favorite ice cream. Because I knew her. I knew everything about her. Well, everything but a few things. My gaze wandered to her lips for just a beat.

"Really? They had the forbidden chocolate? I haven't had this in years." She reached into the bag and pulled the container to her chest with the most orgasmic sigh.

"Shh, your mom will hear you," I said.

"Hear me sighing?"

"I have no idea what she'll think if she heard the noise that just came out of your mouth. Come on." I grabbed her around the waist and lifted her in the air.

"What are you doing?" she said with a laugh as I flipped her upside down over my shoulder. "Matt, put me down."

"No, I'm taking you back to the couch where you belong." I leaned down with her still balancing on my shoulder to grab the ice pack she'd discarded on the floor. Somehow one of her hands slid down to my butt.

My whole body tensed. Not because I didn't like it. Because I did. But I didn't know if she knew her hand was perched precariously on my left ass cheek. And it seemed like a good idea to tell her just in case it was an accident.

"Kennedy, I need to inform you that your hand is on my ass."

"Would you just put me down, you big oaf?"

I laughed and tried to gently put her down. I collapsed on the couch next to her. "You touched my butt," I said and pulled out the French fries I'd picked up after I'd gotten her ice cream.

"I didn't mean to."

"Sure," I said. But I was pretty sure she'd meant to.

"You're really drunk."

"Am not."

"You're talking so much louder than you realize," she said with a laugh. "Oh my God, this reminds me of one night when Brooklyn and I came home drunk. Do you remember that party at Felix's place?"

"Yeah, I remember." Brooklyn had looked so beautifully out of place at that party. I hadn't been able to stay away from her.

"Oh no, wait. Uncle Jim was pissed after that. But not as pissed as he was after the party at your house. Because we came back drunk again. He tried to ground her for life."

I shook my head.

Kennedy leaned forward and for a second I thought she was going to kiss me. But then she just gently touched my neck, right below my ear. I tried not to orgasmically sigh like she had. I may have groaned though. Just a little.

"Why do you have mud on your neck? Or is that chocolate?"

I scratched the side of my neck where there absolutely was mud. That was going to look great in Poppy's pictures. *Serves her right.* I rubbed it off on my sweatpants. "Don't eat that," I said and grabbed Kennedy's hand in case she was about to put her fingers in her mouth. I pulled her hand onto my lap just to ensure she wouldn't do something crazy. "It's definitely mud. I have the best story," I said and started laughing.

Kennedy just shook her head as she smiled back at me. "Aren't you going to tell me the story?"

"So I went on a terrible blind date a few weeks ago. So bad that the girl actually jumped in a lake to try to avoid me tonight. I helped her out. She must have gotten some lake gunk on me. Oh, but get this…"

"I'm still stuck on the fact that this woman jumped in a lake to avoid you. What the hell happened on your date?"

"She was super late and tried to set my dick on fire."

Kennedy laughed and somehow her fingers wound up intertwined with mine.

I didn't pull away. And neither did she.

"Wait, I need more than that," Kennedy said.

"Right. I was about to tell you more. She was married to Cupcake."

Kennedy cringed.

I would have missed it if I hadn't been staring right at her. *Fuck*. Why had I mentioned Cupcake to Kennedy after everything he'd done to her? That was a sure-fire way to ruin the night. "I'm sorry…"

"It's fine. Really."

I held her hand a little tighter as she fidgeted with a strand of hair that had fallen from her bun. "I was actually asking for more details about how this girl set your penis on fire."

"Almost. She didn't succeed in her attempts. My dick is fine. But it was crazy. Just picture a candle and some of that oil you dip bread in. It was an accident. I think."

Kennedy laughed. "Well, phew. Close call, huh?"

"Very close." And speaking of close, her hand was pretty close to touching my dick right now. Except I was holding it still. And as much as I wanted her hand on my dick, I actually really liked holding it.

"Did she say why they got divorced?"

"Hm?" My mind had been preoccupied with thoughts of Kennedy touching me. "What did you say?"

"The woman you went on a date with. She divorced Cupcake?"

I knew what she was wondering. If he'd hurt Ash too. He had, but not in the same way. At least, I was pretty sure. "He cheated on her."

"What a dick."

"What a dick," I said. "Someone should set him on fire."

Kennedy laughed and placed her chin in the palm of her hand. And she just stared at me.

It was unnerving. I felt like I needed to get up and run around her small apartment. But I didn't want to move because I didn't want to let go of her hand. So I just stared back at her. "What are you thinking about over there?"

She sighed. "Do you ever just feel like you're stuck?"

It was like she was speaking to my soul. "Every day. Like I'll never actually leave high school."

"Being the football coach was an interesting choice then," Kennedy said.

I looked down at my t-shirt. We'd talked a lot during dinner with her mom last night. I could tell she thought it was an odd decision for me to choose to go back to Empire High all the time. "Like I said. I'm stuck."

"Well, you said you went on that bad blind date. So you're dating. That's good."

"I'm not really dating. I'm not taking that app Penny has me on seriously."

"But what about your dinner tonight?"

"Business."

"Ah. Right, you did say that. So you're not seeing anyone?"

Technically I was dating Poppy now. *Barf.* The pictures would be plastered all over tomorrow morning's tabloids. It was just like Poppy had said. The whole city would know by tomorrow night. But my relationship with Poppy wasn't real. This though? Holding Kennedy's hand? This felt real. And I didn't want to talk about Poppy or anyone else with Kennedy. I just wanted to be here right now and be happy for five fucking seconds of my miserable life. So I shook my head. "What about you?"

"I just uprooted my whole life and moved back here. How would I have met someone so quickly?"

"That doesn't really answer my question."

She smiled. "I didn't leave anyone behind, if that's what you're asking."

"What was your last serious relationship?"

"You're full of questions tonight, Matt. I think it's time for me to ask one. A very important one. What's in the other bag?" She eyed the other plastic bag I'd walked in with.

"French fries," I said and went to grab them. I immediately regretted it. Because my hand fell from hers and my whole body suddenly felt empty.

"Now French fries sound good," Kennedy said and plucked one out. "Mmm. Just what I was craving." She grabbed another instead of opening up her ice cream container.

Kennedy had a bad habit of never ordering the right food. She'd stolen so many fries from me while we were in school. I put the takeout bag between us so she could keep stealing my food. I'd never minded then. And I didn't mind it now either.

She hugged her knees to her chest and watched me.

"What?" I asked.

"Nothing."

"You should be elevating that," I said. I reached out and grabbed her ankle, pulling it onto my lap. I placed the ice pack on top. If I couldn't have her hand, I would at least take her foot.

She just kept silently watching me.

"What?" I asked again.

"On a scale of one to ten, how drunk are you? Like are you going to remember this when you wake up tomorrow?"

"There's like a 50-50 chance." As if those odds were somehow in my favor, I lightly ran my thumb along the inside of her ankle, tracing slow circles. She felt it too, right? That it was easier to breathe when we were touching?

She didn't pull away. "You know, when I was little, I kind of just thought the perfect guy would come find me. Like in all the Disney movies. But the only guy that showed up was Cupcake."

"That would be a terrible Disney movie."

"The worst," she said with a laugh. But her face didn't look very happy anymore. It looked like she wanted to cry. "And I…I stopped trying."

"What do you mean you stopped?"

"You asked me what my last serious relationship was. That was it."

I just stared at her. "With Cupcake?"

She closed her eyes. "He broke me, Matt." Her voice trembled.

I didn't want her to be sad. Wasn't I sad enough for the both of us? "Only if you let him."

She laughed, even though it was forced. "Right. Sorry." She wiped at her eyes even though I hadn't seen a tear actually fall. "We need to pick a movie. And eat French fries and ice cream." She grabbed the remote.

"I don't want to do any of those things," I said.

"But it's forbidden chocolate."

"I don't like forbidden chocolate."

She looked at me instead of turning on the TV. "Right, you don't." She scrunched her mouth to the side like she was trying to remember what I'd liked in high school.

But I wasn't talking about ice cream right now.

"What flavor do you prefer?"

My gaze dropped to her lips. "You." The word just tumbled out of me. I couldn't lie to her about why I was here. It wasn't for food or a movie. It was to be with her. She was the only person who understood what I'd been through. And she'd just admitted it. She was as broken as me. And in some weird, twisted way, it felt like she'd been waiting all this time for me. Cupcake had been her last serious relationship. She'd never been mine back then. But we were tied together. We were both stuck. Why not be stuck together?

"I'm not an ice cream flavor," she said, her voice barely a whisper.

I moved slowly, worried she'd shove me away. But somehow moving slowly toward her, over top of her, just made the heat even more palpable. It was like my whole body was on fire. And not in an Ash accident kind of way. I was hovering over her, my lips a fraction of an inch away from hers, when she broke the silence.

"You'll regret kissing me in the morning."

"Who said I was going to kiss you?"

She laughed. "Matt…"

I grabbed the side of her face. "Fine. Yeah, I'm going to kiss you."

There were tears in her eyes now. "You can't, Matt. We need to pick a movie and eat ice cream before it melts." But she didn't push me away.

I dropped my forehead to hers. "I just need to know if you feel this too."

The sound of her light breathing was speeding up. "Matt, you're drunk."

"I'm not that drunk." I pulled back ever so slightly and traced my thumb along one of her tears. "Why are you crying?"

"Because I'm not her." Kennedy's voice cracked. "I'll never be her."

"You're real. You're here. I can touch you." I let my hand wander down the side of her neck. "I can taste you." I felt tears forming in my eyes too. "I'm so sick of chasing a ghost, Kennedy. I don't want to be stuck anymore. I want you."

"But you still love her."

I nodded. I knew what she was getting at. And maybe she was right. But what if she was wrong? "I don't know if I can ever love someone else." *Why the hell did I say that?!*

"Matt." Her tears fell freely from her eyes now, cascading down her chin.

It felt like I was crying too. But I didn't think I was. It was like I could feel her tears. Like they were somehow mine. "I'm not okay, Kennedy. I'm really fucking not okay."

She didn't say anything.

"But I feel less shitty when I'm with you."

"I know." She reached up and ran her fingers gently through my hair. "I feel a lot less shitty when you're here too. But there's a 50-50 chance you won't remember any of this in the morning."

There was no fucking way I wouldn't remember kissing this girl.

"And I don't gamble with my heart anymore," she added. "I can't."

Is that what I was asking her to do? *Fuck*. It was. I was asking her to take a chance when I just told her I wasn't sure if I could ever love someone else. And just like that, it wasn't as easy to breathe again.

"Can we maybe just..." her voice trailed off. "Can we just watch the movie? And if you remember any of this in the morning, maybe we can talk about this more then?"

I wiped away the remaining tears from her cheeks, hating that I'd caused them. "Okay." Instead of sitting back up though, I lay down behind her, pulling her against my chest. Because if I couldn't kiss her, I could at least hold her. I needed this. I needed to be next to her.

A very contented sigh escaped her lips.

"Just for the record, I'm not that drunk," I said from behind her.

She laughed, not caring when my arms tightened around her. "You are. I don't even think you'd be here right now if you weren't."

That wasn't true. I couldn't get her out of my mind. And I had to prove that to her. "I'm going to remember to bring this up in the morning."

"We'll see about that." She turned on a movie. I wasn't sure which one, because I was staring down at the top of her head. And I was hit again with how much she smelled like...home.

She'd said Cupcake had broken her. I didn't think that was true. But if it was, I was going to be the one to piece her back together. I kissed the top of her head.

"Matt, watch the movie," she whispered.

I kissed the top of her head again. "Okay."

"Okay then."

I continued to stare at the back of her perfect head. I'd been focused on my own problems for long enough. Fixing hers sounded like a better use of time. Besides, maybe it would fix both of us. I really wanted it to fix both of us. I closed my eyes.

Despite what she thought, I would never gamble with her heart. Because I knew how easy hearts were to break.

CHAPTER 32

Thursday

The sound of someone clearing their throat made me slowly open my eyes.

Mrs. Alcaraz was standing there with her hand on her hip staring down at Kennedy and me intertwined on the couch. She was shaking her head back and forth like she couldn't believe what she was seeing.

Shit.

"Mama," Kennedy groaned, stirring in her sleep. "One more minute."

Mrs. Alcaraz raised her eyebrow at me. "Omelet?"

Was she asking me if I wanted breakfast or did that mean something in Spanish like…I'm going to kill you for sleeping with my daughter? "Yes?" I replied.

"Sí." She turned away without another word and I breathed a sigh of relief.

"Kennedy," I whispered and shook her shoulder.

Her eyes flew open and then she smiled. "Whenever I wake up and you're there it nearly gives me a heart attack."

Very funny. "Um, your mom is up."

Kennedy quickly sat up. "Good morning, Mama."

"Mhm," Mrs. Alcaraz said. She was already at the stove cooking.

Kennedy put her face in her hands. "Well, that's embarrassing," she whispered to me. "She probably thinks we're sleeping together." She laughed like that was hilarious.

It wasn't funny to me. I pulled her hands away from her face. "Is that really that funny?"

"Are you still drunk?" She climbed off the couch. "I need to go freshen up. Make yourself at home."

"Don't leave me here…"

But she was already hurrying toward the bathroom.

This was probably the most awkward morning after ever. Especially because we hadn't even kissed, let alone had sex. And honestly, I never did mornings after. Normally I would have been long gone…*shit.* I pulled out my phone. Dozens of missed calls from Tanner. He was going to kill me for staying out all night again. I wasn't used to having a stupid curfew.

"Sit, sit," Mrs. Alcaraz said before I could figure out what to do.

I didn't want to tell her no. And maybe this could help me clear up whatever she thought. "We just fell asleep watching a movie, Mrs. Alcaraz."

She tilted her pan, sliding the omelet perfectly onto a plate, and then handed it to me.

"Thank you."

For a second we both just stared at each other.

Mrs. Alcaraz sighed and then reached out, putting her hands on both sides of my face. "Mi amor." She shook her head back and forth. "She just came back home to me. Por favor. Don't break my Kennedy's heart and send her running."

"I won't."

"Bueno." She patted my cheek before letting her hands fall. "Now eat. It's getting cold."

Kennedy reemerged in a dress that accentuated her long legs. And those worn boots looked perfect on her. "I'm running late," she said. "I'll have to skip breakfast this morning."

"Nonsense." Mrs. Alcaraz slid an omelet onto a plate for Kennedy. "You eat your breakfast."

Kennedy made a funny face at me, then grabbed her plate and sat down. She started eating as quickly as possible. That seemed like the go-ahead on mine. I took one bite and it was so spicy that I could feel my throat closing up. I'd eaten here dozens of times when I was in high school. And never had Mrs. Alcaraz tried to kill me. I started coughing into my hand.

Mrs. Alcaraz laughed at the stove.

"Mama, did you put extra spices in his?" Kennedy scolded and grabbed a container of milk out of the fridge. She poured me a glass and handed it to me. "Drink that." She turned back to her mom as I downed half the glass. "It was my fault. We fell asleep watching a movie. Nothing happened."

"No boys sleep over," Mrs. Alcaraz said.

"It wasn't a sleepover. It was an accident. And it was my fault."

Sweet hell. What was in that omelet? A whole cayenne pepper? I downed half the glass of milk.

"No boys," Mrs. Alcaraz said.

Kennedy sighed. "Yes, Mama."

"I'm so sorry," Kennedy said to me. "You okay?"

I finished the milk and nodded. "Yes," I croaked.

Kennedy laughed.

"It's not funny."

"It's a little funny." She couldn't even hide her smile.

Which made me smile too.

"Here." She swapped plates with me and devoured the rest of my poisoned omelet in record time.

I was very impressed. How was she not crying? I was pretty sure I'd cried after one bite. But the omelet her mom had made for her was significantly more palatable than mine.

Mrs. Alcaraz sat down at the table with her own omelet. "Lo siento," she said and patted my cheek. "Now off to work. Both of you."

Kennedy kissed her mom on the cheek before grabbing my hand and pulling me toward the door. She laughed as we ran through the hallway. I had no idea why we were running. But for some reason we kept going. Like we were escaping.

"I'm so so sorry, Matt," she said as we hurried down the stairs. "She has a no boys rule when it comes to sleepovers. And obviously we're just friends so we didn't break it. But…" her voice got stuck in her throat when I stopped her on the stairs.

"Just friends?"

She blinked up at me. "Yes?"

"I remember everything about last night." I took a step toward her.

She swallowed hard. "You do?"

I leaned forward slowly.

"I'm pretty sure you're still drunk," Kennedy said.

"I swear I'm not. A little hungover. And your mom tried to poison me…but I'm not drunk."

"It was just a little spicy."

"A little?"

She laughed and put her hand on my chest. "We both know that you'll regret it if you kiss me."

I drew a fraction of an inch closer. "I won't."

She seemed to realize I was serious now. "I'm not a temporary fix, Matt."

"I know that."

"Do you? Because I'm not so sure. You said you remember last night. Do you remember what you said to me? That you're not sure if you could love anyone else…"

My lips collided with hers.

Her hand was still pressed against my chest. For a second I thought she was going to shove me away. But instead, her hand crept up my chest to the side of my neck, pulling me closer.

It should have felt wrong. But it didn't. It felt anything but wrong. So didn't that make it right?

But then she did shove me away.

"God, what am I doing?" She started blinking fast. "I can't believe I just kissed you. I can't believe you just kissed me. I have to go." She started running down the steps.

"Kennedy!"

She didn't stop, so I ran after her. She pushed through the doors of the apartment building, blasting us with the cool autumn air. The smell of fallen leaves always reminded me of Brooklyn. But for the first time in a long time, Brooklyn wasn't the one on my mind.

I grabbed Kennedy's hand as she tried to hail a cab. "I don't know how to be okay with her gone," I said. "I've spent the last 16 years trying to be. It's true, I'm a fucking mess."

She was blinking away tears. "Matt..."

"But I know you're not a temporary fix." I reached out and touched the side of her face. "What if you're the cure?"

"I can't fix you. I'm barely standing after..."

I kissed her again. Because anything I said wasn't helping. But she had to feel this. She had to.

And again she kissed me back.

Her lips tasted salty from her tears. And all I knew was that this flavor was way better than anything in that ice cream container. I'd been right.

The soft moan escaping from her lips nearly drove me insane. I wanted her. I wanted to fucking rip her clothes off and take her right here in the middle of the sidewalk. I wanted to know what it would sound like for her to moan my name.

Instead, I just kept kissing her. And kissing her. And kissing her. I wasn't sure whether it was for a few seconds or a few minutes. But I kept my hands firmly planted on her hips. I needed her to know that I wasn't a shmuck like Cupcake. I needed her to know that I meant what I said. That I thought this was the real deal. That maybe we could both be okay.

Her fingers dug into the back of my neck, begging me for more. *Fuck.*

She felt it too.

God, I needed her. How long had I been waiting to feel like this again?

I could tell Kennedy needed this too. She needed me. And it had been a really long fucking time since I'd felt needed.

I pulled away before I accidentally did try to fuck her in the middle of a busy sidewalk.

She opened her mouth and then closed it again, tears still on her flushed cheeks.

"Come to my practice today." I wiped her tears away with my thumbs.

"What?"

"Come to Empire High. I want to show you that you're not stuck. That we're allowed to live outside those walls."

"Matt…"

"Do you trust me?"

She nodded.

"3 o'clock, okay?" I reached out my hand and hailed a taxi.

"That was stupid fast," she said as a taxi pulled to a stop right away.

I laughed and opened the door for her.

For a second, the silence between us felt awkward. Did she regret the first kiss? The second? Both? Had I pushed her too far? I never wanted her to feel the way she had with Cupcake. *Fuck*. She'd told me it was a bad idea…

"I might be a little late," she said. "I have a photo shoot at 1:30, and the client always runs over."

"That's fine. Practice doesn't end until 5."

"Okay."

I smiled. "Okay then."

She smiled back before climbing into the taxi.

I wanted to do some kind of victory dance as the taxi sped off. But my phone buzzed in my pocket. First I had to deal with Tanner.

***

Tanner's apartment was pitch black again when I walked in. With all the windows, it should have been impossible. It was like he'd installed blackout curtains just for this occasion. I stumbled into the great room and Tanner turned on the small lamp he'd set up yesterday morning.

But this time there were two wingback chairs. One for Tanner and one for Nigel. They were both pretending to read newspapers and I cringed, wondering if there was a picture of Poppy and me plastered somewhere in there.

"You broke curfew again," Nigel said and slammed his paper on the ground. "We were worried sick, Mr. Caldwell. How could you…"

"Nigel, please, you sound hysterical," Tanner said and folded his paper neatly. "Matt, we were worried sick! How could you do this to me two nights in a row!"

He sounded almost exactly as hysterical as Nigel had been. "I'm really sorry…"

"Sorry? You're…you're grounded, young man."

I laughed. "What?"

"Go to your room immediately."

"Tanner."

"Fine, I can't ground you because you're practically an adult." He threw his paper on the ground. "But seriously, what the actual hell?"

I walked over to him. "I'm really sorry, man."

"Actions speak louder than words."

"What if I told you I have a really good reason?" Honestly, Tanner was more invested in my love life than anyone else. He was going to be thrilled when he heard about Kennedy.

Tanner sighed. "Out with it then."

"Tanner?" a girl called from somewhere down the hall. "Are you coming back to bed?"

I laughed. "So you weren't that worried," I said.

"It's better to be distracted while worried. It makes time fly." He turned around. "I'll be back in a minute!" he called to her.

"Isn't the saying that time flies when you're having fun?"

He shrugged. "Yeah, distractions can be fun. Tell me your thing."

For once I could make him wait. Yes, I'd kept him worried all night. But he'd been busy with that girl. Surely he wasn't that worried. And he always made me wait for stuff. "I'll tell you tonight."

"What, when you don't come home before curfew?"

"Sick burn, Master," Nigel said. He lifted up his hand and Tanner slapped it. But it seemed like Nigel was going for more of a handshake. Because he ended up awkwardly grabbing Tanner's hand mid-high-five.

"Nigel, whatever are you doing?" Tanner pulled away. "High-fives are the protocol right now. We've discussed this."

Nigel nodded. "Yes, Master."

So weird.

"Ignore Nigel. He's forgetful," Tanner said. "When can I expect you home this evening? Don't answer that. I have the perfect restaurant. And before you roll your eyes, you owe me."

"I never roll my eyes," I said.

"Internally. And before you even ask, yes, I'll be scoping out the place for events. And yes, you do have to pretend to be my date. So come to terms with your masculinity and get over it. If you'll excuse me, Veronica needs my assistance."

"Your assistance?"

Tanner laughed. "I may have tied her up. It's truly refreshing. Women get kinkier and kinkier as time marches on."

"What, since you were in high school?"

"Hmm? Yes. Exactly." He picked up the paper off the floor. I didn't see any sign of Poppy's forced pictures on the page he'd been on.

"Nigel will send you the location of the restaurant," Tanner said. "7 o'clock sharp. I don't want to be late for our reservation." He walked away, knowing that I wouldn't say no. I was kind of at his mercy here.

"Here you go, Mr. Caldwell," Nigel said and produced one of those green hangover smoothies. "Just in case."

"Thanks, Nigel. What's the secret ingredient in this anyway?" I took a sip and the little bit of pressure in my head faded instantly.

"It's a secret," Nigel said with a wink.

I forced myself to swallow down the sip I'd taken. The way Nigel said it made it really seem like he'd skeeted in it or something. "Um…I should get to work." I tried to hand it back to him.

"Once you finish that. And your lunch is packed. I'll draw you another bath tonight, but no rose petals this time. They're a pain to fish out of cold, unused bath water."

"I'm sorry about the last two nights. But I don't need you to draw me a bath, Nigel. We've been over this."

"It's no problem. I like preparing it for you. Have a good day at work, Mr. Caldwell." He turned on his heel and walked away too.

Tanner was really generous for letting me stay with him. But tonight I would fill him in on the deal I'd made with Poppy. As long as I kept pretending to be Poppy's boyfriend, I could be safe back at my place. I wasn't sure how much more I could take of Nigel. I picked up one of their discarded papers and flipped through it.

There was a picture of Poppy holding my hand on top of the table. It looked intimate and quite real. I cringed and threw out both papers. I needed to explain this to Kennedy. And to my friends before they all jumped to a wild conclusion. Well, not that wild, considering the picture. I shot off a text to James asking him to meet up, already knowing what his reaction would be. He'd tell me not to get mixed up with someone from Mr. Pruitt's family. Because there was no way out.

CHAPTER 33

Thursday

I kept looking over my shoulder. But it wasn't because I was scared someone was out there watching me. I was just excited for Kennedy to arrive. Inviting her here may not have been my best idea. But I thought if she could stand on this field and feel okay with it…then we could figure everything else out.

Mrs. Alcaraz had implied that Kennedy was a flight risk. I'd never seen her that way, though. She was loyal. Moving out of the city hadn't made her forget about Brooklyn. It had just given her the space she needed to live. I hadn't allowed myself that space. But maybe I was ready. Honestly, if I wasn't coaching this team, I'd probably convince Kennedy to jump on a flight with me today. I'd go anywhere as long as it was far away from here. I think I needed some distance. I think I was allowed that.

I exhaled slowly. Brooklyn would have wanted me to be happy. Just like she would have wanted me to make sure things were right with James. I was going to stop by his place after dinner with Tanner. I'd fix it. I'd fix everything I'd made a mess of.

I watched Jefferson's extra point attempt. This time the ball didn't even leave the ground. It just rolled along the grass, looking as sad and defeated as Jefferson.

I blew my whistle to call him over.

"You're hitting your laces again."

"Am I?" He looked like he had no idea he'd made any kind of mistake.

How many times had we talked about this? This kid was going to be the death of me. "Take a deep breath for me." I'd read that meditation could really help with focus.

Jefferson breathed in for a second and then sneezed. "Sorry, Coach Caldwell. I have really bad fall allergies."

Of course you do. "That's okay. Don't worry about breathing deeply. What I want you to do is go out there. And instead of focusing on kicking the ball, focus on the sound of your breath. In and out."

"So don't kick the ball?" he asked.

"No, kick the ball. Just don't think about it."

Jefferson shrugged. "I'll try." He jogged back out onto the field. He stared at the ball like he was concentrating on it even more than usual.

"Sorry I'm late," Kennedy said. "My client was being excruciatingly...specific."

I laughed and pulled her into a hug. My first thought had been to kiss her. But I didn't want to overwhelm her. Being here was a lot. I knew that. I pulled back, but kept my arm draped over her shoulders. She didn't move away.

We both watched as Jefferson studied the football like he had never seen one before. Seriously, what was he doing? That was the exact opposite of what I'd asked him to do.

"Breathe, Jefferson!" I shouted, my arm slipping from Kennedy's shoulders.

He proceeded to sneeze as he kicked the ball. It went way left and into the stands.

At least he had some power behind it that time.

Jefferson ran after the ball to retrieve it.

"Wow, you found someone as bad as Prescott to be your kicker?" Kennedy whispered. "Is it like a nostalgia thing...or..."

I laughed. "No. It's a popularity thing." I watched as Jefferson leaned over, out of breath from running up the bleachers.

"Really? He's part of a new group of young Untouchables, huh?" She tilted her head as she looked at him. "Times really do change."

I lightly jabbed her with my elbow. "No, I'm trying to make him popular."

She raised her eyebrows at me.

"I figured if I could teach him how to be an amazing kicker he'd win some points with the other guys. Maybe get a girlfriend or something. Or just a few friends in general."

"And he usually kicks the way I just witnessed?"

"It's a work in progress."

Kennedy shook her head. "Wait, so let me get this straight. You think that having him on the team missing extra points and field goals…"

"I rarely let him attempt a field goal."

"Matt. How is that supposed to help him? You're making it worse. Can't you see that?"

I'd had a sinking feeling that was true as the weeks had progressed.

"You wouldn't understand because you were born popular," she said.

"That's not true."

"Mason was a golden boy before you even stepped foot in the school. You were a god immediately because of association. And then you topped it all off by being a star wide receiver. Abs of steel. A perfect smile. You had it easy. Don't pretend you didn't."

She thought I had a perfect smile? I couldn't help but flash her one. "Just for the record, I've worked really hard on my abs of steel."

She laughed and shook her head. "Tell me about your kicker."

"He's a freshman. He walked onto the field all on his own. I didn't scout him or anything. But I heard the other kids making fun of him for being a scholarship student. And I didn't want to turn him away."

Kennedy's eyes softened. "He's a scholarship student?"

"Yeah."

"Well, I know that's no fun." She pressed her lips together and fidgeted with a strand of loose hair hanging from her bun. "I'll fix this. I used to think of how I could help Prescott back in the day in case he'd ever thought I was cool enough to talk to."

I laughed. "So what's your grand plan?"

"Watch and learn, Coach Caldwell." She patted my chest as Jefferson walked up to us.

"Hey," Kennedy said. "I'm Kennedy, a friend of Coach Caldwell's. What's your name?" She put her hand out for him to shake.

"Henry Jefferson." He shook her hand.

"Nice to meet you, Henry. What's your favorite subject in school?"

"I like English."

Kennedy nodded and seemed to think for a moment. "Anything else? Coach mentioned that you're a scholarship student here. When I went to Empire High, I was one too."

"You were?"

"Mhm. And as a fellow scholarship student, I know for a fact that you must be good at a lot of subjects. Better than any of these guys." She gestured behind her at the field. "Right?"

Jefferson laughed.

"Tell me, what's another class you're really great in? A star student?"

"Umm…" Jefferson looked at me and then back at Kennedy. "I'm really good at geometry."

Kennedy smiled. "Perfect. Matt, do you mind if I help Henry study some geometry?"

What? That was surprisingly unhelpful of her. But honestly what did it matter if he spent the rest of practice doing geometry instead of practicing? He wasn't getting any better. And I was running out of ideas. Besides, I hadn't seen Jefferson smile at practice in a while. And he was smiling now. That was a win in my book. "Sure."

I watched Kennedy and Jefferson sit down on one of the benches. They were talking animatedly as Jefferson pulled out a textbook.

I'd planned to hang out with Kennedy during practice. Show her how normal it was to be here. How the ghosts were at bay. Except when I'd see Brooklyn's face during a crowded game. Or if I went into the school. I wouldn't be going back in there any time soon.

I watched Kennedy laughing with Jefferson. But she seemed okay. Actually, she seemed more than okay. She looked genuinely happy. A feeling I'd been chasing for a while. She looked up at me watching her and smiled.

My eyes flitted between her and the field throughout the rest of practice. It was hard not to watch her. She was so full of life. And watching how she made Jefferson laugh made my chest feel a little lighter. Maybe she was right. Maybe I didn't really understand him like she could.

Right before practice ended, Jefferson ran back out onto the field. Kennedy joined me by my side.

"Hold your breath," she said.

I looked down at her. "What?"

She grabbed my hand. "It's good luck, Matt. Just hold your breath and watch." She squeezed my hand tighter.

I did as I was told. I held my breath as Jefferson swung and his foot made contact with the football. The ball went up into the air, straighter than I had ever seen him hit it before. Higher, higher. A perfect arc. And straight through the uprights.

Kennedy started screaming. She pulled her hand out of mine and threw both of hers up into the air. "Go, Henry!!!"

I started cheering too.

And the whole team joined in. Jumping and cheering, and chanting Jefferson's name. A few of his teammates hoisted him up on their shoulders.

"Jeff-er-son! Jeff-er-son! Jeff-er-son!"

I felt tears in the corners of my eyes. He did it. He fucking did it!

Kennedy was jumping up and down clapping.

I leaned down and lifted her into my arms, twirling her around as she laughed. She wrapped her legs around my waist. "He did it!" she yelled. "Go, Henry!" She clasped her hands behind my neck, laughing.

"You did it," I said in awe. "How the hell did you get through to him?" The chants of Jefferson's name seemed to fade away as I stared at her.

"It's all about the angles," Kennedy said. "We figured out what angle he needed to hit it at. He's really good at geometry."

"You're incredible."

She laughed. "I just used his strengths…"

I kissed her. Not caring that the whole team could see. Not caring that I was standing in the middle of the Empire High football stadium. Not caring that she was supposed to be my friend and only my friend. Kennedy Alcaraz was a rock star. And she deserved to be told that every day. Brooklyn would always be my first love. But that didn't mean she had to be my last. It didn't mean I had to be miserable every day. I laughed as Kennedy pulled away to cheer for Jefferson again.

I wanted to be happy with her.

I put her back down on the ground and she grabbed my hand so we could run into the middle of the field to celebrate with the team.

"You okay, Coach?" Smith asked. "Looks like you're about to cry."

"Shut it, Smith." I wasn't about to cry. I was just...happy. Well, not entirely happy. I didn't love the way some of the players were ogling Kennedy.

Smith laughed. "There's no way we won't go undefeated now. Hell, I'm about to cry too. Go, Jefferson!"

I pulled Smith into a hug. Because for once in his life, it seemed like he'd stopped being an ass. Today was a good day.

"Your girlfriend's hot," he said.

Nope, moment over. I blew my whistle. "Great practice everyone!" And this time, I actually meant it. For the first time, every single player was an all-star. "Now get out of here before I change my mind and make you do sprints!" I watched as the players left, Jefferson actually running in the pack for once.

Kennedy started helping me pick up the practice balls.

"You don't have to help," I said.

"It's fine." She grabbed another ball balancing a pile of them in her arms. "I'm basically a coach now too, don't you think?"

I laughed as I picked up the last one. "Coach Alcaraz has a nice ring to it, huh?"

"Absolutely."

We dumped the balls in my equipment bag and I hoisted it over my shoulder. "You know…I don't actually have an assistant coach."

"Are you asking me to be your number two?"

I smiled at her as we made our way to the parking lot. "Yes." I stared at her. Maybe in more ways than one. "I am."

"It was really fun seeing Henry smile so hard."

"You know everyone calls him Jefferson, right?"

She shrugged. "I like first names. It's more personal. Maybe you should give it a try. I might implement first names only as assistant coach."

"You can't do that."

"Watch me. We'll go undefeated under me."

"We're already undefeated."

"Whatever you say."

"Don't let this go to your head, Alcaraz. I'm still the head coach. And you have to respect my authority."

She laughed as we stopped by my car. "I will never respect your authority. And Alcaraz? Seriously? Don't call me that."

"What do you want me to call you?" I stepped forward and she backed up until her ass hit the passenger's side door.

She didn't say a word, she just stared at me. But I could tell her mind was racing.

"How about baby?" I suggested. "Or babe? Sugar muffin?"

She'd started smiling halfway through the options.

"No? Sex rocket?"

Now she was full on laughing. "Sex rocket? Who the hell would want to be called that?" She started laughing harder.

"Okay. How about I call you my girlfriend?" It was a cheesy thing to say. I felt like an idiot as soon as her laughter died in her throat. What the hell was I thinking? It was too fast. She'd barely agreed to kiss me this morning. But when you spent 16 years being miserable, it was easy to latch on to happiness. And standing here with her? It didn't feel like I'd wasted half my life away. I felt like I was 16 years old again. I felt young and alive and happy. Didn't she?

"Girlfriend? I can't be your girlfriend," she whispered.

I dropped the equipment bag and put my hands on either side of the car, caging her in. "Why not?"

"You know why not. Matt, what are we doing?"

"Dating."

"We're not dating. I didn't say yes."

I leaned forward and kissed her. Despite her words, she kissed me back. Her throat making that adorable moaning noise I was starting to crave at all hours of the day. I pulled away just as she started to pull me closer. "Then what do you call this?"

"Kissing."

I raised my eyebrow. "That's it?"

"Really good kissing?"

"Don't overthink this." I dropped my forehead to hers.

"How can I not overthink this? You and I can't be together. It breaks all the rules of friendship. I…I can't. I shouldn't have even kissed you. I've been twisted up inside all day."

She didn't think I'd been thinking of that? About how wrong this was? But I was fucking sick of living like this. Kennedy made me happy. And I just wanted to be happy. "Fine, I'll call you Alcaraz."

She groaned. "I don't want you to call me that."

"No? Well, it's either that or girlfriend. Your choice."

"You're impossible." She leaned back, folding her arms across her chest. "Fine. Whatever. Call me your girlfriend."

I smiled.

"Stop smiling so hard. You're not supposed to be happy about this. It's weird."

"It's not that weird. But is this better?" I gave her an exaggerated frown.

She reached out, touching the corners of my mouth. "No. I changed my mind. Keep the smile."

I smiled and her hands slid to my neck.

"Okay, first serious question since we made it exclusive," I said.

She rolled her eyes.

"How is your ankle doing?"

"What? Oh." Her cheeks turned rosy. "It's doing a lot better today."

"Really? Wasn't it still hurting pretty bad last night?" I'd been wondering about this all day. She'd run away from me this morning without a single grimace. I was starting to think she was a dirty liar. A very sexy dirty liar.

"Yes," she said. "It hurt a lot last night."

"Are you sure about that? You didn't just want me to come over?"

"*You* texted *me*."

I stared at her.

"It did hurt last night still. But fine, I may have over-exaggerated slightly. Because I like hanging out with you. Is that a crime?" She lightly shoved my shoulder.

I was smiling so hard it hurt.

"You already asked me to be your girlfriend and there's no takesie-backsies."

I laughed. "Get in the car."

She turned around. "What are you doing driving in the city? There's a subway. And taxis. And no reason to own a car. It's one of the best parts of being here."

"Do you want a ride?"

She smiled. "Yes. I was just kidding. I hate the subway, it smells like pee. And taxis are for people who aren't assistant coaches."

I laughed and opened the passenger door for her. "The team has a bye this week. But next week be ready to take that title seriously."

"Oh, I'll take it very seriously. I promise." She smiled at me and ducked in.

We were quiet as I pulled out of the parking lot.

"It's too weird," she finally said, breaking the silence. "We can't date."

"You already said no takesie-backsies."

She smiled. "Fine. But we need a test drive. Where are we going for dinner?"

Oh. Shit. "I have dinner with a friend tonight. But tomorrow?"

She nodded. "Yeah, that's fine." But her face didn't scream "it's fine." She looked worried. Like she'd just made a deal with the devil. Yesterday I'd had a business dinner. Today I had dinner with a friend. I knew what was going on in her mind. And she didn't have a thing to worry about.

"Tomorrow," I said more firmly. "It's a date."

She smiled up at me. "Okay then."

"Our first official date. The pressure is on," I said.

"Don't make it even weirder."

I smiled over at her. "I promise there will be nothing weird about our date tomorrow. It's going to be the best date of your life."

Normally when I said stuff like that, women would practically swoon.

But Kennedy just laughed. "More like the best date of *your* life. Because you'll be eating dinner with the best assistant coach in town, and I'm not even planning on trying to set your dick on fire."

I really shouldn't have told her about that.

CHAPTER 34

Thursday

I couldn't wipe the smile off my face as I walked toward the romantic restaurant Tanner had picked. The rose petals all over the marble floors in the entranceway didn't bother me. And I didn't care that the hostess practically forced me to take a complimentary rose for my date. Or the fact that the dim lighting was dangerously close to being erotic instead of romantic. Honestly, this was probably a great place for a Club Onyx event. Tanner would be pleased.

The hostess rearranged her bucket of roses to accommodate the missing space, then checked her book for the reservation.

This was going to be epically gay. But I was too happy to care. I'd play along with Tanner's restaurant scouting tonight to apologize for making him worry two nights in a row. And he could celebrate my good news and commiserate with me on my bad news. I just couldn't stop smiling. *Fuck Poppy.* I didn't even care about that. But I was hoping Tanner would have some advice on how to delicately explain my relationship with Poppy to Kennedy. He was good at stuff like that. Finagling his way out of a crunch. I needed to figure out a way to tell Kennedy that wouldn't result in her dumping me. I really liked her. I just needed to sort out this mess.

"Right this way," the hostess said.

Tanner was already seated at our table.

I knew he'd reprimand me if I didn't pretend we were on a date. For the sake of leaning into the role and tricking the waiters into giving us the full treatment, I handed Tanner the rose that the hostess had made me take. "Your rose, monsieur," I said in a terrible French accent. Hopefully that was good enough.

Tanner stood up. "You magnificent, secretive beast! I knew it! You're in love, you're in love, and you don't care who knows it!" He grabbed both sides of my face and planted a kiss right on my lips.

What the actual fuck? I made a gagging noise.

Tanner ignored it. He pulled back and patted my cheeks. "I knew it, you scoundrel. Tell me everything."

I swatted his hands away. I'd seen him mouth kiss random people at bars when he was excited. I preferred he did that instead of planting one on me. I wiped my mouth off with the back of my hand. Sometimes I forgot that he grew up overseas. Or went to school overseas. Or did something overseas for some vague period of time he'd never tell me about. Had I somehow reminded him of those memories? It was probably the French accent. I'd have to make sure never to speak a foreign language in front of him again.

"You're speechless," Tanner said. "I understand. Love makes people lose their thoughts." He leaned forward and hugged me super tight, practically lifting me off the ground.

At least he wasn't kissing me again. "Tanner, I'm pretty sure you sold the whole dating act to everyone in the restaurant. Let me go."

"What?" He released me from his embrace. "Sold what? Matt, we're celebrating the fact that you're officially in a relationship again." He picked up a magazine off the table and waved it in the air.

I grabbed it to see what he was talking about. Poppy and I were making out on the front page. Or at least, it looked like we were. I'd gagged as much during that kiss as

I had when Tanner just planted one on me. "It's not what it looks like."

"I'm going to give you two a moment," the hostess said and quickly walked away.

"Damn," Tanner said. "Now she's going to think we're not together."

"Tanner everyone in the fucking restaurant thinks we're together. You just kissed me."

"I didn't kiss you," he said and sat down like he hadn't just put his lips directly on mine.

I sat down too and leaned forward, hoping that a lower voice would make everyone stop staring at us. "What the fuck do you mean you didn't just kiss me? I spoke in French and you literally tried to put your tongue down my throat."

He laughed. "Gross. I don't want my tongue anywhere near your tonsils. I was simply congratulating you with a platonic celebratory peck. And I feel sorry for you for never having received one in your few years on this earth."

"You are so weird."

"You're weird," he said, even though he didn't look very insulted by my comment. "Americans are so basic."

I laughed and shook my head. He was technically an American too.

"Next time I won't congratulate you then. I'll just sit here brooding eating my pastrami and bagels," he said in an overexaggerated New York City accent, that sounded very mobstery. "Actually, I don't think they have either of those things. Maybe a New York City style cheesecake for your basic ass."

"Okay, I get it. I'm basic. Don't kiss me again."

Tanner sighed. "Don't make it sound so gay. It wasn't a gay thing. Now pretend we're on a date so the waiters treat us the right way."

"So don't be gay? But be gay?"

"What? No. You're just not getting it. We're straight men on a fake gay date. Now let's talk about your actual kiss. I thought you said you didn't like Poppy? But you're on the front page of a dozen tabloids right now giving her an un-congratulatory kiss. I need to meet her immediately. Please tell me you haven't sealed the deal yet."

"Gross. She made me do it."

"Are you telling me she put hands on you without permission?" He looked very concerned as he leaned forward. "You can tell me."

"No. What? Are you seriously asking me if I got raped?"

"If you don't want to talk about it, but it's true, blink twice. If you're in a fragile state, I don't mind talking to the police on your behalf. But if you could at least write down the details it would be helpful for the statement."

I didn't blink at all. "Poppy and I just made an arrangement."

"Of the sexual variety? What was the contract like? I'd love to see it, just in case it gives me a few more ideas."

"No, not of the sexual variety. She agreed to not hurt Scarlett as long as I pretend to date her."

"Well that's a boring contract."

"I didn't sign anything. It's just a verbal agreement. Poppy wants to take over the family business and doesn't think Mr. Pruitt will step down until she seems like she can handle the finances. She thinks dating me will show her uncle that she's serious about every aspect of the business. And the deal is only going to last as long as it takes for her to take over for Mr. Pruitt."

Tanner just stared at me. "So have you had sex with her yet or not?"

"I'm not going to sleep with her."

"Oh." Tanner sighed. "Well, what a waste of a congratulatory kiss."

"Yeah, if you ever try to kiss me again, I'll punch you in the face."

He laughed. "In your dreams. Both the kissing and the punching. You couldn't punch me. I'm much too quick. I'd have you rolling on the floor in pain before you even lifted your hand."

"Yeah right."

"Indeed. I am right."

I reached out, not to punch him, but maybe just to slap him to prove my point.

But he grabbed my hand before it came anywhere close to him. He slammed it onto the table, twisting my arm so I was leaning over. He'd somehow grabbed a steak knife at the same time and was hovering it over my hand too.

"What the fuck?" I said.

He let me go, then twirled the knife in his hand and stabbed it into the bread on the table. "Can't touch me."

I rubbed my hand. Now I really did want to slap him. But I'd wait until I got a better opportunity. It would have to be a sneak slap-attack.

"Shall we order?" he asked and lifted up his menu.

"Where did you learn to do that?" I rubbed my hand again.

"Do what?"

"That kung fu shit you just did."

"Oh, I just picked it up over the years. Oh wow, they do have cheesecake. Should I order you some?"

"I'm good." I picked up the menu to look at the options.

"I'm just messing with you anyway," Tanner said and set down the menu. "I hope you're hungry because I already know what I'm going to order for us."

Of course he did. He'd want to know how delectable their specialties were.

He waved over the waiter and ordered half the menu. When the waiter finally walked away, looking a little frazzled, Tanner sighed.

"They don't seem to handle stress here very well," he said. "That's telling. They probably wouldn't like surprises either." He jotted something down in his notebook. "Could you imagine one of those big cages over there with some models dancing in it?"

I looked over to where he was pointing. "Sure. It would probably fit."

"Excellent."

"So..." I let my voice trail off. I needed to word this as nicely as possible. "I really appreciate you letting me stay with you during all this craziness with Mr. Pruitt. But now that I have that deal with Poppy...I should be safe to go back to my house."

"You're sure she's trustworthy?" he asked.

No. Not really. But Nigel was driving me crazy. I couldn't stay with Tanner any longer unless I wanted Nigel to...get the wrong idea or something. "Yeah, Poppy will stick to her word."

Tanner nodded. "Well, regardless, you'll have to speak to Nigel about it. He'll need to coordinate your move back."

"I can't talk to Nigel about it. He'll never let me leave."

"Of course he will. I'll tell him to be accommodating. Surely he has room in his schedule. He moved you out of your house in record time if I remember correctly."

Yeah, but that was because I was coming to live with him. Not moving out. "Did you know that he writes me letters and puts them in my lunches?" I pulled out the one Nigel gave me today and handed it to Tanner.

"You kept it? That's cute."

"I kept it in case I show up murdered and they're looking for a suspect."

"Nigel isn't violent. He's a caretaker if anything."

"Maybe to you. He creeps me out. Look at what your weird little houseboy said to me."

Tanner unfolded the letter and started reading aloud.

Mr. Caldwell,

You never told me if you liked meat, but I assume since you didn't complain about your last lunch that you really like it. So I gave you double today.

As always, I want to make you as comfortable as possible in Master Tanner's abode. Please let me know if there's anything else you need me to acquire. I'm at your disposal any time. Day or night. I put my number below again because you haven't called or texted yet. It's best to send me special requests that way. It's a private line, in case you're worried about interlopers.

Have a lovely and fetching day at work. No fighting with the other boys, remember. The last thing I want to have to do is reprimand you again. Speaking of which, I forgive you for making me worry last night. But I will need details to fully recover from the agony. I'll let you explain where you were last night to me during your bath.

Yours,
-Nigel
XOXO

P.S. I will keep giving you meat until you text me otherwise.

Tanner folded the letter and handed it back to me. "That's so sweet of him. He never leaves me notes. Well, maybe he used to at first. I can't remember, it's been so long."

"Sweet? More like murdery."

"It seemed normal enough to me. What from that lovely note would possibly make you think he wants to lop off your head?"

"Poor choice of words. I think he probably wants to give me head."

Tanner laughed. "Nigel isn't gay. You're leaning into this role here tonight a little too hard. Really, the note was kind and caring. Like I said, he's a caretaker if anything."

"He wants to watch me bathe."

"Surely there will be bubbles hiding anything unseemly."

"Tanner, Nigel is clearly into me. He makes me very uncomfortable."

Tanner sighed. "Please don't tell him that. His sole purpose is to make you feel comfortable. He said it in his note. He'd be devastated."

"Well, I don't want to devastate him."

"Your parents were moderately wealthy," Tanner said. "I can't believe you didn't grow up with a houseboy. They just take some getting used to. It took me forever to think of Nigel as more of a friend than the little nuisance he sometimes insists on being."

Moderately wealthy? All my life I would have said exorbitantly. But that was before I'd met Tanner. "If you didn't like him originally, why didn't you fire him?"

"Oh it wasn't my choice, believe me. I'm stuck with him. But we've set our boundaries now and my house runs seamlessly."

And Tanner thinks I'm the weird one?

"Enough about Nigel. Tell me more about your contract with Poppy. Is it ironclad?"

It wasn't. "Actually, I have some other non-Poppy related news that I want to discuss with you. But I want to make it clear that you shouldn't mouth kiss me again." I was suddenly nervous and I had no idea why. Brooklyn had been my one and only girlfriend. I'd been adamant about not dating anyone else after her death. This was a big deal for me. And as one of my best friends, I wanted Tanner to be happy for me. But I had this weird feeling he'd make me feel like shit. For breaking my vow to love Brooklyn and only Brooklyn.

Tanner laughed. "I promise to not celebrate whatever it is you're about to say."

I pressed my lips together for a second. "I'm not dating Poppy. But I am dating Kennedy, Brooklyn's best friend. I asked her to make it official."

Tanner's smile grew with each word. "I'd celebratorily peck you so hard right now if you hadn't made me promise I wouldn't. I'm really happy for you, man."

"Yeah?"

"Of course. I've been wanting to set you up for ages. And look at you. You're practically glowing."

I laughed. "Well, I doubt I'm glowing. But...you really think it's okay? That I'm dating her?"

"Why wouldn't it be?" Tanner held up his hand. "Whatever you're thinking right now, cut it out. You're allowed to be happy, Matt. You're allowed to live your life. You only get one. It's over in the blink of an eye. You've already wasted enough years being miserable. This is a good thing."

I nodded. "I am happy."

"Champagne!" Tanner yelled. "Champagne for everyone!"

"You don't need to do that."

"Actually, you're doing it, because you're paying."

I opened my mouth to protest, but then closed it. *Fuck it.* "Champagne for everyone!" I yelled.

The restaurant started cheering.

"Oooh, they cheer when they're surprised," Tanner said. "I like that." He jotted it down in his notebook and then looked back up at me. "So Kennedy is fine with your ruse with Poppy?"

"Kennedy doesn't exactly know about that. Yet. I need to tell her. I'm just trying to figure out how."

Tanner sighed. "Sabotaging it from the very beginning, are we? Not on my watch. We won't leave until we have a plan, you have my word."

"Good. Because I really don't want to screw this up."

"I have one condition for my help though. You have to give me your word that I can meet Kennedy before you sleep with her."

"No problem. We're taking things slow." Kennedy wanted to be swept off her feet like she was in a Disney movie. I wasn't a prince. But I knew how to make her laugh. And I had a few ideas to keep a smile on her beautiful face.

CHAPTER 35

Thursday

"You really don't need to come with me," I said as Tanner and I exited the elevator on James' floor. "It's kind of a private conversation."

Tanner slapped me on the back. "There is no privacy between best friends. Besides, it's on the way home. And I hate sitting in the car."

Fair enough. I knocked on James' door.

A second later, Scarlett opened it.

What the actual fuck? "Scarlett we talked about this. You're not supposed to answer the door alone."

She blinked up at me. "It was another accident."

"Scarlett, you're in big trouble…"

"Nuh uh, Uncle Matt. *You're* in big trouble. Mommy said so."

"Your mom said that?"

Scarlett nodded and then looked over at Tanner. "She talked about you too, Mr. Tanner."

Tanner smiled. "Am I in trouble too?"

"No. She said you and Uncle Matt were…" Scarlett scrunched her face up as she thought. "I didn't know the word. And I forgot it."

"Like you forgot you're not supposed to answer doors?" I asked.

Scarlett smiled. "Yes?"

Luckily for her, I had her back. She'd be safe now. At least from the Pruitts and Cannavaros. But from random strangers at the door? "Scar," I said and crouched down to look at her. "How many times are we going to need to have this conversation?"

"Maybe…once more."

"Stop opening up the door, kiddo."

"I don't think you're allowed to tell me what to do, Uncle Matt. You're not my daddy."

"So you want me to tell your dad what you did?"

She stuck her hand out. "Deal."

I'd taught her about the art of negotiation a few months ago. She didn't quite get it. But I'm pretty sure she thought the deal was that I wouldn't tell her dad. Not the deal she'd actually just accidentally made where I would tell him. "And you won't do it again?"

"Deal."

I shook her hand.

"Is that present for me?" She gestured to the gift bag I was holding.

"Not today." I patted her head.

"Who's it for?"

"Your dad."

"Oh." She sighed. "He's working. I'll get my mommy." She ran off. "Mommy! Mommy! Uncle Matt is here!"

"Such a cute kid," Tanner said. "Pretty terrible at the negotiation table though."

I laughed. "Yeah, she could use some work in that area. And in the area involving telling the truth. Why does she keep saying she accidentally opened the door? You can't accidentally do that."

"Did you accidentally shove your tongue down this horrid woman's throat?" Penny said as she stormed into the foyer. She lifted up a tabloid with a picture of Poppy and me kissing before hitting me with it. "She's a Pruitt!"

I grabbed the tabloid out of her hand. "Technically she's a Cannavaro…"

"Are you kidding me, Matt? You know what that family's capable of. She just threatened my daughter and you're making out with her?"

This was a funny misunderstanding. Maybe that's why I couldn't seem to wipe the smile off my face. Or maybe it was because I hadn't stopped smiling since I asked Kennedy out. "I can see how that looks but…"

Tanner started laughing.

"And you," Penny said turning to him. "Of all people, you should be upset about this too, Tanner."

"Why me exactly?" Tanner asked. "I've never actually met the woman." He lifted the tabloid from my hand. "She's rather attractive, albeit apparently insane."

Penny looked back and forth between us. "I don't know what the hell is going on. Or why you both look so happy. But Matt, I am so done with whatever mind games you're playing. Sending me on a wild goose chase trying to set you up with people when the whole time you were…I honestly have no idea what you're doing. But you can't come into my house if you're seeing that woman."

"Penny," James said as he joined us in the foyer. "I can handle this."

"I'm serious, Matt," Penny said, ignoring James. "She'll never step foot in here. I don't trust anyone from that family. And if you do, you're completely insane."

"Penny," James said more sternly.

I'd never heard him talk to Penny like that. His short temper was usually reserved for…well, me. And I understood why what she said upset him. He was worried that I'd be offended that Penny had said *that family*. Because of Brooklyn. But honestly? I was just happy tonight. And the Pruitts did suck balls.

"Good luck," Penny said to James. "He's clearly lost his mind. Poppy Cannavaro. What is it with you men and evil brunettes from crime families?" She left the foyer as quickly as she had come in.

"Still a little touchy about what happened with Isabella, I see?" Tanner said. "It's best to let things go, I always say."

"Tanner, if you'll excuse us, I need to have a word with Matt in private," James said.

Every word that left his mouth made him look more and more agitated. I'd been on the other side of one of his fists before. And I didn't feel like icing a black eye tonight. Kennedy would have too many questions about that.

"It's fine," I said. "Anything you want to say to me you can say in front of Tanner."

Tanner nodded.

"Whatever you want," James said. "Both of you come this way then." He turned around and started walking toward his study.

Tanner looked at me.

I shrugged and we both followed him.

The lights were off in James' study, and as soon as we stepped in, the door was slammed and locked behind us. Then the lights turned on.

James, Rob, and Mason were all sitting in a semi-circle staring at me.

"Um, what's up, guys?" I asked. They were all looking up at me awkwardly. It felt like I'd just walked in on something really weird. "I thought guys' night was tomorrow?" Actually, this was good. I could apologize to all of them at once. *Wonderful.*

"For fuck's sake," Rob said. "Who invited Tanner to the intervention?"

"Intervention?" I asked. I stared at them staring at me. *Oh.* I should have expected this. I'd been a fucking mess recently. But not tonight. Not now. So I just did the only thing I could do and laughed.

"Why are you laughing?" Rob asked. "This is serious."

I tried to wipe the smile off my face to no avail. At least now I knew why James looked so serious. "And what exactly is this intervention for?"

"You being...sad," Mason said. He was staring at the smile on my face that I couldn't get rid of.

I shrugged. "Right, that. I'm good. Actually, I'm great. I appreciate you guys worrying about me, but I'm seriously doing a lot better." I would have told them about Kennedy. But I wanted it to be a surprise when I brought her to guys' night tomorrow. It was a silly idea for our first date. It would make her smile though. And that's all I really cared about. She wouldn't be impressed by a fancy dinner or anything. Kennedy wasn't like that.

"Are you high or something?" Rob asked.

"Nope. I've had a few drinks, but I'm sober enough to know that I feel amazing. I actually came by to apologize to James, but now I can apologize to all of you, so this is perfect. But I wished I knew you were all coming because I only got an apology present for James." I handed him the gift bag.

James just stared at me.

"What exactly are you apologizing for?" Rob asked.

"Great question. First off, I'm sorry that I made you all lie to your wives about Brooklyn ever existing. I shouldn't have done that. Real shitty move on my part."

Mason nodded.

"And for really not letting any of you talk about Brooklyn for all these years. Not talking about something doesn't make those feelings just go away. I know she was a friend to all of you too. I wasn't the only one that lost someone, and it was rather selfish of me to act like I was."

Rob just stared at me like he still thought I was high.

"And I think I'm most sorry for the fact that I blamed you two for her death." I pointed at Rob and James. "That was ridiculous. Yes, the last time I saw Brooklyn alive I had a fight with her because of the prank you all pulled. I blamed you two for my last words to her. For making Brooklyn feel like she had no one on her side when she died. I just needed someone else to blame. Because I hate that I did that. I hate what I said to her. I hate that I left her. I promised her I would never walk away from us. I promised her. And I lied. I walked away and left her with Mr. Pruitt. I know it's not your guys' fault that she died. Because it's mine." *It's my fucking fault.*

Mason shook his head. "It's not your fault."

"It's Mr. Pruitt's," Rob said.

I nodded, the smile suddenly gone from my face. "But if I'd stayed by her side…"

"Mr. Pruitt still would have found a way to get what he wanted from her," James said. "You know that. You never could have prevented Brooklyn from hanging out with her dad one-on-one. And I'm sorry that the two of you got in a fight because of what Rob and I did. I truly am. And I'm sorry I wasn't sober enough to make better choices back then. I'm sorry that you were worried I'd take my own life. I'm sorry I ever made you worry about that."

Mason and Rob were quiet.

"All of you," James said. "I'm sorry, guys. I was in a bad place. But I never meant to drag any of you down there with me. I didn't realize I was doing that."

I was surprised James brought that up. I was supposed to be apologizing to him for snapping at him the other night. Not the other way around.

I'm sure we'd all been worried about James hurting himself over the years. But I was done holding grudges.

"You don't have to apologize." I tried to shake away that feeling in my stomach that talking about Brooklyn always stirred up. The guilt that had been eating me away for 16 years. I needed to forgive my friends. But I needed to forgive myself too. If I had any chance of giving Kennedy a life she deserved, I needed to let this go. It was time. Past time, really. Besides, I'd made Mrs. Alcaraz a new promise. And promises to the living were more important than promises to the dead. They had to be. Because I couldn't keep going like this. I took a deep breath.

"I'm just really fucking sorry, guys," I said. "For everything. And I don't want there to be any resentment between us. I don't want you to walk on eggshells around me or worry about me being okay. Because I am okay. I think I'm more okay right now than I've been since Brooklyn died." I shook my head. "I just want all of us to be happy. You guys are my best friends."

Tanner cleared his throat.

"All of you," I said. "Can we just try to…move on from the past?"

"We all made a lot of mistakes," Rob said. "I'm sorry too."

"You have nothing to apologize for," I said.

"Does this mean you're done with that fake smile bullshit you've been doing for the last 16 years?" Mason asked. "Because you may have tricked mom with that, but you look insane when you do that."

Wow, I'd thought I'd nailed the fake smile thing. "No more fake smiles necessary."

Mason looked relieved.

"So you guys forgive me?" I asked. This conversation had been easier than I thought it would be.

Mason and Rob both nodded.

"Of course," Mason said. "We weren't looking for an apology. We just wanted to make sure you were okay."

Rob nodded.

But James stared at me. "When you were worried about me, you had my back," he said. "And I need to return the favor. Because despite everything you just said, I think we're all still worried about you, Matt."

"I don't know," Rob said. "He looks pretty happy to me."

"I promise you," I said. "I'm good. Better than good. I feel fucking fantastic." For the first time in years I actually meant it. I was in a good place. I'd been lying to myself for years. Trying to put all this blame on myself when it came to Brooklyn. But I couldn't go back in time. And if I'd learned anything from her, it was to never take any days for granted. She'd instilled that in me. She'd be horrified that I'd been wasting my life away. And it was like seeing Kennedy had jump started something in my heart. I was done being pissed and angry with everyone. I just wanted to be me again.

"Well, that was easy," Rob said. "We kind of nailed this intervention thing, huh?" He started to stand up.

"Not so fast," James said. "Matt, how on earth can you stand there and say you're okay? Is dating Poppy a cry for help or something? I don't agree with everything Penny said back there, because I know Brooklyn was a Pruitt and she wasn't like the others. But Poppy? Seriously? She's awful. She's just as bad as Isabella. Is this some kind of cry for help?"

"It's complicated," I said.

"You know how the Pruitts operate," James said. "Of all the people in this city, you had to choose her? Didn't you learn anything from my mistakes? There is no out with those people."

"We have a deal..."

"Don't tell me you signed something," James said.

"No, nothing like that."

They all just stared at me.

"I think I can help explain," Tanner said. "Matt and I will let you in on our secret, but you have to promise not to tell anyone. Everyone else in the city needs to believe the tabloids."

Rob frowned, but all three of them nodded.

"Matt isn't actually dating Poppy," Tanner said. "I can't believe you guys would actually believe that." He said it like he hadn't just kissed me earlier to congratulate me on the same thing. Him knowing first was really getting to his head. "Poppy promised not to kidnap Scarlett if Matt pretends to date her. Just until Richard lets her take over the family business. Apparently Matt's expertise in the realm of finance is of the utmost importance to Richard."

"You're going to help them launder money?" Mason asked.

I shook my head. "I'd never do that. I'm just..."

"Keeping Scarlett safe," James said. He leaned forward in his chair, his elbows balancing on his knees. "I'm not asking you to do that, Matt."

"You didn't have to." I shrugged. "We're family."

"Is that why you're always trying to sleep with Penny?" Rob asked.

Fuck. "About that. James open your present."

James pulled out the framed picture of me, Mason, Rob, and him from high school. He looked up at me.

"You have the life I wanted," I said. "The wife. The family. I've been jealous of you for years. Penny's always kind of reminded me of Brooklyn. And yeah, I may have had a little crush on her. Or a big one. Whatever, it doesn't matter. I don't want to destroy your life. I know you didn't destroy mine. And I really want to put this all behind us. I want us to go back to being as happy as we all were in that picture."

"Thanks," James said. "That means a lot. Even though I was probably high out of my mind in this picture," he said with a laugh.

"So not exactly like that picture," I said.

"And we're absolutely sure that Matt isn't high right now?" Rob asked.

I laughed. "I swear I'm not."

James looked up from the photo. "So…no more flirting with Penny?"

"Yeah. I really am sorry."

"It's okay. I'm just glad you're not actually dating Poppy."

"Could you imagine?" Mason said. "I feel like we only just got rid of Wizzy."

We all laughed.

"But you really don't have to go through with that charade," James said. "I can figure something out…"

"I know you can. But you don't have to," I said. "That's the whole point. I've got your back, man,"

"This is wonderful," Tanner said. "Here, Matt, you should celebrate with some green juice." He handed me a to-go cup filled with Nigel's secret hangover elixir. "You did have a lot to drink tonight. Just for preventative measures."

"Where did you even get this?" I asked.

"I slipped out real quick while you guys were talking."

Had he? Whatever. If he'd made this, it meant Nigel's skeet wasn't in it. I'd never drink one of these Nigel made ever again. I took a huge sip.

"What's up, Mason?" Rob asked. "You look…weird."

Mason laughed. "Nothing. I just…never really thought about how much Penny reminds me of Brooklyn. In just like…the way she always has all our backs. And her sense of humor. And a little how she looks too."

We were all quiet.

"Well, James did propose to Brooklyn all those years ago…" Rob said.

James laughed. "Don't bring that up. Not one of my finest friendship moments. And just for the record, you both married girls from Delaware too."

"Huh," Rob said. "I never really thought about it like that either."

"It's fine," I said. "Really." And for the first time, I really meant it. It may have been a good idea to mention the fact that I was dating Kennedy. But I was planning on surprising them tomorrow night. By bringing her to our guys' night. She was going to have so much fun catching up with everyone.

"So we can tell everyone now?" Rob asked. "About Brooklyn?"

"Just let me tell Penny," I said. "I owe her an apology too for lying about wanting to be set up. For lying about everything really."

"Maybe give her a little while to cool down?" James said. "She's pretty heated."

I nodded. Penny definitely did seem mad at me. I'd fix that next.

"This was highly productive," Tanner said. "And I think we're all even now. My job here is done." He looked down.

I followed his gaze. "What the fuck?" My pants were tenting. I didn't even feel a little aroused. What the hell was my dick doing? *Shit.*

Rob started laughing. "I've never seen someone get so excited by an apology before."

I covered my growing erection with my hand and looked over at Tanner. "You said your job here is done. What the hell did you do?"

He grabbed the green juice from my hand. "Nothing you didn't deserve."

"Did you slip something in my drink? What the fuck was it? A boner pill?" If I was still holding the glass I would have thrown the green juice in his face.

"You drugged James at his bachelor party when you were being spiteful. So it only seemed fitting that you got drugged in return. And no one seemed to want to do it. So I stepped up. Like the saying goes…revenge is best served hard."

Rob laughed. "Okay, I have to admit that's pretty funny. Nice one, Tanner."

Tanner smiled. "Thanks, Robert."

"Revenge is best served hard." Mason laughed. "Have you been planning this since our last guys' night? When you insisted that was a phrase?"

"Well, it was a simple plan," Tanner said. "I was just trying to fix Matt's mistakes. What do you say, James?"

James chuckled. "Honestly I don't even really remember that night at the Blue Parrot Resort. But we'll all remember this. Well played, Tanner."

Tanner smiled. "So we're all good here? Shall we head home, Matt?"

"We're not all good," I said. Having a boner in front of all my friends seemed a lot worse than tripping balls to me. No one deserved this hell. They all laughed at me while I tried to get it under control. "Undo what you just did, Tanner."

"No can do," Tanner said with a laugh. "You'll have to…take care of it. Actually, I'm not sure that's how it works. It might just remain like that for about 4 hours. I didn't read the label."

"Four hours?! I can't let Nigel see me like this!"

"Wait, who is Nigel?" Rob asked.

"My houseboy," Tanner said.

"Houseboy? What the hell is that even?"

"Like a personal assistant with a bath fetish," I said. "And I'm not going home so he can see me like this."

"Whoa, wait," Rob said. "You're living with Tanner? When the hell did this happen?"

"Cool your loins, Young Robert," Tanner said. "Best friends usually do live together."

"Right, which is why he should be living with me," Rob said.

I ignored them. "When I was worried about the hit-woman, Tanner offered to let me stay with him…"

"You could have stayed with me," Rob said. "You know that."

"It was just for a few nights. I'm moving out tomorrow."

"Depending on Nigel's schedule," Tanner added. "Speaking of which, he will be worried. Let's get going." He slapped me on the back like a good friend that hadn't just given me a boner in front of all my other friends.

James started laughing harder. "In the handbook about interventions I read, you're supposed to hug at the end. Can we skip that part so Matt doesn't try to sword fight us?"

"Shut up," I mumbled. But I couldn't help but laugh. This was too ridiculous not to. "And I'm good without a hug."

"We can tell you're good," Mason said.

"Well, only as good as a Caldwell can get," Rob said. He pretended to cough. "Tiny dicks." He coughed again.

"Yeah right, Rob," Mason said. "Drink some juice and prove you're bigger."

"Fine." Rob got up. "I will. Hunters for the win."

But before he could grab the glass, Tanner dumped it into a houseplant. "You won't be wanting to drink that. There were a lot of pills in there."

"What the fuck?" I said. "Do I need to go to a hospital?"

"The houseplant is probably worse off than you are. You just need some rest. We'll see you tomorrow for guys' night," Tanner said, inviting himself as usual. "Ciao."

He put his arm around my shoulders to lead me out of the study.

I pushed him off. "Dude, don't touch me when I have a boner."

"It's not a real boner. It's a fake one."

"It sure feels real to me."

Tanner laughed. "Well, I hope you learned your lesson. Next time don't drug someone."

"Same advice to you, man."

"You'll be fine in no time. I'll have Nigel whip you up something to alleviate that."

"Don't you dare tell Nigel I have a boner." I heard more laughter and turned around.

James was standing there shaking his head. "Just for the record, I wasn't mad at you about my bachelor party. But we're definitely even now."

"Good to know that this wasn't necessary," I groaned.

"See you tomorrow," said James.

"Daddy, Daddy!" Scarlett ran into the foyer.

"Pumpkin, what are you doing out of bed?"

Scarlett slid to a stop. "I was thirsty." Her eyes grew round. "What's in Uncle Matt's pants?"

"Um…" James started.

I cleared my throat. "It's not…"

"It's a snake," Tanner said.

Scarlett screamed and ran out of the room.

James shook his head. "I'm going to go deal with that. She has a thing about snakes. Later, guys."

Tanner opened up the door.

"I'm going to kill you," I grumbled.

"Is it going to be a feeble attempt like when you tried to slap me at dinner? Good luck, Matt. You can't touch me. And I did you a favor. I fixed your relationship with your other, lesser friends."

"I had already done that by apologizing."

He shrugged. "Well, I'm sure this was the cherry on top for all of them."

"Rob's my best friend now," I said.

Tanner laughed. "That's just your boner talking." He frowned. "Wow that sounded really gay." He shook his head. "What a night, huh?"

CHAPTER 36

Thursday

Nigel stared at me as I held ice on my dick.

"Please stop looking at it," I said.

"Then how else are we going to know if the swelling goes down?" he asked.

"I'll tell you." *Stop staring at my penis, Nigel.*

"The hitwoman has been called off," Tanner said. "So Matt is safe to move home. Could you coordinate the arrangements, Nigel?"

"I'll have to check my calendar," he said.

Tanner just stared at him.

"Would you like me to check it now, Master Tanner?"

"Yes."

Nigel nodded. "Let me go get my planner." He bowed and ran off.

"Thanks for bringing it up to him," I said.

"No problem. Now if you'll excuse me, I have company."

"Who?" I asked. There was no one else here.

There was a knock on the door.

"Here she is. Have fun with your ice. Maybe you should invite Kennedy over. If you do, knock on my door so I can meet her before she takes care of that for you."

"I'm not inviting Kennedy over right now." She'd never let me live this down. Plus she'd wonder why I was living in this weird apartment with Tanner instead of at my own house. A whole restaurant already thought we were gay after that kiss. I didn't want a fake relationship with Tanner to be in the tabloids next.

"Wow," said a petite brunette as she walked into the kitchen. She ran her hand along the granite countertops. "This place is amazing. I would die to cook in this kitchen."

"What would you make?" Tanner asked, resting his elbows on the counter, staring at her.

"Hmm..." she said with a seductive smile. "Homemade whipped cream perhaps?"

"And what would you do with whipped cream when you have nothing to put it on?"

"I could think of a few things to put it on."

Tanner pulled her close. "Is that so?"

She laughed.

I cleared my throat.

The girl screamed. "I didn't realize anyone else was here." Her face turned bright red.

"Ignore him," Tanner said. "He was just retiring for the evening. Right, Matt?" He nodded toward the hall, trying to tell me to get lost, not at all subtly.

It was for the best. I probably needed to be alone with my stupid raging boner. "Yup," I said, making a mental note to not eat anything that ever touched that counter. Because they were 100% about to have sex in this kitchen. "Night."

"Night," Tanner said to me and then looked back at his date. "Now where were we?" He lifted her up on the counter.

Yup, that kitchen was disgusting. I wandered down the hall. There was a Post-it note on my bedroom door.

Meet me at the pool.
Yours,
-Nigel

What the hell was that weird little man even talking about? There was no pool in Tanner's apartment. And I wasn't about to wander around One57 with a boner. I went to open up my door, only to realize that there was a second Post-it note where the first had been.

Two doors down on the left. I have news.
Yours,
-Nigel

What the…? I looked down the hall. There was no way this place was big enough for a pool. It wasn't possible. I walked down the hall and opened the door Nigel had directed me to. And sure enough, there was a pool. Nigel was floating in the middle of it, wearing his butler outfit, sipping on some drink with an umbrella in it.

"Um…Nigel?" I said.

"Ah, Mr. Caldwell, I'm glad you found it. Join me." He gestured to a float beside him.

This should have felt safer than him staring at me in a bath. But somehow it felt even worse. I was still holding ice on my junk. He had to see it was weird to request for me to get in this pool when I'd consumed who knew how many boner pills. "I'm good."

Nigel sighed and slowly paddled over to me, keeping his drink steady. "I have bad news, Mr. Caldwell. Well, possibly good depending on what you think of it. I think it's a positive."

"What's the news?"

"My schedule is booked solid for two months. So I'm afraid it will be some time before I can assist you with your move."

Two months? "You're literally relaxing in a pool right now."

"Scheduled-in relaxation." He pulled out a notebook I hadn't seen a minute ago. "I'm allowed one minute of relaxation for every minute served. But that includes sleeping. So it really cuts into my free time. And I'm not very pleasant unless I get my R&R in." He skipped a few pages. "And now that I'm looking closer, it might be more like three months. I'll schedule you in for sometime after the new year."

"Nigel…I need to move back home."

"Are you not comfortable here?"

"No, that's not it." *It's partially it.* "This isn't my home."

"I'll do better."

"Nigel, it has nothing to do with you."

He blinked at me. "Is it about the meat in your lunch? You never texted me to say whether or not you liked it."

"No. I mean, yes, the meat is fine. But no, it's not about that."

"Do you have a specific thing I can do to make your time more comfortable here?"

I sighed. "I'll just hire movers. Don't worry about it."

Nigel shook his head. "I'm afraid I can't approve that. Master Tanner is very specific about what company is allowed into his home."

"He literally has a different girl here every night."

"And I vet them before they're allowed up."

"Then you can vet my movers."

"Vetting Master Tanner's mistresses is in my schedule." He jabbed a page with his finger. "Vetting big strong movers is not. I can schedule your mover vetting for January as well, if that is what you'd prefer. But I wouldn't trust movers with all your personal possessions. It would be best if I did it for you."

"In January?"

"Yes. Speaking of which, do you prefer a traditional Thanksgiving feast? Or more of a modern one?"

"I honestly have no idea what that means."

"Modern it is. I'm so excited to spend the holidays with you. Now, if you'll excuse me, I'm late for drawing you a bath."

"Nigel, I don't celebrate Thanksgiving."

He stopped. "What do you mean you don't celebrate Thanksgiving? It's a treasured American tradition."

"I just...don't." I hadn't since Brooklyn died. I always spent the day alone. I didn't want a traditional or modern Thanksgiving. My stomach churned. But what would Kennedy think about that? I took a deep breath. "Actually, put me down for two for a modern Thanksgiving meal."

"You're inviting a friend, Mr. Caldwell?"

"Yup."

Nigel stared at me. "I'll see what I can do. The guest list is already extensive. And there's only so much room at the table."

"You mean that huge dining room table?"

"It's smaller today. I removed some leaves."

"Then you can add them back."

He lifted up his notebook. "Not until January. I'll go draw your bath. Do you want another ice pack?"

"I'm good."

He bowed and ran away.

So strange. I pulled out my phone as I made my way back to my room. There was a text from Kennedy: "What's the dress code for tomorrow? I don't want to embarrass myself on our first official date."

I smiled and texted her back. "Business casual."

"Are you taking me to an office event?"

"I'm kidding. Casual. Super casual. But not slippers casual."

"You needed me. I didn't have time to change. And my slippers are adorable."

I laughed. "They really are."

"Good. I'll wear them then."

"Are you wearing them right now?"

She didn't write me back right away. Fuck. Why had I asked her that? She was going to think I was a pervert. I shifted the ice pack on my boner. It wasn't my fault that I was drugged. But right before I set my phone down on my nightstand, another text came through.

"Are you asking me if I'm wearing lingerie and sitting on a bed seductively all alone?"

"Yes."

"I hate to break it to you, Matt, but that is not how I dress when I'm alone. Think more along the lines of a baggy t-shirt."

"No bra?"

"You're a terrible boyfriend."

"I'm a great boyfriend."

"That's yet to be seen. We haven't even been on one date yet and you're asking me the 'what are you wearing' question."

"I'm taking that as a yes to the no bra."

"Good guess."

I sat down on the edge of my bed. "I like picturing you like that." Honestly, her in an old t-shirt waiting for me in bed sounded pretty great to me.

"Oh, do messy updos turn you on?" she asked.

"Well, I'm definitely turned on." I swallowed hard as another text didn't come through. *Fuck*. Too much. Sexting wasn't exactly a Disney prince kind of move. But I was so fucking hard.

Another text came through: "Is that so?"

I couldn't take it anymore. I unzipped my pants and wrapped my hand around my cock. It was cold from the ice and my hand felt amazingly warm. I could imagine it being Kennedy's mouth around me. "I wish I was with you right now," I said.

"Me too."

I closed my eyes and ran my hand down my shaft. I imagined Kennedy on her knees looking up at me. Her nipples hard against the fabric of her shirt. I pictured her leaning forward, running her tongue along my tip.

Someone cleared their throat.

I opened my eyes to see Nigel staring at me. "Nigel, what the fuck?" I pulled up my pants.

"I was drawing you a bath."

"You've been in here this whole time? Get out!"

"But..."

"Nigel, get out of my room."

"Yes, Mr. Caldwell. Enjoy your...bath. The water is the perfect temperature. I'll be back in a minute to check on you." He bowed and left.

The image of Kennedy on her knees had disappeared as quickly as it had come. But the good news was that my boner was finally receding. Apparently seeing Nigel watching me stroke myself was the key to making my dick soft. I should have known.

This was for the best. I'd been masturbating to a ghost for years. I didn't need to imagine this with Kennedy. I could have the real thing.

I just needed to wait until she was ready. Although if her flirting was any indication, I wouldn't have to wait that long. But we couldn't go back to her mom's place to do it. And I didn't really feel comfortable bringing her here. I'd figure it out.

I texted her. "What do you think about getting a hotel room for tomorrow night?" I pressed send before I could talk myself out of it. I always took women to hotels. Kennedy was different. I would have taken her home but I didn't have a bed there anymore. And we were going to need a bed. Well…maybe. A bed wasn't entirely necessary.

"That depends on how our date goes," she wrote back.

"It's going to be a great date."

"So cocky."

I smiled. "Goodnight, Kennedy."

"Goodnight, Matt."

I looked down at the tub full of bubbles. Honestly, it looked pretty relaxing. I looked over my shoulder to make sure Nigel wasn't watching, and then stripped and climbed in. I rested the back of my head on the edge of the tub. Tomorrow night was going to change everything. I'd had sex with too many women to remember. But I only ever loved one of them. I knew how that felt. And I'd be lying if I said I wasn't starting to feel that way again. Kissing Kennedy was intoxicating. And I just wanted more. All I could think of was more.

My friends were right. I'd needed an intervention a week ago. But now? I really was happy.

I heard footsteps, but didn't bother to open my eyes. "Nigel, I really don't need any assistance."

"Are you sure?" He asked. "I could…"

"I'm sure." I was also positive that I didn't want to hear the end of his sentence. "See you in the morning."

"You don't want me to check on the swelling?"

Are you kidding me? "No, Nigel, I don't need you to look at the swelling. I'm fine."

He sighed. "As you wish, Mr. Caldwell."

I opened my eyes to make sure he was retreating. If I was being forced to stay here for three months, I'd need to set some boundaries. *What am I even thinking?* I wasn't going to stay here for three months. Tanner would sort it out.

I sunk lower in the bubbles. Nigel was weird, but this place did have its perks. I lifted up the snifter of cognac that Nigel had promised. The life of a billionaire, I guess. Or was it? James was the only other billionaire I knew, and I was pretty sure he didn't have a weird little servant trying to examine his cock all the time. I'd have to ask him about it. When I crossed that line into being a billionaire, I wouldn't be hiring a houseboy.

My phone buzzed and I looked down, hoping it was another text from Kennedy.

Poppy's name showed up. I pushed the phone away. I didn't want anyone to disturb my bath.

CHAPTER 37

Friday

We were all hanging out at James' place tonight. I was waiting outside for my surprise guest. I'd been looking forward to seeing Kennedy all day. We had a reservation at a hotel within walking distance of James' place. Not at my usual hotel. Because I knew she wasn't just some random hookup. And I'd never treat her like she was.

Not that the hotel or anything about tonight mattered until I told her what was going on with Poppy. I didn't purposely keep Kennedy in the dark. I was just looking for the best possible way to explain the situation. Because I hated how it was all tied up with Brooklyn. Kennedy and I needed a fresh start. And this was the exact opposite. Tanner had helped me with a good plan though. A simple one that involved flowers and the truth.

I looked down at the bouquet in my hand. I had no idea what kind of flowers Kennedy liked. Maybe this was a bad idea. I should have brought her French fries. Relationship advice from Tanner couldn't be that great. I'd never seen him with the same woman more than twice.

My phone buzzed in my pocket. My mom was calling. I still hadn't called her back. Kennedy wouldn't be arriving for another few minutes. I could use the distraction. And I honestly owed my mom an apology too. "Hey, Mom," I said as I answered the phone.

"Matthew!" She sounded so relieved. "I've been trying to reach you."

"I know. I just..."

"I know."

We were both quiet. I thought about what Mason had said. That my fake smile may have fooled mom, but not him. I wasn't so sure that was true. If it was, she wouldn't always be so worried about me during this time of year. "I'm really sorry, Mom."

"For what, sweetheart?"

"For lying to you for years about being fine. I don't even know if half the time I realized I was lying. But…I realize it now. Because I'm actually happy." I took a deep breath. "I met someone."

I heard her inhale.

I didn't want to make her guess. "Or rather, ran into someone I used to know. Do you remember Kennedy?"

"Kennedy Alcaraz? She was so sweet."

My parents never bothered with tabloids. They wouldn't know about Poppy. And I didn't want to go into that. I just wanted my mom to know I was okay. "I really like her, Mom. And I know I shouldn't because…"

"No." Her voice sounded so firm. Like when she'd yell at Mason or me for fighting. "Don't do that. Don't push away a good thing. You deserve happiness. I know how much you loved Brooklyn. But that doesn't mean your heart isn't big enough to love someone else too. Don't you think you've tortured yourself enough?"

I blinked fast, hoping I wouldn't start crying in the middle of a busy Manhattan sidewalk. "So does that mean you like Kennedy?"

She laughed and sniffed at the same time, and I could tell she was laughing through tears. "I liked her when she was a teenager. But I haven't seen her since you two graduated. You'll have to bring her by for dinner."

My mom would definitely still like Kennedy. This was just her way of getting me to come over. "I can do that."

"We miss you."

"I miss you too, Mom." My phone started buzzing. It was probably Kennedy. I needed to take it. "Tell Dad I miss him too. Text me and we can set up a time for dinner."

"Alright. I love you so much. I don't think I have to tell you how happy this call has made me."

I smiled. "I love you too, Mom." I hung up and looked down at my phone. But it wasn't a call from Kennedy. It was several texts all in a row from Poppy. She'd been messaging me all day, trying to get me to go to some stupid event. And she wasn't taking no for an answer.

I quickly responded. "I told you, I have plans tonight." My phone started ringing. *Shit.* I made sure Kennedy was nowhere to be seen and answered the call. "Not now, Poppy."

"This was part of the deal, Matthew. For you to come when I need you. And I need you tonight. Uncle Richard is going to be there. I wanted tonight to be our big society debut."

"We'll have to do it another night."

"You know he doesn't go to many events now."

I actually didn't know that. I made a habit of not being in the same social circles as that monster. "Just tell him we're dating."

"He'll want to see us together for himself. Talk is just hearsay. You know this. You know him. Why aren't you coming?!"

"I'm sorry, Poppy. You should have given me more warning."

"I only just found out last night that he'd be in attendance. And you're supposed to be my boyfriend. Which means you're supposed to want to hang out with me on Friday nights."

"I can't pretend tonight," I said.

"But why?" Her voice was even whinier than normal.

"Because…" I couldn't tell her I had a date. That was exactly the kind of excuse that would not get me out of this last-minute obligation. "Because tonight I'm telling my friends about the fact that I'm dating you. If we want this to work, they need to know."

"Oh. Well, that's good." She sighed. "But can't you meet up with me after though? Please."

"Guys' night usually goes until at least midnight." It didn't. But I had other plans tonight involving Kennedy naked.

"We had a deal, Matthew. And I don't want to have to break my side of it."

Fuck. I ran my hand down my face. That hotel room was calling to me. But Poppy had me, and she knew it. I'd have to postpone my alone time with Kennedy. *Again.* "I'll see if I can get away."

"I'd say make sure of it. See you in a few hours. And wear a tux. If you bring flowers it'll certainly be a bonus." She hung up.

I looked down at the flowers I'd brought for Kennedy. What was I doing? Flowers definitely weren't Kennedy's thing. But I didn't have time to go get her some French fries because her taxi pulled to the curb and she stepped out. She leaned in and told the taxi driver something, and when she closed the door, he didn't drive off.

I met her in the middle of the sidewalk. I could tell something was wrong because her normal smile was nowhere to be seen. And I just hoped to God I wasn't too late to tell her about…

She slapped me hard across the face. "I can't believe you."

Shit. "Kennedy…"

Before I could say anything else she slapped me again.

Damn, she was stronger than I thought she was. I rubbed my jaw.

"I'm such an idiot," she said. "No. Actually, you're the idiot. What the hell is wrong with you? Why are you still playing the same games you did as a teenager? We're not in high school anymore!"

"I can explain."

"You made Brooklyn feel like a dirty little secret, Matt. And I won't give you a chance to make me feel the same way." She turned back to the taxi.

I caught her hand so she couldn't leave. "Please just let me explain."

She turned around. It looked like she wanted to slap me again but she didn't. "Explain how you were making out with someone else on the cover of every tabloid in the city? Or the fact that I found out because I overheard two of my employees gossiping about the city's most eligible bachelor being taken off the market? What could you possibly have to explain? Because it seems quite simple to me. You're a cheater. You're disgusting. And I want nothing to do with you."

I'd been called a lot of bad things over the past 16 years. But never with such vehemence.

"Kennedy, please just let me explain what's going on. This is a huge misunderstanding. Can I just talk to you inside for a minute?"

"Why? Because you can't let anyone in the city know about your mistress?" She grabbed the flowers out of my hand and whacked my arm with them like she was brandishing a sword.

"Would you stop yelling for one second?" I grabbed the flowers from her and threw them on the ground.

She pulled the taxi door open, ignoring me.

I slammed it shut. "Kennedy…."

She shoved my chest. "Puta mierda."

I grabbed her hands so that she'd stop hitting me. "Look, I agree with you okay? I'm an idiot."

"You've got that right."

I tried to lower my voice so that no passersby would hear us. "But that kiss in the tabloids? It wasn't real."

"Your lips were on hers."

"Just so the photographers could snap a stupid picture to spread the rumor. I swear it meant nothing. I had to enter into a fake relationship with Poppy Cannavaro in order to ensure the safety of James' daughter. It's a verbal contract that will expire when Poppy acquires Mr. Pruitt's business holdings."

"What are you even talking about?"

"Poppy is Mr. Pruitt's niece. And she thinks being with me will somehow show Mr. Pruitt that she's serious about taking over the company. That's it. It's basically a business transaction. And believe me when I say that there is *nothing* real about the relationship at all. Because I'm falling for you, Kennedy. I can't stop thinking about you."

She just stared at me.

"You changed everything, Kennedy. I was fucking drowning before you came crashing back into my life."

A tear slid down her cheek.

I risked her slapping me again and reached out to wipe her tears away. "So please just come inside. And we can talk this through."

She opened her mouth and then closed it again. She shook her head. "I can't do this with you, Matt."

"Do what?"

"Get tangled up in whatever you just said. If you owe some kind of debt to Brooklyn's dad…"

"I don't. I swear I don't. Scarlett was in danger. And I'd do anything to keep that little girl safe. This was the only way. I swear if I think of something else, you'll be the first to know."

"So James has a kid?"

I smiled. "Two actually."

"I can't picture him being a dad. When did we all get so old?"

"You look anything but old."

She looked down at her shoes.

"That's what the date is, by the way. Mason, Rob, and James are all inside for guys' night. I was kinda thinking I could surprise them with…you. And the fact that we're dating."

"So they don't even know I'm coming?"

I shook my head.

"And they don't know that we're dating?"

"Not yet." I smiled down at her. "That's kind of what tonight was for."

She took a deep breath. "I think maybe we should keep it that way."

"You want to do something else tonight?"

"I mean the dating thing. We're not dating, Matt. Not anymore. I've been in a toxic relationship before. And I'm not putting myself in a situation to get stepped all over again. I can't."

"Kennedy…"

"We'll be friends. Until you get this sorted out with Poppy. Okay?"

"Just friends?"

She nodded. "Just friends."

I was so close. So close to getting to be happy. So close to getting the girl for once. I didn't know how long this shit with Poppy was going to take. Days? Months? Longer? I tried to ignore the sinking feeling in my stomach. But I had to respect Kennedy's decision. I'd never force her to be with me in secret. Despite what she'd said, I'd learned my lesson on that. "Okay."

"Okay." She exhaled slowly. "So I'm just going to go then."

"You can still come up, Kennedy. All the guys are going to be thrilled to see you."

"I don't really feel like hanging out with everyone when I feel like I'm about to start crying."

"I'm sure Rob will make you smile."

She laughed. "That's true. I have to admit, I kind of miss his jokes. But won't it be weird?"

"Why would it be weird? You and I have always been friends. Nothing will change that." But it was a lie. Everything changed as soon as I kissed her. I didn't want to go back. I didn't know how to go back.

"Right." She tucked a loose strand of hair behind her ear.

I could already feel her slipping away. "Come on. It'll be fun." I put my hand out for her.

She ignored my offered hand. But she leaned in to tell the taxi driver he didn't have to wait any longer. "I'm sorry about the flowers," she said as the taxi sped off.

"It's okay. At the last minute I realized you'd probably prefer French fries anyway."

She laughed. "Very true. But for the record, when you've done something wrong and want to bring flowers, my favorites are tulips. I can't even remember where my mom and I were going. But we were on a trip and we passed by this huge field of tulips. It was the most beautiful thing I'd ever seen."

I didn't say a word as we walked side by side into James' building. But if she thought she wasn't getting a tulip every day until she took me back, she was sorely mistaken. We got on the elevator and I could feel the distance between us. She leaned against the wall on the opposite side of me. And all I could think about was closing the distance between us.

CHAPTER 38

Friday

"Stop looking at me like that," Kennedy said.

"Like what?"

"Like more than friends."

"I don't know how to not do that," I said.

Kennedy shook her head. "You're making this harder than it has to be. It's like you said earlier, we've always been friends."

"That was before I kissed you." I watched as her cheeks grew rosy.

"Cut it out," she said.

"I'm not doing anything."

"Yes you are," she said with a laugh. "You're over there looking all sexy, staring at me."

I smiled. "You think I'm sexy?"

"Try harder to look at me like we're just friends," she said, ignoring me.

I closed the distance between us in the elevator.

She looked up at me. "Matt…"

"You can't deny that you feel this too."

"Of course I feel this." She put her hand on my chest and then quickly removed it. "I didn't say this wasn't hard for me. I just…I don't want to be with someone that isn't all in. And you can't be all in right now."

"I am all in."

"Except in public where you're all in with another woman?"

I pressed my lips together.

"We're just hitting pause," she said. But her words didn't fit her actions, because she drew a fraction of an inch closer.

I didn't say a word. I just stared down at her.

She leaned forward, her lips stopping by my ear. Her hand rested on my shoulder.

It took every ounce of restraint I had not to hit the emergency button on the elevator to bring it to a halt. I couldn't remember the last time I wanted something so badly.

"Try harder," she whispered and then took a step back.

Kennedy Alcaraz was a tease. And I was pretty sure I was falling in love with her. "Maybe you should try harder to keep your hands to yourself, Alcaraz."

"Don't call me that," she said with a laugh.

"You know the alternative."

She rolled her eyes.

And the elevator doors dinged open, ending our conversation. Because Tanner was standing there.

He looked at us standing on opposite sides of the elevator.

"I guess the conversation didn't go as planned?" he asked.

Kennedy stared at me.

"Not exactly," I said. I didn't try to take her hand as I stepped off the elevator. "Kennedy, this is Tanner."

"Matt's best friend," he said. "It's lovely to finally meet you."

"From one of Matt's friends to another, it's nice to meet you too, Tanner."

"Friends?" Tanner looked at me. "Oh, it really didn't go as planned then."

"I thought you said no one knew about us yet?" Kennedy asked me.

I smiled. "Don't worry. Only Tanner knows."

"Okay. Well, Matt and I decided to just be friends until he sorts out whatever he needs to do with Poppy. So, maybe just don't mention that we dated for all of two seconds to anyone else?"

Tanner smiled. "Luckily for you, I happen to be an excellent secret keeper."

"Now which apartment is James'?" she asked.

There were only two doors on the floor. One for James' apartment. And one that led to his security team. I knocked on the closer door. "Why hadn't you gone in yet?" I asked Tanner.

"I was waiting for you two. You know how uncomfortable Robert makes me."

Kennedy laughed. "Please don't tell me Rob goes by Robert now?"

"Only I call him that," Tanner said. "Because he hates it and we're sworn enemies."

"Why?"

"He loves to claim that he's Matt's best friend when that title clearly belongs to me. And his jokes are rarely funny. And his haircut is stupid."

Kennedy looked up at him. "It kind of sounds like you're jealous of him."

"Of Young Robert?" Tanner laughed. "Never."

"Young Robert? How old are you?"

Tanner cleared his throat. "Age is only a number."

"So...Rob's actually older than you?"

"It doesn't matter either way. What matters is that he certainly doesn't act like it."

"Hmm," Kennedy said.

"What? What was the hmm for?"

"It's just…your sense of humor is actually a lot like Rob's. I feel like you two are more similar than you think."

Oh, this wasn't good. I knocked on the door louder this time. We needed more people so that Tanner wouldn't flip out.

Tanner gaped at her. "Similar to Robert? If Matt wasn't in love with you I'd tell you to wash your whore mouth."

I didn't know what was more shocking. The fact that he'd dropped the "L" word when I hadn't or that he'd told her to wash her whore mouth. "Tanner, what the hell?" I said.

But Kennedy started laughing really hard. "I guess it's a good thing Matt's in love with me then."

I glared at Tanner.

"I take it back," Kennedy said to him. "I think you're funnier than Rob."

"I can tell we're going to get along swimmingly," Tanner said and put his arm around her shoulders.

"What else has Matt told you about me?"

"What hasn't he told me?" Tanner said. "Where do I even begin?"

Fuck my life.

James finally opened the door, but he wasn't paying attention to me. "It's the button that has a pause sign on it!" he yelled over his shoulder. When he turned around, the smile faltered from his face. But not because he was upset. Just because he was probably as surprised as me when I'd first seen Kennedy again. Or maybe he was confused because Tanner's arm was around her shoulders when it should have been my arm there. "Kennedy? What are you doing here? When did you move back to the city?" He leaned down to hug her before she had a chance to respond.

"It's good to see you too," Kennedy said.

"Guys!" James yelled. "Kennedy's here!"

"Who?" Rob asked as he walked into the foyer holding the remote. "Holy shit. Is that you, Kennedy?"

Kennedy laughed. "It's good to see you too, Rob."

"Decided to crash our guys' night?" Mason asked as he leaned down to hug her.

"Actually, I was invited by my friend here," Kennedy said and lightly punched my arm.

Friend. It sounded more like a challenge than anything.

"How long have you known she's been back in town?" Rob asked.

"A few days."

"A few days, huh?" Mason asked. "Interesting."

"Why is that interesting?" Kennedy said.

Mason shrugged. "No reason. Want a beer?"

"I'd rather have a tour." She stepped into the living room. "What a view." She wandered over to the windows overlooking Central Park. Everyone started to follow her. But I grabbed Tanner's arm to hold him back.

"What the hell was that?" I asked.

"What was what?"

"You called her a whore and told her I loved her."

"No, I said I would never call her a whore because you love her."

"Same thing!"

"Actually it's quite different."

"Kennedy and I just had a fight outside. We agreed to be friends. The last thing I need is to scare her off by tossing out the L word."

"I don't know," he said and looked over at Kennedy with the guys.

I followed his gaze.

Kennedy was staring at me instead of the amazing view. She blushed and turned back to listen to what James was saying.

"It seems like maybe that was the exact word she needed to hear," Tanner said.

Kennedy stole another glance at me over her shoulder.

God she was sexy. I smiled and she smiled back.

"I told you I was good at helping people find true love," Tanner said. "Just trust me."

"You own a sex club."

"That's a matter of interpretation. But this is all going according to plan. Quite perfectly as a matter of fact."

"What plan?"

"You and Kennedy falling for each other."

"You had nothing to do with that."

"Of course I did. I admit, I was a little perturbed that you asked Penny to be your matchmaker instead of me. So I decided to interfere. I recently acquired the real estate company your agent Bill works for. I had the owner hire Kennedy's photography company. It was a huge contract. I knew she'd been considering moving back to the city and just needed one final push."

"What? How did you…"

"And I hired a security team to follow you after all the hitwoman nonsense. So they knew you went straight home the other night instead of coming to my place. Which I'm still quite angry about. But it was a good opportunity, so I let it go. I arranged for Kennedy to show up to take your listing pictures that night. And bam. True love. You're welcome."

"But last night…you thought I was dating Poppy. You were all excited about it."

"No, I knew you weren't. It was all a ruse. Because you hadn't told me about Kennedy yet and I was trying to force your hand. It worked, didn't it? You told me everything. Before you told Rob by the way. Just saying."

Wow. He'd orchestrated this whole thing?

"And Penny thought she was your matchmaker the whole time." Tanner laughed. "I win." He lifted his hand for a high-five.

I literally had nothing to say. Because I was pretty sure he had in fact won. I just had no idea he'd had anything to do with it. I high-fived him. "Wait, you've been having me tailed?"

"For your own safety. Don't look at me like that. It's like you have a penchant for getting into trouble."

Well that explained why it still felt like someone was watching me.

"So you can tell Penny that you no longer need her services. And I'll send you the bill for mine."

I couldn't even imagine how much he was going to charge me for all that. Was I going to own the real estate company after this? What the hell was I going to do with a real estate company?

He laughed. "Just kidding. I did it gratis for that."

"For what?"

"Take a look in the mirror, Matt. I haven't seen you this happy in years."

He was right about that. "But your plan failed. She just wants to be friends."

"Give me till the end of the night. I'll have her in your bed by midnight." He slapped me on the back and hurried over to where everyone else was still talking.

I didn't doubt him at all. He'd brought Kennedy back to the city. He'd made the two of us run into each other.

I watched Kennedy laugh at something Tanner said. She smiled over at me again.

Damn, Tanner was a pretty great matchmaker. He was wrong about one thing though…he hadn't gotten me to fall in love with her. Kennedy had done that all on her own. And I wasn't about to be put back in the friend zone.

CHAPTER 39

Friday

I couldn't pull my eyes away from Kennedy's smiling face.

"So he did it butt naked," Rob said.

Kennedy started laughing again. "No." You could barely hear the word through her laughter. "You didn't." She put her hand on my knee.

All night long she'd been doing things like that. Grabbing my arm. Touching my thigh. I wasn't even sure she realized she was doing it. It was like her body just gravitated to mine.

I smiled at her. "They dared me to. Of course I did."

"You could have gotten arrested," she said. "Who runs butt naked into a convenience store for a bottle of water?"

"One lesson you learn in college is that while breaking the law you should break said law naked," Rob said. "It's a lot easier to slip away from an officer when he's trying not to touch your junk."

Kennedy shook her head. "I didn't learn that lesson in college."

"Oh, well it's different for girls," I said. "I think police officers like when women are naked. They'll probably grab you even faster."

"There are girl officers too, you know," Kennedy said.

"Which I'm sure aren't all straight," Rob said.

Kennedy laughed. "Well surely there were some gay officers that would have loved to grab your junk."

"Fair point," Rob said. "I'm sure there are plenty of men that would like to feel me up. It's just a general principle that usually works."

Kennedy shook her head. "You're all ridiculous."

"Only Rob is ridiculous," said Tanner. "And I have a much less ridiculous topic to discuss with you. Do you believe in true love?"

"Who, me?" Kennedy asked.

"Yes, you."

She eyed me for a second but then looked back at Tanner. "It depends on what your definition of true love is."

"Soulmates. Two people that are perfect together." Tanner smiled. "Destined to be together, even if it takes them a while to figure it out."

Kennedy's cheeks flushed. "Yeah, maybe." She locked eyes with me for a second, but quickly looked away. "It's certainly a nice idea."

"It's more than an idea. Let's take you and Matt for example. You were friends when you were teenagers. Who's to say you aren't destined to be more?"

"We're still just friends," Kennedy said with a half-hearted laugh. "Right, buddy?" She elbowed me in the side.

It took all my restraint not to pull her onto my lap and kiss her. "Right." *For now.*

All my friends stared at us.

"But time changes people," Tanner said. "It certainly changes circumstances."

What was Tanner doing? Trying to scare her away? I was already doing that well enough thanks to Poppy. I was about to change the subject, but Kennedy started talking again.

"Well, what about you, Tanner?" she asked. "Do you believe in true love?"

"Of course I do."

"So have you found it?"

Tanner leaned back in his chair. "No. Not yet."

I knew that wasn't the whole story. He'd had it and lost it like me.

"Rumor has it that Penny's pretty good at matchmaking," Kennedy said. "Maybe you should ask her for help."

Tanner lowered his eyebrows. "Maybe someday. But not right now."

"Trust me," James said. "Penny's not a very good matchmaker. Her intentions are good, but her setup ideas have been a little out there recently."

My dick that was almost set on fire could vouch for that.

Kennedy laughed. "It must be hard though, Tanner. Everyone around you falling in love while you're still single." She cleared her throat. "I mean, you and Matt. The both of you are single."

Smooth one, Kennedy. At least it seemed like she believed we were only friends just as much as I believed it. Which was not at all.

"Yeah," Tanner said. "Let's just say I'm a little…cursed in the love department. At least for now. Besides, I'm focusing on growing my empire."

I laughed. "Pretty sure you've grown that quite enough."

Tanner shrugged. "If I ever want to retire, I'm going to need a lot more."

Everyone just stared at him.

He cleared his throat. "I mean, with the average person living so much longer these days and everything. It's just wise."

I was pretty sure Tanner could shut his whole business down tomorrow and still have enough money to send his great, great, great grandchildren to an Ivy League school.

"What exactly are you planning on doing during your retirement?" Mason asked. "Randomly buying million-dollar corporations and immediately shutting them down so you never see a dollar of a return? Because that's literally the only way you could blow through so much money."

Rob laughed. "Or are you just worried that Matt's so bad at his job of handling your finances that you have to be extra careful?"

"I'm great at my job," I said and threw a pillow at him.

Rob caught it and stuck his tongue out at me.

"Actually, I have to admit it," James said. "You are great at it, Matt. My portfolio is insane. And it's insane that I just said that sentence out loud. When did we get so old?"

"Speak for yourself," Kennedy said. "Matt, Rob, and I are practically still teenagers. Sorry, Tanner, I have no idea how old you are."

"Older than I look," he said.

"Hmm." Kennedy scrunched her mouth to the side as she stared at him. "Let me guess…37?"

Tanner laughed.

"He's just messing with you, Kennedy," Rob said. "Tanner's younger than all of us. He's only 28. Which is why it's extra annoying that he calls me Young Robert."

"Maybe if you acted a little more mature, Young Robert…"

Rob pelted the pillow at Tanner's head.

Tanner caught it in his hand before it collided with his face.

"Seriously," Kennedy said. "Why don't the two of you get along? You have the same sense of humor…"

"As Robert?" Tanner asked. "We've been over this. Never."

"Never," Rob said.

Kennedy laughed. "You two literally just agreed on something."

"Never," Rob and Tanner both said at the same time and then glared at each other.

"Well, I certainly won't be using that word again," Tanner said.

"Just say nunca," I said.

Kennedy smiled up at me.

"Anyone want another drink?" Tanner asked. "Kennedy, will you come help me?" He wandered into the kitchen before she had a chance to respond.

"I feel like I've been summoned," Kennedy whispered to me.

"Just ignore him."

She smiled. "It's important for your friends to like me." Her face flushed again. "I mean, just so that we can all be friends. I'll be right back." She followed Tanner into the kitchen.

What the hell was he going to say to her?

James and Rob's phones started buzzing at the same time.

They looked at each other and sighed.

"Probably something with the kids," James said. "I gotta take this."

"Me too," Rob said.

They both answered their phones and wandered out of the room.

"So..." Mason said as he stared at me. "Does Kennedy have anything to do with your good mood last night?"

"You heard her," I said. "We're just friends."

"Huh."

I laughed. "What?"

"Nothing." He folded his arms in front of his chest. "It's just that the two of you were pretty close years ago. I always wondered if maybe there was something more there."

There hadn't been before. She was just the only person who understood what I was going through. But now? It was actually exactly like Tanner had said. People changed. Circumstances changed. I was wondering if he had been talking more to me than he was to Kennedy. "Can you keep a secret?" I asked.

"Probably not."

I shook my head. It didn't matter. I was pretty sure it was all over my face. And I'd already told my mom. I was surprised she hadn't called Mason yet with the good news. "I think I'm falling for her."

Mason didn't say anything for a long moment. "Can you keep a secret?"

"Better than you can because Bee won't be bugging me about it."

He laughed. "I always thought you and Kennedy might get together. I was hoping you would, actually. She gets it."

She did. I think there was a part of me that always realized that. And now that she was finally here? All I wanted was to be close to her.

"And she's a cool girl," Mason said. "I've always gotten along well with her. I think Bee would like her too."

"Yeah. I think she would." I shook my head. "Wait, that's your secret? That you've been secretly wanting me and Kennedy to get together all these years?"

"No. My secret is that you should fall a little faster. Because my kid's going to want a best friend. And he's going to be younger than all James and Rob's kids, so I need you to step up."

"Bee's pregnant?"

He laughed. "Not yet. But we're going to start trying."

"That's awesome." A few weeks ago, this would have been the worst news ever. But it didn't feel like bad news tonight. Because I wasn't stuck anymore. I knew what I wanted. I smiled as I heard Kennedy's laughter filter into the great room. I wanted her. "Wait, but you said 'he'?"

"Yeah, I'm planning on having all boys."

"I don't think that's something that you can just decide."

"Just watch and learn. I'm much too masculine to have a girl." He raised his beer bottle.

"That's definitely not how it works."

"We'll see."

Despite Mason's flawed logic, I was going to be an uncle. A real one. Not that Scarlett, Liam, Sophie, and RJ didn't count. But this was a big deal. "That's going to be you soon then," I said and gestured over to James and Rob who were most likely talking to their wives.

"What do you think is wrong?" he asked.

"I'm guessing someone has a tummy ache."

"Hmm…maybe. But I'm thinking Liam pulled Sophie's hair again."

I laughed. "The audacity of that little baby to pull pigtails."

Mason shook his head. "Want to bet on it? Loser drinks all those shots," he said.

I looked over to see Kennedy and Tanner walking back into the room. They were each carrying a few shots in their hands.

I had a feeling tonight was about to get significantly more interesting. "Deal," I said to Mason.

CHAPTER 40

Friday

Kennedy's eyes locked with mine as she put the shots down on the coffee table. I was wondering what she and Tanner had been talking about in the kitchen. But it couldn't be bad, because she looked really happy. I found my gaze wandering to her lips.

She sat down next to me, closer than before. "What?" she whispered.

"Nothing."

She shook her head with a smile. "Anyone want another drink?" Kennedy asked. "Tanner tried to convince me to play spin the bottle, but I had to explain the rules to him. Because he didn't seem to realize that when there's only one girl it'll end up being some boy-on-boy action."

Tanner laughed. "I've never played before."

"It's okay," Kennedy said. "I never played before either. I was super lame in high school too."

"Right," agreed Tanner. "That's exactly why I don't know what it was like. I was just super lame." He laughed like the idea of him being lame at any point in his life was the funniest thing he'd ever heard.

I had no idea what he was up to, but hopefully whatever he said to her in private would help. And I knew he'd only mentioned spin the bottle so I could make out with Kennedy. Or maybe he really was just misinformed. He didn't go to school in the states. Who knew what they did in…Greece? I vaguely remember him saying he'd been in Greece for high school. Or was it Germany?

"But I can't imagine you being lame," Tanner said. "Matt pretends he was cool in high school and he told me the two of you were friends."

"Matt was cool," Kennedy said. "And he only hung out with me out of obligation."

"That's not true." I lightly touched her back and she didn't push me away. "I always thought you were cool, Kennedy."

She laughed. "No way. You were just being nice because I didn't have any other friends my junior and senior years. You just didn't want me to have to sit alone at lunch." She patted my leg and let her hand linger.

That wasn't true. I'd gotten used to eating lunch with her and Brooklyn. And I just…didn't want to stop. But before I could correct her, James and Rob came back over.

Kennedy removed her hand from my thigh but didn't seem to care that my hand was on her back.

"Sounds like girls' night is ending early," James said. "Penny will be home any minute. So you guys better…down those shots?" he said looking at the coffee table. "Since when were we doing shots?"

"They're actually only for Matt," Mason said.

"No way. Which one of them is sick?" I asked.

Rob laughed. "How did you know that? Liam and RJ are both fussy. Daphne thinks their tummies are upset."

"Boom," I said. "Drink up." I pointed to Mason.

"Fuck." Mason shook his head, but started downing shot after shot.

"What the heck did we miss?" James asked.

"Mason bet me that your wives were calling because Liam pulled Sophie's hair again."

Mason cringed on the fourth shot but kept going.

"And I bet it was because one of them had a tummy ache. I won."

Mason slammed the last glass down on the coffee table. "Bee's going to be so pissed that I'm coming home this drunk. Well, not this drunk. Drunk as in drunk me 15 minutes from now." He coughed. "I'm pretty sure that tequila is in my veins."

Kennedy laughed. "In my defense, I thought we were each going to take a shot. I didn't know you guys were making a bet."

The front door opened. "Daddy!" Scarlett called from the hallway. "Liam's doing the burping thing!"

James laughed. "Excuse me for a sec. Liam has the cutest burps."

"Gross," I said.

James lightly slapped the back of my head as he made his way past me. After a few seconds, Scarlett came running into the room. Heading right for me.

"Uncle Matt, Uncle Matt!" She ran into the great room and climbed up onto my lap. "I got to eat chocolate cake tonight! A whole piece all on my own. This big." She showed me with her hands how big the ginormous slice of cake she'd eaten was. She seemed…very hyped up on sugar. "You should've seen it." She turned to look at Kennedy and then ducked under my arm to hide from her. "Who is she?"

Kennedy smiled. "I'm a friend of your uncle's."

"Which one?" Scarlett asked from her hiding spot.

"Matt. Well, all of them, actually."

"It's okay, kiddo," I said and ruffled her hair. "Kennedy's really nice. How about you come say hi to her."

Scarlett shook her head.

"For me? Please?"

Scarlett peered out. "So you're my aunt?"

"Oh." Kennedy laughed. "No."

"But all my other uncles are married. So that means you're dating Uncle Matt. Which means you're my aunt. It's nice to meet you." She sat back down on my lap, her fear of Kennedy completely gone.

"Your uncle and I are just friends."

"No."

Kennedy laughed. "Yes we are."

"No, boys and girls can't be just friends. That's what Axel says."

"And who is Axel?" Kennedy asked.

"My boyfriend."

"You have a boyfriend?"

"Yes. And we're going to have ten babies because he doesn't care that I like playing with dolls. And he's going to be on the TV with the football."

Kennedy smiled. "It sounds like you have it all figured out."

Scarlett nodded. "You too." She grabbed my hand and Kennedy's and put them together. "You can have ten babies too if you want. It's okay."

Kennedy and I looked at each other.

I knew Scarlett had no idea what was going on outside the world of her dolls and Axel. But to me, this felt like her blessing. Like maybe she was telling me I should take a chance on being happy. That maybe it was worth the risk.

"Pumpkin, it's time for bed," James said and lifted Scarlett upside down.

Kennedy pulled her hand out of mine. I didn't want to be put in the friend zone. And I didn't want to wait around being Poppy's puppet. I'd been waiting my whole life. Just letting it pass by in one big blur. Scarlett wanted me to be happy. And James would understand. Hell, he'd already said he understood. I'd find another way to ensure that

Scarlett was safe. But I couldn't put my life on pause again. Not when I'd finally figured out how to start living again.

Scarlett laughed. "Daddy, I had the biggest piece of cake."

"I can tell," James said as he righted her in his arms and peppered her face with kisses.

She squealed.

I grabbed Kennedy's hand and pulled her off the couch.

"What are you..." her voice trailed off as I brought her into the kitchen.

"I'm done," I said when we were alone.

Kennedy shook her head. "Done what?"

"I'm not going to make the same mistakes I did before. I'm not going to keep how I feel about you a secret. I would never do that to you, Kennedy. You deserve more than that. So much more."

"Matt..."

"I'm telling Poppy I'm pulling out of our deal."

Kennedy took a deep breath. "I can't let you do that."

I stared down at her.

"Maybe if you had said this downstairs earlier, I would have agreed. But I just met that cute little girl. Scarlett's adorable. And the way she ran right over to you?" She shook her head. "I can't let you risk Poppy hurting her. I can't."

"I've already made up my mind. I'll find another way to keep Scarlett safe."

"You're a great uncle. And I'm not going to get in the way of that." She grabbed both my hands. "And I hope you do find another way to keep her safe."

"I will. And in the meantime we can..."

"No. In the meantime nothing. We can't do anything until you have a backup plan in place. I couldn't bear it if anything happened to Scarlett. Not because of me. I already live with so much guilt because of what I said to Brooklyn..."

"Brooklyn knew you didn't hate her."

"Did she though?" A tear ran down Kennedy's cheek. "Because I never got a chance to apologize."

"She knew, Kennedy. She knew."

Kennedy took a shaky breath.

"Is everything alright?" Penny asked.

Kennedy took a step away from me and wiped beneath her eyes. "Yes," she said with a laugh. "Matt just made me laugh so hard I was literally crying."

Penny smiled. She was patting Liam on the back and he made the most adorable little burping noise.

I would have said "aw" if I hadn't just made fun of James for thinking it was cute.

"Excuse you, baby boy," Penny said and kissed the top of his head. "I'm so sorry, I'm being rude. Can I get either of you something to drink or anything?"

"Your hands are full," Kennedy said. "I should be offering you something to drink."

Penny laughed. "Thank you, but I'm okay. I'm just going to go put this one down. But before I do..." she looked back and forth between us. "I have to ask. Please tell me you two are dating."

I glanced at Kennedy, who looked down at the ground.

"We're just friends," I said. Every time I said it, it killed me a little more.

"Oh my God, I'm so sorry," Penny said. "I feel like I keep jumping to wild conclusions that are wrong."

"It's fine, Penny," I said.

"So you're not dating Kennedy," Penny said. "Or anyone else?"

"Nope."

"Definitely not me," Kennedy said. "We've been friends for forever. It would just be…weird. Right?" she said and looked up at me.

I swallowed hard. "Right."

"If you'll excuse me." Kennedy left Penny and me alone in the kitchen.

Penny sighed. "Being your matchmaker is hard work. Say goodnight, Liam." She turned around so I could see Liam's cute little face.

I booped him on the nose and he burped.

Awww.

"I'm exhausted so I'm going to call it an early night too. It was nice seeing Kennedy again. I'm sad that she's not the one for you."

I wanted to tell her that she was right. That Kennedy was the one for me. But I held my tongue. I felt guilty for hiding another secret from her. I was pretty sure Mason had already told Bee about Brooklyn by now. And Rob had probably told Daphne. I'd asked them to let me tell Penny though. And it didn't seem like she knew yet. I was lucky that they hadn't spilled it at girls' night. I'd tell Penny soon. But not right here where our friends could probably overhear.

Before Penny left the kitchen, she turned around. "You know what? Let's have dinner. You and me tomorrow night."

Well that was easy. Tomorrow would be a perfect chance to tell her everything. "Sure. That sounds great." I already felt a little relieved. Penny was right. Secrets sucked.

She gave me a weird grin. "Despite what James thinks, I'm pretty sure I have everything figured out."

Wait, what? "I have no idea what you're talking about."

"I know. It's a surprise. Besides, I owe you an apology dinner after freaking out on you about Poppy. James told me you're doing it for Scarlett. And you know we're both so grateful. Really, I can't thank you enough for putting yourself into this mess. Dinner is the least I can do. See you tomorrow night."

"Goodnight, Penny." I shoved my hands into my pockets as she walked out of the room. And my fingers collided with a piece of paper. I pulled out one of the notes Nigel had put in my lunch. I had no idea where the washing machine was in Tanner's apartment and didn't feel comfortable asking Nigel about it. I was pretty sure he'd insist on washing all my stuff himself and do something strange with my boxers or something. So I'd worn the same pants a few days this week. And it was a damn good thing I had.

Because I was pretty sure Nigel was the answer to all my problems. He was a sneaky little man who would literally do anything for me. As Tanner had put it, serving people was Nigel's sole purpose in life. Nigel had told me if I ever needed anything all I had to do was text him. And I needed his help to bring Poppy down.

CHAPTER 41

Friday

I pulled out my phone, ignored the unread messages from Poppy, and shot Nigel a text. "I need your help with something."

His response came immediately. "Mr. Caldwell? Is that you?"

"Yes."

"I'll be right there. I just need to dry off."

I hoped he meant he'd been swimming again. And not that he was bathing and texting me right now. Or something somehow worse than that. "No need. I can just text you," I wrote back.

"I only need 15 minutes. Please, Mr. Caldwell. Let me come to you. Let me serve you properly."

First I had to see if he could even help. "Do you have connections to other house managers?" I wasn't really sure of Nigel's official title. Surely he didn't consider himself a houseboy or whatever Tanner called him.

"Every single one on the Upper East Side," he replied. "And several others. And all of them know several others. I have access to anyone you desire. At a moment's notice."

"Do you know Poppy Cannavaro's house manager?"

"Yes, sir."

Perfect. I really hoped I wouldn't regret this. "Great. I'm at James' place."

"I know."

Creepy. "I'll meet you outside in 15 then."

"I won't be tardy."

I have no idea why, but I had a feeling he'd resisted texting, "And if I am tardy, punish me." I shoved my phone into my pocket and headed back out into the great room. I glanced at the texts from Poppy. Two just asking me when I was coming. I shot her one back saying I'd be there in an hour.

Kennedy was laughing when I walked out of the kitchen and I couldn't ignore how that sound warmed my heart.

"I never called you Tiger," Kennedy said.

"I swear you did," Rob said. "Homecoming sophomore year. You were plastered and you called me Tiger and rawred at me. Legit rawred."

"Oh God." Kennedy cringed. "I really don't remember much about that night. But I do vaguely remember hearing about something like that."

Rob laughed. "Don't be embarrassed. I know I'm the hottest of the four of us. I don't blame you for having a thing for me back then."

Kennedy looked over at me. And she didn't need to say it. I could see it all over her face. She didn't think Rob was the hottest. She thought I was.

"Sorry to cut the night short," I said. "But I have to get going. Kennedy, can I walk you out?"

"Yeah, sure." She stood up. "It was really nice seeing you guys again. We definitely need to do this again sometime."

"Anytime," Mason said. "I'm so glad you're back in the city." He hugged her goodbye, giving me a not at all subtle thumbs up behind Kennedy's back.

She gave hugs to everyone else too. Tanner whispered something in her ear and her face flushed.

Seriously, what kind of stuff had he been saying to her all night?

"Later, guys," I said as Kennedy joined me by my side. I didn't care that we'd just told all of them we were friends. I put my arm around her shoulders as I led her to the door. Friends did that too, right?

"You're really bad at this," Kennedy said as we stopped in front of the elevator.

"At what?"

"The friends thing." She lifted my arm off of her.

"Friends touch each other too," I said.

She laughed. "Not the way you want to touch me."

I smiled. "And how do you think I want to touch you?"

She rolled her eyes and stared at the elevator doors. "I think Tanner's right about you."

"What did Tanner say about me?"

"Oh, a lot of things. He was wingmanning hard for you tonight. I like him. He's an interesting guy."

"That he is."

"And the things he was saying were particularly interesting."

"Are you going to make me beg you to tell me what lies he was spewing?" I asked.

"Lies? I highly doubt that he said anything untruthful." The smile playing at the corner of her mouth was driving me insane.

All I wanted to do was kiss it right off her face. I was having an increasingly hard time keeping my hands to myself. "What did he say?"

The elevator doors dinged open.

She walked in backward so she could keep her eyes trained on mine. "That you're madly, desperately, insanely in love with me."

The doors started to close and I quickly hopped in, closing the distance between us. She stepped to the side, trying to move away from me. But I kept advancing until her back was pressed against the side of the elevator. I couldn't even be mad at Tanner. Because Kennedy was looking up at me like she felt the same way I did. Her chest rising and falling faster and faster as she stared into my eyes.

"And how did that make you feel?" I asked.

"Terrified."

I swallowed hard. "Are you scared of me, Kennedy?" I reached out and touched the side of her face. "Or of what we could be?"

"It's just…what if Tanner's right? What if it was always supposed to be me and you? And it just took us some time to find our way to each other?"

I knew Tanner had a meddling hand in that. But I believed it too. She was standing here in front of me for a reason. There was a reason I couldn't stop smiling for the first time in years. There was a reason why it had been easier to breathe since Kennedy had come back into my life. There was a reason for all of this. There had to be.

My fingers slid to the side of her neck. "What can I do to make you feel less scared?"

She stared at me. "I don't know."

"Would it help if I told you I might have a way out of this thing with Poppy? I'm meeting up with a friend tonight." Since when had I considered Nigel a friend? "He has connections all over the city. If anyone can help me dig up dirt on Poppy, it's him. I'm going to keep Scarlett safe. And I'm going to get to be with you. You have my word."

"Well…" she bit the inside of her lip as she looked up at me. "I mean, I guess that makes me feel a little less scared."

"What else?"

She didn't say a word.

I smiled at her. "It seems like all you really want is for me to get down on my knees and beg you for information tonight."

She laughed as I got down on my knees in front of her. I leaned forward and kissed the inside of her thigh, right beneath the hem of her skirt. Her smile faded and her lips parted with a sigh that made me instantly hard.

I kissed a fraction of an inch higher. "Tell me what you want," I whispered against her thigh. I'd been trying to go slow for her. A whole life of one-night stands made it difficult. I'd been dreaming of this moment. Waiting for her to say she was ready.

She didn't say a word as I kissed higher, pushing her skirt up her hips.

"Tell me what you need." I kissed higher still. "Or tell me to stop." I ran my thumb along the front of her lacy thong. "Just say the words and I'll stop, baby."

"Please don't stop." Her voice was barely a whisper.

I slowly pushed her thong to the side, letting my thumb brush against her clit.

She shuddered.

"Do you ever touch yourself when you think of me?" I whispered as I slid my index finger along her wetness.

"Yes," she moaned.

"I thought about you last night when I had my hand wrapped around my cock. About how your lips would feel wrapped around me. Have you thought about my lips on you?"

She gripped the back of my head, pulling me closer.

I took that as another yes. I leaned forward and tasted her for the first time. *Fuck*. She was so wet for me. I pulled one of her legs over my shoulder to get better access to her. And I tasted and tasted until she was practically shaking in my arms.

The elevator doors started to open. Kennedy stepped away from me. But instead of running out of the elevator she hit the doors closed button. And then hit the emergency button.

I stared at her. With random women, this would normally be the moment I fucked them. Where I told them to turn around and put their hands against the wall. Where I'd try to focus on them for a few minutes instead of the woman who haunted my dreams every night.

But Kennedy wasn't most women. And she'd be the only one in my dreams tonight. I wanted her to feel safe with me. I wanted her to know that I'd take care of her. Always. I stepped forward, caging her against the wall as I kissed her.

"It's impossible to resist you," she said against my lips.

"How hard have you been trying?"

"Really freaking hard, Matt."

I would have stopped there, just kissing her, but I couldn't resist going a little further. She'd let me taste her. And I wanted to make her come. I wanted to hear her moan my name. I needed to remind her that we weren't just friends.

"Spread your legs for me," I whispered into her ear.

She did as she was told.

I slid one finger inside of her and then another, a whimper escaping from her lips. "I want you to come for me." I ran my thumb along her clit. "And I'm going to make you come like this as many times as it takes for you to trust me." I kissed the side of her neck. "Only with my fingers. And my tongue. Until you're ready for more."

"Matt."

"Until you're the one kneeling before me begging me for more." I kissed her hard as her fingers dug into the back of my neck. "Come for me, baby." I pressed my thumb down on her clit. I felt her tighten around my fingers as her whole body shuddered.

And she chanted my name like I'd just caught a touchdown pass. *God I loved hearing her moan my name like that.* I ignored the raging erection in my pants as I slowly pulled my fingers out from beneath her skirt.

She was breathing hard. "You."

I had no idea what she was talking about. So I just stared at her flushed cheeks and mussed up hair. She looked appropriately sated. And I'd be picturing her just like this when I dreamt about her tonight.

"To answer your questions from earlier. About what I need? What I want?" Her eyes searched mine. "You. I think I've needed you for years. But I was scared you didn't need me back."

"I need you back."

"As soon as you figure out the Poppy thing? I'll be waiting for you, Matt."

I smiled. "To be continued?"

She hit the button to open the doors and then pressed a soft kiss against my lips. "To be continued. Hopefully soon," she said with a smile. "And next time, I get to please you." She walked out of the elevator, knowing perfectly well how she'd left me dying for her.

I shifted my erection in my pants, hoping to hide it from the concierge at the front desk. I didn't make eye contact with him as I hurried outside.

But apparently I'd done a bad job of hiding my erection, because Nigel was waiting for me outside and his eyes traveled right down to my tenting pants.

"Oh," Nigel said. "This isn't about my connections is it, Mr. Caldwell? You have something else in mind for us tonight?"

"What? No. I mean, yes, it is about your connections. Eyes up here," I said.

"Did Master Tanner do that to you again?"

"No."

Nigel's eyes traveled down to my groin again.

"Nigel, focus. Like I said, I could have just told you this via text, but you insisted on meeting. I need to find dirt on Poppy. That's it. I just need something on Poppy that will make her leave me alone."

"Leave you alone? In what way?"

"In the way of making me not need to fake date her. I just need something that either connects the Pruitts or Cannavaros to murders they've been behind. Or money they've laundered. Or any laws they've broken. Or shady business dealings. Or something. Anything."

"You're only faking with her?" he asked, ignoring what I was asking for.

"Yes." I thought Tanner would have told him that.

Nigel shook his head. "I will take care of it then, Master. I mean, Mr. Caldwell."

This was getting hella creepy. "Okay, great."

"Give me 48 hours to serve you."

"Sure," I said.

"I'll make sure to remove your plus one from the modern Thanksgiving feast as well."

I didn't bother correcting him. I had a feeling that if he knew about Kennedy, he wouldn't help me out of this mess with Poppy. And I really needed his help.

"Is there anything else I can help with?" Nigel asked.

If he was talking about helping me with my boner, he actually already had. Talking to him had made it disappear in a flash. "Nope, that's it."

"Do you want to share a taxi back home? I have some free time. We could play a round of cards. Or I can draw you a bath and we can chat."

I couldn't help but think about the fact that he had time for this but not for helping me move out. That didn't matter right now though. I needed him to be on my good side, and calling him out would probably not help matters. "I wish I could, Nigel…"

He looked so excited.

"…But I have a stupid date with Poppy tonight. Boy do I wish I had some dirt on her so I wouldn't have to do stuff like this. And have more time for my new friend." I lightly tapped him on the shoulder.

He looked more excited than before. "So that we can have more time together." Nigel nodded. "I will get to work. What time will you be home tonight?"

"Um…midnight?"

"Perfect. I'll have your bath ready." He hailed down a taxi.

"Nigel?"

"Yes?"

"Thank you for this. I owe you one." What the hell possessed me to say that? I didn't want to owe him anything.

"Anything for you, Mr. Caldwell."

I nodded. "Just email me anything you find out right away."

"Email? I prefer faxing."

I just stared at him. "Why? Faxing is the absolute worst."

"Oh. When did that happen? I thought everyone faxed things."

"Maybe like twenty years ago."

Nigel nodded. "Right, faxing is the worst. Don't you think? It's terrible. I agree with you 100%. Who would want a piece of paper that you wanted to immediately show up with very little work? Lame."

Okay.

"But forget texting and stupid faxing. It's best to do this in person. We don't want to leave a trail. I'll text you the time and place we can meet once I find what you are seeking."

"Sounds good, Nigel."

A taxi pulled up in front of him. "Have a pleasant evening. Text me if you'll be late for your evening bath."

"Will do." I was pretty sure I'd just promised him a favor. And to meet up with him in 48 hours in some most likely weird way. And that we had another bath date tonight. I shrugged. It was worth it. Getting my life back was worth it. Kennedy was worth it.

Nigel rolled down the window. "And if Master Tanner asks where I am, tell him I'm picking up the dry cleaning. This is going to be our little secret." He winked at me.

It's going to be worth it, I reminded myself. I smiled and winked back. For some reason I even pointed finger guns at him. Apparently I'd lost my fucking mind.

He pointed his own back at me. "Pew, pew! Secrets!" He blew on his pointer fingers like his gun was smoking.

I couldn't even make fun of him. I'd started that weirdness. And now I had a weird secret thing that Nigel and I did together. What had I just done?

The taxi pulled away.

I'd worry about how to get out of a bath chat later. Right now I had to go appease Poppy for the last time.

CHAPTER 42

Friday

"What the hell are you wearing?" Poppy grabbed my arm and pulled me back towards the ballroom entrance.

"I didn't have time to change," I said.

"I told you to wear a tux and you don't even have a suit jacket?" She looked like she wanted to scream. "It doesn't matter. Hopefully everyone will be staring at my dress." She stared at me like she was waiting for me to comment on how she looked.

The answer...she looked fine. I wasn't attracted to her. At all. I couldn't help it, but whenever I looked at her I saw Isabella. I'd never been attracted to Wizzy either. "Or you could just tell everyone the truth. That you're blackmailing me and I had no choice but to be here tonight."

"Very funny. Just stand there and look pretty and don't say a word." She pulled me back into the ballroom. "God, people are staring."

She'd told me not to speak, so I didn't bother telling her that people were probably staring at her because she was demon spawn.

"Maybe someone took off their jacket before dancing." She perused the room for a jacket to steal.

"I'm not going to wear an ill-fitting stolen jacket."

"So now you care what you look like?" She leaned in to whisper. "This wasn't part of the deal. You're embarrassing me."

"I don't actually remember impeccable dress being part of the deal."

"New amendment. Dress better."

I looked fine. Why did people always diss my clothes? "If I'm embarrassing you, I'm happy to leave."

"Not until Uncle Richard sees us being a happy couple. Come on, let's find him." She grabbed my hand, her nails digging into my palm. She probably didn't even realize her fake nails were stabbing me.

I wasn't sure what was worse...being clawed to death by Poppy or having to see Mr. Pruitt. The last time I'd seen him, I'd said a lot of nasty, albeit true, things. He brought out the worst in me. But tonight I had to be on my best behavior. Angering him wasn't going to help matters. It would probably just lead to Poppy realizing a relationship with me was useless and offing Scarlett without any kind of deal. That couldn't happen.

"Where did he go?" Poppy asked. "I swear he was just here." She froze. "You know what? I have a great idea to pass the time while we wait for him. Let's dance." She pulled me to the dance floor, moved my hands to her hips, and laced her fingers behind my neck. Her eyes darted around, searching for her uncle.

But when she led us over to a table of men much younger than Mr. Pruitt, I had a sickening feeling this had nothing to do with her uncle. "Is he even here?"

"Who?" Poppy asked.

"Mr. Pruitt."

She looked up at me. "Yeah. Of course. He probably just went to the bathroom or something. Dip me."

"What?"

"Dip. Me." She started leaning backward.

Fuck. I caught her before she fell onto the dance floor. "What are you doing right now?"

She pulled back up and started laughing. "You're so funny, Matthew. You always make me laugh," she said way too loudly for polite conversation.

"Poppy, what the hell is going on?"

She leaned forward and whispered in my ear. "Be cool. My ex is here. And now he's staring at us and just...just be cool, Matthew." She moved in a little closer to me, pressing her hips to mine.

For fuck's sake. It was one thing to pretend for Mr. Pruitt. But making her ex jealous? Now I understood why she was so insistent on tonight. Definitely not part of the deal. "Poppy..."

She grabbed both sides of my face and kissed me.

Gag. I was pretty sure I threw up in my mouth a little. I turned my head away from her. "Cut it out. I'm not here to make your ex jealous. I'm here to convince your uncle that you're ready to take over the company. Period."

"Two birds, one stone." She leaned in for another kiss.

I turned it into an awkward hug in the middle of the dance floor.

She started swaying to make it look like we were just a couple in love instead of strangers arguing. "Just kiss me," she hissed.

"No."

"Fine. Deal off." She shoved my chest in a playful way like I'd just made another pretend joke. All just a show for her ex apparently. But her eyes were deadly serious.

Damn it. I caught her hand and pulled her to my chest. I could still taste Kennedy on my lips. I didn't want to kiss Poppy again. I'd literally rather be doing anything else. A bath and chat with Nigel included. "Deal not off," I said. *Yet.* "But you got it all wrong. You don't make an ex jealous with sloppy kisses with someone new. You do it with dance moves. And it just so happens I'm a pretty great dancer. So let's make him jealous of our sick moves." I backed up, spun around, and pointed at her.

"What are you doing?" she said. "Don't draw attention to yourself."

"Don't leave me hanging here," I said and shimmied my shoulders.

She actually laughed. "You're an idiot."

I wasn't going to stop until she joined in. I started doing the robot.

She grabbed my arm. "If I say deal back on, will you please stop?"

I nodded.

"Deal back on."

I froze on the dance floor, my arm still dangling down in the perfect robot. I moved it just an inch.

She slapped my robot arm and then pulled me back in. "Sorry," she said. "I just figured since you were here it wouldn't hurt to rub it in my ex's face that I'm so happy."

"You know what will probably make you happy?"

She looked up at me. "Don't tell me you moonlight as a therapist. I hate therapists."

Yeah, me too. "No. But I do know that being in a real relationship is better than being in a fake one."

"That's the plan. We'll grow on each other."

I clenched my jaw. That wasn't what was going to happen. It was hard enough to stand here with her, let alone thinking about being in a relationship with her. *Please, Nigel. Do your thing.*

"Ah, there he is." She pointed over to Mr. Pruitt. "Let's get him to believe we're in love. He's going to be thrilled. Look at me like you can't see your life with anyone else."

I tried to picture her like Kennedy. But I couldn't. But the thought that Kennedy popped into my head made me smile.

"Perfect." She looped her arm through mine and walked us over to her uncle.

"Poppy," Mr. Pruitt said and leaned in to give her a hug and a kiss on the cheek. "And…Matthew. What is this?" He looked back and forth between us.

"We're dating, Uncle Richard." Poppy reached out like she was about to straighten my tie, but then remembered I wasn't wearing one. She laughed and patted my chest.

"You're dating…each other?" He lowered his eyebrows.

"That's right. When I went to visit him the other day we got to talking. And talking. Talking at his office turned into dinner." She shrugged like it had all happened without threats and bribery. "And we have so much in common. Plus, he's such a finance whiz. I know you mentioned that a while ago." She waved her hand through the air. "But I'd completely forgotten. He's so smart. And I was telling him how I'm not so great with budgets and all that. He's been kind of tutoring me on the side when we're not busy canoodling." She booped me on the nose. "Isn't that right, sugar tits?" She batted her fake eyelashes at me.

Sugar tits? What the hell kind of nickname was that for a grown ass man?

Mr. Pruitt just stared at her. And then his scrutinizing gaze landed on me. "Is this true?"

Honestly, the last thing I wanted to do was lie to Mr. Pruitt. But I was kind of in a sticky situation here. I just nodded.

"I thought you loved my daughter," he said.

It felt like a slap in the face. "I do." I shook my head. "I did." A lump had formed in my throat and it wouldn't go away. "She's gone."

"We really need to talk," he said. He glanced at Poppy and then back at me. "In private."

"Anything you need to say in front of my boyfriend you can say in front of me, Uncle Richard." Poppy snuggled into my side like a leech.

"Very well." Mr. Pruitt stared at me. "Then both of you come with me." He turned around and walked toward a door marked *Personnel Only*.

We started to follow him.

"Sugar tits?" I whispered to Poppy. "Really?"

"I panicked. It was the first thing that popped into my head. And we're stuck with it now, so just roll with it."

I shook my head as we walked into the hotel kitchen. There were only a few people inside. Caterers refilling their trays with little desserts.

"Out," Mr. Pruitt said to them.

One of them looked up. "But…"

"I said get out!" He picked up one of the half full trays and threw it against the wall.

The caterers scattered, running out of the kitchen.

I tried to bite my tongue, but I couldn't. "You know who would have hated you talking to them like that?" I asked. "Brooklyn."

Mr. Pruitt turned to me. "I don't think you knew Brooklyn as well as you believe you did."

What was that supposed to mean? I opened my mouth but Poppy grabbed my hand.

"Uncle Richard, you seem a little upset," Poppy said.

A little upset? He just threw a bunch of miniature cheesecakes at a wall. If this was a little upset, I didn't want to see what really upset was.

Mr. Pruitt ignored her. "I've always thought of you as family," he said to me. "Despite everything. Despite my past with your father. But I should have known. Maxwell put you up to this, didn't he?"

What did my dad have to do with any of this? "No."

"Don't lie to me."

"I'm not lying to you. My dad has nothing to do with who I do and don't date."

Mr. Pruitt glared at me. "He's been trying to ruin me for decades." Mr. Pruitt started pacing. "End this, Poppy. Matthew's just trying to con his way into our family to get inside information. He doesn't love you. He only loves himself."

What the actual fuck? "I loved your daughter."

He stared at me.

"I never see you leaving flowers on her grave," I said. "Fake crying once doesn't count. You basically harvested her organs. So don't you dare stand there and say she meant nothing to me when she meant everything." I could feel myself cracking. I was saying everything I wasn't supposed to say.

"Are you finished?" he asked.

God I wanted to punch his smug face. I clenched my hand into a fist and then unclenched it. Over and over. "Yeah, I'm done."

"So you loved Brooklyn? And you expect me to believe that now you love Poppy? The two of them couldn't be more different."

"Opposites attract."

"I know that. That's why Brooklyn liked you. She was pure and wonderful and good. And you're cruel and cold and uncaring." He turned to Poppy. "Poppy dear, he doesn't love you. Cut him loose."

"Are you saying that I'm cruel and cold and uncaring too, Uncle Richard?"

"No, that's not what I meant. You know I think the world of you."

"Then why don't you trust me?" she asked. "It's like you have no faith in me at all. Uncle Richard, this isn't some big con. I'm in love with him."

Love? I tried to smile and nod when all I felt like doing was throwing up. I didn't want to talk about Brooklyn. I didn't want to be standing here with her dad and Poppy. I wanted my fresh start.

Mr. Pruitt nodded. "Truly?"

"Truly, madly, desperately in love with him. Why aren't you happy for me?"

For a second Mr. Pruitt said nothing at all. But then he cleared his throat. "Of course I'm happy for you, darling. And Matthew. You feel the same way about Poppy?"

"Yes." My voice sounded strange as the lie twisted in my throat.

A smile spread across Mr. Pruitt's face. "Well, this is wonderful then, yes?"

The fact that he was suddenly so happy was somehow more terrifying than when he was throwing food. I nodded.

Poppy smiled up at me with pretend sweetness. "So wonderful, isn't it, sugar tits?"

Stop calling me that.

"I have to say, I'm surprised," Mr. Pruitt said. "But relieved." He slapped me on the back. "I've been worried about you over the years."

"Right. All your texts. I'm sorry I didn't respond, but I wasn't in the right…headspace." *I hate you and I always will, murderer.* "You said you wanted to talk to me about something?"

"Not necessary now." He shook his head. "Not necessary at all."

What did that mean? Not necessary now that I was…dating Poppy? Happy? What? "The last time we spoke, you mentioned that I was in danger."

"Ah, yes. A little unrest in the family again. But there's nothing to worry about now. It's been taken care of."

"Tit for tat," Poppy said. "And I got to find out that car bombs are delightfully fun. Boom."

My stomach rolled. I honestly had no idea what she was talking about, and I wanted to keep it that way. In less than 48 hours I'd be out. I had to be. I couldn't be pulled into car bombings and evil plots. I didn't want any part of that.

"It warms my heart that you've found happiness again, Matthew," Mr. Pruitt said. "Warms my heart indeed. If the two of you love birds will excuse me, I don't want my absence to be noted."

He hugged Poppy and then turned to me. "Just so we're clear. If you hurt her, I'll kill you. Slowly. Understand?"

I nodded.

"And I'll have a relationship contract sent over to your residence immediately. Please return the signed copy as soon as possible."

Just like that I'd been pulled back in. This was worse than just a lie with Poppy if I had to sign a contract. I couldn't let it get that far.

Mr. Pruitt nodded and then strolled back out of the kitchen.

As soon as he was gone, Poppy elbowed me in my side. "What were you doing, purposely antagonizing him?"

"He…"

"And don't you ever bring Brooklyn up again in front of my uncle. The last thing we need is for him to think you're still in love with her."

"I'll always love Brooklyn."

"Keep saying idiotic things like that and I'll kill you slowly myself."

"I'm sorry, Poppy." I didn't want to end up six feet under when I finally felt like I was living again. "It won't happen again." But only because this would be the last time I'd be seeing her before I had a way out of this shit show.

"Good boy."

How many times was she going to make me throw up in my mouth tonight?

"Shall we get back out there?" she asked.

"Actually…you're right. I'm completely underdressed. And we already chatted with your uncle. I should probably just head out."

She assessed my outfit again. "You're probably right. You're certainly not making my ex jealous tonight."

I'd take that as a compliment.

"But let's go out again tomorrow night. There's this new restaurant…"

"I have dinner plans tomorrow with a friend." I wasn't going to put off this dinner with Penny. I'd been putting off telling her about Brooklyn for years. Enough was enough.

"You can't keep blowing me off, Matthew."

"I'm here tonight, aren't I?"

She sighed. "But you were late. Who are you having dinner with tomorrow?"

"A friend."

"Be more specific, will you?"

"Penny. Scarlett's mother."

"Is there something there I should know about?"

"We're just friends. And you better add her to the list of people you're not allowed to hurt. All my friends, actually. And my family."

"I won't touch any of them. I promise. I need to get back out there."

I caught her arm before she could leave. "I want to be very clear here. I don't just mean touch. I mean harm in any way. Including your newfound love for car bombs."

She pouted. "You're no fun."

"Promise me."

"I promise." She pulled her arm away from me. "Make sure to clear your schedule next weekend for only me."

Nope. I'll be out of your clutches by then. "Sure thing, sugar tits."

"Don't call me that. It's your nickname, sugar tits." She pushed through the doors, leaving me alone.

I rubbed the back of my neck. All this stress was really starting to mess with me. I thought about the bath that was most likely waiting for me back at Tanner's place. Honestly? A bath sounded pretty great right now. And I assumed I'd have to have a bath if I wanted any updates from Nigel. It was a win-win scenario, minus the whole him ogling me thing. At least he didn't call me sugar tits. Yet.

CHAPTER 43

Saturday

Penny said she had a surprise for me tonight. I had no idea what that was about. But it didn't really matter. All that mattered was what I needed to tell her. And I'd be lying if I said I wasn't nervous.

I handed the valet my keys and walked up to the restaurant. It had been a while since I'd been out to dinner with anyone other than Tanner. And it would be nice to not have to pretend to be gay for a meal.

But there was still a sense of dread in my stomach. All Penny knew were my lies. For years I'd told her I'd never been in love. Half the time I was lying to myself about it. But I was done lying. In a lot of ways, Penny had been the closest person to me the past few years. Well, her and Tanner. And Tanner knew the truth about my past. Penny didn't. I owed it to her to tell her. She deserved that much for putting up with me.

I also needed to apologize for flirting with her. I owed that to her and James. And I'd tell her about Kennedy too. After tonight, everything would be out there. I'd be an open book. For once in my life.

I took a deep breath and tried to get rid of my nerves. Penny would understand. She was very understanding, that was one of the reasons why we got along so well. *I got this.*

Instead of walking up to the hostess stand, I scanned the restaurant looking for Penny for a moment. She was usually easy to spot with her red hair. But I didn't see her.

"Hi," I said to the hostess. "I'm meeting someone here. I'm pretty sure the reservation is either under Caldwell or Hunter."

"Ah, yes. Hunter. Right this way."

It felt like I was just a few steps away from my fresh start. Especially because Nigel had told me last night that he was pulling together some great dirt on Poppy. He refused to share any of it yet, but he looked really happy. And as Tanner liked to say, Nigel was happiest when he was serving others. I considered his gleefulness a sign of the job being done well.

The hostess stopped at a table where someone was sitting. Someone that was definitely not Penny. Because that someone was a man.

I stared at him. "Justin?"

He looked back up at me. Yup, it was definitely Justin.

He recognized me. I knew he did. But then he shook his head and pretended to be confused.

"Sorry, do I know you?" he asked with way too much extra sass for someone who 100% knew me.

"Justin, cut it out. Why do you always pretend you don't recognize me?"

He stared at me. "It's just...you're not ringing any bells, honey."

The hostess smiled. "I'm just going to leave you two on your date." She placed the menus down and hurried off.

Damn it. The one night I wasn't going on a pretend gay date and the waitress thought I was gay anyway. "Come on Justin, stop messing around." I sat down across from him, leaving Penny plenty of room to join us.

"What's your name again?" Justin asked, squinting at me. "To be perfectly honest with you, I need reading glasses. But I don't like to admit that to anyone. Especially strangers."

"It's me. Matt."

"Matt?" He shook his head. "I'm so sorry, I just have zero clue who you are. Well, I mean, I know you're friends with Penny and James. Obviously. Or else we wouldn't be sitting here together." He laughed. "Wait a second, were you at their wedding?"

"Justin, what the hell? You know who I am."

He patted his index finger against his lips. "No. I have a stellar memory. And I have no recollection of a grown man that's so poorly dressed."

I looked down at my suit. Seriously, what the fuck was wrong with how I dressed? And why did everyone keep bringing it up? I got it when I was in my coach gear. But I'd dressed up for tonight. Nigel had even pressed my suit for me. "I'm well dressed."

His eyes ran up and down my body. "Oh no." He leaned forward. "Are you colorblind? I know that makes things excruciatingly difficult. For matching purposes."

"I'm not colorblind."

"Oh my. Well that's shocking. I don't even know where to start. And it seems harsh to critique a stranger's poor outfit selection."

He was one to talk. I was pretty sure he was wearing a parka or something. It didn't seem fashionable at all. "I'm Matthew Caldwell. Brooklyn's…"

"Don't." He ran his fingers through his hair. "Can you please not bring her up?"

I stared at him. "So you do know who I am?"

"Fine. Okay?' He sighed. "Of course I know who you are. And I always try to avoid you. Because I get very emotional when I hear Brooklyn's name."

Oh. "I'm sorry."

Justin sniffled. "It's fine. I just…like to pretend I don't recognize you. Because I don't like talking about her. Not because I didn't love her. The opposite, really. She was such a dear friend of mine. And I…I miss her. You know?"

I nodded.

"You may not know this, but she was so kind to me. She believed in me when no one else did."

"Yeah. She believed in me too." I could feel myself getting teary eyed because he was getting teary eyed.

"I don't even think I'd be a wedding planner if she hadn't told me I could do it. I owe that girl everything. And she never got to see me living my dream." He grabbed a napkin and blew his nose. "See!? Now I'm a blubbering mess. Oy vey."

"It's fine, Justin. Trust me, I understand."

Justin blotted away the rest of his tears and smiled. "And here we both are. Crying over a girl. Whoever thought two gay men would be doing that on a date? We're acting like straight guys."

"Uh…what now?" Was he talking about me? Were we expecting a fourth person? "Where's Penny?"

"How should I know?"

"Because we're meeting her here?" It was a guess. Because I honestly had no idea Justin was going to be here. I guess he was the surprise? A blast from the past. Shit, did this mean Penny did know about Brooklyn?

"No, honey. This is a date. Penny set us up. She told me all about how you've been hiding in the closet all these years…"

"I haven't been hiding in the closet."

"Oh. Oh, no. You're not out yet? I swear to God, that girl promised you'd be excited about this."

"I'm not gay, Justin."

"Of course you are. I mean, I totally get it. I heard what you said at the funeral. That you'd love Brooklyn and only Brooklyn until you died. And hopping onto the other team doesn't really feel like breaking that promise. Because at least it's not another woman. So technically it's kosher. We're all good. I'm not judging you. I'm actually really happy that you're here."

"Justin, I'm seriously not gay."

"Penny told me everything." He reached out across the table and grabbed my hand. "She said she was out to dinner the other night with James, and she saw you kissing a man."

"I never kissed a…" my voice trailed off. *Fucking Tanner.* I pulled my hand away from Justin. "This is a big misunderstanding. That wasn't a kiss. It was just a celebratory peck between two male friends."

"Yeah…that's not a thing," Justin said.

"He's foreign."

"Oh. Well then." Justin shrugged. "Maybe it's a thing. But the question is…did you like it?"

"No."

"You seem awfully defensive. And a tad too sassy for a straight man if you ask me."

"Justin, I'm not gay."

"Someone maybe needs to spend a little more time in the closet," he whispered.

"I'm not gay!" I yelled. *Oh fuck.* People were staring at us. "Not that anything is wrong with that," I said. "I love gay people." Shit, this was coming out so wrong.

"I am so sorry," James said.

I looked up. Where the hell had he come from? He seemed out of breath like he'd just run here from his apartment. "James, what are you doing here?"

"I came as soon as Penny told me what she'd done. I'm so sorry, man. I had no idea what she was planning. Hey, Justin. Nice to see you again." He put out his hand for Justin.

"Oh, the pleasure is all mine," Justin said. "Are you joining us too? This is seriously my lucky night."

"Um. No. I'm just here because..."

"Stop," Penny said. She was just as winded as James. "You run so freaking fast, James." She put her hands on her knees, trying to catch her breath. "Don't ruin this for Matt. He needs space to find himself."

"What the hell is going on?" I asked.

"We support you, Matt," Penny said. "No matter who you love. And I know you love men. And Justin's one of the greatest guys I know..."

"I'm not gay."

"James." She turned to him. "Don't stifle him."

"I'm not stifling him, baby. Matt isn't gay."

"Of course he is," she said and turned to me. "I've finally put the pieces together. It makes total sense. You passed on so many great options on the dating app. And then someone from your past literally falls into your lap and you pass on her too. I've rarely seen you with the same girl more than once. And everyone I've ever met that's slept with you says you're an emotional brick wall. That's a quote straight from Jen."

"Oh God," James said. "Please don't bring up my sister banging Matt."

"It's important," Penny said. "You're an emotional brick wall during sex because...you know...you wish you were having sex with men instead."

"What the fuck?" I said.

"And James and I saw you kissing Tanner at that romantic restaurant. I'm so sorry he doesn't want to be more than friends. My heart hurts for you. And I know he cares for you of course, but he's clearly not gay."

"Neither am I!"

"Matt. It's okay. We're here for you no matter what. And I'm so sorry you never felt comfortable enough to tell us that you've been gay this whole time. We love you no matter what."

"I haven't been secretly gay this whole time. I've never been gay," I added, just to make sure I was being clear enough.

"Well he definitely didn't used to be gay," Justin said. "Since he was engaged to Brooklyn and everything."

It felt like all the air left my lungs.

"What?" Penny said. "Brooklyn?" She turned to me. "Who is Justin talking about?"

"His fiancée," Justin said. "They were high school sweethearts. But she passed away…"

"Stop," I said. I felt like I was choking.

"Oh my God, Matt." Penny put her hand over her mouth.

This wasn't how I wanted to tell her. It wasn't supposed to come out like this. I couldn't breathe. I got up from the table. I couldn't look at any of them. I couldn't do this right now. I couldn't breathe.

"Wait, Matt," Penny said.

"Penny, stop." James ran after me instead. "Matt!" He caught up with me outside the restaurant. "I'm sorry. As soon as I found out she sent you on a blind date with Justin, I tried to stop it."

"I just need to be alone." I waved my hand at the valet. He went to get my car.

"Where are you going?" James asked.

I didn't respond.

"Matt?"

I ignored him as the valet pulled my car up and handed me my keys.

"You're not the only one that's ever worried about someone else," James said. "I worried about you back then. After Brooklyn died. I worried that you knew what it felt like to not want to keep going too. You were right about me. I hated my life. I hated everything. And you looked out for me. And now I'm looking out for you." He grabbed the keys from my hand. "Now where are we going?"

I wasn't going to fight with him. "I need to go home."

"Okay." He unlocked my car and we both climbed in.

He didn't say a word to me as he drove through the city streets. Not a single word until he pulled up outside my place and cut the engine. "Brooklyn would have wanted you to be happy."

"I meant what I said last night. I am happy."

"You don't look happy, man," James said.

"I feel guilty. For moving on. I can't help it. I am happy, but I feel like shit for being happy."

"We all like Kennedy," James said.

I looked over at him.

"You weren't fooling anyone with that 'just friends' stunt. Except for Penny I guess."

I laughed. "Yeah."

"I used to feel guilty too. For being happy. For being with Penny when I broke the rules to have her. But I don't regret breaking the rules. I'd do it all over again in a heartbeat."

I didn't say anything.

"You made a promise when you were 16 years old. You're allowed to break it."

"I know. I just...I need to be alone for a few minutes. You can take the car back for Penny."

"I'll take a taxi." He tossed the keys at me. "Call me if you need anything, okay?"

I nodded and climbed out of the car. I knew he was right. I'd told myself as much. But I just needed a minute to breathe.

CHAPTER 44

Saturday

I was sitting in the middle of all the portraits I'd painted of Brooklyn. They used to make me feel close to her. But tonight, she'd never felt further away.

I wasn't sure how long I sat there staring. But I felt the wetness on my cheeks. I never did get the blue of Brooklyn's eyes right in the most recent painting. And I realized right then that I didn't really remember how her eyes looked. She was drifting away. I opened up the photo album that Kennedy had given me all those years ago. But instead of my eyes gravitating to Brooklyn like they always used to, they gravitated to Kennedy. I slammed the album closed.

"You paint?"

I turned around to see Penny leaning against the doorjamb. "I'm sorry. Your door was unlocked and..."

"It's okay."

"No. It's not." She sat down next to me on the floor. "I really messed up. I..."

"Thought I was gay. Yeah, I got that. I loved all your evidence too." I smiled over at her.

She hit her shoulder against mine. "In my defense, I literally saw you kiss Tanner. What was I supposed to think?"

"It probably would have helped if I'd told you the truth about Brooklyn."

"You can tell me now."

"It's a long story."

She shrugged. "I've got time."

"I'm pretty sure I fell in love with her the first moment I ever saw her." I looked at the painting in front of me with Brooklyn's smiling face. "She stuck out. Not because of her worn uniform or anything like that. But because she was…she was just a really good person. She wasn't tainted by this world yet. She was pure. And perfect. And she was mine." I filled Penny in on the story. All the way up to the vows I never got to say to Brooklyn. The ones I said at her funeral instead. I even told her our bitter last words to each other.

I looked over at Penny. She was wiping tears off her cheeks. "My heart hurts for you."

It was something exactly like Brooklyn would say.

"I had no idea," Penny said. "I'm so sorry."

"How could you have known? I never told you."

"Why not?"

"Because I didn't want you to look at me like you're looking at me right now. Like I'm broken."

She leaned over and hugged me. "I don't think you're broken, Matt. I think you're in pain. And that's when you're supposed to let friends in."

"I'm sorry," I said. "About everything. And while I'm at it. For the past few years…I didn't think of you as a friend. I lied. You remind me of her. And I think I…I just liked being close to you. I definitely had a little crush on you."

She pulled away from my hug. "Wow, the guys were right? They're never going to let me live this down." She laughed even though it was forced. She tried to wipe her remaining tears away.

"She's beautiful," Penny said as she stared at the paintings.

"She was." I needed to get used to talking about Brooklyn in the past tense. I needed to get used to talking about her at all.

"So that's it?" Penny said. "You're going to keep your promise to her and never date anyone else?"

"Would you date someone else if James died?"

She pulled her knees to her chest and rested her chin on one of them. "That's an impossible question. If I waited 16 years? Our kids would be in high school and college." She smiled. "God, 16 years is a long time. I don't know how to answer that." She looked over at me. "My gut reaction is no. I can't imagine my life without him. And I'm sorry you're living your life without her."

We were both quiet.

"I almost lost him before. And it felt like a piece of my heart had been ripped out. Like I was slowly dying too." She cringed as if the memory was too painful.

I knew the feeling.

"But James and I have lived a life that I'm proud of. We're a family. We have kids. Is that something you want?"

"Yes." I was so sick of lying to myself. "I really want that."

"You're not a bad person for wanting that," she said.

"Am I a bad person for wanting to love someone else?"

"No. Not even a little bit." She looked over at me. "The emotional brick wall thing makes sense in this context too. You were trying not to love anyone else."

"I've never loved anyone else. I've kept my promise."

"And now?"

I didn't respond.

"It's scary," she said. "Facing the unknown. But what's the alternative? Not living?"

I didn't know what to say.

"You should see the way Kennedy looks at you."

I knew how Kennedy looked at me.

"I'm sorry too," she said

"What are you sorry about?"

"I gave you this huge lecture about how toxic keeping secrets was. And you were right. I had one too. It's okay to be scared. I know what it's like to have the future you wanted pulled away from you."

I pressed my lips together.

"And if you don't want to talk, that's fine. I know how to fill up the silence. You were wondering what I've been sad about, right?" She shrugged. "You thought it was about James. It has nothing to do with him, but also everything to do with him. He's given me this amazing life. More than I could have possibly dreamed of. And I just wanted to give him one thing in return." She closed her eyes. "A house full of children. And I can't." Her voice cracked. "I can't have any more children."

Fuck.

She wiped the tears that were trailing down her cheeks and opened up her eyes. "There was a complication with the surgery when I had Liam. I can't have any more kids. And I'm trying to be fine. I want to be fine. But I'm not fine. I feel like my future was ripped away from me. And I'm trying to be strong and I'm trying to be present but some days are harder than others."

She pulled her knees tighter to her chest. "So now you know. I'm not crying because I'm unhappy in my marriage. I'm crying because I want to give James the whole world like he's given me. Because I love him so much that it hurts. And I love his friends like they're my own family." She shook her head.

I felt about two inches tall. I was so wrapped up in my own problems that I hadn't seen it. "You're everything to James. He doesn't need anything else."

"I know that. He's told me a million times that Scarlett and Liam are enough. That I'm enough. But some days I don't wake up feeling like enough. So now you know." She wiped away her remaining tears. "Please don't stare at me like I'm broken."

I smiled at her. "I don't think you're broken either."

She looked down at her stomach. "But I actually am."

"You're not, Penny. You're perfect."

Her fingers splayed across her stomach. "I'm not. No one's perfect. But I do believe that everyone has a perfect fit. Someone that sees their flaws as anything but. And that's what James is for me. And maybe that's what Kennedy is for you. She's seen you at your lowest lows. And she still looks at you with stars in her eyes."

"It's wrong, right? To be in love with Brooklyn's best friend?"

Penny smiled. "I don't know. You're one of James' best friends and rumor has it that you had a crush on me."

I laughed. "You're never going to let me live that down, are you?"

"Probably not. But in all seriousness, I think that if you keep hiding out in here..." she gestured around the room, "...instead of taking a chance on something that could be great? You'll regret it. More than you regret the last 16 years of pushing everyone away."

"I don't want her to fade away. I don't want her to think that I stopped loving her. I'll always love her too."

"She may fade away a little. But she'll never fade away completely. She's a part of you. But you have to say goodbye. You can't keep coming into this room and agonizing about the past. You have to see that that's not healthy. You're amazingly talented. But this…it's a lot, Matt."

I'd been afraid for anyone to see this room. I thought my friends would get me shipped off to a loony bin. Which was a valid fear. Because this was legit crazy. What was I doing? Wallowing my life away? Penny was right. I needed to say goodbye. But I couldn't do that here. "You're right. I know what I have to do."

Penny nodded.

"But could you maybe just sit here with me for a while?" I asked.

"Of course. Tell me more about her."

I smiled. I had a million stories to fill the time. And I'd always found it easy to talk to Penny. She always listened. Staring at me with her big blue eyes. I stared into them for a second. They were the same color as Brooklyn's. Almost the exact same hue. I blinked and turned back to one of the paintings as I told Penny about the performance I did on the homecoming float to win Brooklyn back.

"You're a terrible singer," Penny said with a laugh. "I can't believe you did that."

"I'm not a terrible singer."

She stared at me. "Please."

I laughed.

It was so weird. For years I'd been jealous of James' life. I'd resented him for having everything I wanted when it felt like he'd stolen it from me. But sitting here right now with Penny? I wouldn't have had it any other way. I'd needed Penny. As a friend. And if James hadn't met her, I think I probably would have still been stuck.

Penny was a terrible matchmaker. But she was one hell of a good friend.

***

I sat down on Brooklyn's grave. "Hey."

The silence of the night was all that greeted me.

I picked up a tulip that was on Brooklyn's grave. "Kennedy's back in town. But I guess you already knew that." I wondered what Kennedy had talked to her about when she was here. Had she apologized for falling for me? That's what I thought I'd be doing. But now that I was sitting here, I knew that wasn't what I needed to do. I put the tulip back down.

"I'm sorry that I haven't been living my life. I'm sorry that I've been wasting time. You'd be so pissed at me if you were here." I smiled.

"I asked you for a sign the last time I was here. And I know Tanner meddled and technically the person I saw here was Jefferson's mom." I shook my head. "But I think you sent Kennedy back here. I think you knew she could fix me. She was my wake-up call."

I slowly exhaled. "Everyone knows about our past now. I'm sorry I kept you a secret. It's been really lonely. I've been really fucked up, Brooklyn."

I knew it was crazy, but it felt like she was listening. So I said the words I never thought I'd say. "I want a wife. I want kids. I want a family. And I can't have any of that with you. I'll always love you. But I can't stop living. You'd hate me for it."

I swallowed hard. "I think I love her." I ran my fingers along the grass to where I thought my aunt's ring was. The one I'd given to Brooklyn when I'd asked her to marry me. "And I need to see this through. I need to give us a chance." I looked down. The ring was right around here. I had been pissed that Mr. Pruitt had given it back to me. It had belonged here with Brooklyn, so I'd buried it here after her funeral. But I needed it back. I needed my heart back. I let my fingers sink into the dirt, digging tiny holes, until my fingers collided with the ring. I pulled it out. It looked terrible. Caked with mud and grime. I wiped my finger against the diamond and it caught a sparkle in the moonlight.

"Everyone said time would help. But it hasn't helped at all. It was like I felt guiltier and guiltier every day that went by. Until I wasn't even sure it was because of my last words to you or because in my heart I knew that I wanted to live my life again." I wiped away my tears. "I wanted you. I wanted you to be my wife. The mother of my kids. My family. But I can't have you. And I can't keep living like this. I can't."

"This is goodbye," I said. "Not forever. I just…need some space to give Kennedy and me a real chance. You understand, right? You'd want this, wouldn't you?" I'd want it for her. I'd never want her to be miserable. She couldn't possibly want me to keep living in hell.

"I would do anything to go back in time and do things differently. Say anything else to you. Tell you anything so you didn't hurt when you left this world. Something to make your heart happy. And I don't ever want to forget about you. Or what we had. But I have to let this go before I drown."

I slowly stood up. "I love you." *But I'm ready to move on.* I touched the top of her gravestone. And then patted Uncle Jim's too before walking out of the graveyard. I wasn't going to waste another second of my life. I slid the engagement ring into my pocket. I needed to talk to Kennedy.

CHAPTER 45

Saturday

Kennedy

The teakettle started whistling. I immediately pulled it off the stove before it made too much noise. My mom was sleeping and I didn't want to wake her. But I couldn't sleep. And tea always seemed to help.

I poured the hot water into a mug and added a tea bag. I wiped the tears off my cheeks. I wasn't sure how much tea would help the fact that I couldn't stop crying.

"Mi amor, what are you doing up this late?"

I tried to wipe away the rest of my tears. "I'm sorry, Mama. Did I wake you?" I cleared my throat. "I just needed some tea. You should go back to sleep."

"Kennedy." She lightly touched my chin so that I'd look at her. "Why the tears?"

I couldn't help my bottom lip shaking. "I messed everything up."

"Nunca." She pulled my head down onto her shoulder. "You couldn't possibly."

"I did."

She rubbed her hand up and down my back. "Was it Matt? Did he hurt you?"

I lifted my head. "No." I shook my head. "No, nothing like that." I sniffed. "Quite the opposite." It was scary to say the words I needed to say out loud. It made them too real. It made it so easy for me to get hurt. But if I couldn't even say them to my mom, how would I ever say them to Matt? "I think I might love him."

My mom just nodded. And then turned and poured herself a cup of tea too. "Tell me everything." She sat down on the couch.

"I didn't mean for it to happen." I sat down next to her. "I wasn't even going to look him up when I got back to the city. But we ran into each other. And one thing led to another. And…I just…he understands me. He respects me, Mama. He's kind and caring. And everything I've never had before. But I don't know what I'm doing. He was engaged to Brooklyn. What the hell am I doing?"

My mom grabbed my hand. "Life is short. And you can't help who you love. But you can help if you curse."

I would have laughed if my insides weren't all twisted up. "But Matt? I can't fall in love with him. It's wrong."

"I think the damage is already done."

I shook my head.

"Mija." She held my hand between hers. "You said you're falling in love with him. Has he fallen too?"

"I think so." I thought about how he didn't deny loving me when I brought up what Tanner had said. And how he'd kissed me. And how he'd kept pursuing me even after I tried to stop it. I tried. I did. But I didn't want to fight it anymore.

Matthew Caldwell wasn't mine to have. But it had happened anyway. "She'd be so angry with me."

"The dead can't talk."

"I visited her grave. And there were so many dead flowers on it. I think he visits her all the time. I think I'm falling in love with someone who will never love me most. Why do I keep doing this? Why do I keep choosing the wrong people?"

"He's not wrong people. He's a good boy."

"But not for me. I feel so guilty. It feels like the guilt is going to swallow me whole. My stomach is twisted in knots and I can't sleep. I'm miserable. Love isn't supposed to feel this way."

"That's because you're fighting it. Feel happy, mi amor. Be happy. You deserve everything in this world. You deserve to be happy if happiness finds you. Embrace it."

I'd been through so much pain. And therapy. I'd spent years trying to piece myself back together after what happened with Cupcake. I felt like I was finally okay. And I wasn't sure if I'd felt that way before Matt had crashed back into my life. I told him I couldn't fix him. But what if he'd fixed me? I loved him for that alone. "But he can't possibly love me. Brooklyn was his one great love."

"Fairy tales." She shook her head. "He'll love you differently. The way you need to be loved. Different isn't less."

Different isn't less. I didn't know if that was true. But I wanted it to be. Because no matter how torn up I was inside, I didn't know how to tell Matt no. I'd tried. But he'd broken down all my walls. I couldn't get him out of my head. And I didn't want to. Even though I knew he shouldn't be there. Not in that way. *God, what am I doing?* "I miss her so much."

"I know." She pulled me into her side. "Me too." She kissed the top of my head and yawned.

"It's okay, Mama. You can go to bed. I'm going to be fine."

She slowly stood up. Slower than she used to move. I tried not to let that worry me.

"You have nothing to fear." She patted my cheek. "He already promised me he wouldn't break your heart."

"He did?" He'd promised her that? When? *That night he slept over.*

"Sí. He loves you too. A mother knows these things."

He loves me too. I wanted her to be right. Desperately. And I didn't really have any reason to doubt it. He'd asked me to be his girlfriend. I was the one pushing him away. Not the other way around.

My mom kissed the top of my head.

"Goodnight," I said to her as she retreated back to her room.

I leaned my head back on the couch. "Give me a sign, Brooklyn," I said into the silence. "Tell me it's okay." Because it hadn't felt okay at her grave. It felt like I was stomping all over her memory. And I never wanted to do that. I loved her. I'd never had a friend like her before or since. Neither one of us was perfect though. She'd dated Felix when I thought it was pretty clear that I liked him. And now...I was going to date Matt. *That's okay, right? Please, just give me a sign.*

My phone buzzed.

I looked down at a text from Matt. "Are you up? I need to see you."

My heart started racing. If that wasn't a sign, I didn't know what was. "Actually, I can't sleep."

"Too busy thinking about me?"

I smiled. One of the many reasons why I was falling for him. He was good at making a heavy situation feel light. "Always." I didn't want to lie.

"I'm coming over now. Keep that train of thought. I have an important question for you."

"What kind of question?"

"You'll see."

I wanted to be able to push him away. I did. But my body had a mind of its own. There were suddenly butterflies in my stomach instead of that twisting guilt. And my pulse was racing. I couldn't turn him away even if I wanted to. Maybe Tanner was right. Maybe Matt and I were always supposed to be together. It was just a long, hard route to get there. But sometimes the hardest loves were the ever-lasting ones. The real ones.

Another text came through. "What are you wearing?"

I laughed out loud. "The usual. A very sexy pair of sweatpants." I was crying a minute ago and now he had me laughing. I ignored the way my stomach twisted. I wasn't just falling for him. I was in love with Matthew Caldwell.

"Perfect. Just the way I like you. Are you rocking that sexy bun too?"

"Don't you know it. I'm all ready for you." I was smiling so hard it hurt.

"Just for the record, whatever you're wearing won't be on for long."

I felt my cheeks flush. "Is that your question? Whether or not I'm ready to go all the way?"

"I'd probably word it more on the lines of are you ready for me to properly worship your body. I hope the answer is yes to that. But that's not my question. And it's okay if you're not ready."

I was smiling so hard my cheeks hurt. What was he going to ask me? "I'm ready."

He sent about ten eggplant emojis which made me laugh again.

"It's a shame that we're just friends, Matt."

He sent ten more eggplant emojis. He was such a dork. Apparently I loved dorks. "Could I have a side of fries with that eggplant?"

"What kind of boyfriend would I be if I didn't bring fries and tulips with me?"

Well, that was that. He was officially perfect.

The call button buzzed. I hit the button to let him up.

I was ready for this. I was ready for him. I glanced in the mirror real quick to make myself look at least a little more presentable. I had no idea what Matt was planning. But I had a feeling it involved me repaying him for our little elevator shindig earlier. He'd promised he was getting out of the thing with Poppy. Maybe that was it. But honestly? I'd sneak around with him for a few days. Hadn't I already been doing that? *That was probably the question.*

He wasn't hiding me like some dirty little secret. He wasn't the same guy he was in high school. We'd both changed. And somehow wound up a pretty perfect fit.

He knocked on the door. I put on a little lip gloss and then hurried over. I looked out the peephole just as my hand grabbed the doorknob.

Oh my God. "Puta mierda." My hand froze. I blinked and stared at the peephole again. This wasn't happening. This couldn't be happening. But every time I blinked, nothing changed.

The butterflies in my stomach turned to lead. I felt like I was going to be sick. What the hell had I done?

I threw open the door. I wanted to curse and scream and cry. I wanted to hit the redo button. I wanted to be doing anything other than staring at the ghost in my doorway. A ghost that very much was not a ghost at all.

No.

It wasn't possible.

Never.

And yet…

Nunca.

"Brooklyn?"

WHAT'S NEXT?

Brooklyn's back! Brooklyn's back! If she'd come back a few weeks sooner, everything would have been perfect. But now... Oopsies.

Will Matt go back to Brooklyn? And where has Brooklyn been all this time? Find out in *Runaway*, available now.

While you wait, see what Matt was thinking when he first met Brooklyn back in high school.

To get your free copy of Matt's point-of-view, go to:

www.ivysmoak.com/ehm-pb

A NOTE FROM IVY

She's alive, she's alive!!!! But things are a little messy now, huh?

I always knew Brooklyn was alive. But I feel my characters' emotions so intensely. So in my head, Brooklyn was dead the whole time until she reappeared. I cried during Kennedy's last scene with Brooklyn in Book 3, because I knew what was coming. I cried in Matt's last scene with her and throughout all of Matt's perspective in Book 3. I was as devastated as you, I promise you that. I made myself believe she was dead in order to write the emotions as purely as I could. I felt that death. It was like losing my best friend. I was devastated and emotional and honestly, a little depressed after going through those emotions while writing book 3 and 4.

And then while I was feeling down…the hate mail started coming in. Hate mail for the ending of Book 3 came in droves via email, private messages, and social media posts. I've seen it in every way. So much hate. About how I'm a terrible person for that ending. How could I be so cruel? How could I think as a romance author I had the right to write such an ending? I was told to stay in my lane. I was told I was a monster. I was told I didn't care about my fans. I was told no one would ever read a thing I wrote ever again. I was cursed at. Called names. Told that I was worse than Isabella – and no wonder I could write an evil character like that so easily. And I was told that I should be the one that was dead, not Brooklyn. I was told so many hateful, untrue things. I'm not going to lie, it's hurt me.

And I had to bite my tongue. Because I knew Brooklyn was alive. But there was no way in hell I was going to ruin the surprise by telling the haters that.

And the hardest part of the last few months? I wrote about bullying in my dedication and author note in Book 2 of this series. About how destructive it is. At the essence of this whole series is the effects of bullying. Words hurt. People telling me I'm an awful human every day for the past 6 months has hurt me. I'm actually crying writing this because I'm so tired of the hate. I'm not naïve. I know the hate won't stop now because a lot of readers will still stop after book 3 and never know the truth. But I'm hoping that sharing this story reminds us all that being cruel is never the answer. This whole series is a warning to not behave this way. And I'm horrified that so many people missed that pretty important message. But I'm also grateful that this happened. Because I don't want anyone reading my books who thinks it's okay to talk to another person that way.

Takes a deep breath. I no longer read hate mail. I delete it as soon as a message starts out negatively. Because as I said in my previous dedication, I won't let anyone silence me. I will never stop writing. And for all those "fans" I lost over the "death" of Brooklyn....your loss. You'll never get to see how amazing Brooklyn is as an adult. You're the one missing out. Because Book 5 is going to be epic, I promise you that. And my true readers are reading this and hopefully knowing how much I love them. Because I do. I love you all so much!

And for all you wonderful readers, get ready for a bumpy ride. Because you know Book 5 is going to be a rollercoaster. I wouldn't have it any other way.

Ivy Smoak
Wilmington, DE
www.ivysmoak.com

ABOUT THE AUTHOR

Ivy Smoak is the USA Today and Wall Street Journal best-selling author of *The Hunted Series*. Her books have sold over 3 million copies worldwide.

When she's not writing, you can find Ivy binge watching too many TV shows, taking long walks, playing outside, and generally refusing to act like an adult. She lives with her husband in Delaware.

TikTok: @IvySmoak
Facebook: IvySmoakAuthor
Instagram: @IvySmoakAuthor
Goodreads: IvySmoak